THE PROPHECY OF BEES

R.S. PATEMAN

First published in Great Britain in 2014 by Orion Books,
an imprint of The Orion Publishing Group Ltd
Orion House, 5 Upper Saint Martin's Lane
London WC2H 9EA

An Hachette Livre UK Company

1 3 5 7 9 10 8 6 4 2

A CIP catalogue record for this book
is available from the British Library.

ISBN (Hardback) 978 1 4091 2859 5
ISBN (Trade Paperback) 978 1 4091 2861 8
ISBN (Ebook) 978 1 4091 2860 1

Typeset by Deltatype Ltd, Birkenhead, Merseyside

Printed in Great Britain by Clays Ltd, St Ives plc

The Orion Publishing Group's policy is to use papers that
are natural, renewable and recyclable products and made from
wood grown in sustainable forests. The logging and manufacturing
processes are expected to conform to the environmental
regulations of the country of origin.

www.orionbooks.co.uk

THE
PROPHECY
OF
BEES

Also by R.S. Pateman

The Second Life of Amy Archer

For Mum

The gun doesn't make me feel any safer.

Until a few hours ago I'd not even held a gun before, let alone loaded one. My fingers shook so much I had to concentrate to slide the bullets home. Those tremors make me even warier of the trigger. Make me doubt my aim. I'm not even sure what it is I will be shooting at. If I'll get the chance to do so. If a bullet will be of any use.

But that doesn't stop me checking to see if the gun is still beside me, propped up against the windowsill. Reaching for it. There's an alarming comfort in the smooth and shiny chill of the long thin barrel. I am not reassured for long. It's a gun, after all.

I can hardly believe I'm going to have to use it. I shouldn't even be here, I always said so. If only people had listened.

But it's much too late for that now.

My mouth's so dry I can't swallow. The knot in my throat doesn't help. I can hear nothing but the thump of blood in my ears.

I stand guard at the window. It's so dark outside. Too dark even to make out the shapes of the hills and the trees that I know are there. They've been swallowed by dense and impenetrable blackness. Even the moon is hiding.

I thought I knew every type of dark there was until I came to Stagcote. It's so remote and empty that night snaps over it like a lid. It holds in secrets. Hides demons and spells. Covers up death and disaster.

And even in daylight, those secrets linger. They've been here for centuries. In the earth. In the bricks. The air and the water.

1

Now they're coming to get me and Stagcote Manor's history will be repeated once again. Now I see that it deserves its nickname. Now I know why local people call it Heartbreak Hall.

Mr Eaves, the estate agent, hadn't mentioned Stagcote Manor's nickname. Not to me anyway. He might have told Mum but he probably hadn't. It's not the sort of quaint detail to make someone rush to buy the house, although, of course, that's precisely what Mum did.

She hadn't even been to see the house before she put in her offer. She didn't tell me about moving out of London either. When she called me into the drawing room at the house in Eaton Square, it wasn't to float the suggestion that a move might be good for us. It was more than an idea. It was an instruction.

She was sitting at the table by the window, her auburn hair scraped back into an immaculate bun and speared with a pearl-capped pin. Long, pale fingers collated the small stack of paper spread out in front of her. There was the glint of something in her eyes – not exactly mischief, but a smug self-satisfaction. Like the punchline of a joke she hadn't shared yet.

The joke, as ever, was on me. She'd secured a place for me at Cheltenham Ladies' College where I was going to have to start my A levels from scratch in September.

'You've missed so much of the first year,' she sighed, 'you haven't a hope of catching up. Starting over's the only way.'

I could almost picture Mum in the head's office, squirming on the seat as she fudged some reason for me having to leave my old school. God knows I've given her plenty to choose from over the years but I bet she didn't use any of those.

The truth was rather too painful. Too revealing about her. Me. *Us*. She'd probably gone for something vague and persuaded the head at my old school to back her up, should the new head check. Mum likes to cover her back. She likes to get her way too. And then she wonders where *I* get it from?

'I'm not going to boarding school!' I snapped.

'You're not boarding, Isabella. You're a day pupil. We need the time together if we're to build some bridges. That's why I've bought Stagcote Manor.'

There it was. A done deal. No questions asked. No opinions sought. None were necessary, least of all mine. My helplessness was fuel to my fury. I had no choice. No say. My ranting got me nowhere. She just stood there with a bored look on her face, waiting for me to finish. I didn't give her the opportunity to come back at me; I stormed out and flew up the stairs to my bedroom. I pummelled the pillows, screamed into them. It wasn't fair. *She* wasn't fair. I had a life too – or would have if she'd let me.

She stopped by my bedroom door a little later on and said I should get an early night as we were travelling up the next day so the head could give me the once-over and I could see the house. *As if it mattered if I liked it or not.*

Next morning, I watched her from the car as she dithered at the front door of the house. Some last-minute instructions for Olga, the housekeeper, and a quick pat and a kiss for the chihuahua struggling to escape from Olga's arms. Olga nodded quickly and shot me a sympathetic glance; Mum had probably said something about me to her. Maybe she just felt sorry for me. She usually did.

Mum straightened out her grey linen suit, dropped the keys into her glossy black handbag and glided down the steps. Toes pointed. Shoulders straight. Eyes fixed ahead. Her smile faded when she saw me.

I hadn't even gone too mad with the make-up this time but I knew it would be too much for Mum. My eyes were pools of black, my lips a glossy aubergine. Stiff tufts of jet-black hair poked at the roof of the car.

I knew I wouldn't get away with my dirty protest but that wasn't the point. I had to make the effort. For my sake. But that's just what Mum could never get. Me looking the way I do is all about me, not her. At least it wasn't, not initially. It was about my feelings towards the world, towards myself. Inevitably it became a protest against all that Mum represented, not because I hated it per se, but because it made no space for who *I* wanted to be.

Mum opened the car door, slid into the seat. My hand was held out before she'd even opened her handbag and retrieved a bottle of make-up remover and passed it to me. I'd have been more surprised if she *hadn't* been equipped and ready.

That was part of the problem; beating her to something, just surprising her even, pushed me on to ever more outrageous behaviour. If only she would listen to me as much as she said she loved me. If only she didn't always think she had the answer – the *only* answer to *everything*.

I took the cotton wool and lotion from Mum's hand and removed the thick black make-up with slow, belligerent strokes. I let the balls drop into her outstretched palm and turned my head towards the window. I heard her wrap the balls in a tissue, the snap as she closed her handbag, the sigh of satisfaction.

'Well,' she said, starting the car, 'I suppose I should be grateful you've worn something reasonably sensible.'

I looked down at the black shirt, short purple and green tartan skirt and black lace leggings.

'I can always change. It wouldn't take long.'

She released the handbrake and pulled off. There was a softness in her eyes as she gazed back at the house.

'Next time we drive away from here it will be for good.'

4

Her accent never grated on me more than when she was trying to be sincere or wistful. It was a hybrid of Hicksville Massachusetts and Belgravia salons and spas. I may have inherited my mother's auburn hair and green eyes, but I'd fought off her accent at all costs and hid all trace of my natural hair colour with regular doses of dye. If I looked like my mother, I thought and talked like my father and I was glad of that.

'It's been a good home to us, hasn't it?' Mum said. 'Most of the time anyway.'

The good times she was referring to were the cocktail parties, the soirées and receptions with her pals from the opera, ballet and various charities. The bad times were pretty much everything to do with me. And losing Dad. That was another reason why I wanted to stay. Eaton Square was the only real home I'd ever known and it was the last place I'd seen Dad alive.

'If it's been that good a home then why are we leaving?' I said. My tone was hopeful, conciliatory. Persuasive.

Mum looked over at me. Apologetic but resolved.

'You know why, honey,' she said. 'You need a change of scene. A fresh start. Somewhere you won't be tempted or distracted from what's important.'

'A prison, you mean.'

'Not at all. Just somewhere . . . out of harm's way.'

I closed my eyes as she burbled on about colour schemes and soft furnishings, landscaping the garden, recruiting staff, how London traffic was becoming intolerable, how nice it would be to live in air unpolluted by fumes and police sirens. All the things I would miss.

Cosmo too, of course. Cosmo more than anything. The wing mirror was crowded with cars and buses, people darting between them. I hoped to catch a glimpse of Cosmo among them, as if he might have somehow found out I was leaving London and was going to leap in front of the car, arms out, beseeching and tearful. Wanting me back. But this wasn't some dozy romcom.

It had seemed so at the start. That shy glance he'd given me as he passed me a flyer for a gig his band was playing. That look he'd shot me from the stage, his crooked smile all the more dazzling for the spotlights. And after he'd played his set, the smell of Pernod on his breath, the gloss of blackcurrant on his lips. The quiet way he'd asked for my mobile number, his insistence that he'd use it. My delight that he had. Beginnings. If only they didn't have to end.

I nibbled at the soft, red skin around my fingernails. Tasted blood.

'It's a fresh start for both of us,' Mum said brightly. 'We've got to really try and make this work. I need you to meet me halfway.'

She didn't need that at all. Her idea of halfway was her way. We both knew that – it was the pretence of there being room for negotiation that maddened me and made me fight back. Play dirty if I had to.

The school was pretty much what I expected. Lush playing fields and ivy-clad buildings, the arched windows like a cathedral. Groups of freshly pressed, make-up-free girls with clear-skinned smiles walked along the pavement, giggling and texting. They were sure to be every bit as good with hockey sticks as they were with violins, Shakespeare, Pythagoras, Palmerston and potassium. No different to the girls at the other schools I'd been to. I hadn't fitted in there either. The familiarity of it all – the predictability – was deadening.

The headmistress was a small, bony woman with sharp blue eyes and a clipped way of talking. The sort who thought she'd be able to keep me in line. We would see.

She leafed through a file on her desk, said that the reports from my previous teachers were consistent.

'You have real academic promise, especially with regard to English, it seems. We'll do all we can here to help you realise it, Isabella, as long as you make the effort too.' She tilted her head sympathetically. 'With your cooperation, your history will be just that – a thing of the past.'

Mum beamed. I ached.

An hour later we were on our way to meet Mr Eaves at Stagcote Manor. The black glossy railings of the houses in Cheltenham gave way to thick hedgerows that snaked across endless fields, their umpteen shades of green occasionally interrupted by a splash of acid yellow.

The roads got narrower, bumpier.

'We'll have to get another car,' Mum said. 'Range Rover or something like it.'

'We could always get another house,' I said.

'Come on, honey. You haven't even seen it yet! Give it a chance.'

'I've seen enough. It's in the middle of nowhere. Look!' I pointed out of the window. 'There's nothing here. God, with the school and now this . . . I'm going to go mad.'

Mum glared at me.

'We agreed we'd give it a go.'

My laugh was short and bitter.

'I didn't agree to anything. *I* had no choice.'

'Neither did I,' she said. '*You* didn't give me one.'

The events that brought us here had begun long ago, each one a painful step further along the drive to Stagcote Manor. It was my confusion, my anger, my gut-wrenching loss that had sent me into free fall. Stagcote was no soft landing place. No feather bed. Mum may have thought she was cushioning the blows but all she was doing was smothering me.

She put her foot down and the car bucked and dipped along the road. The satnav bleeped with confusion as we bumped our way along the track and crested a hill.

'That must be it,' Mum said, stopping the car and waving her hand into the distance.

The cluster of grey-beige cottages at the foot of the hill were like prey trapped beneath a heavy paw.

'How pretty!' Mum said, leaning forward then turning to me. The green of her eyes glittered with excitement. 'Isn't it, honey?'

She took my silence as approval and drove on.

As we drew closer, we turned off the track into a long driveway. She slowed down at the house on the junction. Its brickwork was a mellow gold, the garden large but a little wild.

'Is this it?' I said. I couldn't believe that it would be. It was too much like an ordinary house. Not enough of a statement.

Mum laughed and pointed to a sign on the wall. *Gate House.*

'Our neighbours,' she said. 'The house isn't part of the manor's estate although I seem to remember the estate agent's catalogue saying that it had been. At some point.' She craned her neck as we drove past. 'Pretty little place, isn't it?'

We drove on for a half a mile, the line of tall straight trees freckling the driveway with shade and sunlight. About a hundred metres ahead of us, something moved. Mum slowed down and leant forward, frowning.

A group of people walked towards us, at the front a couple of young girls dressed in white and carrying a large garland of white flowers. Behind them was a white-smocked vicar with an open book in his hands, followed by around thirty men and women and a handful of children. Above the indistinct words of the vicar came the cry of a baby and the bark of the dog at the back of the procession.

They stopped walking and the smaller boys in the party

stepped forward, towards the drystone wall on the right of the drive. The vicar laid the book upon their heads then pushed them until their foreheads gently touched the wall. When they withdrew, a man with a bucket and a brush freshened up the white paint on one of the stones in the wall.

Everyone turned and moved along the driveway, towards our car. The girls at the front slowed but the vicar waved them along. When they drew level with us, Mum opened the car window.

'Good morning!' she said. 'This looks interesting. What's going on?'

The girls blushed and shifted on their feet. The vicar walked up to the car and closed the book – the Bible – holding his place with his finger.

'Good morning,' he said, bowing his head. He was a tall, gaunt man and the thin gauze of white hair barely masked the pink of his scalp or its liver spots. His eyes were an intense blue. 'I'm Father Wright. From St James's Church in Stagcote.' He bent down even further. Almost bowing. 'And you, if I'm not mistaken, must be Lady Griffin-Clark.' He glanced at me. 'And Isabella. The new owners of the manor.'

Mum blinked, obviously delighted.

'How clever of you to know!' she said.

Father Wright shrugged.

'Ah, well, I can't claim to be clairvoyant,' he said. 'Stagcote is a very small village and news travels fast. Especially big news like a new resident of the manor. It's been some time since it's been occupied, you see.'

'So I understand from Mr Eaves,' Mum said.

Father Wright nodded then jerked his head down the driveway, in the direction of the manor.

'We saw him earlier, on our way past. He told us you were coming today.'

Mum smiled.

'Wow, and you're the welcoming committee!' she said.

Father Wright winced. The others in the ground moved their feet, mumbled.

'Not quite,' the vicar said, 'although we're happy to be that as well, of course . . .' He looked awkward. 'It's Rogationtide, you see, so we *had* to be here today, although we'd hoped to be away before you arrived. Ordinarily, we'd have asked permission, of course.'

Mum turned to me, puzzled.

'Don't look at me,' I said. 'I can't help you. Should have done your homework before you dragged us here.'

The villagers were pretty much what I'd expected. Drab, slow, all with the same expression; bewildered or awed at the incursion of the real world. No doubt Mum would just see it as contentment. I wondered if this was everyone from the village as there was no one near my age, no teenagers at all, it seemed – at least, none the right side of fourteen.

I wasn't ready for another boyfriend – it was too soon after Cosmo and anyway, he might still come for me – but teaming up with a girl could have passed the time even if she wasn't into my sort of music and clothes. It might have been fun to lead a country bumpkin astray. To be the snake in the garden of Eden. But even that little pleasure had been denied to me. If I were to have any friends of my own age, I'd have to find them among the dowdy swots at school. My world was suddenly even smaller and dimmer.

Mum turned back to the vicar.

'Rogationtide?' she said. 'Permission? For what? Sorry. I don't understand.'

'To come through the grounds of the manor, of course.' He cringed slightly. 'Technically, we're trespassing but, as there wasn't anybody to ask, we just went ahead. We have to come this way, you see, when we're beating the bounds.'

Mum sat up, her back stiffened.

'You're beating your hounds?' she said, indignantly.

'Not hounds, Your Ladyship,' Father Wright said. '*Bounds*. The village boundaries.'

'Oh, right.' Mum's body relaxed.

'It's something we do each year,' Father Wright said. 'Something Stagcote has done since . . . well, for ever.'

'How fascinating!' Mum said, lowering the window further. 'What does it actually involve?'

Father Wright smiled again.

'I can tell from your accent that you're not from this part of the world,' he said.

Mum nodded.

'Boston, Massachusetts.' She said it like she deserved a prize. 'But I've lived here for twenty-five years.' She said that like she deserved a prize too.

'Then you'll be aware that the British have some funny ways,' Father Wright said.

'Amen to that,' Mum said. 'Driving on the left still makes no sense to me.'

Father Wright nodded patiently.

'This little ceremony is one of our ways,' he said. 'Well, in places like Stagcote at least.'

'Oh?'

'Yes, each year we process around the parish and mark its boundaries by repainting the posts or the stones that mark it.'

'And we get our heads bashed!' a little boy in the crowd said.

'Hardly bashed,' Father Wright said, laughing. 'We "hit" the children's heads against the posts so that they remember where the boundaries are. They need to know the limits.'

'Amen to that too,' Mum said, glancing at me. 'And what do *you* do?' she said to the girls with the flowers.

They put their heads down and fiddled with the garland.

'Look pretty,' one of them mumbled.

The other girl nudged her.

'We make the flowers and the crops grow,' she said.

'Fertility and renewal and remembrance,' Father Wright said, 'that's what it's all about.'

'It's charming, isn't it, honey?' Mum said.

It was all I could do not to laugh. Trooping round the countryside with the Bible and flowers and a pot of paint? Knocking kids' heads against walls because they were too stupid to remember where they lived? They didn't need permission. They needed help.

I did too. If this was what passed for fun in Stagcote, then there was no telling what other horrors lay in store for me. Communal jam-making maybe. Morris dancing. Basket weaving. Oh God.

'So you don't mind us being here, then?' Father Wright said.

'Not at all!' Mum waved her hand away. 'If it's been going on for all this time, who am I to stop it?'

'You're the lady of the manor,' one of the little girls said, sulkily. 'You can do what you want.'

There was a murmur among the rest of the group. It was hard to tell if they were agreeing or not.

'Well,' Mum said, 'I don't know about that.'

'I do,' I muttered.

Mum shot me a stern look then turned back to Father Wright.

'We'd best not keep Mr Eaves waiting,' she said.

Father Wright bowed again.

'I'm sure we'll see you again soon,' he said. 'Hopefully at the church?'

Church? As if.

Mum nodded, took off the handbrake and drove on.

'How about that? Beating the bounds. Who knew?' she said, chuckling. 'Wasn't it the cutest thing? Those little girls were adorable.'

There was a faraway look in her eyes and I knew she was thinking about me when I was the same age. I was too.

Then I was the sweet little girl with the auburn ponytail, bright green eyes, ready smile and immaculate manners. I liked nothing more than spreading out my clothes next to Barbie's on the bed, Barbie and I advising each other what to wear and then asking Mum to settle any disputes.

And I was still riding at that age too. I'd go out every day with Mum around Hyde Park, my grey pony, Shenandoah, ambling alongside Mum's grey mare, Fleur. Apart from the size of the horses we were mirror images; backs straight, hair in nets beneath jet-black hats, our leather boots and saddles squeaking a duet.

By the time I outgrew Shenandoah, I'd outgrown aping Mum, too. I declined the offer of another, bigger horse and haven't ridden since, despite Mum's efforts to persuade me.

As we drove along the driveway, Mum glanced over.

'I bet there are some wonderful rides around here, don't you, honey?'

I was sure there were. I was equally sure that she'd be riding out alone. But there was just a part of me – the smallest, tiniest part, too small to be given any credence – that wondered if I still knew how to ride. If there'd still be a thrill in it. What it might be like to ride alongside her once again.

The thought disturbed me. Made me wonder if the move to Stagcote was going to have the miraculous effect on our relationship that Mum had hoped for. I shut the thought away.

From the moment Mum first told me that she'd bought Stagcote Manor, I was determined to hate it. It could have been the most beautiful house in the world and it would have made no difference.

What it represented was ugly. So it seemed only right that the house turned out to be ugly too.

A hotchpotch of architectural styles, it slumbered at the bottom of the hill, as dark and quiet as the shadows it cast across the lawns.

The sleek symmetry of Georgian windows and balsa-coloured stone was disrupted by sludge-grey towers crimped by crenellations and crowded by a huge, stopped clock and a rusty bell. Ballustraded balconies hung over bricked-up doorways, a strip of driveway lapping at each one, like a tide.

Despite my best efforts, I couldn't deny the flutter in my heart. It was a mess of a house, unruly and unkempt, twisted and restless, as if at war with itself. The manor's turrets, towers and wonky, ivy-clad walls created my very own Gothic castle.

Cosmo would have loved it. I bit my lip at the thought of him, of knowing he would never see it or be part of my life here. Of knowing he would never want to be. That was as good a reason to hate the manor as anything else.

Mum exhaled deeply.

'There it is,' she said. 'Home.'

I couldn't tell from her tone if she was pleased with the house or not. I watched her carefully for any sign of disappointment or uncertainty. If it wasn't what she was expecting, she might change her mind about the move and we could stay in London. But her face glowed with a quiet fire that couldn't be faked, although her experiences with me had given her the knack of putting a high gloss on things for appearance's sake.

Even if she hated the house there was no way she would let me know. And she certainly wouldn't even think about selling it. That would be giving up at the first obstacle. Giving in to me.

Besides, the appearance of the house was incidental. I'd seen a lot of property shows on television when I was taking a break from pretending to do some homework. All they banged on about was location, location, location. And that's what mattered with Mum. The manor was miles from anywhere, removed from all distractions but within driving distance of a good school, so it ticked all the right boxes.

As we pulled into the forecourt, the front door opened and a man came out, buttoning up the jacket of his blue suit. A horseshoe of brown hair exposed the ruddy brown of his scalp. When we got out of the car, his smile was quick and slick. His handshake was too.

'Welcome to Stagcote Manor, Your Ladyship,' he said, standing back, arm out like a chat-show host introducing a guest. 'Or should I say welcome home.'

Mum gave him her most gracious smile, turned to full beam.

'You're the second welcoming party we've had today,' she said.

Eaves frowned for a moment, then raised a finger in under-standing.

'Ah, the vicar and his troop.' His frown was back. 'I hope you didn't mind, Lady Griffin-Clark. I would have asked you first but—'

Mum waved him away.

'It's not like it's going to be happening every day of the week, is it?' Now it was her turn to frown. 'Or is it? How

15

often does . . . Rogationtide come along anyway? Didn't the vicar say once a year, honey?'

I shrugged.

'I believe so,' Eaves said, with a deferential nod. 'Now, if you'd like to look around on your own I can wait in my car.'

'Nonsense,' Mum said. 'We want the full tour.' She shielded her eyes and leant back to look up at the house. 'This part is eighteenth century, yes?'

Eaves nodded. Mum smiled, pleased to have got it right.

'Mostly, yes. The bell tower is from around 1750, we believe. And there are parts of the house that we think go back much further than that.' He lowered his voice. 'If only walls could talk, Your Ladyship. I'm sure it would have some wonderful tales to tell.'

'I bet,' Mum said, dropping her gaze and focusing on Eaves. 'I can almost guarantee there'll be a few stories about ghosts.'

'Indeed,' he said.

'Not that I go in for all that bunkum, of course,' Mum said.

Eaves held his arm out in invitation.

'After you,' he said.

I didn't follow on behind her. The longer I left going into the house the better. It wasn't my new plaything, but hers. The house wasn't going anywhere; it could wait for me as much as I could wait to see its dubious attractions. Ghosts included. At least Eaves hadn't tried to use the ghost stories as a marketing angle. Mum was many things but gullible wasn't one of them. At least I take after her in some ways.

'You go on,' I said. 'I'll catch you up. I want a fag.'

Mum glared at me and shook her head.

'All this fresh, country air and you want your lungs full of that . . . filth instead?'

'I'll take it every time,' I said, rummaging in my bag for my tobacco.

Mum sighed. Eaves smiled weakly and took a step towards the house, eager to get away from our tiff.

She'd been on at me about smoking ever since she found a crumpled packet of Rothmans in my pencil case when I was twelve. She screamed that I was killing myself and demanded to know who'd bought them for me. I screamed back that she should never have been looking through my things anyway.

Dad said we both had a point, which only made Mum angrier and me love him all the more. I never did let on – to either of them – that it was Dad's chauffeur who'd bought the cigarettes for me.

A year later I was able to buy my own, a growth spurt that added a couple of inches to my bust and height, belying Mum's claims that smoking would stunt my development. A couple of inches of backcombed hair, plenty of make-up and even more attitude ensured no newsagent ever questioned my age again.

I rolled my cigarette and gazed at the manor through a cloud of smoke. Even when the wind had whipped away the smoke, the house seemed blurred, the fine lines I'd noticed from a distance somehow less distinct now that I was closer. I leant back and looked up at the towers. The hands on the clock had stopped at ten to two. A giant, rusty, V-sign. The wall was stained and streaked with ochre, like dried blood.

It could never be home.

I turned and headed away from the house, back up the driveway. An early escape bid or reconnaissance for future attempts. It was a shame there was no sign of the people in the procession as they'd be sure to know the quickest way back to civilisation. Or maybe not.

I ended up near the Gate House. I sat down on a tree stump, took out my tobacco and papers and rolled another cigarette. As I exhaled I shifted back onto the stump, my hand flat on its rough, crumbling surface. Something stuck into me. Something sharp.

I jumped up.

'Shit!' I yelled, flapping my hand about.

I opened up my palm, saw a small splinter sticking into the skin, an angry red spot appearing around it.

'Are you OK?'

I jumped and turned, my cigarette falling to the ground.

He was coming out of the garden of the Gate House. Something about him resonated with me. The slightly uneven gait. The grey crew-cut hair. The wonky smile with perfectly straight, clinically white teeth. If he was our new neighbour then I was encouraged; he didn't look like the others I'd seen in the procession. I mean, he was still old – just not *as* old. At least he didn't look it. If he had a daughter she could be around my age. For a moment I forgot about my stinging palm.

'Hello again,' he said.

I frowned at him.

'It's Isabella, isn't it?'

'Yes,' I said hesitantly. The vicar wasn't wrong. News really *did* travel fast in Stagcote.

'How did—'

'I was in the procession earlier on,' he said.

That's why he'd struck a chord with me, although I didn't recall actually seeing him there. I must have caught him in my peripheral vision. Sensed him somehow.

'I was at the back,' he said. 'Hiding my blushes. All a bit twee for me.'

'And me,' I said.

'Howard Thompson,' he said, putting his hand out. I winced as I shook it. 'What happened to your hand?' he asked.

'The ruddy countryside, that's what happened!' I said, looking at my palm. 'I've got a splinter.'

'I wouldn't be so sure about that,' he said, and walked towards me. 'Let me see.'

He took my hand. His skin was brown, rough to the touch.

'Just as I thought,' he said. 'Not a splinter. A bee sting.
Hold still.'

He pinched the fine, black stem of the sting between his
thumb and forefinger and quickly pulled it away, before
brushing it off on his trousers.

The red and tender welt on my palm was already swollen
with venom.

'You're not allergic to bee stings, are you?' he said. 'Some
people are.'

'No,' I said, shaking my hand. 'Ow, that hurts.'

He looked at the tree stump.

'There's the culprit,' he said, flicking away the curled up
bee. 'A straggler.'

'You can tell what sort of bee it is just by looking at it?'

He laughed. A rich, throaty chuckle.

'God no,' he said. 'But there are plenty of folks around here
who can. What I meant was that it must have got separated
from the swarm.'

I stopped and looked around me nervously.

'Swarm?'

He steered me through the garden gate.

'Don't worry, it's all sorted now. Cedric's on the case.'

He pointed towards the far end of the garden where a
chubby man with a white beard carried a large straw basket
towards a cluster of beehives, one of which had its roof open.

I looked at Cedric and then at Howard.

'What? You're telling me he's got a swarm of bees in there?'

Howard nodded.

'But . . . he must be mad! He hasn't even got one of those

19

protective suit things on. Shouldn't he have one of those hats on too . . . you know, with the veil thingy?'

'Cedric doesn't use them. Or need them. Apparently, the more often you're stung, the greater your immunity to the venom. Cedric says he's been stung more times than he can remember. But he's got another more miraculous weapon in his arsenal too.' He leant in closer. 'You've heard the phrase about someone being able to charm the birds from the trees?'

'Yeah, of course.'

'Well, Cedric's got the measure of *all* living things. Bees included. He's like the Pied Piper. Only he doesn't need a flute. Just his know-how and his voice. Listen.'

It was hard to hear Cedric above the thrum of bees and the rush of wind in the leaves, but I could just make out the words in a light, mellifluous tone and a languid, comforting rhythm.

'Come by, come by, my beauties,' he said. 'Here's home now. Your new home.'

I couldn't believe he actually thought the bees were listening to him and doing as he asked them. Like he was Doctor Doolittle or something. My laughter was easier to swallow than my scepticism.

I flinched as he tapped the end of the basket and a solid clump of bees fell into the open hive. The grass around it undulated as stragglers walked towards the hive entrance, their backs and wings glinting in the sunlight like wet coal.

Cedric placed the roof on the hive and walked towards us, stroking his beard.

'All done,' he said slowly. 'For nows, anyhow.'

I thought maybe he'd just adopted a light, sing-songy voice for the bees, but it turned out that was his normal way of talking. His accent was thick and rolled around his mouth. Father Wright's had too, I realised. So did Howard's, although his was less pronounced.

Cedric stopped when he saw me. His eyes swept over me with a mix of curiosity and distrust, the glare I'd grown accustomed to because of the way I dressed and made up my face.

''Ow do,' he said, dipping his head at me before turning to Howard and flicking his eyebrows skywards. 'They'll be OK, Howard. They be settling in now.'

'Excellent,' Howard said. 'So they won't be causing any more trouble for people?' He pointed at me. 'This young lady got stung.'

Cedric frowned.

'You's been unlucky then, miss. They're normally right docile when they're swarming, see. So filled up on honey they can't bend their body to get the sting into you.'

I looked at my hand.

'That'll be right,' I said. 'Just my luck.' I blew on my palm. 'To be fair, I didn't give it much choice. I squashed it. By accident, of course,' I added quickly, not sure why I felt I needed to explain. It was only a bee and I hadn't meant to do it.

'Well, Howard here can take care of that sting for you, right enough,' Cedric said.

Howard put a finger to his forehead and gave a quick salute.

'I can rub your palm with some onion if you like,' he said.

'Onion?' I wasn't sure I'd heard him properly.

'Been used for bee stings for centuries, so Cedric told me.'

'That's right,' Cedric said. 'Well-known fact, that is. Stings and onions.'

'Well known around here anyway,' Howard said with a sly wink. 'And, bizarrely enough, it works. I mean, who knew?' He jerked his head towards Cedric. 'Apart from Cedric and the rest of Stagcote, that is.'

'Have you got any onion?' Cedric asked.

Howard said he had.

'Aye, well,' Cedric said, shaking his head, 'that's the sting taken care of. The little one, anyways. The big sting though . . .' He sucked in his breath and shook his head again. 'Not an onion in the world can do much against that.'

'Big one?' I said.

Howard laughed and put his hand on Cedric's shoulder.

'He's got this notion that there's trouble ahead,' he said.

'Ain't no notion about it.' Cedric's eyes flashed with anger. 'It's the truth. You mark my words. The bees know.'

I wanted to laugh. No one in their right mind could believe that bees knew much about anything other than flowers and honey and stuff they were meant to know. Bee stuff. But *he* did. I wondered if he was Stagcote's village idiot; that would explain why Howard humoured him. I followed suit.

'The bees know what?' I asked, with as much interest and innocence I could muster.

Howard held out his arm, inviting Cedric to speak.

'The prophecy of bees.' Cedric's voice was low and grave. 'When a swarm is found on a dead tree, it's a warning that death is nearby.' He pointed vaguely over his shoulder. 'We found this swarm earlier. During the procession. On a dead elder tree. *Inside* the parish boundary.' He rubbed his chin thoughtfully and shook his head. 'Not good, miss. Someone in this parish is not long for this world.'

I nearly said I hoped it was my departure from Stagcote the bees were referring to, but he looked so serious and intent I didn't dare. I hoped the bees were right though; I couldn't stand the idea of living in a world where banging kids' heads against stone walls was considered normal and the stings of clairvoyant bees were treated with vegetables.

'All the other villagers are just as perturbed,' Howard said to me, hunching his shoulders, as if he too was struggling not to laugh. 'There was such a fuss when we found it this morning you'd have thought a siren had gone off, warning of an imminent nuclear attack.'

'It's no laughing matter,' Cedric said sharply. 'Nothing to laugh at, at all.'

Howard grimaced.

'Sorry, I shouldn't mock you.'

'No,' Cedric said. 'No you shouldn't. Nor the bees neither. Theys deserve respect. Theys know things – looong before they happens.'

'Well,' Howard said, 'let's hope they've got it wrong on this occasion, eh?'

'Hope?' Cedric snorted. 'You can hope all you like. Now the bees are safely home, I'm off to the church to pray. I won't be the only one there neither, you watch. You'd do right to follow suit too,' he said to Howard. 'And you, miss, especially as you're living at Heartbreak Hall. Some would say *you* need prayers more than most.'

'Heartbreak Hall?' I repeated.

'It's what the locals call the manor,' Howard explained.

'For good reason too,' Cedric said. 'Nothing good ever happens up there.'

He wouldn't let his eyes meet mine.

'It's supposed to be cursed, would you believe?' Howard said, arching his eyebrows.

'Yeah right,' I said, smiling. 'Nice try.'

'What?' Howard said.

'Winding me up! Look, I might be young *and* the new kid in town, but I'm not ditzy enough to believe in curses and whatever.'

'It's the truth,' Cedric said.

'Sure, about as real as the bees doing what you tell them.'

Cedric glared at me.

'It's all true, I tell you. All of it.'

23

He looked crestfallen. Hurt. He was an old man. A little simple. I had to humour him.

'What sort of curse is it then?' I said. 'What's meant to happen?'

But Cedric must have sensed my insincerity and just muttered to himself and started to wander away.

'I've said too much as it is,' he said when I pressed him. 'I'd best be off to the church.' He dipped his head at me and walked quickly to the garden gate.

'Right,' Howard said, turning to me. 'Let's get this sting taken care of, shall we?'

'There's no need, really.' I checked my hand. The red lump in the middle of my palm was larger and darker now. I winced when I touched it with my fingertip, felt the warm throb of pain.

'I know it sounds daft but it *will* help,' Howard said. 'It won't take a minute.'

I'd already upset one of the villagers and I hadn't even moved in yet. I didn't want to upset our nearest neighbour as well, especially as he seemed to find old Cedric's ways eccentric too. If everyone in Stagcote was as wacky as Cedric, then Howard might be as close to normal as I could hope for.

I followed him through the back door of the Gate House, into the kitchen. He pointed to the old wooden table and chairs at the far end and told me to take a seat. I walked through a pool of heat emitted by the blood-red Aga. Howard took an onion from the vegetable rack next to the sink and a knife from the collection sprouting like wigwam poles from the cutlery drainer.

'So,' he said, as he rested the onion on the sideboard and pressed down on the knife, 'what do you make of the manor? Can you see yourself living there?'

I laughed cynically.

'No. But Mum's really set on it. Not even a curse is gonna shift her.'

The onion split into two. He turned over one of the halves and sliced it; thin opaque waves fell slowly onto the counter.

'Ah,' he said, picking up a slice and passing it to me. 'What about your father?'

'Dad's . . . Dad died a few years ago.' I winced as the cold of the onion touched the heat of the sting.

'Just leave it there,' Howard said softly. 'Let it do whatever it is it does.'

The tone of his voice was as soothing as the balm of the onion. I was suddenly four years old again, sitting on a dazzlingly white beach as Dad gave the kiss of life to Barbie after she'd been swept into the sea by a wave.

I looked around the kitchen. Mismatched wooden furniture. Country-coloured pottery vases. Cast-iron cookware on a scratched slate shelf. Hessian place mats. The Aga was the only thing with a definite colour, as red and glossy as it was warm.

'*My* dad passed away a few years ago too,' he said, as he put the kettle onto the Aga's hotplate. 'It's kind of what brought me here.'

'So you're not from Stagcote then?' I nodded. 'Thought so.'

'Bristol,' he said. 'Originally. I ended up here via Exeter University, London and Frankfurt.' He gazed off into the distance. Then sighed. 'That's where I was when Dad died.' He pulled a face. 'I was working in banking. Married. Disillusioned. Classic mid-life crisis I guess. I took early retirement and Ulle, my wife, came back to the UK with me. We thought we'd make a go of it in the country, but . . .' He shook his head. 'I've not had the energy to move on.' The smile was back on his face. 'But then, my house isn't cursed, is it? Maybe if it was I'd be out of here a bit sharpish.'

He took two mugs from the draining board and added a heaped spoon of coffee from the jar on the windowsill.

I smiled and shook my head.

'Is it for real, all this stuff? Obedient bees and curses, I mean. It's like the land that time forgot around here.'

'It's real enough to Cedric.'

'What about the rest of them? You said they use onions on stings too so they must be just as weird.'

He poured in water from the kettle. Steam wreathed around him.

'People can't help what they believe.'

I bit my lip and shook my head.

'But it's ludicrous, isn't it?'

The teaspoon clattered against the mug as Howard stirred the coffee.

'People believe in more ludicrous things. God, for one. An invisible, all-knowing spirit who lives in the sky? Really?'

'That's different . . . and anyway, I don't believe in God.' I took the mug from Howard. 'What's supposed to happen with this so-called curse then?' I said.

'No idea. I'm not privy to stuff like that, being the incomer I am. Two years I've been here and they still won't let me in on it. That should tell you all you need to know about Stagcote and the people who live here. I only got to join in with the beating the bounds jamboree as they couldn't really leave me out, seeing as it comes by my house.'

I sipped my coffee slowly.

'Of course, it might be different for you,' he said, blowing on his coffee. 'You're from the manor. The lady of the manor – sort of. Maybe that will make them open up more.'

I put the mug down and lifted up the slice of onion; the bump of the sting was less pronounced, the redness slightly paler. I raised my eyebrows in surprise.

'Told you it would work,' Howard said. 'These people know a thing or two.'

The phone in my pocket vibrated.

Voicemail. Mum.

'Isabella? Where on earth are you? I hope you haven't run off . . . you really need to give the manor a chance. It's got so much potential, honey. I just know we'll be really happy here. Come back and have a good look around. See for yourself.'

I deleted the message and dangled the phone between my fingers.

'I'd better be going.'

'Well, I guess I'll be seeing you again soon, now that we're neighbours.' He clicked his fingers. 'Which reminds me . . .'

He opened one of the cupboards and took out a jar filled with a dark amber honey. 'Thank you,' he said, and passed it to me.

'What are you thanking me for?'

'Cedric told me it's customary for the beekeeper to give a jar of honey to his neighbour, as a thank you for letting the bees feed on the plants in their garden.'

I rolled the jar in my uninjured hand.

'Thanks, but to be honest I don't really like honey.' I put my hand to my mouth. 'But don't tell the bees that, will you?'

Howard laughed and beckoned me outside.

'One more thing,' he said. 'Come on.'

I followed him down to the bottom of the garden. The air hummed with the wings of thousands of bees; the ground trembled with bass.

'Not too close,' Howard said. 'And don't make any sudden movements or loud noise.'

My mouth was dry, my heart thumping. There was something unsettling about being so close to something so natural and vital. Something so potentially dangerous.

Howard knelt down slowly and beckoned me to do the same. I checked to see there were no bees on the grass and knelt down next to him.

'What are you doing?' I said.

'Sssh,' he said, his finger to his lips. 'We've got to tell the bees the news.'

'What? You expect me to talk to the bees?' I said, incredulous.

'They need to be told whenever big stuff happens around here. Weddings, deaths, births. That sort of thing.'

'What, they're going to send a condolence card, are they? Or a helium balloon?' I said, starting to stand up. The touch from Howard's hand on my arm stopped me halfway. That and the buzz of the bees.

'You don't believe in all this, surely?' I said, lowering my voice.

'No, but we have to do it. Out of courtesy.'

'But they're bees, for God's sake!'

'Not just courtesy to them, but to Cedric. They're *his* bees. He can't keep them in his garden as his neighbours have got dogs and young children. So he keeps them up here, out of the way. If we don't tell them your news, they'll stop producing honey for him.'

'But that's mental!' I said, tossing my head back and laughing.

The bees buzzed a little louder.

'Sssh,' Howard whispered. 'I told you to keep still and quiet.'

The zip of black bodies in the air stirred up a flutter of fear inside me. It was nonsense. Talking to bees. Mysterious curses. It almost made Mum seem sane. I just wanted to get away.

'What do we do?'

'Just tell them your name and who you are,' Howard said.

'You're joking me,' I said.

'Just say it. Come on. For Cedric's sake.'

'I'm Isabella,' I said, in a poor copy of Cedric's singsong voice. 'But you . . .' I pointed at the hives with a single finger, 'you can call me Izzy.'

Howard glared at me.

'My name's Izzy,' I said, enunciating clearly. 'And I live at Stagcote Manor.'

The thrum of the hive intensified.

A date was set. The removal company booked. Packing cases delivered. Rolls of bubble wrap sprouted in every room. Mum launched herself into sorting things out and sticking labels onto furniture and boxes of books, paintings, ceramics and lamps.

I was surprised she was taking so much of it. Relieved too. At least Dad wasn't being left behind, even if Mum didn't like a lot of the things he'd bought, such as the painting that took up the length of the hall wall, with its alternate strips of blue and red and splat of yellow at the centre. Or the collection of intricately twisted filaments of glassware he'd picked up on a trip in Venice.

'Because it was fragile and complicated,' he said. 'Like love.'

Mum took the glassware as a criticism – elegant and eye-catching, certainly – but a criticism nonetheless. Which was why I was surprised to see it packed away and put into one of the boxes marked Stagcote.

Dad's favourite chair got the nod for the trip to Stagcote too, even though it was a little saggy and didn't match the rest of the suite. I liked to sit in it, nestle my head into the dent left by his, feel the shape of his arms and back support mine. When I breathed in deeply, there was a trace of him; clean and sharp and tangy. Gradually, the scent had faded, subsumed by time and the familiar notes of Mum's solid, earthy perfume.

I understood why she would want to sit in the chair too. It felt wrong to resent her for doing so, but I did. She got in the way of the last tangible sense of him. Of my memories. Perhaps she thought the same of me.

I'd heard the story of how they met and their lives together countless times but, in the last few years, when she'd started to tell the tale I've had to get up and walk away. I just couldn't bear to hear the whole commercial.

How she'd grown up in a dowdy house in a run-of-the-mill suburb of Boston, her presence barely acknowledged by a father too easily distracted by a bottle of Jack Daniel's and the Red Sox games on the TV. How her mother tried hard to fit in with the others at the school gates, but was too timid and apologetic to be noticed and took refuge behind a diet of pizzas and burgers, antidepressants and easy credit at the mall.

How neither of her parents noticed their daughter's intelligence and abilities, but one of her teachers *did* and secured her a scholarship that eventually took her on to Penn University, where she juggled waiting tables and shifts at the multiplex cinema to help pay for her degree in International Relations.

How a trip to Europe ended in a grotty sandwich bar in Old Street, whose best customer was Adam, the geeky guy who lived above the shop and spent all day fiddling with circuit boards and computer programmes, wires and bits of gadgets. How they spent their evenings making spaghetti bolognese and curries and sharing a bottle of Costcutter's finest plonk.

And how, afterwards, Adam would tire of watching television and challenge her to a game of Pong, which she pretended to enjoy despite its simplicity and monotonous beeps. How she fell in love with a quiet and unthreatening man who had a quick sense of humour and answers to all of her questions.

How it transpired that the computer games weren't the hobby of a bored young man with too much time on his hands, but the foundations of a business empire. How his mind worked like a logic board, making connections, making things work, making computer games that made money. Lots and lots of money. How his biggest hit, Million Dollar Heist, was aptly named. And how he'd then moved on to telecoms – and made money all over again.

How they had enjoyed giving money away, funding scholarships and science blocks at Warwick University and bankrolling charities that built wells in Africa, hospitals in Haiti and schools for Indian street kids. How with his own brain making clean and quick connections, he became fascinated by brains which didn't work as they should, and became a champion for Alzheimer's and autism charities.

And how his success and philanthropy landed him on the first honours list of the Blair government, making Adam a life peer and Lindy a lady.

How having a title never stopped her from forgetting how lucky she was, how grateful she was at all the chances she'd been given throughout her life and how she'd taken each and every one. That the properties around the world, the fistfuls of jewels, the chauffeured cars, theatre premieres, polo ponies, galas and yachts were never taken for granted – but that none of them were more precious than their daughter, the biggest blessing of them all.

How she couldn't understand that I didn't realise my good fortune. How she was going to make sure I didn't throw my opportunities away.

But she never understood how the things that *I* wanted – not homes, horses or holidays, not clothes or tiaras – but freedom and individualism, got overlooked.

How I've fantasised about things being different.

About going to an ordinary comprehensive instead of umpteen uptight private schools, living in a suburban semi rather than a Belgravia mansion, and spending my holidays snogging boys in a Greek beach bar instead of sitting in my room avoiding the guests at the St Kitts villa or Klosters ski lodge.

Maybe then I would have been allowed to do what I wanted to do, rather than what was expected. Not have to be Daddy's little girl, or Mum's Barbie princess.

Maybe I wouldn't have broken into the drinks cabinet and made vodka jellies for my eleventh birthday party or got a taste for cigarettes. Maybe I'd have got a buzz from scoring the winning goal at hockey or making perfect cupcakes instead of digging scalpels, knives and paperclips into my legs and being fascinated by the blood.

Maybe I wouldn't have had my head turned so easily by a wonky-smiled bass player in a goth band, or been so completely possessed by him. Maybe. But I expect I would. First love bit deep, drew blood. I was still bleeding.

Maybe Dad wouldn't have cheated on Mum and spared her the hurt and humiliation that fuelled their arguments, which in turn made Dad even more reluctant to come home from his office. Maybe he wouldn't have worked his way into an early grave, and me and Cosmo would still be together.

Perhaps. Maybe. *If only.*

My own packing wasn't as efficient or as rigorous as Mum's. Black clothing seeped across my bedroom carpet like an oil slick. Piles of books teetered on tables. When I'd come across the deluxe editions of Neil Gaiman's *The Sandman* comics, I'd curled up on the bed to read them for the first time in years.

I'd always liked them, but now there was a special resonance to the story of its main character, Morpheus, Lord of Dreams, who escapes after being a prisoner of an occult group, takes his revenge and rebuilds his kingdom. It seemed so apt and pertinent to me, although it might have struck a chord with Mum too.

I took down framed posters of gnarled, moonlit forests where strange, hooded figures skulked in the shadows while demons flew overhead. There were fistfuls of flyers for club nights Cosmo had taken me to.

Antichrist, its letters made out of stylised axes, daggers and cobwebs. That was where I first saw him play live and where I heard the girls behind me wondering if he was smiling at them. I can still feel the thrill of knowing that it wasn't.

Blood and Velvet. Where I told him that I loved him and went into agonies of doubt and shame when he didn't say he loved me too.

Dead and Buried. Where he finally told me that he felt the same. His kiss was dazzling, hot as a spotlight. Love lit me up, threw the shadows from the world and convinced me I could do the same with the chains.

Hex. Where I spent the evening watching him from the darkest alcove, sipping a Coke, wondering how he'd feel about being a parent. Scared he'd be as frightened as I was, but also confident we could cope. We were in love, after all.

All of the flyers were like a slap in the face but I couldn't bring myself to throw them away so I buried them among a drift of DVDs. *Sleepy Hollow. The Crow. Suspiria.* Just looking at the covers I could almost feel Cosmo's arm around my shoulder, hear his heartbeat as I rested my head against his chest, the pair of us lit by the shadows and flicker of the TV screen. Until he switched it off, of course, like he did his love, and I was left in the dark, looking for my happy ending. Empty. Only not.

The pain of the memories couldn't be packed or thrown away – even if I wanted to. And I didn't. My counsellor, Dr Ingram, was always trying to get me to find a different groove. Look forward, not back. Don't do what you always do. Do something different. But I couldn't because I didn't want to let Cosmo go. First love was a loop. And so is a noose.

I crawled over the debris onto the bed. Tears scorched my eyes.

I swept them away at a knock on the door. Two short taps. A pause. Then a third knock.

'Come in, Olga,' I said, wiping a smudge of mascara onto my skirt.

She slipped into the room without fully opening the door, like a spy. Dove-grey eyes scanned the room. Her head tilted sympathetically; a strand of dirty-blonde hair fell across her face. She tucked it back behind her ear and walked towards me, perching on the bed. She smelt of fabric softener and warm laundry.

'This won't get us packed,' she said. 'We need you up and about. We never get to the new house if you stay on the bed.'

'Suits me fine.'

She'd been the housekeeper for the last three years, after Mrs Brady had been forced to retire because of complications after surgery on her knee. The domestic agency sent over a number of candidates, Olga included, only Mum wasn't certain at first as she worried that Olga's English wasn't up to scratch.

I told Mum not to be so stuffy about it; *she* was an immigrant too. How would it have been if the sandwich shop in Old Street hadn't given her a chance?

'You're always banging on about getting an opportunity and taking it,' I said. 'Doesn't it apply to other people too?'

I admired Olga for having the guts to make a break from her life in Riga for a shot at something new, something better. Like I wished I could. Like I would when I was old enough.

Within her week's trial period, Olga had made herself indispensable, proving herself more capable and flexible than Mrs Brady and yet still having time to sit at the kitchen table, hunched over puzzle books.

'Crosswords good for my English, Miss Isabella. Make me

look here,' she said, pointing her pen at the dictionary on the table. 'But why you have so many words the same that mean not the same? Re*fuse* or *refuse*? Patient, sick. Patient, no hurry. Why no just make up more words? Different words?' She tutted. 'And why give different words different meanings and spellings but same sound? There. Their. They're.' She shrugged and went back to her puzzle.

There. Their. They're. Even her confusion was soothing.

Every day, her English improved. Every day, my fondness for her grew. I've lost count of the number of times she has comforted or helped me. I can still remember the smell and warmth of her apron as I sobbed into it after Dad died; earthy, with a floral hint of detergent. She didn't tell Mum about me smoking in my bedroom and masked the smell with vigorous spurts of air freshener. She let me use her phone to call Cosmo when Mum confiscated mine. And she left the basement door unlocked when I sneaked out to go clubbing.

Mum never knew Olga was such an ally or that it was Olga who made the house feel like home. I hoped she'd do the same at the manor.

'It's exciting, Miss Isabella,' she said. 'New home. Like for me when I first think about coming from Riga to London.'

'To London, yes. Not to Stagcote.'

She screwed her face up.

'It's better,' she said. 'For me, anyway. Much better.' She leant in closer. 'I only stay in London because there's nothing for me in Riga. House. Money. Husband. Pff,' she said, snapping her fingers. 'All gone. But here,' she sat back and smiled, 'I have a house and a job. Both very good.'

'No husband though,' I said. 'And you won't find one of those in Stagcote.'

'Why?' she said with mock indignation. 'Are you saying I'm ugly?'

'No!' I laughed. 'It's not *you*. It's Stagcote. You just don't understand. There's nothing there. And the people! God, you don't want to know.'

'You and Lady Lindy are both there. That's all I need to know.'

'You won't miss it here?'

'Miss what? It's noisy. Dirty. Too many people. All the time rush, rush, rushing. Sirens. Dog dirt. Boys with knives. Crazies. Drugs.'

'Well, don't you worry there are crazies in Stagcote too. Believe me.'

She shook her head. 'Out in the countryside it's quiet. Nothing noisier than animals. Sheeps and birds and flowers.'

'And bees. You'll have to make friends with them. It's compulsory. Watch what you tell them, mind. Or they'll put a curse on you.'

Olga frowned.

'What?'

'Don't mind me,' I said. 'It's just nonsense. But you better get used to it.' I squeezed her hand. 'Thank God you're coming, Olga,' I said. 'I couldn't bear it if you weren't. It would feel like an even bigger punishment.'

She sighed.

'You know, this isn't so easy for Lady Lindy either,' she said. 'Tough for her to leave here too.'

'She doesn't give that impression.'

'She hides it. But I see it.'

'See what exactly?'

She pointed to her eyes.

'It's in here. The sadness. She's leaving a lot behind too. All the parties, concerts. Friends. And she lived here a long time with your father. Many memories. Good ones. Bad ones. For you too, of course.'

She was right. It hadn't all been bad. There had been laughter and joy here; Mum and me in our socks having sliding races down the polished wood corridors, Dad singing to me when light summer evenings kept me from sleeping, the glow and shadows of the pure white candles on our Christmas tree, Frisbee and pogo sticks in the garden, ice-cream floats, chirruping budgerigars. Love.

Longing and regret burned like acid in my belly. The thought of Mum feeling the same way intensified the burn. It wouldn't be the same at Stagcote – couldn't be, not with all that had happened, not without Dad. But we could try. Mum, Olga and me.

'It will be fine,' Olga said. 'Finger crossed.'

I laughed.

'*Fingers* crossed,' I said. 'You're going to fit right in at Stagcote, I promise you.'

I coiled my hand so tight my fingernails bit into my palm. The tender skin around the bee sting smarted.

We moved a week later. An army of men in brown overalls loaded the furniture, boxes and crates into a fleet of purple removal trucks. Each was loaded up then driven off, and the next one summoned by the supervisor on a walkie-talkie. The hiss of the static and the pitch of the voices set my teeth on edge.

Mum flapped around, watching anxiously as each item was picked up and carried outside. Room by room, the house was emptied. The flush on Mum's face deepened; the light in her eyes grew brighter. Her back seemed to straighten and she looked taller, as if she'd been compressed, shouldering the weight of the house, and was finally being freed of the burden brick by brick.

I wanted to feel the same but I couldn't. I drifted from one

39

empty room to the next, shuddering at the echoes and dragging my fingers along the walls, just to make sure they were still there. That *I* was still there.

All the other things in the house had been wrapped up against breakages. I was broken before I even left and Stagcote would not make me whole again. How I wished the walls would close around me.

In the end, the supervisor asked if I could wait outside as I was holding things up.

'We'd best be on our way as it is, honey,' Mum said to me. 'Everything seems to be going OK at this end. Let's hope it's the same at the other.'

Olga had driven up first thing that morning, taking the dog, Sasha, with her. Someone from the stables would bring Mum's horses up a few weeks later.

I blinked back the tears as I stepped out of the house for the last time. I ground my foot into the step, as if I might take root. How many times had I crossed that threshold? No more. Life was closing behind me, leaving me to drown in Stagcote's cold and barren murk. The 'Sold' sign was like a flag celebrating Mum's triumph. I looked the other way as I went past it, through the gate and got into the car.

I could see Mum's silhouette in the hallway. At first I thought she was giving last-minute instructions to the removal men, but I noticed she was standing still, arms by her side. When she moved, she did so in increments as if committing everything she could see to memory. A hand drifted up to her face and brushed beneath her eyes. She straightened her back and walked out of the door and down the steps.

She gave me a soft, sad smile as she slid into the driving seat. How I wished she would suddenly put up her hand and call the removal men back. From the look in her eyes I wondered if she felt the same way too but the glimmer of doubt and sorrow only lasted for a moment.

I didn't dare to look back as we pulled away. I don't think Mum did either, but I caught her glancing at me out of the corner of her eyes. The green of her eyes was darker, more liquid. Several times she drew breath as if about to speak then let the air out in a quiet sigh.

'Well,' she said, about ten minutes into the journey. 'That's that then.'

As if it was as simple as that, when we both knew that it wasn't.

'Yes,' I said. 'I suppose it is.'

'We'll be OK, honey. You'll see.' She put her foot down to get through an amber light. '*More* than OK.'

'I wonder if the people who'd had the manor before us thought the same thing,' I said.

'The Gilbeys, you mean?' Mum said.

It turned out Mum's solicitor knew the owners, a pair of hotshot lawyers who specialised in acrimonious, asset-rich divorce cases. They were so renowned for winning large pay-offs that if one half of a divorcing couple appointed James Gilbey, the other half would appoint his wife, Ingrid. Ripping other people's marriages apart in the divorce courts seemed to keep their own marriage afloat.

'Nice couple apparently,' she said. 'I should imagine we know a lot of the same people. It's a wonder our paths haven't crossed before.'

'They're still alive then?'

Mum laughed and gave me a quizzical look.

'What a question! Of course they're alive.'

So much for the curse. Just a load of bull, as I suspected.

'The solicitor said they sold up as the manor was too far from London.'

'They're not wrong there.'

'Yes, but they weren't worried about being away from nightclubs and such,' she said. 'One of their kids was diagnosed with leukaemia not long after they bought the place and they wanted to be closer to their consultant.'

It was just a terrible coincidence. Nothing more. A fluke.

I leant my head against the window, felt the thrum of the engine, the life of the city streets reverberate through me. Each pulling me in a different direction to the other. I closed my eyes.

When I opened them some time later, the traffic was thinner and moving faster. Concrete and lamp posts had segued into fields and telegraph poles.

As we turned off the road into the driveway to the manor, I deliberately made a point of not looking through the hedge at the Gate House. Turning my back on the bees. It was daft really. But even by consciously ignoring them I was giving them attention too. Giving credence to their power.

I looked through the hedge. There was no sign of Howard but the white of the beehives flashed like code through the leaves.

'Boo!' I said quietly, smiling at my defiance. But as they faded into the distance in the wing mirror, I wondered if I'd said it quietly to keep it from Mum or the bees. My circumspection made me smile again. Mum was the bigger danger. She'd already proved that.

'We should invite our new neighbour over at some point,' Mum said.

She'd been thrilled with the jar of honey he'd given us even though, like me, she had no taste for it. What mattered was what it represented: neighbourliness and being welcomed. Accepted. Although she'd shipped me out to the countryside because of the plans she had for me, she had ambitions of her own too.

She loved films about English history, where knights jousted for the honour of their ladies, and kings had their heads turned by pretty young women with eyes on a title. The houses in those films didn't look too different from the manor and the local lord and lady were the axis around which the whole world spun. They provided the work that put food in their bellies. They set examples of polite behaviour, led thought and fashion, showed people right from wrong.

She enjoyed having the title of 'Lady' but it meant nothing on its own, particularly as she'd only got it by default. Now that Dad had gone, she wanted to play up to the title in her own right and taking over the manor was the perfect opportunity.

I shuddered at the thought of her in some 'official' capacity; cutting the ribbon at the opening of a shop, perhaps, judging cakes and watercolours at the annual fête or taking salutes from competitors at the gymkhana. She needed that affirmation. Tradition and custom could be relied on to point the way and keep her head above water. That's why she'd been so charmed about the beating the bounds ceremony. And the jar of honey.

As we moved down the driveway, she had a smile on her face and a distant look in her eyes. I could almost see the village idyll taking shape inside her mind, where rosy-cheeked girls danced around maypoles while grizzled men with bad teeth arm-wrestled for a flagon of amber cider.

She looked enraptured. Happy. I was tempted to ruin the moment for her by telling her about the curse and the prophecy of the bees. It was almost enough to make me wish I believed it.

The manor's forecourt was a jigsaw of vans and removal lorries. Men scurried around between them, shouting and grunting as they eased crates and furniture along the lorry to the platform at the back, which juddered the goods to the ground with an air-pressured hiss.

I got out of the car and looked up at the house. Once again its turrets and towers and tall, arching windows gave me a sharp kick of pleasure. But there were shadows in its nooks and crannies, the drainpipes like blackened veins. The weathered gargoyles could as easily have been prowling, hissing demons as proud, roaring lions. The V-sign in the hands of the clock was resolute.

The large hall was teeming with removal men pushing trolleys loaded with tea chests and boxes or heaving furniture up the worn steps and through the wide open double doors. The floor was a maze of boxes and misshapen objects hidden beneath waves of plastic and bubble wrap. The grunts of men shunting a piano across the floor punctuated the hubbub.

I hadn't bothered going inside last time, so it should have been a surprise. Only it was pretty much as I imagined it would be.

Ribs of wood fretted the hall's vaulted ceiling. Its dark, lacklustre patina matched the oak of the panelled walls and the steps and balustrades of the staircase that sprouted from the black and white marble floor. The long sweep of windows on either side of the main door admitted a faltering, uneven light; dust motes hung like mist. The chilly air had the musty smell of history.

I suppose it looked elegant but there was something about the place I couldn't quite put my finger on. It seemed restless, brooding, unwelcoming, like Cosmo's flatmates the first time he took me back to his squat. Their reception had been grudging and half-hearted. This felt the same. But there was something else too; a sense of foreboding, like I was walking into a trap. A prison.

And I was; keeping me under control was the whole point of moving. My anxiety about the manor was more to do with my feelings about the move and my mother than the house itself. It would never be my home. If we were to turn around there and then and abandon our move, I suspected the house would be as happy about it as I would.

I felt Mum's gaze burn into me and realised she was expecting a reaction. She widened her eyes and leaned towards me, hands out.

'Well?' she said, spinning on her heels. 'What do you think? Isn't it something, honey?'

'It's . . . something all right,' I said.

'It needs some TLC, of course,' she said firmly, her head gazing up at the ceiling. 'But I've got loads of ideas for what we can do to the place. To make it *our* home.'

If she hadn't been in such a hurry to get me out of London, the renovation and decoration could have been done before we moved. But she'd got it into her head that doing the house up would bring us together, that we'd find common ground over paint samples and fabric swatches. It would take more than plaster and paint to cover up the cracks in our relationship. What she had made me do, the torment she had caused me, could not be hidden by a well-placed sofa and rug.

'Great,' I mumbled. 'I know what I want for my room.'

Mum smiled and cocked her head.

'Oh yes?'

'A bomb. Or a wrecking ball.'

'Honey, please,' she said. 'Give it a chance, OK?'

She took my shrug for a yes.

'Your father would have loved it here,' Mum said, her voice a little tight. She took my hand and squeezed it. 'And he'd have loved the idea of you and me pulling together to get the place right. I bet he's looking down on us now, cheering us on.'

45

I squeezed her hand back.

'Yeah,' I said. 'But I'd rather he was here.' My lip trembled and I tried to hide it with a laugh. And a joke. 'We could do with the extra pair of hands.'

Sasha's shrill bark echoed along one of the corridors. Mum called out to him and he appeared a moment later, weaving past the furniture and removal men, his tail twitching and eyes bulging.

Mum swept him up into her arms, out of harm's way, and moved further into the maze of boxes. She leant over a large box, peering beyond it.

'What . . . what on earth is that?' she said.

She pushed at the box with her knee but it was too heavy so she asked one of the removal men to move it aside. She squeezed through the gap and stood in front of the massive fireplace in the hallway, frowning. Sasha licked at her hand.

'Any suggestions, Isabella?' she said over her shoulder.

I slouched across the hallway, leant over a crate and looked into the fireplace. Slabs of beige stone had been carefully laid out, filling the fireplace with a pyramid, at the apex of which were the two halves of an eggshell.

'It could be feng shui?' Mum said. 'Or ikebana maybe . . . although I don't see any sign of any flowers . . .' She moved away from the fireplace and looked around her, a hand on her head, the other cradling Sasha. 'Whatever it is, I don't remember it being here when we came to view the house, do you?'

'How would I know? I didn't come inside, remember?' I stood back from the fireplace and frowned at her. 'You were probably so gooey-eyed about the place you missed it . . . too busy looking up at the ceiling.'

'Maybe,' Mum said, quietly. She screwed her eyes up in concentration. 'But . . . it's so big and . . . it's opposite the front door. It would have been the first thing I saw!'

46

'Then it couldn't have been there, could it?'

Olga bustled into the hallway, her hair swept under a polka-dotted headscarf, a sheen of sweat on her forehead and a clipboard in her hand.

'Ah, Lady Lindy. Sorry, I didn't hear you arrive,' she said.

Her eyes looked brighter than they had in London and she seemed relaxed despite the pressure of the move.

'Everything gone very well, Lady Lindy,' Olga said, tapping the clipboard with a pen. 'Things are just about in the right place and nothing's broken . . . so far . . . I think.'

Mum nodded.

'Very good,' she said. 'We were wondering if you knew anything about this?'

Olga squeezed between the boxes and stood in front of the fireplace.

'Looks good, I think,' she said, 'but not so good for keeping warm.'

'You put it there?'

Olga started with surprise.

'Me? I've plenty to do already,' she said. 'And if *I* built a fire, it would be one you could actually use.'

Mum raised a hand in apology. Sasha tried to lick it.

'So it was here when you arrived this morning?' Mum said.

Olga nodded.

'And the alarms were on?'

'Yes,' Olga said. 'Very loud. Not so easy to turn off as the ones in London.'

'And there wasn't anybody about?'

'No.'

'And you've not seen any broken windows? Open doors?'

'No.' Olga frowned. 'Sorry. I don't understand. Don't you like the stones? It's art, no?'

'No, I do *not* like the stones,' Mum said, her eyes darting

47

around the hall. 'Someone has been in the house. Someone who has keys and knows the alarm code.'

Olga's eyes widened.

Outside, the gravel on the driveway popped beneath the wheels of a car. A few moments later, Mr Eaves appeared at the open door.

'Good morning,' he said. 'Just thought I'd drop by to see how things are going.'

He wiped his feet on the steps and walked towards us, zig-zagging boxes and smiling hello at the removal men.

'Mr Eaves,' Mum said. 'You're just the person who should be able to help.'

Eaves opened his hands in invitation.

'Fire away.'

'I need the number of the alarm company and a good lock-smith,' Mum said quickly. 'We've had a break-in. Of sorts.'

'Of sorts?' he said.

His concern dissolved as soon as Mum pointed towards the fireplace.

'This?' he said. 'Yes, I thought you might be a bit baffled by it. That's one of the reasons I called in. I was hoping to get here earlier so I could allay any fears you might have had. But there's really nothing to worry about.'

'*You* did it?' I said.

'No, not me. Some of the people from the village. I just let them in.'

Mum cleared her throat and put Sasha on the ground. The dog sniffed around Eaves's feet then trotted off among the boxes.

'Is your company in the habit of giving access to a private home to anyone who asks? I know some country mansions are open to the public but Stagcote isn't one of them. Nor will it be. It's *our home*.'

Eaves shifted uncomfortably, his grin tense and embarrassed.

'I understand, Your Ladyship. But if you'll let me explain.'

Mum puffed her cheeks out. 'Go on,' she said.

He reminded Mum that she'd asked him to come to the manor to let the surveyor and the utility company engineers in.

'When the locals heard I was here,' he explained, 'a couple of men and their children came up and asked if they could put the stones in the fireplace. It's a Stagcote custom, you see.' He held his hands out. 'Like the little procession we encountered when you first came to see the house?'

Mum and I nodded.

'Well, this is another one of their funny little ways, apparently. They said how interested you'd been in the beating the bounds ceremony and thought you'd like this too.' He held his hands out. 'And, seeing as you'd told me yourself how charming you'd found the procession, I agreed. I'm very sorry if I was mistaken.'

Mum cleared her throat.

'There's a big difference between letting people pass through my private property,' she said, 'and letting them into my house.'

'Of course. I'm sorry. If it's any consolation I was with them the whole time. No one went any further than the hall.'

'You could have told us about it,' Mum said. 'Saved us the stress.'

Eaves inclined his head to her.

'But then I would have spared you the surprise too,' he said imploringly. 'And they were so keen that it *should* be a surprise. If you could have seen the children's faces . . . They'll be so upset if they knew you were angry.'

'But what's it supposed to mean?' Mum said. Her tone was less terse, relieved.

'They told me it's Stagcote's way of saying "welcome", and also a good luck charm . . . a wish that you enjoy a comfortable life here, with fuel for the fire and food to cook on it.'

'Oh God,' I muttered. 'More cutesy custom. Haven't these people got anything better to do?' I clicked my fingers. 'Scratch that. I already know the answer to that one.'

But Mum's pursed lips slowly ripened into a smile.

'Well, it's really rather quaint, isn't it?' she said. 'Very . . . thoughtful.'

'I'm glad you think so, Your Ladyship,' Eaves said. 'That's what I'd hoped.'

Mum eyed him coolly.

'I still don't like the idea of you letting people into the house.'

He grinned sheepishly.

'I'm sorry. I can arrange to have the stones removed, of course.'

'Don't worry,' Mum said, 'we'll get one of the removal men to shift them.'

Olga made a note on her clipboard.

Eaves knelt down by the stones and peered up the chimney.

'You might want to get a chimney sweep in before you go too far with the decoration.'

Olga wrote that down too.

'So,' Eaves said, standing up and brushing soot from his hands. 'I hope you'll agree there's really no need for new locks or to call out the alarm people.'

'No,' Mum said, apologetically. 'There's no need to worry. Everything's fine.'

Only it wasn't. That was our mistake.

I'd gone upstairs to choose a bedroom. My feet were heavy on the stairs, the treacle-coloured wood groaning with each step. How many other people had used the stairs? I wondered. How many palms had it taken to wear the handrail so smooth? Had any of those people been happy here?

Despite the light from the window at the top of the staircase, the house felt gloomy upstairs. The air was thicker, stale, as if the previous occupants had sucked up all the oxygen. I was slightly puffed by the time I got to the top and my breathlessness unnerved me. The fags were taking their toll.

The staircase divided halfway up and the corridors running off to either side shrank away from me as I stood there deciding which way to go. I turned left and found myself in a long passage flanked by large windows, the light filtered by a gauze of dust and dirt. This had to be the Long Gallery – Mum had mentioned it when she'd been trying to sell the house to me.

Apparently residents used to take exercise here when bad weather prevented them from walking in the grounds, the large sweep of glass affording them a view of what they were 'missing' outside.

My steps echoed on the floor and I found myself tiptoeing, reluctant to walk in the footsteps of those other unfortunate souls, condemned to walk up and down the same corridor over and over again. Their sorrows and frustration snapped at my heels.

My sleeve left a greasy, murky arc as I rubbed at one of the windows. Something about the light, the green of the trees outside, the shadows, took me back to the view I'd had of St

James's Park from the counsellor's suite where Dr Ingram – Jenny, as she insisted I call her, like she was some kind of friend – tried to get me to work through my anger and forgive Mum.

I went once a week for a couple of months and spent most of the time staring out of the windows, watching birds fly off into the distance and wishing I could join them. Jenny droned on behind me, trying to get me to talk, sometimes succeeding. When the words came, they were always the same. Just anger and recriminations and blame.

'My mother hates me!'

'Why do you think that? Why do you think she doesn't love you?' God, that simpering sincerity in her every word.

'She made me kill my baby.'

'It was your decision, Isabella.'

'She gave me no choice.'

'You're over sixteen. You didn't need her consent to keep the baby. She couldn't have stopped you having the abortion. So . . .' and here she'd lower her voice, coat it in a little more sugar, 'perhaps there was a part of you – just a tiny part – that didn't want the baby either. Is it possible you're blaming your mother for something *you wanted* to do . . . that you knew, deep down, was for the best?'

'No! She never listens to me!'

And off we'd go again. The usual round of cajoling and encouragement foundering in the face of my stubborn silence, my back turned to the room, my eyes blank, burdened with grief, guilt, the wish just to be left alone.

I turned away from the grubby rainbow I'd left on the Long Gallery window and walked on, treading heavily in the footsteps of those who'd gone before, their exercise every bit as enervating and futile as my time with the counsellor.

I sought refuge in the rooms leading off the Long Gallery and found them to be surprisingly small, and ill-lit by cramped windows set in mottled stone walls. Mum would have her work cut out to make these rooms look anything other than a perfect cell. The garden below was snared in an elaborate tangle of weeds, a forest of rose bushes frothy with blooms overwhelmed the crumbling walls. Beyond, the spire of a small, squat church.

Adjacent to the rose beds, dilapidated greenhouses watched over unruly allotment plots. I went on tiptoes to try and see what was inside the circular wall a metre or so high. It could only be a well. I shivered, as if icy water had trickled down my spine, and turned away from the window.

There was no radiator and the grate was empty and dirty, not with coal or smoke, but dust and bits of twigs dropped by birds down the chimney. Which made me think Mr Eaves had been right about the need for a chimney sweep.

I left the room and crossed to the corridor to the right of the landing. The stonework wasn't the same uniform colour, but brindled with lighter patches and seamed with paler mortar. The windows were wider, the cross-hatching of leading in the glass less dense. The swirls of stucco were less effusive, the cornices deeper.

I was no expert but even I could tell this part of the house was newer than the other part. But even though it had been built during a different period, it retained the same grudging, brooding air, the cold, stale smell of history. It fell around me, like a cloak.

The rooms, though, were larger, brighter and warmer, although still not warm. The fireplaces were more capable of a decent, toasty blaze than the meagre ones promised on the west wing.

I folded my arms and pressed my forehead against the window. Fields and trees rode the undulations in the earth beneath them. Birds skittered in the air and pheasants dawdled across stretches of unkempt lawn.

It wasn't a view I'd ever like, but it was better than the one from the other side as it had more hedgerows than walls, and the few walls I could see were low. Surmountable. Incapable of keeping me in.

And beyond the hedge, just peeping above the brow of the hill, I could see the roof of the Gate House. I decided to take that room as mine.

That's when I heard a noise coming from the garden. A rattling, rumbling noise. Groaning and heavy breaths.

I crossed to the room on the other side and looked out of the window. Below me, one of the removal men staggered across the kitchen garden, pushing a trolley loaded with the stones from the fireplace. He stopped at the well to wipe his forehead on his sleeve, the sweat shimmering in the sunlight.

Then he bent down, got right under the trolley handles, and pushed them up and forward. A blizzard of rock and rubble crashed into the well.

A pile of rocks as a house-warming gift? What were they thinking? These people were on a different planet. Apart from anything else, it would take a lot more than a stack of stones to make the manor feel anywhere close to home.

The removal man picked up a few stones that had fallen to the ground and lobbed them into the well, before peering over the edge. A backdraught of dust billowed around him, swallowing him up.

A few seconds later, something rattled in the fireplace behind me, making me jump. A knot of twigs twitched in the grate, haloed by a puff of black dust. I turned back to the window. A sudden gust of wind spilt crows from a tree on the hillside; in the startled calls that rang out across the sky, I thought I heard the cry of a baby.

My hand dropped to my stomach and I bolted out of the

room and down the stairs. A pall of soot swirled in front of the hall fireplace. Dry black dust coated the back of my throat.

'I need some air,' I said, and crossed the hall to the door.

Thank God Mum couldn't see me hawking and gobbing onto the grass. Not quite the impression she'd want to give of the new family at the manor.

The garden was a tangle of weeds and crisped husks of shrubs. Grey stems veined a weathered trellis and ivy grabbed at my ankles. Just walking anywhere in or around the house was such an effort; how the hell was I going to live here?

I gave the well a wide berth as I approached, but something pulled me closer. Curiosity, I suppose. Remembrance too.

I don't know how old I was – six or seven, I suppose – or where we were precisely – some hotel or the other, all glass and marble with an atrium and escalators. Dad was holding on to my hand as we glided down the escalator, the bronze and silver coins at the bottom of the fountain in the lobby shimmering like fish scales. When we got to the bottom, Dad held out a shiny coin and told me to throw it in and make a wish. I told him he had to make one too. The coins plopped and splashed, fluttered to the bottom.

'Don't tell me what you wished for,' Dad said, 'or it won't come true.'

'Or you!' I squealed.

'Ah, I don't mind,' he said, kissing me on the nose. 'I've had too many wishes come true already. I don't want to be greedy.'

I can't remember what I wished for – only that I still believed it possible that wishes could come true.

Traditions. Customs. Superstitions. They were all nonsense. Sideshows to distract us from the grinding reality of things and sow false hope that things can change for the better. To trick us into putting our faith into something other than ourselves.

So I was surprised to find my hand rummaging in my pocket for a coin. It must have been the Stagcote air getting to me, or the proximity to the villagers discarded house-warming gift. Whatever. It felt like something I had to do.

I blew the fluff from the coin and peered over the edge of the well. My eyes took a moment to adjust to the darkness but once they had, I could just about make out the pile of stones from the fireplace at the bottom, about ten metres down. I tossed in my coin, heard it clatter against the wall, an echo, then, as it landed, a couple of clicks, like bones shifting.

I meant to make a wish, to get me back to London as soon as possible, but when I opened my mouth that wasn't what came out.

'Sorry.'

A sadness as deep and impenetrable as the darkness in the well enveloped me. The yawning void seemed to be reaching out to take me down. I pulled away quickly, unsure who the apology was meant for. Cosmo. My baby. Dad. Even Mum. Maybe even me.

I walked on, towards the gnarled and buckled door with rusty hinges in the head-high wall at the end of the garden. I expected it to be locked or too stiff to open, but the latch lifted easily and the door swung free, spilling me out into the churchyard.

Moss-mottled headstones jutted from the ground like uneven teeth. The church walls were a dingy grey, gradually succumbing to the creep of lichen and damp. An unembellished spire prodded at the sky apologetically.

Memories of Dad's funeral flashed through my mind. The curve of the American white oak pews at St Peter's in Eaton Square, the way they filled up with people, most of whom I didn't know or recognise. They were colleagues from the business life that took Dad from me far too early, a couple of the younger women probably the lovers who'd kept him in their bed instead of letting him come home to read me fairy tales in mine.

The images and memories accelerated. The rheumy-eyed vicar's endless eulogy, the sharp scent of the whitest lilies, the grip of Mum's hand as she took mine, the sobs that pounded my ribcage, the hard, bright pain in our eyes.

I put my head down and rushed past the church, through the gate and out onto what I took to be the main road of Stagcote village, even though it was empty of cars and people.

A row of higgledy-piggledy cottages ran either side of the street, the honey-coloured stone glowing in the sunlight. The roofs were bulbous with thick thatch or silvered by slate tiles speckled with moss. A twist of smoke rose from one of the chimneys, despite the warmth of the sun.

Somewhere to my left I heard the quack of ducks; a flotilla of ducklings bobbed by on a slow-moving river that slipped under a goldfish-bowl bridge. Fronds of green vegetation bent and weaved in the flow.

It was Mum's idea of the perfect English village, a fitting backdrop against which to play out her fantasy of the gracious and benevolent Lady. But to me the cottages looked fossilised. The whole place belonged in a museum. Nothing lived here. Nothing could. Especially me. I ached for the noise of London, to feel its shudder in my bones, its dirt, its danger and possibilities.

Halfway down the street, the sign of the Horns Tavern swayed slightly in the breeze, like a beckoning finger I could not resist. It was about the only thing in Stagcote that came anywhere close to normality and I needed to get rid of the taste of coal dust still caught at the back of my throat.

The smell of stale beer and tobacco smoke hit me the moment I walked in. The pub had a worn, flagstone floor; bare stone walls boasted leather straps with horse brasses and faded watercolours of rural views. A wicker basket of logs stood guard over an empty, soot-stained fireplace.

Two men, one in a grey cap, sat at the bar and they turned towards the door as I pushed it open. Eyes widened. Eyebrows arched. The man behind the bar smiled.

I caught my reflection in the mirror behind the bar. My hair was backcombed, big and black, my face pale, even without its usual layer of foundation. Green eyes glittered in a thatch of black, like berries in a hedgerow.

If there'd been more people in the pub I could've left right away before anyone noticed me. It was too awkward to do that now, but stepping up to the bar felt just as awkward. I dithered, a blush heating my cheek.

The barman cleared his throat.

'Afternoon,' he said. 'What can I get you?'

I took a tentative step towards the bar, patting my pockets, then stopped. My wallet was back at the house somewhere.

'Sorry,' I said, 'I've not got any money on me.' I turned to the door.

'Hold up there,' the barman said. 'You can have one on the house. It'll be my pleasure.'

'You never buy me a drink,' the man in the grey cap mumbled into his beer.

'I would if you lived at the manor.' The barman winked at me. 'I'm right, aren't I? You're the new lady of the manor's daughter?'

'Yes.'

God, everyone knew everything. Forget privacy. Everyone would be watching me. Gossiping. Judging.

'Thought so. I saw you sitting in the car when we were

beating the bounds.' He waved his finger around his face. 'You look a bit different now though. Hardly recognised you.'

I was amazed he'd recognised me at all. I hadn't had the slightest trace of make-up on that day and he could only have caught the briefest glimpse of me.

'I'm Ed,' the barman said. 'This is Percy.' He gestured to the man in the cap, who lifted the front of it with his finger but didn't actually take the cap off. 'And this here is Nathan.' He was the youngest of the three and had a chipped front tooth.

'Isabella, isn't it?' Nathan said.

Of course he knew my name. Everyone did. Me and Mum would have been the only topic of discussion for weeks.

'Izzy.'

'Well then, Izzy, what would you like?'

I ordered a vodka and tonic and Nathan pulled out the bar stool next to his. Then he cut a chunk of pale, waxy-looking cheese from the wedge on his plate, popped it into his mouth and chewed quickly.

'So,' Ed said, wiping the bar, 'how are things up at the manor?'

I thought of the well, the soot and the cry of the baby and the call of the crows. The drudgery of the Long Gallery, the V of the clock.

'Fine,' I said quietly. I wasn't going to give them anything else to gossip about. I took a slow sip from my glass, let my teeth settle briefly on its rim.

'Did the move go OK?'

'Yes. It's still going on, actually,' I said.

Percy took an unlit pipe resting in an ashtray and sucked on the end of it.

'Did you see anything . . . unusual?' he said.

Just the house, the entire village and everything in it, I wanted to say. *Nothing interesting though.*

'No, not really,' I said.

The men looked at one another.

'Nothing . . . in the fireplace then?' Nathan said.

'Oh, the stones you mean?' I said. 'Yes. They had Mum worried for a while. She thought we'd had someone in the house.'

'You had.'

'Yes, but . . . not burglars or anything.'

'Not much to steal in an empty house.'

'Not that anyone around here would steal from the manor even if the place was full of gold,' Ed said. 'We're a law-abiding bunch. You've no worries on that score, at least.'

The pub door swung open and Howard breezed in with a smile that broadened further still when he saw me. I was glad to see him too. Not only was he about the most normal person I'd met so far in Stagcote, he was an outsider too. He'd probably undergone the inquisition from the villagers when he first arrived and would hopefully rescue me or at least provide a distraction.

'Afternoon all,' he said, walking towards the bar.

'Howard,' Ed said patiently. Percy and Nathan gave grudging nods of acknowledgement. I sensed their disinterest; my own experience of being rejected and judged for being different made sympathy swell inside me.

'I see you're settling in,' Howard said to me, with a wink.

He offered to buy us all drinks but Nathan and Percy pursed their lips and said no. I was going to decline too but I didn't want Howard to feel slighted so I asked for another vodka.

Ed placed a pint of lager and my glass of vodka on the bar.

'Leaving all the work to your mother, are you?' Howard said.

'Sort of,' I said. 'I should finish these and get back, I suppose.'

'I wouldn't hurry,' Howard said. 'A couple more lorries

60

have just turned up there. It's pretty manic so I didn't stay long. Just introduced myself and dropped off a bottle of wine.' He frowned. 'She said it was more traditional than the other house-warming present she'd received and would be much more fun to dispose of, so God knows what else she's been given.'

I shifted on my chair awkwardly and told him about the stones and the misunderstanding they'd caused.

'Ah,' he said. 'Now it makes sense.'

'We didn't mean no harm with the stones,' Ed said.

'No, I know,' I said quickly. 'Once Mum understood what it was all about she thought it was rather sweet. We both did.' I looked at the floor, hoping to hide the lie in my eyes. 'Thank you.'

When I looked up again, Percy and the others were staring at me. Nathan sliced another chunk of cheese.

'What did your mum mean about Howard's present being more fun to dispose of?' he said, slowly. The note of suspicion in his voice made me squirm. My hesitation made them more curious.

'You've removed them already, have you?' Percy asked a little abruptly.

I fought the blush in my cheeks. Why were they making such a fuss about a pile of stones? It made no sense that they could take them so seriously. It was a gesture. I *got* that. And I'd appreciated it – sort of. And I'd apologised for their gift not lasting very long.

But it seemed to mean so much more to them than that. The offence cut deep. Stagcote had some strange ways – it ran on superstitions and silly customs – and I could only wonder at the people that still clung to them so tenaciously. How I was going to stop myself going mad living amongst them was equally baffling.

'Look,' I said, my stomach tightening, 'I'm really sorry. It wasn't my idea . . . I hope you won't be offended but . . . Mum got the removal men to throw the stones out.'

Ed drummed his fingers on the bar.

'Well, you couldn't keep them for ever, could you?' Howard said, looking to the others for support. They ignored him. 'I mean, who wants to live with a pile of stones?'

I shot him a grateful glance.

Percy took a match from a box, held it over the bowl of his pipe and sucked on it quickly.

'We don't worry about the smoking ban here,' Ed said to me. 'Nobody has complained . . . yet.' He raised his eyebrows to underline his point. His dare.

I'd never been happier that I smoked. I was anxious and embarrassed about the house-warming gift and how stupid I found the men's superstitions and customs. Lighting up would give me cover.

I took my tobacco and papers from my pocket and quickly rolled a cigarette. Percy's eyes fixed on me through the clouds of pungent, sweet-smelling smoke that rolled across the room.

'It would have been nice if the stones lasted a bit longer than just a few hours,' Percy said.

'Yes, but Mum just thought . . . with so much stuff in the house already . . .'

'If you don't want the stones, I could make use of them for plugging a few gaps in my garden wall. I can come and pick them up whenever you say.' At least he had a practical purpose for them. Or did he? Maybe he wanted to use them for some other bizarre custom. Either way, it was too late now.

I gritted my teeth.

'I'm afraid that's not possible.'

'You're using them?'

'No . . . I mean yes.' I sucked quickly on my cigarette,

wishing the smoke would envelope me entirely. 'Look, I'm sorry but . . . the stones were tipped down the well.'

They all flinched. I should have said something different, but I just didn't have time to think of anything but the truth. And why should I lie anyway?

'Down the well, eh?' Nathan said, folding his arms and stretching out his legs. 'I wonder if that will keep him quiet, then?'

'It's one less way out for him, I'd say,' Percy said, lighting his pipe once more.

'Who?' Howard said.

Ed took a glass from behind the bar and began to dry it with a tea towel.

'Edward Ingle,' he said. 'Apprenticed as a sweep to Thomas Dawkins at the age of eight from the workhouse in Cirencester. Stagcote was part of his round.'

Howard turned in his chair, eyes bright with curiosity.

'So?' he said, leaning towards them. 'What about him?'

Ed buffed the glass and put it on the rack above the bar.

'Well,' he said hesitantly, 'it's . . .'

Percy and Nathan nodded at him, as if giving him permission to continue.

'That's the thing, you see,' Ed said, taking his cue. 'No one really knows. The story goes that Dawkins beat Ingle for being lazy and greedy. It weren't like today, remember . . . no child protection officers or health and safety and all that.'

'That's right,' Percy added. 'No one really cared. That's how he got away with it.'

'*If* there was anything to get away with,' Nathan said.

I was confused, lost.

'Sorry,' Howard said. He looked just as bewildered as I did. 'Who got away with what?'

'Dawkins killing Ingle,' Ed said.

63

'Or not,' Nathan said firmly, jabbing his finger on the bar for emphasis.

Ed sighed.

'As you can see,' he said, 'even after a hundred and fifty odd years to think on it, the village jury's still out on this one.'

'Either way,' Howard said, 'we'd still like to hear the story, right, Izzy?'

I didn't know that I did but I couldn't possibly say so. Not after all the gaffs Mum and I had already made, albeit inadvertently. It was only another silly Stagcote story by the sound of it. Hopefully it wouldn't take long. I still had another vodka to finish too.

'Yes,' I said, with what I hoped sounded like real enthusiasm. I nodded for emphasis and blew a cone of smoke across the room.

Ed took another glass and twirled the tea towel inside it.

'Dawkins and Ingle turned up to do their stuff at the manor,' he said, 'and Ingle, well . . . he was never seen again. Dawkins said that Ingle went up through the fireplace and never came back. Said he was lost in the maze of chimneys.'

Nathan raised his shoulders.

'It's feasible!' he said. 'That place has had so many bits grafted on over the years it must be like a bloody big jigsaw inside the walls . . . one with missing bits or pieces that don't fit. Try putting that lot together in the dark, on your own . . . when you're hot and cramped and tired . . . when you've got someone shouting at you, threatening to thump you again once you get out.'

'That poor kid!' Howard said, wincing.

I wondered if he was faking interest too.

'Didn't Dawkins get any help?' I said, stubbing my cigarette out. Playing along with the story might help us get to the end of it sooner although I was already pretty certain where it was heading.

'Dawkins said he tried,' Ed said. 'But the family of the house were in London at the time and the locals – my great-great-great-grandparents included—'

'Mine too,' said Percy, raising his hand.

'Yep, yours too, Percy, *and* those of many, many others still in the village . . . they were all in the fields getting the harvest in.'

Percy nodded.

'Aye,' he said, 'and by the time the alarm was raised and they got to the house, there was no sign or sound of Ingle.'

'Some say Dawkins dumped Ingle's body down the well,' Percy said.

'But others,' Nathan said, leaning forward to put his glass on the bar, 'reckon Dawkins is innocent and that poor Ingle just took another wrong turn and ended up in the well. It's just a different kind of tunnel, I suppose . . . another one he couldn't get out of.'

It started off as a smirk but quickly blossomed into a broad smile. Then into a fit of the giggles.

'I'm sorry,' I said, spluttering into my drink. 'But I knew it! I knew we were going to end up with a ghost.'

'You don't believe us?' Percy said indignantly.

'Come on!' I said. 'A ghost? I mean, they're kind of cool . . . fun . . . but . . . you believe in this stuff? Really?'

Nathan spun his glass in his hand.

'A house with that history certainly has more than one ghost,' he said. 'It's not called Heartbreak Hall for nothing.'

'But any old house gets lumbered with a ghost story!' I cried. 'It's practically the law.'

Howard looked at me and twitched his eyebrows

imperceptibly, the same way Dad used to. I swallowed the sudden lump in my throat.

'At least it's original,' he said. 'A sweep makes a change from a white lady or a headless coachman.'

'It's easy to mock, isn't it?' Ed said.

'I . . . I don't mean to,' I said. 'It's just so . . . so weird. I mean, ghosts and curses? How can you believe this stuff?'

Ed, Nathan and Percy bristled and glanced at one another.

'You know about the curse then?' Ed said.

'Howard told me about it.'

The three men glared at him.

'That figures,' Percy said.

'*We* don't like to talk about it so direct,' Ed said, looking over each shoulder warily.

'We don't like talking about it at all, truth be told,' Nathan added, staring into the bottom of his glass. 'Just in case.'

'You're set on staying, are you?' Ed said. 'Despite everything?'

'I'd be gone in a shot,' I said. 'And not because of some so-called curse. It's Mum's idea we live here, and she's even less likely to believe in ghosts and curses than I am.'

'So you don't believe in the curse?' Percy said.

I felt four sets of eyes drilling into me. The silence hung heavily in the room.

'Look, I'm the sort who goes for minotaurs and goblins. Black magic, Ouija boards . . . anything like that, I'm there . . .'

'But?'

I ran a hand through my hair, scratched my scalp. 'I can't believe in curses and whatever without some kind of proof. Even the last people to own the manor are still alive! OK, yes their child is being treated for leukaemia—'

'Is he?' Nathan said. 'We didn't know that.'

'No surprise though,' Percy said, with a resigned nod.

66

'Not at all,' Ed said.

'But it's not proof of anything,' I said firmly.

Nathan leant forward.

'It isn't just the child though,' he said.

'His parents are fine!' I said. 'My mum's solicitor knows them. They're alive and kicking up a storm in the divorce courts.'

'The parents are, yes,' Nathan said, 'but Mr Gilbey's father, Martin. He moved into the manor with them.'

'And was found drowned in the river just a few months later,' Percy said. 'Lost his footing on his way back from the pub and fell in.'

'I can vouch for this much at least,' Howard said. 'It was me who found him.'

'Oh,' I said, suddenly less sure of myself than I had been before. 'I didn't know about the father dying.'

Percy held a hand out as if offering me absolute proof of the curse.

'But he could have just been drunk!' I said.

'And the little boy could have just been healthy,' Nathan said. 'But he wasn't.'

'Two tragedies in one family in a matter of months?' Ed said with a shrug.

'That's unlucky, really unlucky,' I said. 'I'll give you that. But it's not proof.'

'But unlucky is not unusual at the manor,' Percy said. 'It's the norm.'

'You should listen to him,' Nathan said.

'You should get out,' Percy said, staring at me. Yellow teeth bit into the arm of his pipe.

Even the darkness was dismal. I'd never seen such an impenetrable black, and that was saying something. Black has long been my friend. But Stagcote has taken it and added shades and hues I never thought were possible. The light from the stars and the moon would have broken the interminable stretch of nothingness I gazed upon from my window, but cloud had inked them out.

The darkness was yet another reminder that I was so far from London nights stained with yellow street lamps, the dazzle of headlights, the amber wink of indicators and Belisha beacons, the green of Go. Life.

It was no wonder the villagers had to make up ghost stories and think of occasions for silly customs. What else was there to do? I peered into the darkness. I couldn't even see any lights in the windows of the cottages. No flicker of TVs. Did they even have TVs? Computers? The internet connection was dodgy and unbelievably slow. What did these people do for fun? Woodwork, probably. And knitting. Pressing flowers. Yes. Definitely that.

Oh God.

The locals were right. This place *was* cursed. I smiled. Maybe that wasn't a bad thing; at least it would put an end to this nightmare.

I turned from the window and drifted towards the bed. Mum had wanted to get new beds but I'd insisted I brought the one from London. It wasn't old and besides, it was comfortable. Familiar. I needed that. I slid into the dented facsimile of my body in the mattress and stretched out. The bedframe creaked.

Something rattled. I thought a coin must have slipped from my pocket earlier and got caught in the duvet. I turned over. I'd get it in the morning.

I'd never had any trouble sleeping; it was the quickest and easiest way to escape Mum and everything else. I blanked things out so entirely that I never dreamed or, if I did, I could not recall them when I woke.

But sleep eluded me that first night in the manor. It was hard to settle without the humming lullaby of traffic outside, the murmur of planes circling the city. Mum always said she envied my ability to sleep through anything – alarms, storms. I slept on during the screeching sirens, emergency services radios and swirling blue lights that attended the fire at a house on the other side of Eaton Square.

It was dark here, though. Strange. Quiet. *Silent*. If it hadn't been, I probably wouldn't have heard a thing.

A scratching noise. Faint. By my door.

I shifted position and closed my eyes. The noise came again. A little louder. Longer. I sat up. There it was again.

It sounded like it was coming from outside the door. I stared in that direction, saw nothing but darkness. There was no light under the door. No one was up and about. I checked the clock on my phone: 03.03. Olga wouldn't get up for several hours yet. Even when Mum didn't sleep well she wouldn't get out of bed but read or watch TV.

Every house has its noises, I thought, little ticks and creaks as the walls and floors contract and expand, shifting, like layers of rock adjusting to geological pressure. The manor had been empty for a long time; it would need to readjust to being oc-cupied once more, to the weight of furniture, the tread of feet upon the floorboards, the flow of air and heat. I snuggled down into the bed again and closed my eyes. I heard nothing more.

I didn't give it a moment's thought the next day. Nor when

I went to bed that evening. I was tired. Mum and I had spent the day arguing about where things should go. This picture on that wall or that wall? What about those chairs? That table? I wasn't really bothered either way but was determined to have my say nonetheless. We disagreed constantly. Furniture, paintings and ornaments were moved around like giant and elaborate chess pieces in a game that would have no end. So I was glad to get to bed and fell asleep almost immediately.

Once more I was woken up. The room glowed an eerie grey when I checked the time on my phone. 03.02. The noise was louder this time, closer. I sat up, waited for it again. It wasn't a creak of expanding wood like I'd thought, but a scrabbling noise. And it wasn't outside either. It was in my room. There was a sudden anxious flutter in my heart.

A mouse, running around behind the skirting board or in the rafters. It had to be. I smiled at the thrill of alarm, the thump of my heart.

The next morning I said to Olga that we needed to get the pest controllers in but she told me she hadn't heard anything. Mum said the same.

'And I've been awake during the night too. Could have heard a pin drop.' She gave a little shrug. 'It's not like you to wake up though,' she conceded. 'But it's just being in a new house. Your sleep patterns will be back to normal soon. Just like mine are – unfortunately.'

Sleep deprivation added extra tetchiness to our wranglings over the furniture. In the end I just told Mum to do it her way, like she always did. Usually after a row I'd storm off to my bedroom but I was strangely reluctant to do that this time, in case the noise came again. So I spent the rest of the day with Olga in the kitchen, unwrapping crockery and glasses and checking the inventory as we stacked the silver plates, crockery and tureens in the silver vault.

When I eventually went to bed, I struggled to get off to sleep. Dreams came in fitful flashes. A couple of large oak trees. A London bus. A cradle.

I woke at 02.59, restless and confused, angry with myself for feeling alarmed at the thought of a mouse.

Three minutes later, the scratching started. Closer still than it had been the night before. Louder. Too loud for one mouse. There had to be lots of them, scurrying around, claws on old, dry wood.

I reached for the shoes I'd discarded by the bed and threw one against the wall. The scratching stopped. The clump brought Mum to my door.

'It was that noise again,' I said. 'Didn't you hear it?'

She shook her head.

'Wait here a minute,' I whispered. 'It will come again.'

But it didn't. We just stood there, completely still. All I could hear was our breathing.

'I don't hear anything,' Mum said, 'but we'll get the pest controller in regardless. It's quite likely there are mice around. Big house like this.'

Even though the pest controller found no sign of any mice, no droppings or gnawed wood, the house was mined with traps and poison. When he finished, Olga made him lunch in the kitchen. As he ate his salmon and cress sandwich, he told us how quickly mice could breed. That they could squeeze through any hole wider than a pencil.

'Plenty of those in a place like this,' Olga said.

'You can't put traps everywhere,' he said. 'So best keep them out where you can. Wire wool. They don't like the feel of it and won't squeeze past it. The rougher the better.'

I spent the new few hours plugging any holes I could find which inevitably meant moving bits of furniture – which in turn caused more arguments and forced me into an early night.

I jerked awake. 03.02. I turned the light on and cocked my head. The noise was even closer now. Even louder.

It was behind the wall beneath the window. Then it moved, slowly. Much too slowly for it to be mice.

Towards the fireplace.

Despite myself, my first thought was that it could be Edward Ingle, still looking for a way out of the chimney. I couldn't wait to break the news in the pub. They'd lap it up. It would keep them going for weeks. I didn't know *how* they'd interpret the return of the manor's ghost but I could guess – another dire warning. The bees were probably all abuzz too.

But my flippancy ebbed away as the noise continued. There *was* something there. And it couldn't be mice. It couldn't be a ghost either. Maybe someone was trying to get in the house downstairs and the noise was just echoing up the chimney. The thought was scarier than any ghost.

I pulled the duvet up around me, scooted along the bed and put my back against the headboard. I didn't want to look at the fireplace but didn't dare take my eyes from it. The noise was more regular now, heavier. As if something was being dragged.

My blood was ice as the sound inched away from the fireplace, bit by bit. Up the wall. Following the route of the chimney.

I flew out of bed, the duvet sending the lamp on the bedside table crashing to the floor. The sudden darkness made me panic and I blundered my way to the wall, frantically searching for the light switch and the door. But they weren't there, not where they should have been. I wondered for a moment if I was just dreaming and tried to call out but I couldn't catch my breath to do so.

Suddenly it was light. I turned to see Olga standing in the

doorway, her pale blue towelling dressing gown tied tightly round the waist. Her eyes were heavy with sleep and confusion.

'Miss Isabella? You OK?'

I rushed towards her, through the open door and out onto the landing where I sank to the floor, clutching at one of the banisters. Olga knelt down beside me, pressed a hand to my head.

'What is it? Bad dream?' she said.

I shook my head.

'That noise again! I think . . . there might be someone in the house.'

Olga pulled away from me, alarmed, and stood up to peer over the landing.

'I hear nothing,' she whispered. 'No lights either.' She came back to me. 'Just a bad dream. Like I say.'

'I . . . I couldn't get out,' I said. 'Couldn't find the door.'

Olga smiled and pushed some hair back from my face.

'You were looking in wrong place!' she said. 'You looked for the door where it was in the *old* bedroom,' she said. 'I had the same problem with bathroom. I nearly wash in my toilet. Very strange, eh, being in a new house?'

I flinched at the rattling behind me, turned and saw Mum closing her bedroom door. She was drowsy-eyed, her peach silk nightdress shimmering in the hall light.

'It's OK, Lady Lindy,' Olga said, standing up. 'Miss Isabella's been dreaming again.'

I shook my head.

'It wasn't a dream! It was that noise again. Surely you heard it this time?

Mum and Olga looked at one another with blank expressions.

'I didn't hear anything, honey,' Mum said, kneeling beside me. She smelt of sleep and stale perfume, a hint of perspiration.

Her arm slid around my shoulders. It felt heavy and awkward. 'I told you, it's just being in a new house. Getting used to its little foibles. Like that street lamp outside my bedroom window at Eaton Square that kept me awake for hours. I had to use blinkers, remember? But eventually . . .'

Olga switched the hall lights on and went down the stairs, slowly at first, stopping now and then to listen.

'Hello?' she said. 'Anyone there?'

Nothing.

She stepped from the last stair and turned on more lights, disappeared towards the kitchen. A few moments later she came back upstairs.

'There's no one there, Miss Isabella. No one.'

Mum and I followed her into my bedroom and stood still for a few seconds.

'See?' Olga said. 'All silence.'

'But it . . . he was there,' I said. My hand shook as I pointed at the fireplace. 'Going up the chimney.'

'He?' Mum said.

'The chimney sweep,' I mumbled. I couldn't believe I'd even said it. There was no ghost. It was just a story. I was tired. Mum would just think me stupid – even more stupid than she did already. Clearly I was just a hysterical teenage girl who needed watching over.

'Sweep?'

'*Sleep*. I said I need some sleep.'

'I think we all do,' Mum said. 'Let's get you back into bed, honey. No more dreams tonight, eh?'

It didn't seem possible that I'd dreamt it but it was the only feasible explanation. Ghosts weren't real. Edward Ingle might not even have been real. My imagination had just taken one thread from the last few days and pulled it, harder and faster until it spun loose.

Olga said goodnight and left the room. Mum pulled the duvet up around my chin and for a moment I thought she was going to kiss me on the forehead, like she used to do when I was younger. It used to make me feel safe then. Special.

I closed my eyes, expecting the kiss – maybe even hoping for it. But it didn't come. And when I looked up, I must have looked angry or disappointed – and maybe I was – because she backed off and gave me a smile that could just as easily have been a muscle twitching in her cheek.

The duvet bunched tightly in my fists.

I asked her to leave the light on, slid down the bed and turned away from the fireplace.

Mum smiled when I walked into the kitchen the following morning. Sasha dashed out from under the table, sniffed at my feet then curled up back where he'd been. I breathed in coffee and warm toast.

'You sleep OK in the end, honey?' she said, pouring another cup of coffee from the cafetière on the table. I hadn't but I nodded my head.

'Good.'

The jangle of dropped cutlery on the stone floor made me jump. I turned around and Olga gave me an apologetic smile.

We hadn't yet settled into the routine from Eaton Square, where Mum and I would sit on opposite sides of the table in the morning room, Mum reading the paper and trying to make conversation while I gazed at the trees in the square through the window and Olga bustled in and out with a tray, asking if we wanted anything else.

No doubt Mum hoped we'd go back to that arrangement as soon as possible, but until everything was delivered and unpacked, rooms assigned a function and decorated accordingly, we were eating meals in the kitchen. I preferred the informality, and Olga's constant presence provided some distraction, so much so that even Mum seemed more relaxed with the new regime.

Olga waggled the kettle at me.

'Coffee please,' I said.

'You want some eggs?' Olga said, putting the kettle on the Aga's hot plate. 'Bacon?'

I shook my head.

'Thanks, I couldn't. Not just yet.'

Olga sucked her teeth.

'And you wonder why you has bad dreams,' she said. 'Empty stomach. Full head.'

I sat down at the table, ran my fingers through my hair and yawned.

'It wasn't a dream,' I said. 'There *was* something there.'

Mum took a sip of coffee and then added a scrape of butter to the slice of toast on the plate in front of her. The scratch of the knife on the toast sounded like the noise I'd heard behind the chimney in my room. I pulled my dressing gown around me and shuffled closer to the table.

'Some*thing* there,' Mum said, biting into the toast. 'Well, I suppose that's better than last night.'

Huh?'

'At one point I thought you said something about a chimney sweep.'

I looked down.

'No.'

Olga passed me a mug of coffee and I cupped it in my hands and took slow sips, my shoulders hunched. 'Although . . .'

'Although what?' Mum asked.

'It's nothing. Just some nonsense I heard about the house. *Part* of it anyway. You wouldn't believe the crap they go in for here.'

'Such as?'

I took another sip. Felt a silly smile creep across my face.

'Like ghosts.'

'Ghosts!' Mum smiled. 'Well, this *is* England, I suppose. I should have expected that.'

'And there's a curse too,' I added.

Mum chuckled at that. It struck me how I hadn't heard her laugh in ages. What little laughter I *could* remember had been sarcastic or dismissive, used to underline a point. This sounded different – clear and light, right from the belly. It tickled a response from me, an unfamiliar one, and I realised I hadn't laughed in a long time either. It felt good. It felt good to laugh with Mum. Strange but good.

'A ghost and a curse?' Mum said. 'I wonder if that added a few more grand on the price of the house or got us a discount?'

Olga cleared her throat. I noticed she wasn't laughing.

'What did you hear, Miss Isabella,' she said. 'Who from?'

'I got it from the locals in the pub.'

Mum put her toast down and leant forward, her amusement seeping from her face.

'Pub? You've not been in the pub already, have you?' She shook her head. 'Really, what will the villagers think?'

It wasn't just that Mum wanted to make the right impression with the locals by inviting them to a formal unveiling of the new family at Stagcote. String quartet, platters, champagne and all that. She was worried about who I might meet at the pub. The last thing she needed was for me to take up with some village oik. Cosmo had been bad enough but a villager from Stagcote was even less likely to make the grade and that was saying something. We'd come here for a new start; she didn't want me distracted from my studies, least of all by another unsuitable boy. *That* really would be a curse.

'You're worried about what *they* think of *us*? They should be worrying about what we think of them! Chimney sweeps lost in the chimney and left for dead. Certain death for anyone at the manor. It'll be hobbits at the bottom of the garden next.'

Mum's laughter was back.

'Did you hear this, Olga?' she said, dabbing away some crumbs from her lips with a white napkin. 'It's like something out of *Scooby-Doo*.' She wafted the napkin in front of her face and made a wooing noise.

'Don't!' Olga said. Her forehead was creased with a deep frown and her eyes pinched. 'It's not funny.'

'Oh come on,' Mum said. 'You don't really believe in all this sort of stuff, do you? It's nonsense. Fun – but nonsense.'

It was nice to know we agreed on something. But Olga's anxiety was written all over her face.

'Mum, please,' I said. 'Olga's upset.'

Mum looked crestfallen.

'Oh really! Olga.'

'I can't help it, Lady Lindy. I don't like things like this.' She shuddered. 'Give me the creep.'

Mum let her napkin fall to the table and pushed her chair back.

'Honestly,' she said. 'There's nothing to worry about. I won't let anything get you. Not even the mad axeman under your bed!'

'Mum!'

Olga's lips flattened into a thin line and she began clearing the table.

Mum shook her head and walked out of the kitchen, muttering about it only being a joke. Sasha trotted after her.

'So,' Olga said quietly, as she loaded Mum's plate, cup and cafetière onto a tray. 'What's this curse about?'

I stirred my coffee thoughtfully, trying to remember what I'd heard from Howard and the others.

'*Supposed* curse,' I said gently.

Olga didn't look convinced.

'What did they say? In the pub?'

I swirled my coffee in my mug.

'Oh, I don't know what's meant to happen,' I said. 'Not the specifics, anyway. Just that bad things happen at the manor.'

The crockery rattled as Olga carried the tray over to the sink.

'But bad things happen *everywhere*,' I said. 'It's not a curse. It's just luck. *Life*. Like me ending up here, for example.' I drained my coffee and sighed. 'Maybe there is a curse after all.'

Olga winced and put the tray down. My joke must have been as bad as I thought.

She straightened her back and groaned.

'You OK?'

She nodded and winced again as she rubbed the base of her spine.

'These last few weeks. All this lifting and carrying . . .'

'You should take it easy.'

'Ha!' she said. 'No time for that. Too much to do here.'

'Can I help you?'

Olga's frown lifted and she gently rolled her shoulders.

'You're a good girl, Miss Isabella. But I'll be OK. Mr Eaves say people in the village are looking to work here. Two are coming up this morning for a chat.'

I was glad for Olga that she was to get some help. I was angry – but not surprised – that Mum had neglected to tell me that there would be two other people around the house, in my home. When I tackled her about it, she said she'd intended asking me to sit in on the interviews anyway, but had forgotten to ask me.

'Nothing malicious intended. No agenda.' She sniffed. 'I

was thinking about running an ad to recruit some ghostbusters too,' she said, giving me a little nudge with her elbow. 'What do you think?'

'I think we shouldn't tease Olga,' I said. 'I always go on about you not respecting my views or listening to me. Same applies here.'

Mum sighed and dropped her hands to her lap.

'It was just a bit of fun . . . Anyway, the ghostbuster positions are already filled, aren't they, honey?'

I saw the would-be staff arrive through the library window. Olga had said there were two people coming in for an interview, but it was a man and two women who walked across the forecourt and up the front steps.

The two women were strangers to me, but I recognised Cedric straight away. He looked smarter than he did when I'd first seen him, but not by much.

The white hair on his head and chin looked as if it been combed, but his brown trousers were grubby with mud and the hems frayed. The limp white shirt was creased and the badly knotted green tie failed to hide the missing top button.

The two stout, mousy, middle-aged women had to be twins as they were identical in every way except one; although both had a wonky eye, for one of them it was the left, and the other the right. Standing next to one another, the unsettling effect was of one large, shifting face with a gaze that both stared ahead and either side simultaneously.

Their out-of-kilter gaze threw Mum too. I saw her do a double take as Olga showed them into the library, Cedric right behind them.

The two women bent their knees in a quick bobbing curtsy.

'Morning, ma'am,' the woman on the left said. 'We're the Fletchers. I'm Glenda . . .'

'And I'm Brenda,' said the other.

It was hard to tell which one was talking as they looked identical and neither of them moved their lips very much as they talked. But they both spoke with a broad local accent, the vowels so fat and round in their mouths it slowed them down.

The two women laughed at our confusion. Their laughter was too loud. Too long. I felt awkward on their behalf, embarrassed because *they* weren't.

'Don't worry, ma'am,' Glenda said. 'We get this confusion all the time. We make it easier for people by always standing this way round. Me on the left and Brenda on the right.'

Olga nodded.

'What happens if you don't stand together?' Olga said, her tone and expression only half joking.

'You can tell by this,' Glenda said, tapping her wayward eye. 'Mine's on the left. Brenda's is on the right.'

'Our names make it easy to remember,' Brenda said, boastfully. 'The second letter of Glenda's name is "L" for left.'

'And the second letter of Brenda's name is "R" for right.'

They turned to face one another and blinked in unison, a perfect reflection of imperfect symmetry. I tried not to stare too hard. Or laugh.

'We're used to people staring, miss,' Glenda said. 'We've been like this since we were a month old.'

'That's right,' Brenda said. 'We weren't born like this, you see. Our eyes got twisted when a doctor who didn't know better held us up in front of a mirror. No good for babies to see their own reflection, ma'am, but I'm sure you're aware of that already.'

Olga nodded vaguely. Mum smiled and said nothing. I swallowed my smile. More bloody mumbo-jumbo. Mirrors making your eyes wonky? Where did these people get these ridiculous ideas from?

'But our little . . . disability doesn't stop us doing anything,' Brenda said.

'Not at all,' Glenda said. 'We're experts at searching out even the smallest speck of dirt in the most awkward sort of places. You won't find two more impeccable cleaners.'

'Local too, so you've no worries about us not showing up because the car won't start of an icy morning.'

'No such problems with me either, ma'am,' Cedric said, nodding his head in greeting. 'I live in the village as well.' He looked down sheepishly. 'I hope you don't mind me tagging along with the Fletchers here, but when I heard they were coming to see you about getting their jobs back, I thought I'd try my luck too.'

'You work here before?' Olga said.

'Aye. As the gardener.'

'That's his name too,' Glenda said. 'Gardener by name and profession.'

'Cedric Gardener.' He smiled and tipped his head. 'I know every inch of the gardens here at the manor.'

'And we know the house inside out,' Brenda said.

'And back to front,' Glenda added with a little nod. 'We worked for the Gilbeys, and the Lanchesters before them, the Earlhams . . . the . . .' She clicked her fingers. 'Oh, who was it before them?'

'The Turners,' Brenda said.

'That's right, the Turners.'

'Liked their rhubarb, the Turners,' Cedric said. 'And their plums.'

'Then there was the Worthingt—'

Mum held her hand up.

'OK, I get the idea.' She turned to Olga. 'You see, it can't be such a terrifying place to be after all, can it? The Fletchers and Cedric have survived for years. I'm sure we will too.'

Glenda and Brenda blinked slowly.

'Sorry, ma'am?' Glenda said.

Mum smiled. 'Oh it's nothing. Just a little story we heard about the house being haunted. *And* cursed.' She gave a little laugh. 'Now, when can you start?'

So much for being involved in the recruitment process. Mum had decided. End of story. If she'd asked me, I'd have told her I found them a bit odd – unnerving even – and that having them around all day might drive me mad. But I could see it made sense recruiting local people and, of course, it tied in very neatly with Mum's notion of the ties between the manor and the village. It just would have been nice to be asked, that's all.

'We can start right away, ma'am,' the Fletchers said in unison.

They didn't waste any time. I was up in my bedroom, staring out of the window, when there was a knock on the door and Glenda and Brenda popped their heads in.

They were wearing pink nylon overalls and carrying brooms and a bucket full of dusters and brightly coloured bottles of bleach and polish. Their eyes swept the room greedily, settling here and there for a moment then darting away again.

'Just working out who's in what room and so on, miss,' Glenda said.

Brenda pulled her shoulder up to her neck and wrinkled her nose.

'Oh, it's lovely to be back, miss,' she said. 'I can't tell you how much we've missed it here. I'm itching to get going on the Long Gallery. Need some polish, those floorboards.' She sighed. 'You can just imagine the things those walls have heard over the years, can't you? All those lovely ladies, walking up and down . . . it's my favourite bit of the house. All those windows . . . all that light.'

Despite its large windows the Long Gallery always felt gloomy to me. I did my best to avoid going down it and, if I had to put something into storage in one of the unused rooms at the other end, I picked up my pace. I looked over my shoulder too; it was daft really but the large expanse of floor made me feel vulnerable, as if someone might dash out of one of the doors and chase me.

But it wasn't just the Long Gallery that made me feel uneasy. I was walking through the rest of the house more quickly too. I'd never thought it would be home but it seemed to become less comfortable to me the longer I was there.

Installing furniture from the London house hadn't made the manor familiar. It looked out of place. Every time I went into the drawing room, the sofa and Dad's old armchair seemed to have inched closer to the walls, as if seeking shelter. Tables groaned and creaked as if complaining. Picture frames slipped from the horizontal and several light bulbs had exploded when Olga flicked the switch – even bulbs in different rooms on separate switches.

The house smelt odd too. Its mustiness was still there, and probably always would be as it was so ingrained in the stonework, but beneath the staleness was a trace of something sharper. Ranker. Like something rotting. Mice, perhaps, fooled by the pest-controller's poison.

The smell would soon be masked by the Fletchers' polishes and sprays, the gloom in the Long Gallery lifted by sparkling windows and shiny floorboards. The mice would vanish too.

Brenda coughed and stepped forward.

'Her ladyship mentioned that you'd not been sleeping,' she said. 'We think we know why.' She pointed to the bed. 'We need to turn it round. So your head's pointing north and toes south. Like the needle on a compass. That way the magnetic fields ensure a good night's rest.'

'Right,' I said. 'Of course.' Either they missed the sarcasm in my tone or chose to ignore it.

'And as the earth spins on an east–west axis,' Glenda said, 'it's easier to get comfy by rolling over on your side than it is head over heels. Wouldn't you agree, miss?'

'Er . . . I'd not really thought about it,' I said.

'No,' Brenda said, stepping closer to the bed, Glenda just a heartbeat behind her. 'We can tell.'

I hadn't made the bed and the duvet and pillows were still flat and skew-whiff. Brenda picked up the corners of the duvet and flapped it several times, before letting it settle neatly on the bed.

'I know you might not be used to doing it yourself,' Brenda said, 'given you're the mistress of the house and everything, but if you don't make the bed before you leave the room and go down for breakfast, the next night's sleep will be disturbed.'

Well, that was one way to reduce their workload. Their superstitions could make short work of a to-do list. Maybe employing the Fletchers – anyone from the village – wasn't such a good idea after all.

Glenda plumped the pillows and carefully placed them on the bed.

'And remember to put the pillow cases open ends facing outwards,' she said. 'That way the nightmares can get out.'

'It wasn't a nightmare. I wasn't even asleep,' I said. 'I heard something. Behind the wall.'

'We know, miss. We've heard it too.'

'Several times, actually, over the years we've worked here.' Glenda cleared her throat. 'And it's not mice, despite what her ladyship says.'

'You're going to tell me it was Edward Ingle, aren't you?' I couldn't mask the impatience in my voice.

They looked at one another and then at me.

'So . . . so you don't believe in the ghost or the curse, miss?'

'Of course not! They're just stories. Incomplete stories at that.'

'Incomplete?' Brenda said, squinting.

'People talk about the curse . . . about Heartbreak Hall, but no one ever says what's meant to happen.'

They shook their heads.

'That's because no one likes to talk about it,' Glenda said with a firm nod of her head. 'Just in case it makes it happen.'

'I mean, it will anyway,' Brenda said, 'but talking about it just makes it happen sooner.'

'Makes *what* happen?' I said, the irritation rising in my voice.

They glanced at one another, nervous and anxious, each waiting to see if either of them would break cover.

'Accidents, fires, bad harvests,' Glenda said. 'Money problems, sickness. Death.'

'But *all* of those things are bound to happen over time!' I said, sitting down on the bed. 'Especially in an old house like this. That's not a curse. That's bad luck.'

'I wish it was just bad luck, miss,' Glenda said, 'but it happens too often, too . . . regularly to be that.' Her words evaporated in a resigned sigh. 'You need to be careful.'

'Yeah right, well, if *I'm* in trouble, *you* are too. You're at the manor as well, in case you haven't noticed.'

Brenda nodded. 'We're *at* the manor, yes. Not *of* it.'

'Things only happen to the owners the manor, you see.' Glenda's eyes met mine and darted away. 'And their children.'

It was ludicrous. Impossible. But their earnestness, their utter conviction, was unmistakable and set a flutter going inside me. Not nerves as such and nothing as solid as certain belief. But a glimmer of curiosity in a sky of doubt.

Instinctively I pulled away from them.

'We're not threatening you,' Glenda said. 'Just . . . warning you, that's all.'

'We're concerned for you,' Brenda said, 'of course we are, but . . . we're worried for our sakes too. For our jobs.'

'They never . . . last as long as we'd like,' Glenda said, giving a little shiver. 'And we need the work. Have done ever since the Gilbeys moved out. There's not much else going around here, you see, miss.'

'There's nothing we can do to stop bad things happening here entirely, but our tips and tricks keep the harm at bay and let the better luck flow for as long as it can.' She pointed to the bed. 'Like the stuff with the bed, for example.'

'But they're just superstitions!' I held my hands out imploringly, but the two sisters didn't falter.

'They're precautions,' Brenda said.

'And they work,' Glenda added.

I stood up and walked to the window. Glenda immediately plumped up the duvet again, removing the dent left by my buttocks.

'You won't mind, will you, if we try and help? You know, with some of our little ways?' Brenda said.

Even if I *could* believe I was living under a curse – and that was a big if – I *couldn't* believe that making a bed in a certain way or avoiding walking under ladders would offer any protection.

But it seemed to be so important to them that they did something, and it would have been arrogant and high-handed of me to tell them that they couldn't. What they believed was their business. Who was I to tell them otherwise? Doing so would make me no better than Mum. And even if I told them they couldn't deploy their quack domestic tips, there was no way I would know if they had or hadn't. What they did was as much a mystery to me as why they did it.

'If it makes you happy,' I said.

They both gave a quick bend at the knee.

'Thank you, miss.'

'But I wouldn't mention anything about it to my mother,' I said.

'Right you are, miss. We don't want to be shown the door before we've even started.'

As they were about to leave the room I called them back.

'Don't go upsetting Olga with all this curse stuff either, will you? She's a bit freaked by it.'

They both nodded and closed the door.

'Well,' one of them said as they walked away, 'at least Olga's taking it seriously.'

Mum had no complaints about the quality of the Fletchers' work or their industry. Olga too was impressed. But, somehow, to me the house felt even darker after they'd left than it was before they started. Cobwebs vanished, dust and grit was scooped up into pans, windows polished to a high shine and floorboards gleamed – but to me, it was if shadows fell out of their dusters.

I wondered what little rituals they'd used to conjure a protective veil around the house. Maybe they'd used weird, home-made concoctions to make things sparkle. Whatever they'd used, it hadn't completely masked the underlying odour of rotting vegetables.

There were no fingerprints anywhere but I could feel the Fletchers in every corner. I supposed that meant I was safer. The thought made me smile and I wiped it from my mind. There was nothing I needed protecting from. But curiosity began to settle, slowly and quietly, like dust.

When I went up to my room, I found my bed had been shunted across the room so that it faced the fireplace. The duvet and pillows were fat and soft and pristine. The openings of the pillowcases faced outwards.

An undisturbed night's sleep should have been a certainty. But by five minutes past three I was sitting up in bed, woken once again by scratching at the wall. The pest-controller's poison hadn't done its job. Neither had the Fletchers' ministrations.

My eyes fixed on the wall as the scratching and scrabbling worked its way up the chimney breast. This time, though, it was different. It climbed higher and higher until it paused at the height of the ceiling. I held my breath. Then the noise started once more, moving away from me, further into the room above. I threw back the duvet, slipped from the bed and tiptoed out of the bedroom.

We weren't using the rooms – the former staff quarters – on the next floor and we weren't going to, other than for storage and only then if we had to, seeing as the back staircase was so narrow. It was tucked away in a corner – at the other end of the Long Gallery.

I didn't want to put on the light as I'd wake up Mum and Olga. Mum would just laugh at me for being so stupid and Olga would be scared. So I edged towards the Long Gallery, using the wall to guide me, my feet squeaking on the smooth, polished floor. A mildewed moonlight fell through the windows, illuminating grotesquely shaped smears, like ghosts crowding to get in. The Fletchers hadn't been so fastidious after all.

I ran as quickly as I could on tiptoes, the squeak of my feet like yelps from a pack of hounds in pursuit. When I got to the other end of the Long Gallery I was surprised at the thump of my heart. The rhythm picked up still further as I opened the doorway to the staircase.

There was a light but no handrail, so I steadied myself with a hand on each of the walls, casting truncated shadows. The walls were uneven, the surface rough and cool. Bits of plaster flaked off and fell onto the stairs and beneath my feet, the rattling an echo of the sound that had drawn me up there in the first place.

I turned left at the top of the stairs, towards the room above mine. My hand rested on the door handle and I pressed my ear against the door. Above the thud of blood in my ears, I could hear the scratching on the other side of the door. Loud. Fast. *Frantic.*

I took a deep breath and opened the door. The scratching stopped.

The residual glow of the light in the stairwell cast an eerie nimbus around the door. I flicked the switch on the wall but the light didn't come on. I swallowed hard and stepped inside.

The air was thick and stale. The floor beneath my bare feet was downy with dust and grit and cobwebs and the grate of the meagre fireplace had a rictus grin. Heart pounding, I supported myself with one hand on the chimney breast as I knelt in front of the fireplace.

As I did so, there was an awful whoosh of air and a clattering sound, as something shot out of the chimney and landed in the grate with a thud. The shock of it knocked me off balance and I sprawled on the floor. I sucked in gulps of sooty air and scrabbled to the doorway.

I tried to cry out but all I did was cough and choke. I looked back at the fireplace. It was too dark to see. The scratching had stopped. But there was something in the room. Whatever had fallen down the chimney was too big for a mouse. And it wasn't moving – the room was hushed and still. My skin pricked.

Too big for a mouse maybe, but big enough perhaps for a boy. Edward Ingle. No. It was impossible. It couldn't be. It just couldn't.

I thought about going downstairs to wake Mum and Olga, but worried that whatever it was in the fireplace wouldn't be there by the time I got back. The scratching had stopped when they turned up in my room the night before and I didn't want to risk the same thing happening this time.

I forced myself back into the room, crawling on my hands and knees, closer to the fireplace.

My hand reached out. Touched something soft, making it rattle. I pulled back, scared of what I might find but needing to know what it was. I reached for it once more, half expecting it to move but it didn't. My fingers gradually discerned a bundle of something hard, but light and loose, wrapped in soft, dusty fabric.

I picked it up and shuffled on my knees towards the patch of light by the door.

And that's where Mum and Olga found me screaming and sobbing a few minutes later, surrounded by scattered yellow shards of human bones.

Mum and Olga stood at the door, their faces twisted. Appalled. Frozen. Just as I imagine mine was. Olga had a torch in her hand, its weak batteries adding an awful sickly glow to the room and hooding their eyes with shadows. But I could still see the shock, the revulsion. The incomprehension.

I remember the snap of bones beneath Mum's feet as she came towards me. How the brittle crack made me shudder. Olga brushed the bones to one side with her foot, the dry rattle filling the room. Mum knelt down beside me. Her hand was cool against my face.

'Isabella? Are you OK?' Her hand dropped from my face, and waved vaguely towards the floor. 'What are you doing up here? What happened?'

I rocked backwards and forwards and pointed at the fireplace.

'It's the sweep!' I cried. 'Edward Ingle.'

Mum took me under one arm, Olga took the other. The torch beam swung around the room chaotically; the yellowed bones on the floor twitched in the shadows, as if trying to crawl away.

I groaned. My legs buckled. Mum and Olga wheezed as they hauled me across the room, the bones caught beneath my feet clattering like pencils. Gruesome shapes boiled in the jaundiced light from the torch as we stumbled down the narrow staircase.

I closed my eyes as we went through the Long Gallery but I could tell where we were just by the sense of despair and frustration pressing down on me, buckling my knees once more.

Back in my bedroom, I was lowered onto the bed. My eyes rolled; a wide expanse of ceiling, the cream of the carpet – the gawping maw of the fireplace. I sat up, tried to get out, but Mum's hand on my shoulder pushed me back into the pillow.

'It's OK, honey,' she said gently. 'It's OK.'

'Shall I call the doctor, Lady Lindy?' Olga said, pulling the duvet around me.

Mum nodded her head.

'Yes,' she said. 'And the police.'

Olga scurried out of the room, tightening her dressing gown. Mum sat down on the bed.

'Why don't you tell me what happened?'

'The scratching,' I gasped. 'I followed it . . . I told you I wasn't dreaming!' I closed my eyes. 'It was him. All the time. Edward Ingle!'

Through the window came the broody, tuneless clang of a bell. I opened my eyes. Mum's head turned to the window for a moment too, before snapping back to mine.

'What's that?' I said.

'Sounds like it's coming from the church.'

'I . . . I've never heard it ring before.'

Mum shook her head.

'Me neither. Never mind that now.'

With each chime of the bell, the fireplace opposite me grew larger and blacker, filling the room, until it swallowed me whole. The clang of the bell chased me as I fell into the darkness; the burr of disturbed air reverberated inside me. The vibrations faded, then slowly grew again. Louder, stronger.

I stretched, reaching for something I could sense but couldn't see, until dreams and shadows blended so entirely I didn't know where one ended and the other began. The memories from the imagined.

Ivy raced across the ground, like desperate fingers clutching, scrabbling, then receded, unwinding like pulled thread, revealing a massive slab of stone lit by the crisp clear light of a full moon. The stone shifted, releasing a billowing cloud of bees, their buzz the timbre of just-rung bells.

I felt sweat on my forehead, the creep of the spider tattooed on my shoulder as it moved over my chest to my stomach, its touch the lightest of tickles. A merest breath of air.

I curled up into a ball then felt hands uncoiling me, holding me down. Pale white fingers fluttered around me then morphed into a hundred butterflies that in turn dissolved into a brightly lit room where a man in a white coat looked down at me. The clatter of metal on metal, a murmur of approval gave way to a bell chiming, the hum of chanted prayer, a bloody rose.

A terrible tension gripped me, making me cry out until my spine slackened and ran free like a loose bell rope.

When I woke up, the room was empty and sunlight poured through the open window. I was tangled in the duvet and felt hot and clammy and my pillow was limp and damp.

I sat up and drank from the glass of water on the bedside table. My head ached and I struggled to remember where I was and what had happened. Images flashed into my brain; shadows, shapes. Bones.

Edward Ingle's bones. So the story was true. The villagers would lap it up or, maybe, they'd be disappointed the mystery had been solved once and for all. But just because his body had been found didn't mean there had ever been a ghost. *That* was still a story, just as the curse was.

A few moments later I heard footsteps coming up the stairs and along the corridor. They slowed, then Olga poked her head around my door.

'Ah! Good. You wake up,' she said. 'You've been sleeping for a looong time.'

I rested my head against the wall and propped a pillow in the crook of my back.

'Why? What time is it?'

'Tuesday,' Olga said. 'You've been asleep for one day and a half.'

I screwed my face up. Despite the sunlight and the breeze playing at the open window, I felt groggy and smothered.

'Lady Lindy sat by you for hours and hours,' Olga said, 'even though the doctor say you OK.'

'The doctor was here?'

'Not for long. He couldn't find nothing wrong. He say you needed sleep and . . . well, you were doing that already so . . .' She straightened out the duvet. 'How do you feel now?' Her hand slipped to my forehead. 'I'm sorry, Miss Isabella. Really I am.'

'It's not your fault.'

She took my hand.

'No, it *is* my fault.' She grimaced. 'I didn't call the sweep. I put it on my list but I . . . there's so much to do with moving I just forgot and now this . . . if I remembered, the sweep would have found it, not you. Still not nice, of course, but better he find it than you . . . Lady Lindy has already told me off so . . . if you want to as well . . . go ahead.'

'Don't be daft.' I rubbed my eyes. 'It *was* horrible but it would have been horrible for whoever found it. I'm just relieved it was actually real. The skeleton. Edward Ingle.'

Olga looked at me nervously, her eyes darting away from mine. She stood up and poured some more water from the jug into my glass.

'I wish it *had* been a dream,' she said. 'Horrible. We have to forget it. Somehow. Not easy but . . .' She shuddered and walked to the door. 'But it's gone now. The police have taken it, thank God. So we all get back to normal, yes?'

I was beginning to forget what normal was.

Mum insisted I stay in bed that day. She suggested I change rooms but I couldn't see the point. The skeleton was gone now so the noise would stop too. And it did. That night I slept soundly. In silence.

The next day I was allowed no further than the drawing room. I told Mum I was fine, there was no need to worry but she wouldn't listen. She'd been the same after my abortion. Fussing over me, making sure I didn't overdo it when it was already much too late for that. The baby had gone. That was about as final and overdone as it could be. Mum's hovering around me was like a cat boasting of its prey, helpless and spent. Her eyes seemed to glitter with triumph.

This time, though, her eyes were soft with concern and her touch on my forehead tender. Olga plied me with tea and toast and told me the Fletchers had offered to make me some kind of herbal tonic.

'Lavender and . . . valerian?' Olga said uncertainly. 'Apparently they take it for everything.'

The onion for the bee sting had worked well enough but I wasn't about to try anything else from Stagcote's DIY pharmacy. I was glad Mum kept the Fletchers away from me as I didn't want to have to put up with their questions about Edward Ingle's discovery or what it might mean. Not that I needed to listen to them; their superstitions hadn't kept me out of harm's way after all. Even so, it was best that Olga kept them busy clearing out the stable block in readiness for the arrival of Mum's horses.

I read a bit, watched crap TV, played patience on my laptop. I even borrowed one of Olga's puzzle books. And when Mum wasn't looking I checked to see if Cosmo had been in touch.

He couldn't call me, of course, as Mum had made me change

my number. He must have changed his number too, as I always got the dull drone of the unavailable tone. My email address had changed as well, again on Mum's insistence, but she didn't understand that my old address was still active and any emails sent there would be rerouted to the new one.

There was nothing she could do about my Facebook account. I logged in all the time after Cosmo first vanished, hoping that one of my 'friends' from the squat he lived in would let me know where to find him. Dave, Kirsty, Gretchen, Spud. All of them were silent.

I'd even been round to the flat but there was no one there and the doors and windows were boarded up. They'd been evicted probably, or found somewhere better – somewhere without rancid lino, rising damp and a condemned boiler that rattled the glass in the window frames when it fired up.

It was no surprise to see my email inbox empty. Just like it always was. But that hadn't stopped me sending emails to Cosmo. The *same* email. It had started out as a long plea, pledging my love for him and begging him to come and get me. I didn't care that it sounded desperate. I *was* desperate.

Although the message never changed, the content of the email got shorter and shorter in the face of Cosmo's stubborn silence.

Subject: Where are you? I love you. Come back to me. Please.

The first email I'd sent from the manor had got me excited as it hadn't bounced like those I'd sent from London. But I hadn't noticed how long it took my message to leave; the connection was slow so mail didn't vanish, it dissolved. Eventually.

And it came back to me too, a sluggish boomerang. *Message Failed.* But I was convinced it was a glitch, a bug in the system and had sent it over and over again. Cosmo couldn't resist for ever.

It was all part of my pattern. That's what my therapist – *Jenny* – would have said – a compulsion to keep picking things over, no matter how much it hurt. I had the scars on my arms and legs to prove it, although the fierce red welts have faded now, the crusty scabs long gone. My therapist had been pleased with my progress; Mum delighted.

'You've really turned a corner,' she said. 'This is just the beginning. Well done, darling.'

Only she was wrong. I hadn't cut or gouged myself for some time – that much was true – but I just indulged the same compulsion in other ways. Repeating things over and over, trapped, like the women compelled to trudge up and down the Long Gallery. Sometimes I'd eat and make myself puke over and over again until my stomach was dry of bile and the toilet pan spattered and foamed.

Other times I'd put the same song on repeat and curl up with my headphones on, staring blankly at the window, remembering how Cosmo used to hold me, touch me, push his mouth against my ear and sing the words in hot, quick breaths.

Not a wish or a prayer. But an affirmation. A promise. A spell. *Love You to Death. Beloved. Corpses (A Zombie Love Song).* I'd been intoxicated by the agony each of them roused in me, but resisted the instruction in *Cuts You Up*. Perhaps I was better after all.

But I still hadn't found Cosmo. Maybe I never would.

By the middle of the afternoon the boredom and frustration had grown too much. I had to get out of the house.

It felt good to be away from the manor; its air of neglect, its oppressive sense of history and gloom. The Fletchers had just made it weirder, as if by clearing up the dust they'd disturbed something darker in the shadows.

The village was quiet, the street empty. It gave me hope that the pub might be empty too but, much as I fancied a drink, I didn't want to risk being grilled by the locals about my discovery. I kept walking.

I crossed the river, stopping halfway on the bridge to look over. Brown sinuous streaks weaved in and out of the reeds and hovered beneath the algae, the fish occasionally striking at the haze of flies above the surface. I looked downriver and found myself wondering where Gilbey's father had drowned.

Thinking of one body stirred up thoughts of Ingle's, so I moved on, into the field on the other side of the river. The air was ripe with the sweet scent of newly cut, sun-warmed grass. Five large, golden stones stood in a rough circle around a tree, its branches dotted with yellow flowers.

A man appeared from behind one of the stones, followed by a dog. Cedric and Sasha.

Cedric raised his hand. It was too late for me to turn around. We'd have to talk.

'Feeling better, miss?' he asked, calling Sasha to his side. The dog obeyed instantly, his tail wagging like a stiff worm.

I nodded and he said he was pleased to hear it.

'Bit of a to-do, weren't it, miss? Must have given you quite a fright, finding that.'

'Yes,' I said. 'It did.' It struck me that maybe Ingle's was the death the bees had predicted and I nearly said as much but stopped myself; his death wasn't exactly recent and I didn't want to talk about him or the rumours about his death.

I distracted Cedric by asking about the stones.

'This,' he said with an awestruck look in his eye, ''is Maidens' Reel.'

I stroked one of the stones, felt its pitted surface beneath the nap of warm moss and lichen.

'What is it?'

'Way, way back,' he said, licking his lips, 'six Stagcote virgins came up here to dance on Midsummer's Day. Only the devil wanted to take them for his own, you see, and as he reached up from hell, ready to drag them down, his claws snagged on the ground and snapped off.' He frowned and stared at me for a moment before continuing, his scrutiny making me feel awkward. 'The sixth girl, the lord's daughter, well, she was dancing in the middle and escaped his grip, so the devil wormed a bloody finger into the soil and planted a seed.'

It was a cute story but it was no more than that, although it was possible that this local legend could have spawned the one about the curse. Shaggy dog stories have so many strands.

I followed him as he walked to the tree in the middle of the circle.

'Red elder,' he said, taking a handful of leaves and crushing them. I recognised the stench instantly; it was the same as the one that lingered at the manor. I flapped my hands in front of my nose and stepped back.

'Parts of it are poisonous,' Cedric said.

'You're not kidding.' I looked at the tree. 'Is there one of these in the garden at the manor?'

'No, they likes to be near streams and rivers, do red elders.'

A white butterfly fluttered around him, then settled on a branch of the tree. Cedric gasped and stroked his chin. His eyes, suddenly sad, lowered to the ground. Sasha whined.

'A baby died,' he said. 'That's what that butterfly means.' He shook his head and walked away, Sasha trotting at his heels.

I was too winded to move and had to lean against the tree for support. My hand instinctively slid down to my stomach and rested there.

It was ridiculous. Bees and butterflies. Anywhere else they

were just insects but in Stagcote they were heralds of doom. But ridiculous or not, this superstition had hit home.

I waited a while then made my way back to the manor, the stench of the tree following me. When I got home, there was a police car in the forecourt and Olga was ushering two police officers in through the front door.

It had all looked so routine. Two police constables. A man and a woman. PCs Simpson and Craven, both in uniform, hers a little too big for her. He was in his mid-twenties, with receding brown hair and a slightly ruddy complexion. Craven was younger, a little tubby but keen and smiley.

'Lady Griffin-Clark,' Craven said, 'we've had the results on the skeleton back from forensics.'

Mum nodded and asked them to sit down. They both removed their caps and perched on the edge of the sofa. Simpson's expression made me anxious. He looked confused, as if he'd left something behind and couldn't remember what.

'Would you like some coffee?' Mum said.

'No thank you,' Simpson said. 'We won't keep you long.'

Olga turned to leave but Mum called her back.

'You might as well stay and hear it,' she said. 'I know it's been on your mind. The Fletchers too.'

'They're still out in the stable block,' she said. 'Too messy to come indoors. I'll tell them later.' She hovered by the bookcase, fists clenched.

'Well,' Simpson said, a finger brushing something from his cap, 'we can confirm that the skeleton is that of a female.'

'*Female?*' I said. 'But I thought it was . . .'

'A sweep by the name of Ingle,' Simpson said. 'Yes, your mother told us as much. I'm sorry to disappoint you.'

I wasn't disappointed. Just surprised. Perplexed.

'You're sure?' I asked, perching on the edge of the table.

'Absolutely,' Craven said.

'I didn't think it would be,' Mum said, the gloat in her voice unmistakable. 'The skeleton didn't look right.'

'Oh, and you'd know a male skeleton from a female one in an instant, would you?'

Mum pursed her lips.

'No, not there and then,' she said. 'I meant the size of it.'

'The girl was very young,' Craven said. 'An infant.'

I felt my knees give. A stab of pain from my all too recent past. A child lost. A mother's grief. Crippling guilt. But beneath the emotions flooding me, there was something else, glittering, like a speck of gold in a swirl of mud; surprise at the accuracy of Cedric's prediction about the butterfly at Maidens' Reel.

'A . . . a baby?' My mouth was dry but tears pricked me eyes.

Mum turned away from me.

'How did she die?' I said, my voice wavering.

'Well,' Simpson said, puffing his cheeks out. 'Well, there are only bones of course, no soft tissues, so it's all a bit of a guess . . . But there are no signs of any trauma – like a broken skull, for example, or scars from a knife – so the best the medical team could suggest was she might have suffocated during birth . . . strangled by the umbilical cord perhaps? It's also possible she was stillborn.' He shrugged. 'Natural causes, either way.'

'Oh, thank God for that at least,' Mum said, resting a hand on her chest. 'It's hard enough as it is without the poor girl being murdered.'

'Do you know who she was?' I asked. 'Why she was there?'

Simpson fidgeted on the sofa.

'It might be better not to dwell on it,' he said, 'but, because it—'

'*She*,' I said.

He stopped, tipped his head.

'Sorry, because *she* was found in one of the upstairs rooms – almost certainly a servant's – it's likely she was illegitimate.'

'It's feasible that she was the result of rape,' Craven said. Her forehead creased with a deep frown. 'The lord taking advantage of his superior position . . . it wasn't unusual in those days, was it?' She dropped her gaze to the floor. 'Or now, come to that.'

'That poor little girl,' I said, biting my lip. 'And the mother! She must have been going mental to do that to her child . . . desperate! Damned if the baby didn't survive. Damned if it did.'

Mum flinched and stood up.

'Well, officers,' she said, 'thank you for letting us know.'

Simpson and Craven gave one another an awkward look and didn't move.

'There *was* something else that we thought you might like to know,' Craven said.

Mum feigned curiosity.

'Apart from the date of the bones there were two other aspects of the test results that were . . . well, rather surprising to say the least,' Craven said.

This skeleton – whoever it was – had already caused too many surprises. I didn't need any more but curiosity wouldn't let me go.

'Like what?' I said.

'It seems she's been there for quite some time,' Simpson said. 'Since the sixteenth century, they reckon.'

Olga gasped and quickly put a hand to her mouth. Mum slowly sat down again once more.

'How extraordinary,' Mum said, quietly.

Simpson shifted on the chair.

'There is still some guesswork with these tests, you under-stand,' he said.

'With specific dates, yes,' Craven said. 'But they can set parameters pretty accurately.'

'It make no difference,' Olga said, shaking her head. 'One hundred years. Five hundred years. It's too long to be buried in a chimney.'

'Yes,' Mum said. 'It is amazing that she could be up there for so long without being discovered. Doesn't say much for the chimney sweeps, does it?'

'Ah,' Craven said wincing. 'That was the second thing we had to tell you. They found a few unexpected things in the bones.'

'Yes,' Simpson said, his voice low and slow. 'Traces of soil and seeds. And a ram's horn.'

I remembered seeing it now, a twist of blackened ridges caught in the tangle of bones.

Olga crossed her arms and hugged herself.

'The devil!' she said. 'You sure the girl wasn't killed?'

Mum whirled around.

'Oh, don't be ridiculous, Olga,' Mum said.

Agreeing with Mum was still a new sensation and I felt mean for not supporting Olga. But I couldn't. The circum-stances of the child's burial were surprising – baffling even – but they didn't indicate anything criminal or diabolical.

'Horns were used in sacrifices and devil worship,' Olga cried. 'I see it in films!'

Mum waved her away.

'Films, yes! *Silly films.* But this is real.' She fixed her eyes on Simpson. 'I'm sure there's a perfectly simple explanation for it.'

'We can't vouch for anything quite so dramatic as devil wor-ship or human sacrifice,' he said. 'We think the ram's horn was probably some sort of comforter. Like a rattle. Symbolic only, in this case, seeing as the child probably didn't draw breath.'

'You think,' Olga said. 'You don't *know*.'

Simpson held his hands out.

'No one knows. No one ever will know. But I think a rattle is more likely than some accessory to sacrifice.'

'Quite,' Mum said firmly. 'Seems perfectly logical to me.'

The silence hung in the air.

'What was the other thing?' I said.

'Other thing?' Simpson said.

'You said there were three things about the test results. The date of the bones, the ram's horn and soil you found with them and . . .?'

An awkward glance shot between Simpson and Craven.

'Ah,' Simpson said, 'given our discussion, maybe it would be better if we didn't—'

'What was it?' I said.

'Well,' he said, his expression darkening. 'That's the worst of it, in some ways. They think the soil indicates she was dug up *after* she was buried and then put in the chimney.'

'Oh God!' Olga said, making a sign of the cross in the air. She walked briskly to the door. 'This house! A ghost. A poor baby up the chimney. What they say about this place is right!' She closed the door behind her, silencing her muttering.

Mum shrugged apologetically and folded her arms. 'Exhumation?' she said. 'That *is* too awful to even think about. How long was she buried before . . .?'

I pictured a mother crazed with grief, digging desperately at her child's grave. Picking up the bones. Picking them over. And over. And over . . .

'We can't say, I'm afraid,' Simpson said. 'Sorry.'

I walked towards the window. Clean white roses grazed against the glass.

'The curse,' I mumbled. The words were out of my mouth before I realised. I hadn't meant to say them. It was as if something in my subconscious had pushed them up and out.

'Isabella,' Mum said sternly. 'Don't *you* start! It's bad enough with the others. Olga too, now, it seems.'

'Curse?' Simpson said.

'It's nothing really,' Mum said.

'So you haven't heard anything about the manor being cursed?' I asked.

Simpson glanced at Mum and Craven.

'Erm, no,' he said slowly, 'can't say I have.' He was trying not to laugh. 'What's it supposed to be about?'

'It's just nonsense!' Mum said. 'Ignore it.'

Craven leaned towards me.

'Go on,' she said. 'What have you heard?'

Mum threw her head back and exhaled loudly.

I suddenly felt foolish and conspicuous.

'Just that awful things happen to anyone who owns the manor.'

'News to me,' Simpson said. 'It's barely on our radar, this place. I remember something, a few years back now . . . an accident . . . a drowning, wasn't it?'

Craven shook her head. 'Before my time.'

'Yes, that's right,' I said. 'The father of the last owner.'

'What?' Mum said. 'Who told you that?'

'The people in the pub.'

'Just drunken tittle-tattle.'

'Gilbey's father fell in the river and drowned. *Fact.*'

'To be fair, Your Ladyship,' Simpson said, 'I do remember something along those lines.'

Mum's eyes narrowed with irritation.

'A tragic accident. Nothing more.'

'*And* the Gilbey's child had leukaemia. *You* told me that yourself, Mum.'

'Yes, but that doesn't mean there's a curse on the place!' She looked to Simpson and Craven for support.

'I'm not saying there is,' I said. 'It's just . . . I don't know . . . odd. A bit creepy. Makes you think.'

'Then don't think about it,' Mum said. 'Whatever you give your attention to grows all the quicker and stronger for it. We *both* know that well enough.' Her stare pinched me.

Simpson and Craven exchanged glances.

'Sounds to me like the Gilbeys just had some bad luck,' Craven said. 'Nothing more than that.'

'I suppose,' I said. 'But it is kind of interesting.'

'Sure,' Craven said, 'but there's nothing to warrant an investigation.'

'Not even a baby that's been dug up?' I said. 'Why would anyone do that?'

Simpson coughed.

'It's impossible to say,' he said. 'Her identity will probably always be a mystery . . . so will what actually happened to her. *And* why.'

'So that's it?' I said, turning around quickly.

They both held their hands out, defeated.

'It's difficult to know what else we *can* do,' Craven said. 'It's pretty much the coldest of cold cases.'

But it was somebody's child too. Loved. Missed – yet still present.

'I really don't think this need concern any of us any longer,' Mum said, standing up. 'Thank you for letting us know, officers.'

Simpson and Craven stood up as she did, as if they were joined as one.

'Well, if you won't try and find out who she was, what happened to her, then *I* will,' I said.

'Now you're just being dramatic,' Mum said.

'Why not? It's something to do.'

'There's plenty to do!' Mum said, hands out, gesturing around the room. 'We've got the house to sort out . . . investigations into starting a little farm, some pigs, chickens, maybe some cattle . . .'

'That's *your* stuff.'

'And this is yours?'

'No, it's *ours*.'

Our eyes met. I saw a flicker of understanding. Her jawline hardened.

Simpson and Craven edged towards the door.

'We'll . . . we'd best be on our way,' Simpson said.

'Wait,' I said. 'Please, before you go. What happens to the girl now?'

'Oh, I hadn't thought of that,' Mum said quietly.

'No,' I said, from the side of my mouth.

Simpson put on his cap.

'I assume the local authority will arrange a funeral for her,' he said. 'I can't say for certain. It's a very unusual situation . . . unprecedented. But they do take care of funerals for others when they can't trace any relatives . . . you know, pensioners that are found in their front rooms a year after they've died, the homeless . . . that sort of thing.' He looked up. 'They're a bit basic as funerals go but . . . well, it's better that than nothing.'

'And the cemetery will be better than a chimney,' Craven said.

'Stagcote cemetery?' I said.

Simpson looked doubtful.

'I wouldn't have thought so, no,' he said. 'Probably Cheltenham. That's where these others get taken.'

'No,' I said, sorrow and anger gripping my voice. 'No one deserves such a soulless, functional funeral, *especially* when they've waited for it for so long. I want to do it properly. Give her a proper funeral. A proper grave. At Stagcote.'

Mum snorted with derision.

'Honey, don't you think you're being a little—'

'Thoughtful? Considerate? Kind?' I said.

Mum pinched the bridge of her nose.

'I was going to say over the top.'

'Look,' I said, 'she was found here. She was probably born in the village. Maybe her parents are buried there too.'

'It just seems unnecessary fuss and expense.' She turned to Simpson and Craven. 'I don't understand it.'

'No,' I said. 'You never did. But it might help. No, scratch that. It *will* help me. And it might help us.'

She gazed off into the distance, mouth set firm.

'You know what?' I said. 'Forget it. I don't need your help. Don't worry about coming along to the funeral or about the cost. I'll pay for it. You paid *last time*, after all, remember?'

I ran out of the room up the stairs to my bedroom, slamming the door behind me.

Mum had been just as unequivocal about my abortion. 'You have to do it,' she'd said. 'A girl with your prospects. Of your pedigree? There's no way I'm going to let you be saddled with the child of that . . . creep.'

'His name's Cosmo! And I love him.'

'And he loves you, I suppose?'

'Yes!' I bawled.

'Then where is he, honey? Where is he? How come you've not seen him for a week?'

I clenched my fists and teeth.

'He's on tour with the band. I told you.'

'On tour,' she sneered. 'Is that what they call doing a

runner, now? And anyway, even if he was "on tour", he could still answer your calls, but he doesn't pick up. I wonder why that is?'

'Bad reception,' I said. 'And he's busy.' Even I didn't think I sounded convincing.

I shrugged off the arm she put around my shoulders.

'Oh, honey, I wish that were true. But you've got to see him for what he is. See *this* for what it is.' She rubbed my arm. 'He's freaked out by the baby and left you high and dry. He's probably picked up another girl on this so-called tour already. He's just not good enough for you. Twenty-two and still mucking about in a band? Droning on. Scowling? Hating the world? It's just so . . . depressing. You deserve so much better. You can *get* so much better.'

'I don't want anyone else.'

'Well, I'm sorry to be so brutal but . . . he doesn't want you. Or the baby. And we need to take care of that. Pretty damn quickly.'

I resisted for as long as I could, hoping Cosmo would call me or turn up, contrite about his silence and armed with feasible explanations and that all-conquering smile. His eyes would shimmer through the thick black fringe and that pouty mouth would defy me not to forgive him. And I would.

But the call never came. The doorbell never rang. My inbox was empty.

Mum pressed home her advantage.

'It's for the best,' she said.

We went in Olga's slightly battered Peugeot, as Mum thought the chauffeur-driven Bentley might attract too much attention. And we drove out to a clinic in Surrey, just to be sure we didn't bump into anyone we knew.

The clinic was white, brightly lit and smelt of lemon. The staff's smiles were as quick and expert as the surgeon's hands.

The single red rose in the teardrop-shaped vase on the reception desk mocked me. We drove back in silence, my eyes blank and empty as my belly, my heart and spirit whittled to the core.

Nothing could fill the void, ever – but giving the girl in the fireplace a decent burial was symbolic. It wasn't so much about closure, although that played its part; it was just as much about making amends. Making my peace. Burying my guilt.

I took out my phone, opened the Notes app and tapped on the screen.

Funeral arrangements.

The only event I'd ever arranged was a birthday party for Cosmo and that hadn't taken much planning. I wanted to do more but his bandmates said he wouldn't want too much fuss and I knew they were right, so I kept it simple – a lock-in at the club after the gig, with his band providing the music.

It wasn't much of a template for a funeral, even if the gloomy music and our black clothing made it look and feel like one.

Mum had taken care of everything for Dad. She had to, she said. It wasn't just her duty as his wife, but her duty as a mother to spare me the pain of it.

Spare her the risk of it giving me ideas, more like.

Only three weeks before Dad died I'd been in hospital myself, having vodka and paracetamol pumped from my stomach. I couldn't be trusted with my life, so how could I be trusted with Dad's funeral? Not be encouraged to follow him into the grave?

So I was excluded from the arrangements. The church, the glossy walnut casket with the brass handles, the sprays of white lilies, the thick, black-edged funeral invitations, the text in elegant swirls and loops – Mum saw to it all.

I wouldn't ask her to help with the baby girl's funeral. I didn't want to give her the satisfaction of saying no and the opportunity to laugh at me once again. Olga said no too, but for very different reasons.

'I don't want anything to do with that . . . thing, Miss Isabella. It gives me the creep.'

'Look, even if she *was* a sacrifice or somehow part of this "curse", then surely burying her would help snuff it out?'

She looked dubious.

'It's very good to send the girl back to God,' she said. 'But you'll have to do it without me. Not just because of what the girl is . . . there's Lady Lindy too. She finds out I help you and boom!' She threw up her hands. 'Job gone. No, Miss Isabella, I'm sorry. I will come to the funeral, but I can't help with it.'

I thought maybe Howard would. I remembered him saying that his father had died and assumed that he must have organised the funeral, or at least had some hand in it.

I found him in his garden, scraping at the ground with a trowel, disturbing puffs of dusty earth. He stopped and looked up from under the rim of a straw hat. Smiled. The beads of sweat running down his face were swept away by the back of his hand; mud streaked his cheeks.

'Ah, so you're up and about again then?' he said. 'I heard about that awful business at the manor. I did look in to see you, did your mum say?'

I shook my head. I was touched, glad of his concern and encouraged that it might persuade him to help me.

He pushed his hat back and squinted at me.

'Your discovery has certainly got the village buzzing. They've been quite put out by it not being Edward Ingle. Some of them, anyway. The others are quite pleased. Case isn't proven either way so it's a matter of as you were. Only now, of course, they have another mystery on their doorstep.'

'They haven't heard the half of it yet.'

As I told him about the baby girl's history, he took the hat off and fanned himself slowly, his mouth slightly open.

'Crikey,' he said when I finished, 'that's some story. Of course, you know what sort of spin the villagers will put on it?'

'Yeah,' I said. 'Olga's got it into her head that the girl was sacrificed! A victim of the curse.'

There was a clang as he let the trowel drop to the ground. 'Seriously?'

I smiled, as if Olga's gullibility was my fault.

'How about a drink?' he said.

'I can't face the pub. They'll be on at me the whole time.'

'No, of course. I meant here.' He waved his hat towards the house. 'I've got some lemonade in the fridge. Home-made – by Sissy Bartlett in the village, I hasten to add, not by me. Or there's beer? Also made by Sissy.'

'Beer,' I said, 'thanks.'

He pointed to a worn wooden table and chairs tucked along one side of the house.

The sun was warm on my face – hot even. The shade of the trees along the driveway meant I hadn't noticed quite how warm it was. Lavendered air blew from the bushes alongside me, the purple stems flecked by the black of grazing bees. The sight and smell soothed me.

Howard put two glasses of cloudy beer on the table and sat down opposite me.

'I suppose the bees have been informed about the skeleton at the manor?' I said with a grin.

Howard took a sip.

'Check,' he said. 'Cedric was on it right away. He was like something out of *News at Ten*.'

'Then he'd better give them a heads-up about the funeral too.'

Howard frowned.

'Funeral?'

He looked thoughtful as I told him my plan.

'You think it's over the top, don't you? Like Mum does.'

'No. I was going to say it's very good of you. Bound to get

the locals stirred up too.' He took a sip from his glass then began to laugh. Beer trickled from the side of his mouth and he wiped it away on his sleeve. 'Can you imagine? Who will they blame any untoward events on if the curse has been laid to rest once and for all? This could be the end of Stagcote as we know it.'

His words struck me. I'd not really given the girl's involvement with the curse any credence. Nor the curse, come to that. But, if by some dumb superstitious way she *was* involved, I'd just assumed it would be as a victim. Now Howard had made me think she could be part of the curse itself. The thought was almost as laughable and flashed out of my mind as quickly as it had flown in.

'I was hoping you could help me with the funeral? Please? I mean, you've . . .' My voice trailed away.

'Done it before?' he said. A cloud of sadness passed over him and he put his glass down.

'I'm sorry,' I said. 'I shouldn't have asked.'

'Nonsense. I'd be happy to help.'

'Only if you're sure. If you're not busy.'

He laughed.

'I'll be glad to get away from the gardening,' he said. 'Not really my strong point.'

'OK then,' I said. 'That's great. Thank you.'

He pushed his chair away from the table.

'Just give me a few moments to change my clothes and freshen up, and we'll be off.'

'Where to?'

'Well, given the somewhat unusual circumstances, I doubt we'll need to worry about notifying the registrar about the death. So our next step is to find an undertaker and book the church. Father Wright should be able to help with both.'

*

When I explained what I wanted to do, Father Wright took my hand in his. I could feel the wrinkles in his skin.

'A very good ending to a very bad business,' he said. 'Bringing this unfortunate child to her eternal rest at last.'

The grip on my hand relaxed and his eyes dropped to the ground.

'I only wish we could be as generous,' he said.

'What do you mean? Has my mother been on your case?'

'No, it's nothing to do with your mother. More about God.'

I resisted the temptation to tell him the two were practically the same thing.

'We don't know who the girl was,' he explained, 'so we don't know if she was baptised.' His expression darkened. 'Given the circumstances, I think we should assume that she wasn't.'

I straightened my back.

'Does that matter?'

'In the eyes of God it does, yes.'

Even now the child wasn't wanted. Not even by God.

'But she was buried here before!' I cried, surprised at the sudden rush of anger.

Wright didn't flinch.

'She was *buried* before,' he said slowly. 'That's as much as we know.'

I'd not considered where she'd been buried the first time. The churchyard had just seemed the obvious place but I could have been wrong. Victims of the plague were buried in large pits. A distraught mother, living in an isolated place like Stagcote, might have tried to hide her dead baby anywhere, especially if the child was illegitimate. Under a bush or beneath a wall. It made me all the more determined to give her a proper grave.

'Are you saying you won't have her here?' I said.

Wright shook his head. 'Not at all,' he said. 'God finds room for everyone – whoever they are, whatever they've done . . . or whatever was done *to* them.'

Guilt stabbed at me and I looked away.

Wright stood up and led us round to the other side of the churchyard. The shade was a relief from the bite of the sun. Uneven ground coughed up tufts of grass and blistered, ivy-choked gravestones. Beyond them a forest of thick-stemmed weeds and stinging nettles dwarfed the churchyard wall.

I folded my arms, suddenly chilly.

'It *is* less . . . picturesque than the rest of the churchyard,' Wright said. 'But the northern section is the best we can do for the likes of this poor girl. Alongside the paupers, the suicides and the excommunicated.' He inclined his head towards us, his expression solemn and steadfast. 'It *is* a step up from where she's been for the last several hundred years.'

I wanted to argue with him. The girl was blameless and deserved more than the dark and desolate north churchyard. She was of this parish, one of this church's flock for hundreds of years. This was where she would have been baptised, got married and baptised her own children had she lived. And she would have been buried alongside her family, in the other, more favoured parts of the graveyard.

But his steely expression told me arguing would be futile. The burial was symbolic, a way to bury the past. There was little point in causing ill feeling with my new neighbours in the here and now.

'Fine, I said, 'here will have to do.'

'Now that's settled,' Howard said, 'when would you be able to do the funeral?'

'Sooner would be better for all of us,' Wright said. 'I sat at Old Bess's bedside for an hour this morning and expect to bury her soon.'

'Old Bess?' I said.

'One of the villagers,' Howard said to me.

'She's housebound. Gravely ill,' Wright said. 'As I say, the doctor has told us she doesn't have long. It would be better if we could take care of the girl's funeral sooner rather than later.'

I found myself wondering if it was Old Bess's death the bees had foreseen. I'd thought the same with the skeleton when I was at Maidens' Reel. I'd felt silly for thinking it then and I felt silly for thinking it now. But the thought added a bass to the constant chatter in my head, like the hum of distant traffic or the buzz of a bee.

We agreed to hold the funeral three days later.

'Assuming that gives you time to get the girl's remains back from the police, of course,' Howard said.

'*The girl*,' I said quietly. 'It's so . . . cold . . . anonymous. I can't bear to think of her being buried without a name. It's the very least she deserves.'

Wright agreed.

'It would make it easier for the service too,' he said. 'How about Mary? Or Anne? Katherine, perhaps? They're all proper names from that period of time.'

'*That's* why I don't like them. They're just . . . off the peg. Hand-me-downs from history.'

I gazed at the gravestones nearby. A lot of the writing was lost beneath moss and lichen but I could make out some of the names. Margaret Simkins. Alfred Tym. Cynthia Searchwell. Michael Dobson.

'Let me think on that,' I said. 'I'd like to try a few out and see what feels right.'

'As you wish,' Wright said.

He recommended a funeral director in Stow-on-the-Wold.

'Johnston's,' he said. 'They'll take good care of you.'

We thanked him and walked back through the churchyard. The heat hit us as we stepped out of the shade; the glare made me blink and cover my eyes with my hand. Howard slipped the rim of his hat forward.

I scanned the gravestones for Christian names but was immediately struck by the repetition of the same family names. May. Crichton-Stuart. Sellers.

'Fletcher,' I said, pointing to one grave. Then to another. And another. 'Must be Glenda's and Brenda's relatives.'

'Yes,' Howard said. 'And there's a couple of Gardeners – Cedric's relatives, I would imagine.' He pointed to the right. 'And that's a Bradshaw, I think. One of Ed the barman's.'

We walked on.

'It must be amazing to have that sort of link with the past,' Howard said. 'With your family.'

'Maybe,' I said.

I hadn't had much contact with my maternal grandparents at all. They preferred their quiet lives in Boston to anything my mother could offer them. It suited them both, really, as Mum was as embarrassed by her roots as they were by her success.

Dad's parents weren't as reluctant to share in their son's good fortune, and spent most of the time bobbing around the Med or the Caribbean on their yacht. They were never that keen on Mum and her pretensions and, since Dad's death, had kept away as I reminded them too much of the son they had lost.

I knew little, if anything, of either family beyond that. Sometimes I wondered about where I came from. Mostly, I tried to forget it.

I rubbed my hand over one of the warm, rough stones, like a talisman.

'Whichever of you was her mother,' I said, 'we're bringing her back to you.'

Howard drove me up to Stow-on-the-Wold, a small market town with a square that had probably once been pretty before tourism turned it into a car park. The funeral directors were on the High Street, a single vase of lilies in the window.

The plump woman stood up from behind her desk as we entered. Her solemn expression slowly evaporated once she understood the circumstances of the funeral and realised we weren't suffering with newly inflicted grief.

The time, dates and procedure were all agreed quickly.

'Excellent,' she said, making a last few notes in her note-book. 'Now, perhaps you'd like to choose a coffin.' She slid a catalogue across the desk.

I knew the one I wanted for the girl as soon as I saw it: pure white, the intricate weave of wickerwork making it look as delicate as a butterfly. *The Snowdrop*, the caption below said. The scale of it brought my heart to my throat.

Ten minutes later we were on our way back to the manor.

'Thanks for helping,' I said to Howard as I got out of the car at the top of the driveway.

'I'm sure you'd have managed.'

'Even so, you've made it easier.'

He tipped his hat.

'Let me know if there's anything else you need.'

I said I would and closed the car door.

I was relieved to hear Mum was talking on the phone when I got back. I didn't need another row with her so ran straight up the stairs to my bedroom.

It was hot in there, so I opened the window to its fullest extent. Below me, Cedric snipped at a bed of tangled roses, the breeze carrying their scent into the room. It was sweet and heavy. Intoxicating. My head swam. The single red rose stem in the clinic's reception flashed in my memory.

I thought of the faceless, nameless child I'd lost, the faceless, nameless child I'd found. The scent of the flowers from the garden grew stronger on a freshening breeze.

It was as if the house was whispering into my ear.

'Rose,' I said quietly. 'I'll call her Rose.'

The breeze faltered. Doubt flickered in my heart. I closed my eyes and breathed in.

'No, not Rose. *Rosemary.*'

Despite the heat of the day, my arms flushed with goose pimples.

I didn't sleep well the night before the funeral. I kept thinking I could hear the scratching noise – faint and feeble – but every time I sat up in bed, it was quiet.

There were no mice – the pest controller had said so. And Olga had finally managed to get hold of a chimney sweep. I hadn't expected him to find any more skeletons but I went out into the garden while he worked, just in case. Olga came with me, as much for her sake as for mine, I suspect. We were all relieved when the sweep reported he'd found nothing but soot and old birds' nests.

I wondered if maybe the house was adjusting to the loss of Rosemary. She'd been part of its fabric for centuries. Tiny as she was, she'd left some kind of gap. And something had to fill it and that's what was making the noise. The wind, maybe. What with her removal and the rigours of the sweep, the house had to settle once more.

Even that idea seemed a little wacky. The scratching noise could only have been in my head. I told myself to forget it and go back to sleep. But before I did, the thought came to me that the noise could be Rosemary's mother looking for her daughter. I shivered and pulled the duvet over my head.

It was a relief when dawn broke. I couldn't wait for the funeral to be done and dusted. The shock of Rosemary's discovery – and the murky understanding of the circumstances of her death – had cast an eerie, hesitant atmosphere in the house. Shock, I suppose. Wariness.

The Fletchers hadn't helped. Their superstitions made Olga watchful and jumpy. She told me that every minor accident in the kitchen was made out to be very significant. They were alarmed at the hole found in the loaf she baked, saying it signalled the need for another coffin. A dropped spoon that landed hollow side down meant disappointment wasn't far away, and they'd made her promise she would never sharpen a knife after sunset, as it was an invitation for thieves to call in that night.

'I know it's silly,' Olga said, 'but it's a bit crazy-making too.'

I told her I could have a word with them or get Mum to but Olga said no.

'It's important to them,' she said. 'They couldn't stop it even if they want to. I don't want to give Lady Lindy a reason for sack them. They're good workers and I have plenty much to do already . . .'

It was typical of Olga to be loyal and selfless.

'If you're sure,' I said.

She nodded.

'And maybe it's a good thing. Maybe they make us a bit safer. In this house with . . .' She wriggled uncomfortably and looked over her shoulder. 'You never know.'

It was her circumspection that persuaded me to go along with the Fletchers' superstitions for the funeral. At least that's what I told myself. I didn't like to admit that there was a part of me – just a tiny part – that took some comfort in the protection the superstitions could offer, however nebulous and unlikely. And if I played along, it made the Fletchers happier and made Olga feel less vulnerable.

For the last few days, the Fletchers had made me go over the arrangements so that they could ensure no bad luck was incurred.

We had to turn right out of the house to get to the church, rather than the more direct route to the left.

'Follow the sun, rather than meet it,' Brenda said. 'Otherwise

you'll be burying her *the back way*, and we all know where
that leads to.'

It was no hardship to go round the other way and it made
the procession longer, which was no bad thing given how long
Rosemary had waited for it.

The Fletchers were relieved at the number of people I'd
invited. Six in total, including all the staff and Howard – but
not including Mum, of course. She'd made it quite clear she
wanted nothing to do with it and an invitation would give her
another opportunity to mock and fume.

'Any even number is fine,' Glenda said. 'It's an odd number
you want to avoid or the dead will soon be calling for a com-
panion.'

Sasha was to be kept in the kitchen so that he couldn't cross
the path of the funeral. If he did, it would mean bad luck for
the relatives of the deceased.

'And the only way to avoid it,' Glenda told me, 'would be
to kill the dog.'

The certainty in her tone was chilling. I wondered if she
had it in her to do it and, when I looked into her eyes, the
fervour there told me that she might.

It unsettled me and I found myself listening to their instructions and predictions a little more closely, just as Olga
had. It made me wary of objects I'd barely taken any notice
of, mindful of which direction I stirred my tea or if the hem
of my skirt was turned up. No wonder we were all a little
twitchy by the time the funeral came around.

I was sitting at the dressing table in my room when I heard
the sound of a car outside. It had to be the hearse. I held my
own gaze in the dressing table mirror then looked away; the
guilt was still there. Undimmed. I leant forward, touched up
my eyeliner and applied some mascara, wishing I could cover
the darkness in my eyes just as easily.

I hadn't gone over the top with the make-up; my eyelids were the colour of a winter dawn, my mouth moist with a muted shade of magenta. The same colour scheme I'd had at Dad's funeral.

Outside, the slam of car doors. Voices. I stood up and went to the half-open window. The undertakers opened the back of the hearse, reached in for the coffin. It looked so small and white in the black expanse of the vehicle. So pure. I lifted my chin, swallowed my tears. I didn't have time to reapply my mascara.

There was a rap on my bedroom door.

'They're here, Miss Isabella.'

'Thank you,' I said.

The door opened. Brenda peered in. A wave of panic swept over her face and she rushed across the room at me.

'Oh my goodness, you must get away from the window,' she said. The pressure from the hand on my arm as she guided me towards the bed was firm and insistent. 'You can't watch from there. Not good to see a funeral procession through glass.' She gave a firm nod of her head. 'Not good at all.'

She went back to the window and, with her eyes closed, fiddled with the latch and opened it to its fullest extent.

'There,' she said, brushing her hands together, 'now we're OK. You can look if you want to.'

I got up from the bed, smoothed out my dress. Brenda looked me up and down.

'You promise you're not wearing anything new,' she said.

My calf-length black shift dress was ruched in the middle by a thick, heavily buckled purple belt. The shard of heel on my black patent ankle boots was already making my Achilles tendons sore.

'This is what I wore for my father's funeral,' I said. 'And I've not worn any of these things since.' It was daft following her instructions but I did because it kept the peace. That's what I told myself when, really, there was some comfort in wearing the same clothes; it was a way of connecting with Dad.

'Good,' she said. 'Then I think it's OK to go.'

I went to the window, now safely opened wide, and looked out. Two pall-bearers walked towards the door, the coffin resting on their shoulders.

I opened a drawer in the dressing table, took out a red box and lifted the lid. I'd spotted the antique silver rattle in a jeweller's window when I'd been in Stow with Howard. Its mother-of-pearl handle shimmered under the shop window lights, as if winking at me.

It was similar to one Mum had bought for me when I was born, only mine was older and its silver purer and more finely worked. Both had the head of a jester on top and the little bells on his hat tinkled at the slightest touch.

I'd never really played with mine. It was kept in a glass cabinet, a showpiece, out of harm's way, just like I was. But I remember Mum taking it from the cabinet on a few occasions when I was a toddler, and how special it made me feel. The flash of the silver, the tinkle of the bell. Mum's smile. All pure and joyous.

'One day you can give this to *your* little baby,' she'd say and the glow of love inside me would burn a little more intensely.

I didn't know where that rattle was. Still in one of the crates waiting to be unpacked, probably. I hadn't picked it up in years. Neither had Mum. Despite its glitter and elegance, it was tarnished and ugly.

But as soon as I saw the one in the shop window I knew it was meant for Rosemary. It was more refined than the ram's horn she'd been found with; that was an innocent gift for a tragic little girl from her grieving mother. My gift came from the same place and was wrapped in the same sentiment.

Another thought bubbled up from the back of my mind. If Rosemary wasn't a *victim* of the curse but the *cause*, then this funeral would be the end of it. And the rattle was me having the last laugh. There was joy in the jangle of the bells. A celebration.

I replaced the lid on the box and went downstairs. As I reached the last step, Olga and the pall-bearers came out of the dining room.

'She's in there,' Olga said quietly. 'Just as you asked.'

The pall-bearers dipped their heads at me.

'I won't be long,' I said. 'Please wait here.'

I closed the dining room door and tiptoed towards the coffin. Even if it hadn't been lying on the large, oval table, it would have looked small; I could easily have mistaken it for a sewing basket or a picnic hamper if it hadn't been for the instantly familiar shape. Two unlit candles in long-stemmed silver candlesticks stood guard either side.

The last time I'd been that close to Rosemary I'd ended up hysterical. My heart was just as frantic this time too. When I tried to light the candles, my hand shook, missing the wick completely. I steadied it with my other hand. Held my breath.

The flame was slow to take at first, but then grew, the smudged light reflecting in the shine of the table. The thumping was loud and fast in my ears as I reached out and lifted the coffin lid. The wicker creaked.

There she was. Rosemary, lying on a cushion of white silk, the tatty fabric I'd found her wrapped in tucked under her head, like a pillow. Her yellowed bones were no more than shards. Tiny. The eyes were two small drops of darkness, the mouth open, caught in a lazy yawn after suckling – or muttering eternal curses.

I took the rattle and laid it carefully between her tiny fingers. It looked grotesquely out of proportion. So did the ram's horn lying by her side, although its blackened curves blended in better than the shiny glint of silver.

'Hush now, Rosemary,' I said. 'Hush.'

There was a soft, tap-tap-tapping at the window. Two white butterflies fluttered against the glass.

Ice trickled through my blood.

I went to stroke Rosemary's head but could not bring my-self to do it. I feared she would disintegrate beneath my touch – or that I would disintegrate beneath hers. I batted away the idea that she might turn her head and bite me.

The butterflies grazed the window once more. I wondered about the last face Rosemary had ever seen – if she'd ever seen a face at all. But if she had, I wondered if the eyes that last gazed upon her had been full of love and grief, or crazed with anger and hate.

I wondered what she saw in *my* eyes. If she could read the mix of regret and relief.

'God bless,' I said. 'I'm sorry.'

My stare hardened.

'Goodbye.'

Slowly, I lowered the lid.

I cleared my throat and opened the dining room door. Olga and the Fletchers stood waiting in the hall with the pall-bearers.

'We can go now,' I said.

The pall-bearers nodded and walked past me to collect the coffin. Glenda hurried by too.

'You lit the candles in there, I assume?' she said.

'Yes.'

Glenda smiled.

'Then I'd best make sure they're out,' she said. 'Bad luck to leave lit candles in an empty room.'

'Yes,' I said. 'But that's not superstition. That's just common sense.'

'If you say so, miss,' she said, going through the dining room door. 'If you say so.'

I heard the click of heels on the landing. Mum glided down the stairs, fiddling with an earring, Sasha trotting behind her. When he saw the pall-bearers come out of the dining room he darted towards them. Brenda gasped and made a lunge for him but he was too quick and danced around the men's feet, yapping.

Brenda hurried over and shooed him out of the way, towards the drawing room, and closed the door behind him. When she turned to me, her face was ashen. I felt an illogical pang of concern for Sasha.

'Oh good,' Mum said, 'you haven't left yet.'

She stopped on the final stair and smiled at me. Her navy-blue linen trouser suit and white blouse were crisp and creaseless, her hair swept up in a bun, the pearl-drop earrings accentuating the line of her neck.

'I'd like to come after all,' she said. 'If you don't mind, that is.'

I hesitated.

'You're not coming just so you can mock?'

'No. I can see now just how important this is to you. For whatever reason that might be. I want us to be happy here. If doing this helps you settle, helps *us* put everything behind us so we can crack on building our future, then . . . I'm in. As long as you want me to be.'

'Of course I do,' I said. I kissed her on the cheek and felt her shudder. I did too. 'Thank you.'

She sniffed and dropped her head.

'I'd like to pay for it too,' she said. 'But we can sort that out later, OK?'

She slipped her arm through mine and we followed the pall-bearers out of the door and into the blinding sun outside. I couldn't help a smile as, following the Fletchers' instructions, we turned right, trailing the sun. I glanced over my shoulder. The Fletchers didn't look relieved. They looked agitated.

'There's five of us,' Glenda whispered.

Mum had thrown out the safe symmetry of the funeral party. Seeing Howard and Cedric coming down the driveway added to our numbers but still left us at an unlucky seven.

'Sorry,' he said, a little breathlessly, 'we meant to get here a bit earlier but got held up.'

'Had to lift the bees,' Cedric said. 'Just a few inches . . . they have to be lifted at the same time as the coffin, see. Their way of honouring the dead.'

I sensed Mum bristle, saw her swallow whatever comment she was about to make. I stifled a smile too; I should have guessed the bees had a part to play.

'And then the black crape on the hives came loose,' Howard said. 'I couldn't find any drawing pins anywhere but Cedric was most insistent the hives were decorated properly.' He arched his eyebrows, half in apology and half in impatience for humouring Cedric.

'Black crape?' Mum said, then held her hand up. 'No, don't worry. It's probably best I don't know.' She smiled at Howard, her composure restored. 'I'm glad you were able to come. Apart from anything else it gives me the chance to say thank you for helping Isabella sort things out.'

'Not at all,' he said, and winked at me.

I wondered if Mum sensed his similarity to Dad that I did. She didn't seem to; there wasn't the slightest glimmer of recognition or hesitation. Maybe she didn't want to see it. Maybe I did and it was all just in my imagination.

We walked on together in a respectful silence, but the

urgent and persistent whispering behind us made me turn around. Brenda pointed to each of us in turn.

'Seven of us,' she mouthed.

Glenda held up seven fingers.

They both shook their heads then made the sign of the cross.

But they needn't have worried about the odd number of mourners. As we passed through the gate into the church-yard, there was a crowd of people, all dressed in black, waiting for us outside the church.

There were too many even for the Fletchers to count, but I recognised some of the faces. Ed, Nathan and Percy. Simpson and Craven gave us a nod from the back.

'I didn't know it was going to be such a big funeral,' Mum said.

'Neither did I.'

'You two are part of the attraction, of course,' Howard said. 'This is their chance to gawp at the new ladies of the manor.'

I wondered if that was what had persuaded Mum to come. She straightened her back; a subtle, almost regal smile spread across her face. A few of the villagers dipped their heads; Mum did the same. I squirmed from the scrutiny. No doubt Mum was glad I hadn't gone too mad with my clothes or make-up. No doubt she wished she'd worn something even smarter.

Father Wright stood in the church porch, a Bible in his hand and a soft, sympathetic look on his face. He greeted us and led us into the church.

Inside, the church was spartan, its stone walls a sucked-out shade of grey. The air was slightly damp but, after the heat outside, it was something of a relief. We followed the pall-bearers down the aisle and slid into the front pews. Behind us, the church echoed with shuffling footsteps, coughs and whispers that faded away as Father Wright took his position next to the coffin.

'Welcome,' he said, his tone heartfelt and ponderous. 'Thank you for coming along today to give your respects to . . . Rosemary, one of our own who has too long been forgotten.'

There was a low murmur from the people behind us.

'Why Rosemary?' Mum whispered.

I hadn't told her the name I'd chosen, as she hadn't been at all interested in the funeral. She wouldn't have understood if I'd told her why I'd chosen it. I wasn't sure *I* understood it either.

'Just because.'

Howard peered over and gave me the thumbs up.

Wright waited for the murmuring to fade and announced the first hymn.

I felt Mum stiffen at my choice; at first I thought it was indignation but her hand on my knee told me the hymn had simply stirred up memories of Dad. I wished for a moment I'd gone for something else but then decided it was better this way; Mum's touch was as much about reconciliation as comfort.

When Wright asked us to pray, we shuffled forward in the pew and took the embroidered hassocks hanging from the hooks in front of us. Mine had an image of a large black spider in a thick and intricate web. Mum's had a white dove. Howard's a bejewelled cross.

I felt some sympathy for Wright when it came to the eulogy as the circumstances made it tricky to do well. An unknown girl. Buried centuries ago, exhumed then entombed in a chimney only to be found and consigned to unconsecrated ground once again.

But I didn't really listen anyway; it was all myth. Good or bad, the truth would never be known for certain. She was taking her secrets to the grave. Even that didn't matter. The important thing was that she'd gone.

As we sang the second hymn, and the pall-bearers picked up the coffin and carried it back down the aisle, I felt strangely peaceful. My tread was lighter and the fug in my head clearer. The sun streamed through the stained-glass windows, giving the yellow haloes, the green pastures and the red blood an acid fizz that made my eyes ache.

The last window depicted the Virgin Mary in a luminous blue dress. She cradled a candle in her palm, the flame adding a glow to a pinched, grey face. But once we'd got outside, she had vanished. In her place was a red-headed man in a green tunic, and Mary's candle had morphed into a pile of silver coins. I blinked and put it down to a trick of the light.

We stood in silence as the coffin was lowered into the ground. I took a handful of earth from the graveside. The soil wasn't soft and loamy but crunchy with gravel so when it landed on the wicker coffin, it sounded like a suppressed snort of laughter. I thought I heard the rattle of the bells on the jester's hat too.

I bent my head and brushed the soil from my hands.

'Thank you,' I said to Father Wright.

He smiled. 'Let's hope this time it's permanent.'

As we walked back towards the church door, I pointed at the window with the image of the Virgin Mary.

'I noticed that window during the service,' I said. 'I thought I was seeing things at first.'

Howard looked at me quizzically, then at the window.

'The image is different,' I said. 'The Virgin Mary on the inside and . . . some man this side.'

Mum and Howard shielded their eyes as they studied the window.

'Oh, yes,' Mum said. 'I can see the man.'

'Not just any man,' Wright said gravely. 'Judas. See? He has a pile of coins in his hand.'

'But on the other side,' I said, 'it's Mary holding a candle.'

Howard popped inside the church for a moment and then came out, shaking his head.

'Well, I'd never noticed that before,' he said. He looked down at the ground and shuffled his feet. 'But then, I'm not exactly a regular church attender.'

'No,' Wright said, glaring at Howard. He turned to me. 'It's a curious thing, isn't it? The window, I mean.' He turned back to look at it as if for the first time. 'A neat little trick, made possible by some incredible craftsmanship.' He looked a little bashful. 'Something that can't be said for the bell in the church clock. It has a mind of its own. Rings at the most random moments.'

'Yes,' Mum said. 'We heard it for the first time the other night, didn't we, honey?'

I nodded.

'When . . . when we found Rosemary.'

'Is that so?' Wright said. 'How extraordinary. I must have slept right through that.'

'How old is it?' Mum said, squinting at Wright.

'The clock? Or the window?'

'Both.'

'The church itself is sixteenth century. The windows, we believe could be a little later, maybe as a result of damage during the Civil War. It was quite the Royalist stronghold around here. The clock, I really couldn't say.'

Olga came round the corner, followed by the Fletchers, Cedric and the rest of the villagers. Instead of saying goodbye and drifting away the villagers looked rather curious, like they were waiting for something to happen. I realised with a panic that they were expecting some kind of wake.

I hadn't thought of organising anything; my attention had been focused on the funeral itself, on Rosemary. My cheeks flushed. Howard read my embarrassment and guessed my dilemma.

He cleared his throat.

'Everyone, your attention please. I've been asked to invite you all to join Isabella and Her Ladyship for a drink at the pub.'

There were muted cheers and a spattering of applause.

'Just as well you didn't say it was drinks at the manor,' a thin, spindly woman in a shawl said.

'We don't like to go up to there,' said the man by her side. 'It's not safe, see. But I expect you know that already.'

Mum stiffened with indignation. If the villagers wouldn't come to the manor, her vision of herself as the head of the community was scuppered; the fête on the lawn, the awards for cakes and chutneys, Christmas carols in a candle-lit hall – none of it would ever happen. That suited me but I felt a pang of sympathy for Mum.

'Of course it's safe!' Mum cried. 'You must know that. After all, you were up there for that charming little ritual to do with the village boundaries, weren't you?'

'That's different though,' the spindly woman said. 'We were on parish business. With God's servant along to protect us. *And* we didn't go inside.'

'I can assure you, there's nothing to be afraid of,' Mum said firmly.

'Let's just go to the pub, shall we?' I said to her, muttering under my breath, 'You don't have to stay for long.'

Glenda hurried up to us.

'Thirty-six, miss,' she said. 'I sat at the back and counted them.'

'Counted what?' Howard said.

'The funeral party,' she said, shaking her head with impatience. 'A nice even number.'

'Apparently that's good luck,' I said.

Howard wiped his brow with mock relief.

'What about Sasha?' I said, encouraged by Howard's flippancy. 'Does the even number of mourners wipe out his faux pas with the funeral procession?'

'It doesn't really work like that,' she said. 'And anyway, the bad luck from a dog meeting a funeral procession falls upon the relatives of the deceased. That isn't you or Lady Lindy, is it?'

Howard laughed. I did too, but mine came a little slower than his and was underscored by a sense of relief I wouldn't admit to, let alone explain.

Ed rushed past us to open up the pub and soon the place was full with people crowding the bar and baiting Ed for taking too long to get their drinks to them. Mum stood at the bar before Howard showed her to a table by the window, a gin and tonic in her hand.

The villagers took it in turns to introduce themselves; the names and faces blurred and ran into one another. Parker. Thomas. Rogers. May.

Some of them gossiped about the others, pointing them out in the bustle around the pub. One was Percy Whittingham the blacksmith, who apparently took potshots at birds from his living room window.

'How awful,' Mum said, 'someone should report him.'

'Oh no, ma'am. It's a service to the community. He only kills the yellowhammers cos they're bad luck, see? He leaves the rest alone, especially the robins, martins or swallows.'

There was Ken the Egg, who eked out a living by bartering with the output of his hens; and Mabel James, who preferred the water for her tea to be drawn from the river Windrush instead of the 'factory' stuff from the taps.

Mum smiled at each of them, found a question or two, and said she hoped one day they would be able to come up to the manor. None of them made any promises.

If someone had told me I'd have felt comfortable sitting in a pub with my mother, listening to people talk about livestock having just buried the skeleton of an anonymous and possibly cursed infant, I would have laughed.

But as I looked at the people around me – with their ruddy, broken-veined faces and imperfect teeth, who fell silent at the note from a glass caught on an edge of the bar because a sailor would die if they didn't – I tingled with a curious sense of belonging. Something I hadn't had since Cosmo and his crowd.

We'd never really felt part of the outside world and had never really wanted to be. Nor did the villagers. They were outsiders too, defining themselves with their odd little customs and bizarre superstitions, just as I defined myself with my clothes and make-up. I clung to the dark like they clung to the past. Both had their mysteries, joys and horrors.

Something inside me began to settle. Slowly. Like soot. Not quite happiness, maybe, but the beginning of a sense of peace, an understanding that everything could yet be all right.

A sort of dubious calm persisted for the week after the funeral. So too did the scratching noise, although I didn't hear it every night. Maybe it wasn't really there after all. Maybe I was just getting used to it, which was more than I could say for the rest of the house.

No matter how clean or bright it was, no matter what furniture was placed in what rooms, it always felt as if there was something missing. Or that, after leaving a room or turning around, something had shifted behind my back; the air changed subtly, vibrating with an air of expectation. Or the effort of holding a secret in.

More than once I found myself hesitating at the door, trying to work out if anything had actually moved or altered. On several occasions I had the sense there was someone standing behind the door. When I looked and found nothing, I felt foolish. I laughed it off, my smile hindered by the surprise of my racing heartbeat. I wondered if the house was missing Rosemary, as if her bones had been holding it together like mortar.

I avoided the Long Gallery entirely but I could sense it everywhere. Its heaviness infiltrated the corridors, slipped through cracks, hung in the air like a noxious fug blown by a rusty bellows, its squeak echoed by the occasional clang of the church bell and, beneath that, I thought, the tinkle of a bell.

The smell had become more nuanced too. The stench of rotting vegetables was still pronounced but there was also a fresher, lighter scent I couldn't quite place; it was woody yet had a tang of lemon. It was better than the rotting smell but

I still didn't particularly like it – and that's when I realised what it reminded me of. Honey.

No one else could smell it, not even the Fletchers, which made me think I was even madder than they were. The jar Howard had given me sat, untouched, in the kitchen cupboard. The lid was on securely. I'd not detected any hint of honey when I'd been right next to the hives in Howard's garden so I couldn't see how any smell could waft all the way from there.

Brenda hinted that smelling things was considered a sign of pregnancy. Olga told her not to be so silly and shooed her out of the room.

Thank God Mum hadn't heard her or it might have set back the improvements in our relationship. She'd even suggested getting a gravestone for Rosemary, like a granite olive branch – but she'd left the choice to me. I didn't dither over the decision too much as I wanted to avoid pushing Mum's patience and risking a row.

Most of the options were too elaborate – chubby cherubs, serenely sleeping angels – or too modern – a cutesy puppy, a cartoonish bear. A traditionally shaped, plain stone would have been appropriate as it would blend in with the others in the northern churchyard – which was precisely why I didn't want it.

In the end, I compromised; a normal-shaped tombstone in white marble. On its top edge a butterfly, its wings raised, as if about to fly away.

Mum and I walked down to the churchyard once it had been installed. The earth on the grave was parched and powdery, making the white of the marble all the more stark.

'Good choice,' Mum said. 'Although that isn't surprising. Who knew you had such an eye?'

She was referring to the suggestions I'd made to the choice of colours and fabrics for the manor. Normally I wouldn't have dreamt of sitting down with her to consider the options and she would have known better than to ask. But she made the effort, so I did too.

We were both surprised that poring over shades of pastel greens and yellows didn't provoke me to sarcasm or belligerence. We managed to agree on colours for several rooms without rowing. The shock of it dazed us both.

Mum's mood improved even further when her horses were brought up from the stables in London. Fleur, her mount when we used to go out riding together in Hyde Park, had been retired for a while, and was only kept as company for Ophelia, a four-year-old bay mare.

The white socks on each of her legs caused Cedric some consternation, the root of which he recited in a rhyme as the horse was unloaded from its box.

> 'One white leg, buy a horse
> Two white legs, try a horse
> Three white legs, look about a horse
> Four white legs, go without a horse.'

Mum assured him Ophelia had a sweet temperament and was a dream to ride, although she was jumpy and on her toes that day, her coat frothy with sweat. The man from the London stable explained that she wasn't used to being in the horsebox.

Cedric took the bridle and muttered something under his breath into the horse's ear. The mare settled immediately and even followed him into the stable without him having to lead her. The stable lad cooed with appreciation.

'Very impressive,' Mum said.

'It's his gift, ma'am,' Brenda said. 'Horses, cattle, you name it. All he has to do is talk to them and bingo, they're completely biddable.'

'He got rid of an infestation of rats down at the pub, just by asking them to leave,' Glenda said.

Mum looked doubtful, ready to dismiss it as yet another Stagcote fable.

'I wouldn't put it past him,' I said, 'not after the way he brought in that swarm of bees. He had no suit and no smoke but he didn't get one sting.'

Mum looked impressed. 'I wonder where you learn such a thing,' she said.

'He didn't so much learn it, as take it,' Brenda said.

'That's right,' Glenda said. 'From Stow Fair back when he was a lad.'

Cedric hadn't always been so kind or good with animals, they explained, and had been drawn into a game at the fair, called sparrow mumbling. A young sparrow, its wings clipped, was put in a hat and passers-by were invited to try and bite its head off for a cash prize.

Most missed and came away with nothing but a face pocked with bloody peck marks. Cedric took the bird's head off in one swoop and, in his excitement, accidentally swallowed it.

'He's had the ear of any of God's creatures ever since,' Brenda said.

'But he's never used it to harm any of them, not even a fly,' Glenda said.

Mum's smile was patient. Tolerant. Sceptical.

'Perhaps you should ask him to have a word with the yellowhammers then,' she said. 'Tell them to keep out of range of the blacksmith's rifle.'

She was more amenable to the source of the Fletchers' talents with a needle and thread. She'd stumbled upon their skill when she found them sewing during their mid-morning break and watched as they finished conjuring threads into two samplers, one with an image of the front of the manor, the other depicting it from the reverse.

Their mother had taught them, they said, passing on the skill and passion she'd learned from her father, who in turn had picked it up from his. And so it went, on and on, the tradition stretching back beyond memory. A stitch that ran throughout their genetic code. I envied them that connection to the past; it made my own ties with even my most immediate family seem shallow and shaming.

'It's not just them though,' Mum told me. 'There are plenty in the village who sew, apparently.'

'Yes,' I said, 'they must be at it constantly. I remember seeing some of this stuff on the kneelers in the church.'

'That's right,' Mum said. 'It's quite a Stagcote thing.'

She saw it as part of her role as lady of the manor to encourage the craft, and commissioned the Fletchers to make a couple of cushion covers for the garden room.

Mum even suggested they might teach *us* how to do needlepoint. Olga was keen but I said no; the thought of all of us sitting down and sewing was a bit too close to *Little House on the Prairie* for my liking. Even Mum agreed with me; the shy smile we shared at my joke was a shock.

I couldn't remember the last time we'd smiled at the same thing for the same reason. And having found one smile, we somehow found another, each one a shade more confident than the last and pulling us closer together.

Smiling, I realised, was like pushing a car; hard at first but easier once momentum had got going. The effort, I found, was worth it. And I realised too that Mum didn't have to try as hard as I did; her smile – like her love – had always been there, even if I hadn't always been able to see or feel it.

I wanted to think the same was true of me but I wasn't sure I could convince myself of that. There were only so many miracles you could expect in a week. In time, though, who knew what might happen?

We did not get the time to find out.

For a week after the funeral – a period so calm and surprising I couldn't conceive of thinking even for a second that there might be some truth in the story of the manor being dangerous, or that Rosemary had been anything but an abandoned baby – thoughts of the curse took a firmer grip and would not let me go.

A week. Seven days.

Seven. How innocent that number had once appeared to be. It was just the number of dwarves Snow White had teamed up with. The number of days of the Creation. The number of hills of Rome. It quantified the deadly sins and the members of Enid Blyton's less famous gang of crime-busters. 7-Up. 007. *Seven Brides for Seven Brothers*.

More recently, though, it had been the number of siblings in the sequel to *The Sandman* comics, the brothers and sisters known individually as Dream, Death, Desire, Destruction, Delirium, Despair and Destiny.

All of them soon came knocking at the manor's door.

Mum had tried to persuade me to go out for a ride with her but I declined, saying I didn't think Fleur was up to the task, given her age and the heat. Since we'd arrived at Stagcote the weather had been good and got progressively better until it became apparent that summer had come early, and with real intent.

The sun had a sting, the shadows were sharp and the sky a deep, unblemished blue. Cedric had tamed swathes of the garden; lilacs frothed on one side of the manor, their scent blown on a breeze already loaded with rose and lavender. His burr of contentment was as deep as the thrum of his industrious bees.

The heat wasn't the only reason I declined going out for a hack with Mum. Although things had been much better between us, I didn't want to push it or mislead her into hoping I'd rediscover riding. She'd only begin planning a local hunt or gymkhana in the hope that some hearty, jodhpur-clad public schoolboy would catch my eye. I wasn't ready for any kind of romantic involvement with anyone, let alone some horsey type. My riding days were over.

So I went walking that morning instead. I wasn't heading anywhere in particular and just followed the route dictated by the shade offered by hedgerows or trees. Birds whirred and scuttled in the bushes. The skylark trilling and wittering high above me was made invisible by the glare of the sun.

Once I'd blinked away the dazzle in my eyes, I noticed something in the next field; blocks of golden stone standing in a circle around a tree.

Even before Cedric had explained the legend of Maidens' Reel, it had reminded me of dancers around a maypole. But approaching it from the other side, on a slight hill, it looked like the stones were stalking the tree and closing in for the kill.

I skirted around but my eyes were drawn to the tree. It no longer had the curves and lines of a graceful dancer. The limbs were twisted, raised in panic and the singed leaves of the canopy writhed with white butterflies.

I walked on, strangely uneasy, and sat down on the low stone bridge, my feet dangling over the edge soon numbed by the chill of the water. A woman sat on the riverbank further upstream, a toddler in a nappy and sun hat crawling by her side. A second child in a swimsuit paddled in the river, long blonde hair covering her face as she leant forward, staring into the water intently. Water glistened as it dripped from her fishing net. In her other hand was a small bucket.

She walked closer towards me, wincing and wobbling from the stones at the bottom.

'Hello,' I said. 'Have you caught anything?'

She looked up. Her eyes were red and her bottom lip twitched.

'No fish,' she said. 'Fish are dead.'

'Dead?'

She nodded and held up the bucket. I sat up and leant forward to peer in. The white bellies of three small fish made a grin around the bottom of the bucket.

'Oh dear, that's quite a catch,' I said. 'But you must remember to put water in the bucket too. The fish need it to breathe.'

She glared at me.

'I know!' she snapped. 'I didn't hurt them. They were dead when I found them.'

I looked into the river; the water looked clean enough but maybe that didn't mean it was safe. I swung my legs and pulled my feet clear.

'Oh, I see. That's not good, is it?' I said. 'Something nasty must have got into the water. You haven't drunk any of it, have you?'

She shook her head.

'It's not the water. It's the trumpets.'

'Trumpets?'

'Uh-huh. Mummy told me.'

The woman along the bank was facing the other way, tracking the progress of the toddler as he crawled along the grass bank.

'I don't see how trumpets can kill fish,' I said.

'They can. Mummy said.'

'Right, well . . . maybe Stagcote fish just don't like music very much. Don't blame them. I'm not into brass bands either.'

'Not music!' she said irritably. '*Trumpets*.' She pointed with the net towards the pub.

'Maggie!'

The child turned around. Her mother had the toddler in her arms and was waving her daughter towards her.

'Maggie?' she said. 'Come here now.'

'But I want to help the fish!' the girl wailed.

'Maggie! Did you hear me? Now. It's time for some juice and a biscuit.'

'You'd better go,' I said. 'I don't want to get you into trouble.'

The woman drew closer. She looked agitated and impatient.

'Empty the bucket and let's go,' she said to the girl.

'It's my fault,' I said. 'She was just telling me about the trumpets killing the fish.'

'Really?' she said quickly, without looking at me. 'The things she comes up with. I don't know where she gets them from.'

'*You* told me!' Maggie said. She let the fish slip from the bucket, watched them spin away in the current, then paddled towards the riverbank and clambered out. 'You said there were seven trumpets!'

'I don't think so,' the woman said. 'I don't know what you're talking about. Now, come on.'

'You *did*!' The girl started to cry.

Her mother took her hand and led her away.

A flash of white caught my eye as another dead fish slid under the bridge. I looked upstream; the water was clear, pooled with shadows and undulating wisps of green weed. But there were no more fish.

My gaze drifted to the pub. To the sign above the door. A ram's horn. My stomach dropped. I'd seen the sign before, of course, but not really noticed it since then. It was just one of those things that you simply took for granted or ignored. Any wider significance went undetected – *if* there was any.

I could see the source of Maggie's confusion. Horn. Trumpet. They were both instruments. I wasn't even sure if they weren't the *same* instrument. How was a kid to know? But I couldn't understand why Maggie would think the trumpets had killed the fish.

The door to the pub was open. Ed had his back to me, his shirt damp with sweat as he swept the floor. The bar was empty. I coughed and he looked up. Smiled.

'You're off the mark pretty quickly this morning, aren't you?' he said, glancing at the clock.

'Been out walking,' I said. 'I've earned a drink.'

He leant the broom against a wall.

'Technically, we're not open yet, but . . .' He walked around the bar. 'What can I get you?'

We were both surprised that I asked for a lime and soda. The cool glass felt good in my hand. I took a sip and savoured the tang of iced lime.

He didn't look shocked or surprised when I told him about the dead fish Maggie had found.

'It happens,' he said. 'Some dodgy chemicals found their way into the water. Fertiliser from the farms, maybe.'

'I hadn't thought of that,' I said. 'Maggie said it was something to do with trumpets.'

'Obviously she's heard the village band,' he said, with a smile that didn't reach his eyes. He turned away and fiddled with the pumps behind the bar. 'I need to change the bitter barrel,' he said, and slipped round the back. His footsteps on the wooden stairs were slow and careful.

I rolled a cigarette, lit it and took a long, hard drag. I rolled the smoke around my mouth then tipped my head back and blew it out towards the ceiling in one long breath.

That's when I saw it. A ram's horn on the ceiling. It wasn't mounted up there like the brasses on leather straps attached to the walls. It was pressed into the plaster.

There was another one a few feet away to the right. And another in the left-hand corner. A fourth above the door. I walked around to the other side of the bar. There were three more there. Seven in all.

A jaundiced constellation, yellowed with nicotine and age. No wonder I hadn't noticed them before.

My heart quickened. Familiar shapes flickered in the shadows of my mind, the ghosts of the anxiety and doubts about Rosemary and the curse I thought I'd banished.

I ran behind the bar to the top of the stairs Ed had taken.

'Ed!' I yelled.

There was no answer. Just as I was about go down, he peered up from the bottom, his face shiny with sweat.

'The horns,' I said, pointing towards the bar. 'What are they for?'

He swallowed and wiped his forehead.

'For?'

'Yeah.'

'I didn't put them there.'

'No, I can see they've been there a while.'

'Exactly.'

'But why put them there in the first place?'

He wiped his forehead again.

'It's the wool industry, probably. Pretty big around here back in the day. Less so now, of course . . .'

'That makes sense, I suppose, but . . . why seven?'

'Does there have to be a reason?'

'Yes.'

'Why?'

149

'Because this is Stagcote! And there's always a reason for everything. Even if it doesn't always make sense.'

'I don't know about that.'

'Look, I went to a pub in London once. It's got a fishing net on the ceiling. The net's full of hot cross buns, some of them black and rock hard as they've been there for years . . . hundreds of years, probably. Each Good Friday they chuck another bun in.'

'Well, they do some right funny things in London.'

'But they've a *reason* for doing it! That's my point.'

'Like what?'

'The woman who lived in a cottage where the pub is . . . she had a son who went off to sea. He was meant to come back at Easter so his Mum baked hot cross buns for him . . . only he never came back. She hung a bun in a net from the ceiling and made some more buns the next year . . . and the next . . . like a sign of hope. Expecting him to return. The tradition has carried on ever since.'

'Very interesting, I'm sure,' he said, 'but what's it got to do with my pub?'

'What I'm saying is, if there's a reason a pub in London does things like that, there's bound to be a reason for the horns in your ceiling – *and* for there being seven of them.'

'Maybe,' he said. 'I don't know.' He waved his hand behind him. 'Look, the pump's gone. I'm a bit tied up down here and . . . seeing as we're not really open yet, would you . . .'

He was as keen to get away from me as Maggie's mother had been. And he looked rattled despite his efforts to hide it.

I didn't know what it was that I'd found. All I knew was I'd found *something* and that the locals were reluctant to talk about it. It had to be connected with Rosemary because the horns in the ceiling matched her rattle. It could just have been a coincidence but it seemed unlikely.

I was curious. And I was bored. It was something to do. I might find out who Rosemary was. I might find nothing at all. I didn't know which disturbed me more.

I googled '7 trumpets' and waited. The rainbow-coloured wheel on the screen spun for an age as the World Wide Web struggled to connect with Stagcote. Finally the page loaded.

Seven trumpets are sounded one at a time, to cue apocalyptic events that were seen in the vision of the Revelation of Christ Jesus . . .

The **seven trumpet** blasts are seven plagues that God gives to evil unrepentant people . . .

Bible Prophecy declares that the **7 Trumpets** of Revelation, announcing devastating divine judgments, are to blast soon and in rapid succession!

Oh God. It had to be God, didn't it? I didn't have much time for faith or religion. It was all too vague and unreliable – like the Fletchers' superstitions. I understood that in the past, faith helped people make sense of the world but it baffled me why such antiquated ideas still dictated their beliefs, the things they did and how they lived their lives. If there was a God, He (because it *had* to be a he) was just a bully suffocating individuality and suppressing fun.

I was in half a mind not to continue, but decided to give it a bit longer. I read on, twirling a strand of hair around my finger.

The trumpets appeared in the Book of Revelations, each one

heralding a different catastrophe; raging fires, oceans of blood, poisoned rivers, celestial blackout, lion-toothed locusts and a mighty army mounted on creatures that breathed out plague, smoke, fire and brimstone. The final trumpet was a cue to give thanks to God for the carnage that had cleansed the earth, the destruction finally brought to an end by an earthquake and hailstorm.

I teased myself by thinking that this was the curse. The sudden chill in my heart was thrilling. It was the most alive I'd felt in ages. So I googled '7 horns'.

The reference was also from the Book of Revelations, but concerned a lamb with seven eyes, each one representing characteristics of the Holy Spirit, like wisdom, faith and healing. According to an explanatory note at the bottom, seven was God's number for perfection.

It couldn't have been more benign or more of a contradiction of the results for seven trumpets. It couldn't have confused me more either.

I was surprised at the surge of disappointment, at how much I wanted the two definitions to tally and build a convincing case. It was startling to realise that I half hoped the curse was real. It was one way to get out of the manor, I suppose, although me sprouting wings was more likely.

I leant closer to the screen, stopped fiddling with my hair.

I'd been so disinterested in Stagcote before the move I'd not even bothered to look it up online. I'd let my assumptions lead me. And my search results would not have changed my opinion, as Stagcote was as easy to overlook online as it was in the real world.

The internet skirted around the village, just as the roads did. There was a map, but the pin marking the spot quivered, as if it wasn't quite sure if the location was correct or if there was really anything there to pin down. There were only a few pictures; the deserted high street, the bridge, a couple of the cottages. The manor.

A lot of the links led to pages that, once they eventually opened, were links to non-existent directories of services in Stagcote or adverts for domain names priced in US dollars.

Even *I* could have written the entry on Wikipedia for all the information it contained. My eyes scanned the page so quickly I barely took the details in. A village in the north of the Cotswolds. A farming economy. Sparsely populated. A manor house of little architectural merit.

Built on the site of Stagcote Abbey.

I jolted back from the screen. Blinked. My skin tingled and I read the section once more. Before the Reformation, a community of Cistercian nuns had lived in an abbey on the estate. There were no other details. No photos or illustrations.

I was tantalised.

I'd watched horror films with ghoulish brides of Christ summoned to sacrifice new recruits by a monotonous bell, their chants in the cloisters threaded with laughter and whispers of sexual desire. The notion that Rosemary could have been sacrificed suddenly didn't seem so preposterous. Tremors rippled through me.

But, I reasoned, there was reassurance and refuge in the walls of a church too. I'd experienced it at Dad's funeral and at Rosemary's. The manor had prayers in its foundations, the tread of angels in its soil and meadows, even if it didn't necessarily feel like that to me.

My search for other ruined abbeys found entries for Tintern, Kirkstall and Rievaulx. The photos showed cliff-high walls and arches punctuated by ugly gashes or petering out into nothing. Collapsed pillars crawled like fingers across the grass; stones knuckled through ivy.

Stagcote Abbey must have looked the same. The glimpse of

what was once here made me shiver. I looked up. Outside, the pitch black of night. Inside, the white glow of the screen. The monochrome of a nun's habit. I imagined hushed footsteps as the sisterhood hurried to lose themselves in prayer, rosary beads clicking like bones. The sombre hymns, the sibilance of confession.

It had all happened here.

A barely there touch made my skin bristle. A sound as faint as distant vespers came from somewhere.

I looked up from the laptop, head cocked, listening.

Outside, the rustle of leaves, the bleat of sheep. A hoot of an owl.

I put the laptop on the bedside table, slid into bed and pulled the duvet up to my chin. I'd seen the death of countless virgins announced with the call of an owl in the vampire films I watched with Cosmo in his basement flat in Finsbury Park.

The camera always cut away from the virgins' trembling bodies to a screeching bird, blinking impassively. Fear could be fun. Cosmo and his goth mates had taught me that. We weren't scared to look *in* the dark places – we looked *for* the dark places. That's where we found each other.

I'd pretended to be scared of the films just so Cosmo would put his arm around me and pull me closer to him. Nothing could get to me then. Not even Mum. She'd never understood what I saw in him and only got hurt and angry when I'd tried to explain. Her brand of love was about control. All I learnt of love from Dad was absence.

Cosmo was with me, constant as the stars. Cosmo cared but did not control. His arms told me only that he was there, not that he was trying to restrain me and shape me into something I wasn't and could never wish to be. Now, though, Cosmo was a composite of my experience of love; he was absent, yet he crowded my thoughts, controlling me from who knew where.

The cool white dots on the digital clock pulsed between the numbers. Three o'clock. I waited for the scratching to start but nothing came. The house was completely silent.

The hoot of the owl startled me. It sounded closer; more forlorn and mournful. It called once more. That's three times, I thought, and wondered if that made it luckier. Or more sinister. The Fletchers were sure to know all about the power of three. Lucky numbers. Unlucky thirteen. Abracadabra. Boo!

I turned over. Another call from the owl, raspy and tentative, like a novice attempting their first note on a trumpet.

Mum looked surprised when I told her I wanted to go to the library in Cheltenham.

'That's great, honey,' she said. 'A bit of home study will make sure you're not too far behind when you get back to school.'

I wasn't behind at all. If anything I'd be ahead, seeing as I was a year older than the rest of my classmates would be and had already done half of the first year of sixth form. Repeating a year had its advantages.

I didn't tell her I was going to look into the history of the manor rather than literary criticism on the metaphysical poets and King Lear. Maybe she wouldn't have minded had she known. She could have just seen it as further proof of me settling into the manor and life at Stagcote.

'I'll drop you off,' she said. 'It will be a chance to try out the school run. And I can see what the shops have got in the way of fabrics.'

I was more than happy to be missing out on looking at floral prints and paint swatches.

We left straight after breakfast. I packed my laptop, a pad and a pen into my black leather duffel bag with the rows of metal studs. Mum frowned.

'I'll have a look for bags that are suitable for school while I'm at it,' she said.

She slowed down as we approached the top of the driveway. Howard stood on the corner with a silver camera in his hand. Mum stopped the car and wound the window down.

'Good morning, Howard,' she said.

He winced and raised his hand.

'It was!' he said. 'You've frightened it away now.' He pointed to the camera then to the trees. 'The woodpecker. I was trying to get a snap of it.'

Mum grimaced. 'Sorry!'

'Never mind,' he said. 'Seeing as you're here, you two will do instead. Smile!'

He lifted the camera and pressed the shutter, then checked the photo on the screen.

'I was about to say two English roses,' he said, 'but that wouldn't be right, would it?'

'Why's that?' I said. 'Because only one of us is a rose or because neither of us are?'

'Because I'm not English, of course,' Mum said. She turned to Howard. 'She doesn't normally let me forget it.'

Once we got into town, we parked and got out of the car.

'I go this way,' I said, checking the app on my phone. At least there was a decent signal.

Mum pointed to the sign saying Shopping Centre, the arrow pointing in the opposite direction.

'Give me a ring when you're ready to go home,' she said.

It was odd being with crowds of people, shocking almost. It took me a while to get used to the rush and to slip into the warp and weft of the people coming at me, around me, behind me. It was strangely exhilarating and the realisation made me smile; I'd done the same thing in London and not even noticed it.

Stagcote had opened my eyes. And my ears. The noise of the cars and buses, screaming children, the thump of bass from shop doorways, the beep of pelican crossings – I heard them as if for the first time. Loud. Intrusive. Strangely alien.

It was odd to walk past shops too. Even in London I'd walked past the likes of Next and Mango as their clothes were too strappy and floaty to interest me. But as I got away from a shopping precinct homogenised by the usual names and logos, the sharp whiff from Lush and the earthy fug of Starbucks, the charity canvassers with leaflets and clipboards, I found myself equally disinterested in the shops that would normally pull me in.

I barely glanced at the crusty-looking shops with their tired mannequins swathed in dresses of netting and lace, necks draped with torture-chamber jewellery and shod in boots with more buckles than leather. I breezed past windows mosaicked by record sleeves and books, but the scent of joss sticks in the air brought me to an abrupt halt.

I breathed it in, felt it catch dry and heavy at my throat. It was familiar. I sniffed again. Sweet and citrusy but full and heady. With a trace of honey. The scent I'd detected in the Long Gallery.

'What is that smell?' I asked.

The woman tidying a rack of T-shirts by the door looked up, pushed back her pink tie-dyed headscarf.

'Joss sticks,' she said.

'Yes, but what's the scent?'

The woman smiled.

'Lovely, isn't it?'

I nodded.

'It's not honey?'

The woman took a deep breath.

'I can see where you're coming from with that. There's a

hint of honey, yes, but . . .' She coughed. 'It's frankincense. Like they use in churches. Catholic churches.'

She waved towards the counter, explaining that they sold them in packs of twelve and had loads of other fragrances, but I just thanked her, turned and walked on.

Frankincense. They'd have used it at Stagcote Abbey too. For centuries. It was ridiculous to think it could have lingered, tainted the soil and still be smelt after all this time. It was just my imagination. Maybe there was frankincense in the polish the Fletchers used; one of their home brews. At the very worst it was just a coincidence. I was thinking about Stagcote Abbey – *on a mission about it* – and I happened to come across the smell of frankincense. It meant nothing.

But I'd picked up the smell in the Long Gallery *before* I knew about the Abbey. The woman in the shop had only given it a name, not put the idea in my head.

The library building reminded me of the manor too – the same creamy gold stone, a jumble of towers and little round turrets, arched windows, five worn stone steps. The place was everywhere, it seemed to me. Filling my head with its shadows.

After the bustle and thrum of the street, the library was still, the air stuffy and laced with the smell of new carpet. A few people sat huddled reading newspapers at tables scattered in the main room; a few more tapped away at computers in the corner.

I followed the sign for the Family and Local History Library. The man on reception raised his eyebrows as I approached the desk then remembered to smile.

'Can I help?' he said.

'I hope so,' I said, resting my bag on the desk. 'I'm try- ing to find out about Stagcote, and the manor in particular. I wondered if you could tell me what information you've got and . . . well, where to start really.'

'You've not been here before?'

'No. Never done anything like this before.' I opened my bag and rummaged inside. 'But I've brought some ID and proof of address like it said on your website.'

He angled his head. 'Well, that's more than most people remember to do on their first visit,' he said. He slid a form across the desk. As I filled it in, he checked my passport and the address on my mobile phone statement.

'So,' he said, handing the documents back to me, 'you're here as house detective then.' He nodded. 'Stagcote Manor. Very nice.'

'You know it?'

He shook his head. 'No, not as such. I know it exists but . . .'

'That's more than most.'

'Hmm. I don't recall anyone ever coming to ask about it either. So it's a bit of a mystery tour for me too. I should think we'll have to do some digging.'

He stood up and passed me a reader's badge and a card with a long number on it.

'You'll need to fill out a docket for every document you want to see, quoting your reader number.'

'OK.'

I picked up my bag.

'That has to go in one of the lockers,' he said. 'And no pens or phones are to be used in the reading room.'

Any other time, all the fuss would have irritated me. It was just a load of old books and papers. But the rigmarole made the whole experience richer; I couldn't just rock up and grab what I wanted like I did with make-up or clothes. I had to wait. There were procedures. Etiquette. Stuff that would normally have bored me and put me off. Now it felt like an initiation, or a rite of passage. For a brief moment I had the sense that I was saying goodbye to a part of me. Like a novice entering a convent.

I took my laptop, pad and pencil case from the bag and stored it in a locker.

'Right,' he said, sitting down in front of a computer in the reading room, 'what was it you wanted to know?'

I shrugged.

'Anything really. Photos, pictures. Papers. Especially anything that mentions trumpets. Or horns.'

He frowned.

'As in a band, you mean?'

'Could be. I've no idea, to be honest. I know there was an abbey around there but that's about it. I'd like to know when it was built, when it became the manor, who first lived there. Who's lived there since – not just the lords or whatever, but the staff too.'

'Well, I don't know if we'll be able to help you with *all* that, and certainly not in one go!' he said. 'But let's see.'

He tapped at the keys, waited, sucked his teeth.

'It's as I thought,' he said. 'There's nothing specific, but . . .'

In the Gloucestershire edition of Pevsner's architectural guide, the manor was described as *an unlikely and not altogether palatable confection, a mismatch of styles, periods and conflicting architectural pretensions.*

Pevsner wondered if, at some point in its past, it might not have been preferable for one of the owners to have had the nerve to knock it down and start again, rather than simply adding insult to injury with each successive attempt to make the house work.

The Victoria County History of Gloucestershire had detailed entries for abbeys and priories in Winchcombe, Flaxley, Hayles and Horsley among others – but was silent on Stagcote. The only reference to the abbey was in an entry about Kingswood Abbey in 1131, founded by several of the nuns originally housed at Stagcote.

'We've various local newspapers on microfiche,' the archivist said. 'You might find something there on past owners – but only if they were involved in something newsworthy, of course. The earliest paper we've got is the *Cheltenham Chronicle* from 1809.'

That left me with a gap of some seven hundred years to fill.

'You've got nothing earlier than that?' I said.

He tapped at the computer keys once more, then leant in, his finger running down the screen.

'Ah,' he said, 'there's something over at the archives in Gloucester. They tend to have the older material, the primary sources, original documents, diaries, ledgers and so on. Our collection is more "modern", you might say. Newspapers, guidebooks, maps. Nineteenth century mostly, although Gloucester have some of those too.' He scribbled a number down on a piece of paper. 'There's the reference if you want to follow it up.'

'Does it say what it is?'

He smiled enigmatically. 'A bound volume. Quite large, it would seem. Circa the sixteen hundreds, it says.'

My skin tingled. This sounded promising.

'Great, thank you.' I took the piece of paper from him and rubbed my finger over the number. 'Could be exactly what I wanted.'

The librarian didn't look so sure.

'The book is handwritten,' he said. '*In code.*'

'Code? What sort of code?'

'It doesn't say, I'm afraid. And it doesn't look like anyone's been able to break it either. There's no transcript, you see.' He tutted. 'Sorry. Looks like that's that, then.'

'If no one's read it, how do they know it's about Stagcote?'

'Seems it was among the belongings of one of the lords of the manor.'

'He wrote it?'

The librarian shrugged. 'I really can't tell you any more. That's all the catalogue entry says. Of course, one of my colleagues over at Gloucester might know more.'

'How far away is it?'

'Gloucester? About half an hour.'

I looked at my watch. It was already nearly noon.

'Damn!'

He stood up.

'They're closed today anyway,' he said.

'What about tomorrow?'

'Yep. Open until five for the rest of the week, one o'clock on Saturdays.'

I'd have to wait. Impatience surged. I couldn't believe I was disappointed about a delay in getting to an archive. A few weeks ago I'd have laughed at anyone who suggested that I would be. But here I was. Maybe I *was* changing – and quicker than I realised.

I was about to go but the librarian called me back.

'What about the trumpets? I can do a quick search. Stagcote plus trumpets? You never know.'

But he found nothing.

I thanked the librarian, collected my bag and punched the reference number for the coded book into my phone.

When I rang Mum, she said she'd finished browsing and would see me back at the car. She turned up empty-handed.

'No luck?' I said.

She shook her head and groaned.

'It was a bit of a long shot but I thought it was worth a go. I was hoping to put off going into London for a while but it looks like I may have to. How did you get on? Get much done?'

'OK,' I said. 'I need to go back though.'

I was used to lying to Mum about where I'd been and what I'd been doing, but this felt different. She'd be just as surprised about what I'd been up to as *I* was. Encouraged too, perhaps. There was no real reason I couldn't tell her the truth, I just wasn't used to doing so. There were only so many changes I could take in one day. And anyway, she'd only go on about me wasting time on wild goose chases when I should be doing prep for next term.

Mum beamed.

'I'm so glad you're taking your studies so seriously, honey. I'm very proud of you. The way you've adapted. You've grown up in the last few weeks.' She nodded with satisfaction. 'It was a bit rocky at first but I think Stagcote's going to be the making of us.'

It was certainly changing me, I nearly said, but I didn't want to encourage her, or give her the satisfaction at seeing her plan working out.

The dog came out of nowhere.

A big, black dog. It shot out in front of the car, making Mum swerve sharply and blast the car hooter. Tyres squealed. We both screamed as the car slid into a tree. Metal crumpled. Wood splintered. Airbags ballooned between the front seats and the windscreen.

All I could hear was the tinkle of broken glass, the tick of the engine.

'Mum!' I said. 'Are you OK?'

She seemed to take an age to answer. She was still. Not breathing.

I couldn't count the number of times I'd wished her dead but the shock of it, here, right in front of my eyes, ripped me apart.

'Mum!'

I scrambled out of the car, ran round to her side. Glass crunched beneath my feet. I opened the driver's door. Her hands were gripping the wheel so tightly her knuckles looked like they'd break through the skin. My touch on her shoulder released hard, quick pants of breath.

'Oh thank God! Are you hurt?' I said, frantically trying to undo the seat belt.

'No,' she said, her voice shaking. 'I'm fine. You?'

I rubbed my head where it had hit the side window and the door.

'I'm OK.'

She turned off the ignition and climbed out of the car. She stretched slowly, stiffly and massaged her neck.

'Thank God there was nothing coming the other way. Or behind us.' She looked back, her head moving a little jerkily. 'Bloody dog! What was it doing off the lead? Where's the owner?'

I rubbed my head again.

'You sure you're OK?' Mum said.

'Yes, really. Bit of whiplash but other than that I'm fine.' I pointed to the car. 'I'm in better shape than that is.'

It wasn't as bad as it looked, she said. It could be repaired but not driven. 'At least we were nearly home.'

She took out her phone, called Olga and explained what had happened. She turned up in her Peugeot a few moments later, shaking her head and crossing herself.

'You were very lucky!' she said. 'This time.'

'This time?' Realisation dawned on Mum's face. Followed by a sharp smile. 'Oh come on, Olga! You don't think this is because of the—'

'It could be, Lady Lindy! Couldn't it?'

'No! Of course not. It was just an accident. For pity's sake!'

Olga turned to me for confirmation. I avoided her gaze. I'd

166

be lying if I said the thought hadn't shot through my mind too.

'You've called the police?' she said eventually. 'And an ambulance?'

'No need,' Mum said. 'We're both OK. No one else was involved. We're not blocking the road. Let's just get the car and ourselves home.'

Ten minutes later, a tractor appeared, driven by one of the local farmers, Cedric squeezed into the cab. They hitched up a chain and pulled the car into the road. Glass tinkled. Metal groaned.

'Olga said it was a dog, ma'am?' the farmer said. 'Is that right?'

'Yes,' Mum said. 'I didn't get a good look at it. Everything happened so quickly. But it was a big dog. Really couldn't say what breed. Labrador maybe, but a *big* Labrador. Black.'

The farmer and Cedric gave one another a furtive look.

'A black one, ma'am? All black?'

Mum nodded. 'Must have come from the village,' she said. 'I'm surprised the owner hasn't popped out of the bushes. They've probably not insured it and have run off in case they get sued.'

'Maybe the dog had escaped,' I said. 'They might not even know it's gone.'

Cedric rubbed his chin. 'I don't think so,' he said. 'I know all the dogs in Stagcote. There's no black dogs among them.'

The farmer nodded. 'Not a real one anyway.'

'Real one?' Mum said.

'Legend has it—' Cedric said.

Mum waved them away.

'I'm sorry, I've had Olga getting all wrung out about this being to do with this bloody curse business . . . I really don't have time for . . . for what? Some phantom dog? Please.'

167

'But that dog's bad news, ma'am,' Cedric said. 'I'm telling you. Every time it's seen—'

'What, Cedric? Don't tell me. Every time it's seen, someone dies?'

'Not someone,' the farmer said. 'The person who saw it.' He looked at the ground. 'The *people*.'

'Well, clearly it has lost its touch. Otherwise we'd both be dead or horribly injured.'

'Don't make joke, Lady Lindy,' Olga cried. 'It's not funny.'

'We've been in an *accident*,' Mum said. 'There's nothing funny about that, I can assure you, even if it wasn't too major. But it *was* an accident caused by a *real* dog. Not a phantom. Nothing to do with a curse.' Her voice was wavering with anger as much as shock. Her body began to tremble.

Olga hurried her into the Peugeot and tucked a rug around her, then came back for me.

'You shaking too, Miss Isabella,' she said.

And I was. It was the shock. *Nothing else.*

I'd seen the dog. It was real. I didn't imagine it, like I had the frankincense. I hadn't imagined the scratching either and it turned out there was something there too.

There was comfort in the logic.

But why had the accident happened then, so soon after burying Rosemary? And on the way back from my research in the archive? So soon after I'd stumbled upon the horns at the pub?

That night, the hoot of the owl was drowned out by the sound of the car hooter as we'd swerved to avoid the dog. It rang in my ear. Another kind of horn. A warning. Get out of the way. Move.

That night I slept with light on.

It was hovering over me. Round and pale. Distorted. Blink-ing. Breathing.

I woke up with a start and cried out, scooting up the bed and throwing back the duvet.

'There, there, miss! Where's the fire?'

I looked again.

'Glenda!' I said, catching my breath. 'What the hell are you doing?'

'Just trying to wake you up. Olga wanted to know if you'd be needing breakfast this morning. It's getting late, you see.'

Her lopsided gaze slid over to my bedside clock like jelly from a table. Ten past eleven.

'You're sleeping better now, miss. Seems our little tricks have been working after all, doesn't it?'

'Maybe,' I said through a yawn. 'Probably just the shock from the accident.'

Glenda took my dressing gown from the dressing table chair and handed it to me.

'That too, no doubt.' Her expression darkened. 'The *ac-cident* . . . I saw the state of the car. You were lucky. A very close call.' She pursed her lips in an 'I told you so' kind of way. 'You really must be careful. There's only so much me and Brenda can do.'

It was daft – I knew it was – but she made me feel vulner-able and uneasy, a feeling exaggerated by the sight of Mum moving around downstairs, stiff and slow, as if she was afraid and trying not to be noticed.

It was just whiplash, I told myself. That was all. But it was also a glimpse of the future, her body older, more reluctant and less reliable. She'd always been so healthy, never troubled by anything worse than a bad cold or an occasional bout of asthma.

She said the stiffness in her shoulders and neck didn't hurt but I caught her wincing once or twice when she turned her head too quickly. The vulnerability in her eyes was as much a shock to me as her difficulty in moving. It was as if a veil had lifted, briefly, and we'd seen how things would be one day. It made us both feel strange.

What was stranger was that I wondered if even that frail and shrivelled future might be denied to us if we stayed on at the manor.

I had to get back to the archive.

As Mum couldn't turn her head properly, she wasn't able to drive. I couldn't get a cab. Not even Mum would believe I was *that* keen to study, and telling her the truth just wouldn't be worth the aggro or the mockery. And Olga was too tied up nursing Mum even though she said she didn't need any fuss. But Mum obviously sensed my frustration.

'You know, honey, we should look into getting you fixed up with a driving licence and some lessons.'

I'd never really needed to drive in London – I got around fine on the Tube and buses and cabs and I didn't have to worry about not drinking. Cosmo and the rest didn't drive, so if I'd had a car I'd just have become a chauffeur. And, of course, Mum had never really wanted to me to drive either, as it would have made me even more independent.

Now though, she could see its advantages. She was going to have to drive me to school and back every day. That would be limiting for her and embarrassing for me.

But given what had happened yesterday, the prospect of driving made me nervous.

'Can we leave it for a while?' I said. 'There's been enough to deal with lately and . . . I don't want any more stress.'

'Makes sense to learn whilst you don't have school to think about,' she said. 'I can take you out in between lessons.'

'No!' I said a little too sharply.

She turned her head in small jerky movements to look at me.

'No,' I said, softening my voice. 'I don't want to. We argue enough as it is. It's been great lately, getting on better. I don't want to screw it up.'

Me in the driving seat of a car was an accident waiting to happen – and maybe not just because I was a learner. I didn't want to take any more chances than I had to.

But I needed to get to the archive.

As I walked up the driveway towards the Gate House, I caught a flash of white through the hedge and a trace of smoke on the breeze. I opened the gate and went into the garden. Howard was at the far end, dressed in a white beekeeping suit, a twist of grey smoke trailing from the can in his hand.

'Howard!'

He turned, raised an arm in a slow salute then unzipped the suit's hat and pulled it back. It was Cedric.

'Oh,' I said, walking towards him. 'Hello.'

'Morning, miss.'

'Sorry, I thought you were Howard.'

I was surprised he was wearing the suit. And he kept pumping on the handle of the can in his hand, forcing puffs of smoke from the funnel.

'I didn't think you bothered with the tools of the trade,' I said.

'I don't. Not normally. But they's been really quite uppity since they swarmed.'

'Since *we* arrived, you mean.'

He gave another blast of smoke.

'Just don't get too close,' he said.

There was a warning in his voice. I wondered if it was less to do with my proximity to the bees than my interest in the trumpets at the pub, as word was sure to have spread about that. Maybe I was just overthinking things. Getting twitchy over nothing. My eyes met his. He zipped up the suit, covering his face with the visor.

'Is Howard in?'

Cedric shook his head. 'Cirencester, I think.'

'Bugger! Any idea when he'll be back?'

'He didn't say. Now if you'll excuse me, miss . . .'

Another blast of smoke.

I took the hint and went back to the manor. As I opened the front door I could hear voices, high and excited, coming from the kitchen.

Olga was at the sink, peeling potatoes with brisk, angry strokes, her muttering aimed at the open back door with a toss of her head.

'What's going on?' I said. 'It's not Mum, is it?'

Olga jumped and turned around.

'It's all of us, say those two,' she said, waving her knife at the window. 'The moles. They drive me crazy.'

'The moles?'

'No!' She wiped her forehead with the back of her hand. 'The sisters. Always bad news. And now they disturb Lady Lindy.'

I looked out of the back door; Glenda was pointing at the ground. Brenda waved her arm in a wide arc. Mum moved her head stiffly, following the trajectory. Glenda said something and they all turned towards me as I came out of the kitchen door.

'Is something wrong?' I said.

The Fletchers nodded quickly.

'Yes, miss,' Glenda said. 'This isn't good at all.'

'Molehills,' Brenda said, pointing at the garden. 'Look!'

Mounds of dark soil punctuated the grass.

'All around the house,' Brenda said. 'Death is on its way.'

Mum tried to toss her head back as she laughed but the effort made her grimace.

'Yes,' she said. 'It *is* on its way. For the moles. Look at the mess they've made.'

'But you don't understand—'

'You're right,' Mum said, 'and I never will understand why you believe in this nonsense.'

'It's the—'

'Enough!' Mum said. 'It's upsetting Olga and I won't have it. If you want to continue working here – although God knows why you *do*, given how doomed we all are – this has to stop.'

'But we—'

'Yes, I know, Brenda, it's what you believe. And I'm not going to *stop* you believing it any more than you will make me *start*. OK? So, from now on, you keep all this superstitious bunkum to yourself. A dropped spoon will just be a dropped spoon. If I want red and white flowers in the same vase, *that* is what I'll have, right? No questions, no palpitations, no fire and brimstone. Otherwise we'll have to find our help elsewhere. Understood?'

The two sisters bent their heads. 'Yes, ma'am,' Brenda said.

'Right,' Mum said. 'I'd like one of you to call a mole catcher or pest control or whatever, and get rid of this little problem.' She started to walk away, stopped and half turned towards them. 'Or maybe Cedric could have a polite word with them and they'd oblige by moving on?' She gave a quick smile. '*Joke.*'

The Fletchers didn't laugh. Nor, to my surprise, did I. My thoughts used to echo Mum's and everything she'd just said could easily have come from my mouth as hers. Now my view was kinked, slightly out of kilter; the echo delayed and growing fainter.

I followed her into the kitchen. I should say something about the twist in my attitude. But I couldn't. Not yet. I had nothing really to say and certainly nothing that would convince her. I hadn't even convinced myself.

'Honestly,' Mum said, 'they're grown women!'

Olga swept a pile of potato peelings from the sideboard into the compost bucket.

'It's all over now,' Mum continued. 'You're to tell me if they bother you with any more hocus-pocus, OK, Olga?'

'Yes, Lady Lindy.'

The Fletchers came in behind us, sheepishly.

'And to make up for the upset they've caused you,' Mum said, 'the Fletchers will be taking care of things here today.' She gave them a no-nonsense glance. 'Olga is having the rest of the day off.'

'No need,' Olga said, washing her hands under the tap. 'I'm OK.'

'I insist,' Mum said. 'Their way of doing things has taken up your time too. This is payback.'

'But you—'

'I am quite able to look after myself, Olga,' Mum said. 'And if I want anything, Glenda or Brenda will be here. They won't harm me.'

Olga didn't look so sure.

'Well,' she said, 'I have some things I need to do. Bank. Dry cleaning.'

'That's that sorted then,' Mum said. She glanced at the Fletchers. 'Whilst one of you calls the pest control people, could the other please bring me some coffee in the drawing room?'

She walked out of the kitchen. I waited for Olga to take off her apron then followed her up the stairs.

'Can I cadge a lift from you, please?' I asked her.

'Cadge? What's that?'

'Beg. Scrounge. I need to get into Gloucester.'

'Gloucester?' she said. 'I'm going to Cheltenham.'

'They have banks and dry cleaners in Gloucester too.'

She looked doubtful.

'I have to get sewings things too. Lady Lindy's asked the Fletchers to make more cushion covers. Glenda said there's a good shop in Cheltenham. That's where they go.'

'Fine,' I said. 'Let's go and pick up the sewing stuff and then go on to Gloucester for the rest.'

She frowned. 'What are *you* doing in Gloucester?'

'Library book,' I said.

On the way into Cheltenham, Olga told me to open the plastic bag she'd put on the back seat.

'New designs for the cushions,' she said.

The Fletchers' sketches were as neat and precise as their needlework. A white cross. A horse and plough. A single bee on a beige and orange honeycomb. A ram's horn.

I snatched my hand away.

'What?' Olga said. 'You don't like them?'

'Not really my thing,' I said quickly and put the bag back on the seat. I didn't want to alarm her any further, *if* there was anything to be alarmed about.

All of the images they embroidered were random but they *did* have some connection with rural living in general or life in Stagcote in particular. The ram's horn was part of that. A feature of the local pub. Like a logo, maybe.

But there might be more to it.

If the ram's horn embroidery wasn't just a fluke then the quirky, superstitious things the Fletchers did weren't as mindless as they seemed. I could hardly believe I was even thinking that way, but the chill on my skin was unmistakable.

I stood in the car park, smoking, whilst Olga dashed into the craft shop. She came back, a little breathless.

'So many threads in that shop,' she said. 'Lots of pretty colours.'

As we drove to Gloucester, I opened the bag, slowly, as if it contained a bomb. But there was only a roll of blank, honeycombed canvas surrounded by a palette of luxuriantly coloured threads. What else had I expected? It was only embroidery. Of course it was.

Olga was in the bank for fifteen minutes. The dry cleaners for five. She came out, folding a ticket into her purse and looking disgruntled.

'Too late for same day,' she sighed. 'I knew we should do this in Cheltenham. Now I have to come back tomorrow.'

'Sorry,' I said.

The archive building in Gloucester was a single-storey grey-brick building tucked between a backstreet and a housing estate. Cheltenham library might have the architectural upper hand but it had failed to deliver any useful information; I had higher hopes for the archive.

Olga popped her car door open.

'You're coming in?' I said.

'Why not? It's a library. I *can* read, you know.'

'But—'

I didn't want to scare Olga and didn't want her to unnerve me any further. Nor did I want her to go running to Mum as she'd stop me from doing any more research at all.

'You can't come in,' I said. 'It's a reference library. You need ID.'

Olga angled her head.

'You're up to something, Miss Isabella. I know that look.'

'No,' I said nonchalantly. 'I'm here to study.'

'Then I'll come and study too. See what I learn.'

'But you haven't got any ID.'

Only she had. The driving licence and bank statement she handed over were checked and approved by the receptionist. Olga held up her reader's card with a triumphant smile.

We put our bags in the lockers and went into the cramped but brightly lit reading room. The people sitting around the cluster of tables were invariably grey-haired and bespectacled. Some took slow notes with a pencil and pad, while others tapped on laptops. Several hunched close up to microfiche screens, entranced by a blizzard of print.

The greying woman behind the desk was tiny and birdlike, her small brown eyes darting and alive, her nose sharp. The badge on her cardigan said *Alice*.

I took out my phone and showed her the screen with the reference number I'd been given at Cheltenham.

'Very modern,' she said, smiling. 'But I'm afraid we have to go back to the old-fashioned way now.' She passed me a slip. 'If you could just fill this in, please. Press hard, as it needs to come out on the copies below.'

When I'd finished she dropped it into a wooden tray on the desk.

'The next run's in a few minutes,' she said. 'Find yourself a place at a table. When your document is ready it will be written up on the whiteboard. You can collect your items from here.'

There weren't any tables with two adjoining seats free in the main reading room, so we ended up in an annexe just around the corner. I set up my laptop and notepad and kept watch at the doorway, my heartbeat growing louder each time Alice wrote a name on the board. Excitement vied with anxiety. Curiosity with fear.

'It smells in here,' Olga said, perching on the edge of her chair. 'Sweat. And dust.' She wiped a finger on the table and looked surprised to find it clean.

'Are you going to look around?' I said.

She narrowed her eyes, suspiciously. 'No,' she said. 'I'll wait with you.'

I was up at the desk to collect my document before my name was completed on the board. Alice pushed two pairs of white cotton gloves across the desk.

'You'll need these,' she said. 'The book's in quite good condition given its age but we need to make sure it stays that way. Prop it up on of one of the wooden rests you'll find on the desk as well, please, to prevent the weight damaging the spine.'

She turned and reached under the counter, pulled out a large book with a linen cover, the pages inside thick and yellowed and wrinkled. I pulled on my gloves and picked it up; my arms gave for a moment under its weight.

'Any questions,' Alice said, 'and I'll be right here.'

I thanked her and went back to the table. Olga looked up at me as I approached. Her mouth fell open.

'Big book!' she said. 'We'll never read it all.'

'You don't have to read it at all, if you don't want to,' I said, smoothing out the wrinkles in my gloves.

'Why do you need those?' Olga said. 'Dirty book?'

'Old book. Probably very boring too so if you . . .'

She narrowed her eyes again then picked up the other pair of gloves.

I sat down and placed the book on the wooden supports.

My mouth was as dry as the pages looked. The spine of the book creaked as I turned the cover, releasing the smell of old paper and ink. Of secrets. And a faint hint of frankincense. My heart thumped.

On the first page was a faded drawing of seven rams' horns. There was a falling away inside me, a drop into doubt, the tumbling thrill of discovery. The satisfaction of being right. The fear of what that might mean.

Olga shrank back from the table. 'I don't like it, Miss Isabella.'

'Maybe you'd better wait outside then.'

She pushed her chair back. 'Why are you looking at this?'

'It's about Stagcote.'

'It about the devil. Again!' she said. 'Leave it alone. It's no good, no good!'

A couple of heads in the other room looked up. A bald-headed man in a grey fleece scowled.

'We don't know that.'

She clamped her hand to her chest. 'I feel it,' she said urgently. 'And you do too. I can tell. You're scared, aren't you?'

I glanced away.

'No . . . yes. Oh God, I don't know. A little maybe. But that's how fear works. We're more scared of what we don't know – and it's even more frightening when everybody else *does* know. Like the Fletchers and the rest of the village. It makes me feel . . . stupid. No, not just that. It makes me feel vulnerable.'

'Me too.'

I tapped the book. 'I have no idea what's inside this,' I said, 'but I have to look. *If* there's something bad at Stagcote, I want to know what it is. Otherwise I'll just be making things up in my own head. Scaring myself. Filling the gaps with tales about black dogs and bees and hoping for the best by moving beds around and not sharpening knives of an evening.'

Olga pulled up her chair. Closer to mine this time. She smelt of mints and potato peelings.

I turned over the page.

Elaborate swirling loops and tails sprouted from squat and blocky letters, making them hard to read. But I understood the very first word.

Apocalypsis.

We both pulled back from the page.

'I don't like it,' Olga said again. 'Whatever it is.' But she made no attempt to leave.

The sign above the neighbouring desk said that the computer there had internet access but asked that it only be used for legitimate research and without being monopolised by any one person. I picked up the book and the wooden rests and walked over to the desk.

Olga stood, peering over my shoulder. I typed in the first sentence of the book.

Apocalypsis Iesu Christi.

The results gave me the translation. And the source.

The Revelation of Jesus Christ.

'The Book of Revelations,' I said breathlessly. 'The same as the trumpets.'

'Trumpets?'

'Nothing,' I said.

'It's the Bible, yes?' Olga said, sliding into the seat beside me. She looked perplexed but more than anything she was relieved.

'Yes.'

Olga frowned.

'But that's not how the Bible start,' she said, drawing closer to the book. 'Not in Latvia anyway. "In the beginning . . ."'

'Same the world over,' I said. 'The Christian world anyway.'

The thought struck hard as a hammer. It might have been the Bible but it almost certainly wasn't the good book.

The Latin text only covered one side of each page; the reverse was smothered in symbols and swirls, numbers, dots and slashes, loops and stars and circles, juxtaposed in lines but separated by gaps, giving the impression of words in sentences. It reminded me of a giant word search puzzle crossed with a complicated chemical or algebraic equation.

Olga puffed her cheeks out.

'That's how English looked to me first time at school,' she said. 'Make sense to you?'

'Only those bits,' I said. I pointed to a drawing of a set of scales, a crab and a goat. 'Signs of the zodiac. Maybe?'

I let my hand rest lightly on the page, as if the symbols were in Braille and my fingers would detect their meaning and somehow communicate them to my brain. But nothing came.

No words anyway.

Just the sense of something dark, something brooding. As if there was someone or something on the other side of the page that would tear through at any moment. A hand. A claw. A horn.

I pulled my hand away.

Almost immediately, I was compelled to reach for the book once again, like the needle of a compass is compelled to point north. Whatever the book contained, I had to know. Somehow.

It seemed impossible, but I had to crack the code. Stupidly, I took some encouragement from the fact that I'd always been good at anagrams and logic tests, guessing the next number in the sequence. Maybe I might make sense of it all, given time, a lot of work and plenty of luck. Maybe. It was too much of a long shot.

I stood up and went back to Alice's desk.

'That book,' I said. 'Do you know if anyone has ever translated it? Worked the code out?'

Alice's nose wrinkled. 'I don't believe so,' she said, 'but I can check.' Her fingers were quick and light on the computer keyboard. 'Well, there's no mention of a transcript on the record, I'm afraid. So I'd say no, no one's cracked it.'

'Has anyone tried?'

'It doesn't say. If they *did*, it was a long time ago. That item hasn't been ordered up from the archive for over seventy years.'

If any translation had been made it would have cropped up somewhere by now – if it was going to. And whoever took the book out last was almost certainly dead. Frustration surged through me.

'Does it say where the book came from? I mean, I know it's from Stagcote, but I wondered if there's any record of who wrote it?'

Alice puckered her lips as she read the entry on her laptop.

'There's no author recorded,' she said. 'But there's a note that says it was part of the library of G. A. Crichton-Stuart.'

'Who's he?'

'One of the lords of Stagcote Manor. It seems it was acquired after a sale of the library's contents.'

'Then one of the owners of the manor wrote it?'

Alice sucked on her teeth.

'That's a bit of an assumption,' she said, 'but sometimes you have to take a leap of faith when you're working with primary sources. So, yes, you might be right. The lord *could* have written it. It's best to check where you can though.'

'How?'

'Newspapers, parish records, wills. It's quite a paperchase.'

'Not when it comes to Stagcote Manor, it isn't,' I said. 'There was nothing on it at all in Cheltenham.'

Alice smiled. 'It's not like the internet, I'm afraid,' she said. 'Information isn't instant or obvious. You have to dig a little. Think out of the box. Be prepared to go down a few blind alleys and be diverted by red herrings.'

'That's fine – if you know where to start. All I've got is Stagcote Manor, a backwards Bible and pages of meaningless symbols.'

'Oh no,' Alice said, 'you've a little bit more than that.'

'I have? Like what?'

She looked at the screen. 'Like a certain G. A. Crichton-Stuart.' There was a glint in her eye when she turned to look up at me. The glint of a hunter. 'Let's see what you can find on him, shall we?'

I was nodding but I didn't have the faintest idea where to start. My uncertainty was obvious.

'There are various places to look,' she said. 'The Census, of course, and parish records. It's much easier now that all Census information from 1841 to 1911 is online.'

'But the book is from the *sixteenth* century,' I said.

Alice smiled again. 'We're led to believe the book is from the sixteenth century,' she said, 'but that might not be the case.'

'Are you saying it's fake?'

'I'm saying it could be. Oddities like that need to be taken with a large pinch of salt. Rummaging around in the records, you're very likely to get lost amongst the smoke and mirrors. So keep your eyes and your mind open. Go on a flight of fancy by all means – but don't jump to hasty conclusions or believe everything that you see.'

It was as if she'd described what had been going on in my mind since we'd arrived at the manor. Everything was shifting. Negotiable. Suspect.

It made me feel stupid, vulnerable and way out of my depth.

And it intrigued and scared me too. Somewhere amongst all those names and dates were the threads that made up the story of Stagcote Manor. Rosemary was in there too. I was determined to find it. To find her.

'Right,' I said to Alice, 'where do we start? The Census?'

She shook her head.

'The Census will tell us the facts of the man – name, whether he was married, had kids and so on. The bones of his life, if you like. But if you want to find out about that book, you need to put the meat on the bones.' She reached over to the pile of document request forms and picked up a pencil. 'So I think we should take a look in the newspapers.'

'They'll have written an article about the book?'

'It's possible but I wouldn't hold your breath,' she said.

Her fingers flew over the keyboard then she leant in and wrote a number on the document request form.

'It's one of the newspapers we haven't put onto microfiche yet,' she said. 'So we'll have to wait for the next run.' She dropped the form into the box and checked her watch. 'Should be up in about fifteen minutes. I'll be on my lunch break then so you'll have to look for yourself.'

'Look for what?'

'A sale like the one at the manor would certainly have been advertised, probably in the paper I've requested for you. *The Cheltenham Looker-On*. It was an upmarket local paper – the sort of thing that would be read by people who could afford to buy the items included in the sale at the manor,' Alice said. 'It may well have carried a report on the sale as well. If so, that report might tell us a bit about the man. It might even shed some light on that particular book.' She shrugged. 'But you can't always expect to be lucky.'

I thanked her for her help and went back to my desk. I felt energised and impatient.

'Can we go now?' Olga said.

'Not yet. I'm waiting for something else to be brought up.'

'More books? You've not finish this one.'

'No,' I said. 'I'm going to need more time for that one.' I looked over my shoulder. 'Can you keep watch?'

'Keep watch?'

'Please? Stand up there, pretend to look at the posters on the wall or the books on the shelves. If anyone comes this way, cough. Loudly.'

'Why?'

I pointed to the sign on the wall; a camera with a red cross through it. I took my phone from my pocket and opened up the camera.

'I can't take the book home, so . . . let's just hope the flash doesn't go off.'

Olga got up but as she moved towards the door I stopped her, grabbed a magazine from the shelf and pressed it into her hand.

'Photocopy this,' I whispered. 'It'll make you look less obvious.'

I waited for Olga to get the machine going, then focused in on the first page, close enough for the text to be legible, but not so close that it pixelated. I winced as I pressed the shutter. If the flash went off I could just pretend I hadn't seen the sign – but I'd never get away with doing a second shot, let alone the whole book.

The flash didn't fire.

I glanced up at Olga. She gave me the thumbs up. I turned the page, focused and took the next shot. Ten minutes later, I had all the coded pages of the book. I could find the Bible in Latin online should I need it.

I closed the book and carried it back to the desk. My other item was already listed on the board. A man with half-moon spectacles took the coded book from me then passed me the newspaper.

I'd been expecting a single copy of the paper but it was a volume for the whole year, bound in black leather cracked by age and wear. I could just make out the date on the spine: 1834. I hauled it off the desk and took it back to my seat.

'Can you help me look?' I said to Olga.

'Look for what?'

'Anything about G. A. Crichton-Stuart or a sale held at the manor.'

'Selling what?'

'Anything I suppose . . . furniture, livestock. Books.'

It was a broadsheet, its thin, flesh-coloured pages dense with thick black type. It was easier to read than the Bible or the code, but I still had to concentrate. My eyes pinched with the strain of sifting through story after story.

In between the hand-wringing over the Poor Law Amendment Act and a catastrophic fire at the Palace of Westminster, there were local stories about stolen silverware, sheep rustling, the drunken gypsies at Stow Fair and deliberations on the benefits to the area of the extension of the railway from Bristol to Gloucester. There were adverts for cordials, pills and men's outfitters, notices for plays and concerts and reports of cricket matches.

'There,' Olga said, stabbing her finger at an article at the bottom of the page.

A total of £304 5s 2d was raised Wednesday last from the sale of various effects belonging to G. A. Crichton-Stuart, formerly of Stagcote Manor, Stagcote. A crowd of some seventy-five people attended the auction, which was occasioned by Mr Crichton-Stuart' misfortunes following the defeat of his once invincible filly, Plenipotentiary, in the Derby a result which precipitated a chain of calamitous events, culminating in his incarceration in a lunatic asylum and the death by her own hand of his wife, Mrs Elizabeth Mary Crichton-Stuart.

My eyes slid over the list of items that had been sold – crockery, silverware, tables and chairs, a couple of paintings and the contents of an extensive library. I was disappointed that the coded book wasn't mentioned, but not surprised. I could only assume that no one had wanted it because they couldn't read it and somehow, eventually, it had made its way to the archive.

The archivist was replacing books on the shelves near to our table, so I couldn't risk taking a photo of the article. It was only short so I made quick notes on my laptop.

'Why do you want this?' Olga said. She shook her head but she didn't take her eyes off the page.

'Proof,' I said.

'Of what?'

'I don't know.'

Olga swallowed hard.

'The curse?' she said.

I didn't answer. Her hand gripped my arm.

'Miss Isabella?'

I shook my head.

'I don't know,' I said. 'Maybe.'

I went along the line of graves, pushing aside ivy and scraping off moss so I could see the names. In the northern churchyard, of course. Where the suicides should be.

I found what I was looking for second from the end of a row of graves, the dark ground made darker still by the overhanging yew tree.

Elizabeth Mary Crichton-Stuart
Beloved wife of George Arthur
26th Sept 1788 – 11th July 1834

Even without the ivy and moss, I wouldn't have noticed her gravestone before. It was just one of many. Anonymous. Forgotten. Now she had a name. And a story. Unlike Rosemary, whose name I'd just conjured up and whose story was still in some doubt.

But the comfort I'd found in burying her began to fade, replaced by the nagging pinch of doubt, of realisation, which grew stronger the more I thought on it. Instead of being innocent she was malevolent. Probably part of the curse.

I raced back to the manor, up the stairs and booted up the laptop. The photos flashed on to the screen as they downloaded, making my eyes and head swim. I put them in a separate folder and made sure I kept the pages in chronological order. Breaking the code was already a difficult, if not almost impossible task, and any carelessness would only make it worse.

I clicked on the first photo and enlarged it to a size that made it easier to read but kept the whole page visible at the same time. I edged closer to the screen and stared at every symbol. There were so many and, despite being repeated, there was no discernible pattern or noticeable frequency. The page rained stars and swirls and squiggles.

I blinked and tried again. The symbols seemed to jump away from my scrutiny. The black strokes and loops twitched and squirmed, like bacteria, multiplying and shifting shape, defying me to make sense of them.

I tried the next photo and the next and the one after that. It was like looking at a wall covered in overlapping graffiti, the slogans sly and mocking.

It would be better to print the photos off, I realised. That way, I'd be able to put them alongside one another and look for any patterns or similarities that would be tricky to spot on screen.

I got up and sank onto the bed, massaging my eyes.

There was a knock on the door.

'Come in.'

Olga peered into the room, a pile of neatly folded laundry in her arms.

'Is OK if I just put these away now?' she said.

I glanced at the computer screen. The code stared back at me. I had to be more careful and shut the file down in case of intruders like Mum and the Fletchers.

'I can't make head or tail of it.' I kneaded my temples with my fingertips. 'It's giving me a headache.'

Olga squinted at the screen.

'That book's one big headache,' she said. 'Leave it alone, Miss Isabella. It's no good.'

I watched as she opened the drawers and put the tops and T-shirts away, gently, as if they were precious or fragile. But her eyes kept darting to the screen.

'You're just as interested in it as I am,' I said.

'No. I don't like it.'

'But you've got to help me. Please?'

'Me? No, Miss Isabella. I have no time for the devil work. And even if I did . . .' Her lips creased and tightened.

'But you like doing puzzles and crosswords! You're a demon at sudoko. *That's* the sort of brain you need for something like this. It's just a giant puzzle. We can break it quicker with two of us.'

'Yes,' she said. 'But I maybe win a cash prize for a crossword or sudoko in the paper. What do I get with that?' She tossed her head. 'Trouble.'

189

'But you might get trouble if you stay here too.'

'Stop!' she said, crossing herself. 'You driving me crazier than the Fletchers and the moles. I want to help you. I always help you. You know that. But this . . . *No.*' She closed the drawer firmly with both hands.

I bunched the duvet in my fists and groaned.

'You won't say anything to Mum about the book, will you?'

'She won't like it if she knew.'

'Exactly. Just like she wouldn't have liked it if she knew you let me in to the house in London after a night out.' I arched my eyebrows. 'But you still did it.'

Olga walked towards the door.

'I felt sorry for you, that's why,' she said. 'Now I'm scared for you. But I won't say anything to her.'

'Or the Fletchers?'

Olga looked away guiltily.

'Oh no, you haven't, have you?' I said sitting up.

'Sorry, Miss Isabella. It just came out.'

'What did? What did you tell them?'

'Only that we went to the library.'

'Nothing about the book?'

She blushed again.

'What did they say? I asked.

'Nothing, Miss Isabella. They didn't say nothing.' She shrugged. 'Maybe they'd heard of the book before. It wasn't such big news.'

'I'm pretty sure they *have* heard of the book before. Everybody from Stagcote has. The big news to them will be that *I* know about it too.'

When Olga left I went back to the laptop and tried again. And again. Dusk sucked the light from the room; the birds fell silent. Still I stared at the screen, moving from one page to the next. The symbols stared back at me, inscrutable. They were still there when I tried to sleep, as if they had been scorched onto my eyelids.

I slept fitfully, the heat as oppressive as the diagrams, swirls and slashes crowding my head. But when sleep finally swept over me, it took me so completely, so deeply that I heard no owls or scratching and was awoken the next morning by Mum anxiously knocking on the door.

'Isabella? Is Sasha with you?'

'No, why would he be?'

'Just wondered,' she said. 'I can't find him. He's gone.'

It was easy to explain Sasha's disappearance. He was only small and the grounds of the manor were extensive; Mum never let him off the lead during his walks in Hyde Park. I'd often said I didn't know why God had bothered giving him legs as he spent most of his time in her arms or on her lap. Mum always said it was me who needed a lead.

The reasonable explanations didn't satisfy me any more, even though I picked through them over and over again, as if effort alone were enough to guarantee reassurance.

Sasha had run in front of the funeral procession. Glenda had said that meant bad luck unless the dog was killed. I remembered the unsettling glint in her eye. She *was* fervent. But was she fanatical enough to kill a dog? It didn't seem possible, although . . .

The idea that Sasha's disappearance could be part of the curse kept snagging in my mind. I dismissed it every time, but it soon returned, stronger than ever for being denied. The scratching, Rosemary, the horns, the coded book, our car crash. Now Sasha. It *had* to be more than coincidence. But I couldn't believe that it could be.

I kept these thoughts to myself as our search of the house for Sasha eventually took us out into the forecourt.

'He probably got wind of summat interesting,' Cedric said. 'Mrs Oakley said her bitch was in season last time I saw her. Dachshund, it is.' He looked into the distance. 'Could be interesting, them puppies.'

'Well, he's never run off before,' Mum said, biting her lip.

Cedric chewed on his lips.

'Summat spooked him then.' He looked up at the house. 'Plenty of reasons for that round here.'

Mum tossed her head, the tight muscles in her neck making her wince.

'Not this again,' she said. 'Sasha has never given the slightest indication that there was anything untoward at the manor. No whining, no raised hackles. *If* he was scared by something, it's more likely to be a hunter's gun or low-flying helicopter. Although,' she said, her voice trailing off, 'I don't recall hearing either of those things since we've been here.' Her mouth dropped. 'Oh God. I've just had a thought! What about that black dog we saw? It might have taken Sasha!'

'No, ma'am,' Cedric said. 'Not possible.'

'Why not? It was obviously out of control.'

'Well, it's like we said. That dog weren't real. I mean, its bite is something fearsome – fatal – but it ain't got no teeth. Not like we'd understand them anyways.'

Mum waved him away.

'Utter nonsense, Cedric. I know what I saw.'

Cedric dropped his chin but his eyes held Mum's, more in defiance than apology.

'There's always the Fletchers,' I said. 'Where were they when he went missing?'

Mum looked bewildered. 'What do you mean?'

I knew how she would react but I had to say what was on my mind.

'They said if a dog crossed the path of a funeral it was bad luck.'

'Oh Isabella, for God's sake! I don't have time for this now. Ever!'

'Wait!' I said, taking her by the arm. 'They said the only way to avoid bad luck would be to kill the dog.'

The horror and disbelief that flew around Mum's face had

more to do with me even thinking such a ridiculous idea than it did with the Fletchers actually doing it.

'What?'

I nodded my head. 'I know . . . I know it sounds crazy but . . . and don't tell me they wouldn't do it either,' I said. 'If you'd seen the look in Glenda's eyes—'

'You can't be serious,' Mum cried. 'She wouldn't kill a dog!'

Cedric cleared his throat and raised his hand, like a child asking to speak.

'As I understand it, ma'am, the bad luck only applies to the family of the bereaved. Rosemary wasn't a relative of yours, or theirs, so there'd be no need to kill the dog.'

Mum put her hands over her ears.

'*No one* has killed Sasha. He's out there. Lost. And we're all going to look for him. The Fletchers included.' She shielded her eyes with a hand and looked around the garden, towards the church and the hills beyond. 'Oh God, he could be anywhere!'

'Don't fret, ma'am,' Cedric said. 'We'll find him. You wait and see.'

We split up and searched the grounds, our shouts overlapping like discordant echoes. We checked the stables, outbuildings, greenhouses. The bottom of the well. Olga and the Fletchers went through every room of the house and every cupboard and found nothing.

I couldn't help but notice how hard the Fletchers looked, how genuine their concern was. Maybe I'd got it wrong.

If anyone was going to find Sasha, I was sure it would be Cedric. Mum had been a little put out that Sasha had taken to him so much. The dog was normally so obstinate and aloof, responding to nobody except Mum. But Sasha not only did what Cedric asked him, he would leave Mum's side and search him out. From my bedroom window I'd often seen Cedric working in the garden, Sasha lying on the ground beside him, ears pricked, panting.

But even Cedric drew a blank. That made Mum more anxious. Me too.

We reconvened on the manor's forecourt. Mum went inside to use the computer to make a poster with a photo and a reward. The Fletchers said they'd take them around the village and get them put up in the church and the pub. Olga went back for another look around the house. Cedric and I split the grounds between us.

'Head out a bit further this time, miss,' Cedric said. 'Maybe he's out of earshot.'

I ended up at the top of the driveway. I prayed not to see a twisted, bloody lump in the middle of the road.

'Sasha! Come on then!'

I waited. Called again, walked on.

'Saaa-shaaa!'

I heard something to my right. The rattle of the Gate House front door. Howard looked out and waved.

I hadn't seen him for the last few days as he'd been away and I'd been preoccupied by my research.

'You haven't seen Sasha, have you?'

His smile wavered.

'No, sorry, I haven't. Why?'

'He's been missing since last night. Mum's frantic.'

'I bet,' he said, pulling the door closed behind him. 'Where else have you looked?'

We went back over the same ground, just in case, then pushed on further, to the other side of the river, around fields of corn that hissed in the breeze and meadows flecked by buttercups and cowpats.

Our breathing was hard and fast as we leant into the climb up Stagcote Hill, stopping every now and then to shout as loud as we could. We crested the hill and dropped down, towards the manor, its turrets and towers peeping through the canopy of trees.

As we approached a dense copse halfway between the hill and the manor, the sudden flap of black wings and guttural screeches startled me as several rooks flew out from under the trees. Thick glossy feathers shone in the sunlight. Fierce bills glistened. Wet and red.

Sasha's mangled body lay twisted among dead leaves and ivy, shrouded by shadow. The puny tan torso was punctured and bloody, the empty eye sockets slick with ruddy slime and running with ants and bluebottles.

'Oh Jesus!'

My stomach clenched; a warm rush of puke spouted from my mouth. The splatter was vivid against the leaves and almost made me heave once more. It wasn't like me to be so squeamish. I'd sat through celluloid chainsaw massacres, seen eyeballs carved by chisels and heads turned inside out but had barely flinched. It must have been because it was real. Because it was Sasha. Because of everything else that had happened.

Howard coughed and passed me a handkerchief.

'It's clean,' he said.

I took it and wiped my mouth, forcing myself to look at Sasha's body.

'What was it that killed him, do you think?' I said. 'The rooks?'

'It *might* have been but . . . as far as I know they're scavengers not hunters.' He bent down, picked up a nearby stick and used it to turn the body around. 'Looks like teeth marks there,' he said, pointing with the stick to clean, deep, regular gashes in Sasha's belly. 'Fox, possibly, although I didn't know foxes had such long teeth.' He looked up at me. 'Cedric will have a better idea than I do . . . Christ, what a mess!'

I batted away some flies buzzing around my face. For a moment I thought they were bees and Sasha's the death they'd predicted. Another surge of vomit pulsed in my stomach so I moved further under the trees. The hot stream from my mouth was pale and bitter.

'Shall we take him back?' Howard said.

'We can't leave him here. Mum will want to bury him. Shit, she's going to be gutted.' I wiped my mouth with the hanky.

'I'll have the hanky back when you're done. I'll wrap him in that.'

The stench of vomit wafted on the breeze. I stepped further into the copse.

Perhaps it was the sudden shade, or the smell of decay from the soft and sodden mass of brown leaves beneath my feet. It might have been the trees, shaggy and shapeless with the ivy, the snag of it at my ankles.

Probably it was all of those things. But there was something else that made me feel uneasy. A low, creeping apprehension. A sense of being watched. Of something wrong. Evil.

And yet there was a peace and contentment about the spot too. A calming energy. Flashes of sunlight danced on the carpet of leaves. Birds chirruped high in the canopy above. A shrieking pheasant made me jump. In the quiet that followed, the drone of flies, like mumbled prayers.

I wanted to run away. I wanted to stay.

I took my papers and tobacco from my pocket and sat down on a rotting tree trunk to roll a cigarette. As I smoked, I worked a toe into the moss and leaves, felt the easy give of the mulch, then, beneath it, something firmer. I stamped my foot. The sound was less muffled, less natural. Solid.

I kicked the leaves away and saw a patch of light grey stone sunken into the ground. It looked out of place. Man-made.

I brushed away more leaves, snapped the tangled ivy, each

handful exposing a surface rough and pitted, mottled with moss. My hand felt wet, sticky. Bloody.

At first I thought I'd cut myself on a branch or thorn and hadn't noticed. Then I saw leaves spotted with blood. The smears on the stone.

'Shit!' I said, wiping my hand off on the leaves.

'Izzy?' Howard said, peering into the gloom. 'You OK?'

'More of Sasha's blood,' I said. 'Whatever got him must have dragged him along this way.'

Howard stepped into the copse. He had blood on his shoes.

'What's that?' he said, pointing to the stone.

I followed the edges of the stone in each direction until I'd revealed an oblong slab some twelve feet long and three feet wide.

'Shit!' I said, jumping away. 'It's a grave!'

'No way,' Howard said, bending down. 'It's too big for a grave. For one person anyway. Unless . . . unless it's for two people? Buried head to toe?'

'Why bury someone here when there's a church half a mile away?'

Howard shrugged.

'Is there an inscription?' he said.

I scraped away the moss, collecting a rind of green fuzz under my fingernails. I felt a shallow groove, then another, and excavated with a small twig. The letters were roughly carved, irregular, illegible.

R		T	A	S
C	P	L	R	
	E	N	E	|
\	P	L	R	C
S	/		O	R

'More code!' I said, throwing the stick away. 'Everything about this place is a bloody riddle. The book. Trumpets. *This!*'

'Whoa!' he said, putting a hand on my shoulder. 'What are you on about?'

The book and the horns were real enough so it was easy to tell him about those. But I hesitated to say anything about the doubts I was having about the likelihood of a curse, or the anxiety they were causing me. He'd just take me for a silly little schoolgirl, spooked by a big house. So I tested him out first on the book and the horns.

'I've not been to the library the whole time I've lived here,' he said. 'I'm not much of a reader, although the book sounds interesting.'

'I've taken photos of it if you want to see it.'

'Yes, that would be good.'

'The horns you can see anytime.'

'Yeah,' he said thoughtfully. 'That's the thing though. I like a drink. I'm in the pub several times a week. So I can't believe I haven't seen these horns.'

'But that's just it,' I said. 'You're *not meant* to notice them. But everybody else knows they're there. Just like everybody else knows about the curse.'

A puzzled smile creased his face.

'Curse?' he said. 'You think these horns are connected with that?'

'Maybe,' I said as nonchalantly as I could.

'So that would mean you think the curse might be real?'

I could feel the blush rise in my cheeks. He looked so sceptical, so scornful, I couldn't bring myself to answer him.

'You do, don't you?' There was a tease in his tone.

'No!' I snapped.

He raised his eyebrows slowly, inviting my confidence.

'Well, all right, maybe I do,' I said. 'A bit more than I did before, perhaps.' I didn't dare look at him. 'So much has happened . . . too much to be ignored.' I kicked the stone with my foot. 'Like this. What if it wasn't a fox that killed Sasha? What if it was the Fletchers?'

He looked startled. 'What? Why would they do that?'

'Warning me off, maybe. They *know* I've found the book – Olga told them – so now they want to scare me off.'

'Hang on! That's quite an accusation. You need some proof before you can go shooting your mouth off like that.'

'I'm going to get it.'

'To nail the Fletchers?'

'And the curse. Once and for all. It's starting to do my head in.'

I felt in my pocket but I must have left my phone on the bedside table.

'You got a pen on you?'

He patted his pocket, took out a biro and passed it to me. The nib tickled my palm as I wrote down the letters from the inscription.

'Right,' I said, 'let's get poor Sasha back to the manor.'

I passed the biro and hanky back to Howard and turned away as he picked up Sasha's body. It was too big for the hanky to cover it completely; a tail and buckled legs sprouted from one end, the white fabric spotted with blood.

We ran back to the manor. As we were crossing the forecourt I heard a dreadful wailing. Mum stood at the drawing room window, hand clamped over her mouth, crying. Moments later she was in front of us, transfixed by the bloody mess in Howard's hands. Olga and the Fletchers came out of the front door.

'Stay away!' I yelled at the Fletchers. 'I told you it was them, Mum, didn't I?'

Glenda and Brenda stopped short, their mouths open.

'Us?' Brenda said.

'We . . . we didn't do anything!' Glenda said. 'We couldn't! Why would we?'

'A warning. A sacrifice.'

'Oh, Isabella, please!' Mum said, sniffing back tears. 'Don't you think this is hard enough as it is? Without these ridiculous theories?'

'I know it sounds like nonsense . . . but . . . but you've got to listen. There's a stone up there . . . in the woods. With an inscription. *That's* where they did it.'

'We didn't do anything, ma'am,' Brenda said.

'You've got to believe us!'

'You said you'd do it,' I said.

'We didn't say anything of—'

'And now you've done it. To warn me off from reading the book.'

'No!'

'Enough!' Mum yelled, raising her hands. 'I'm going to put an end to this once and for all.'

'Please don't sack us,' Glenda cried. 'We haven't done anything – except work hard and try to help you.'

Mum nodded and raised her hand once more.

'I know that,' she said. 'But we can't go on like this. Isabella, you said something about a stone? And a book?'

I hadn't wanted to tell Mum about the book – not yet, not until I knew what it said – but I had no choice. She gave sad little shakes of her head as she listened. Sighed wearily. The Fletchers fumed, Cedric gazed into the distance as if scouting for impending disaster. Howard looked dubious, sympathetic, as if I'd lost my mind. Olga fidgeted, the fear that I might be right outweighed by the fear of what might come next and of her involvement being revealed to Mum.

It all felt so familiar. It was me against Mum, against the world, with Olga balancing in between.

'It's magic!' I said. I didn't know where that came from. The idea hadn't really entered my mind, at least not consciously. It was just adrenalin, embarrassment – fear. A desperate attempt to support my claims – claims that even I couldn't really believe I was making. Saying the book was magic just made the claims even more outlandish and made me feel ever more foolish. No wonder the others were smirking.

But, deep inside me, the notion suddenly didn't seem so bizarre.

'Oh yes?' Mum said. 'Is there a wand that goes with it?'

'This isn't a joke.'

Mum arched her eyebrows. 'It is from where I'm standing.' She pinched the bridge of her nose. 'Did the people at the archive tell you it was magic?'

I shuffled on my feet, looked down at the ground.

'No.'

'What did *they* say it was?'

'They . . . they don't know.'

'But *you* do.'

'I can just tell.'

'So you're qualified in the dark arts just because you've watched a few horror films, are you?'

'No! Of course not . . . it's just . . .'

Their sense of expectation was overpowering. I tried to summon up a convincing reason for my certainty, one that would swing the argument my way. Nothing came. How could it? There wasn't one.

'I just . . . I've just got a sense for these things.'

Mum's disdainful laugh drew simpering agreement from the Fletchers.

'You've got an imagination, that's all. I'm beginning to wish that you hadn't.'

'I'm *not* making this up.'

'What about this stone you found?' she said, impatiently.

'Er . . . that's definitely there,' Howard said, shuffling awkwardly. 'I saw it myself.'

'And the inscription?'

He nodded.

'Right here,' I said, turning my palm towards her. Mum screwed her eyes up.

'It's gibberish,' she said. 'No surprise there, I suppose.'

'Don't tell me to just wash it off or forget about it. This is important. I'm going to find out what it means.'

Mum fixed me with her eyes.

'Yes,' she said. '*You are.* This can't go on any longer and you won't settle . . . none of us will, until this is sorted out.' She stepped closer. Pointed her finger. 'So you're going to find out what that inscription means. If it's all death and damnation, then I'll ship us out of here pronto. Maybe even fly us out on a broomstick. But,' she said, shaking her finger, 'if it turns out to be nothing – which I can guarantee it *will be* – then you owe the Fletchers a big apology. *And* you'll have to promise me you'll never bring this curse crap up again. Right?'

'Fine!' I said it with a confidence and finality I didn't really feel. If the book was anything to go by, I'd be stumped before I even got started.

I was stumped anyway; I needed a lift to the archives.

Mum waved my request away.

'Oh no, this is your wild goose chase, not mine. Besides, I can't drive, not with my neck like this. *And* I've got things to do here, not least burying poor Sasha.'

I turned to Olga. She shrank away from me.

'Sorry, I can't go to that place again,' she said.

'Again?' Mum said, her tone rising with incredulity. 'You're on board with all this too, Olga?'

'No, no,' she said, squirming. 'Not . . . not really. But I don't like it. It's scary.'

'There is nothing,' Mum said, '*nothing* to be scared of. I promise you.'

'It was me,' I said. 'I made Olga take me to the archives.'

Mum gave an exasperated laugh.

'And there was me thinking you'd gone to do some studying. How dumb am I? As if all this wasn't bad enough, you were lying to me as well. Same old same old, eh, Isabella?'

'I *was* studying.'

'Sure, and you were sitting alongside Harry Potter, right?'

The Fletchers smiled at one another.

'Well,' Mum said, 'Olga won't be taking you to the archive this time. Looks like you need a spell. Try tapping your heels together à *la* Dorothy. Or wriggling your nose. It worked in *Bewitched.*'

'I'll take her,' Howard said.

I was relieved that someone was on my side at last. Then I wondered if he just agreed with Mum and was only offering me a lift to ingratiate himself. But I was glad of his cooperation anyway.

'You really don't have to,' Mum said. 'I'm sure you've got better things to do.'

'Nothing that can't wait.' He hunched his shoulders, like a guilty schoolboy. 'To be honest I'm . . . I'm kind of intrigued too.'

'Well, if you're sure,' Mum said.

'She can't honour her side of the deal if she can't get to the archives. The sooner we find out, the happier everyone will be.'

Mum nodded. 'I suppose so,' she said. 'And as an independent witness, at least we'll be able to trust what you say.'

'There's that too,' Howard said.

I wrote the letters from my palm onto a piece of paper as I stood at the reception desk. The receptionist asked for Howard's documents then verified them with his application form.

'Thomson,' she said as she tapped into her keyboard, then corrected herself. 'Oops, left the "p" out. Thompson.'

She printed off the card, passed it to him and waved us through to the reading rooms.

I'd hoped Alice would be on the enquiries desk, but instead there was a tubby man in a blue nylon shirt stained with patches of sweat. His face was red and slick.

'How can I help?' he asked.

I passed him the sheet of paper.

'I wondered if you could help with this, please,' I said. 'I know it's Latin but . . .'

The archivist sniffed and took the paper from me.

'Ah, yes,' he said. 'Follow me.'

'Don't we need to fill out a form?' I said, trailing behind him in a pungent backdraught. Howard waved his fingers under his nose discreetly and winked at me.

'No need,' he said, and took a book down from one of the shelves.

I wasn't surprised. I was disappointed. The inscription couldn't be a secret if it was in a book, *an ordinary book*, available to everyone out on the shelves. Maybe Mum was right. I felt my cheeks blush at the accusations I'd made. At the apology I'd have to make. Of feeling foolish.

'Here you are,' he said, putting the book on a desk and flicking through the pages. 'The Sator Square.'

The page showed a stone plaque on a wall. Although the text on the plaque was Latin, the words didn't match the ones I'd seen on the slab at Stagcote.

'I don't understand,' I said, pushing my hair back from my face. 'This isn't the same thing.'

Howard tilted his head, eyes narrowed as the archivist laid the paper out next to the book.

'Yes, it is,' the archivist said. 'It's the same letters, you see, only back to front.' He squinted at my transcription again. 'There's a few letters missing, of course, and some of them are very worn, and that's not helping.'

'No,' I said, looking at Howard. He looked as confused as I was. 'Obviously not.'

I tried to focus; the letters jumped around but didn't take shape or find an order that made any sense.

The archivist took a pen from his top pocket and wrote out the transcription again, using the photo in the book to fill in the missing letters and correct those that had partially faded.

R	O	T	A	S
O	P	E	R	A
T	E	N	E	T
A	R	E	P	O
S	A	T	O	R

Now I could see what he meant; the letters *were* the same but the ones on the transcript were in reverse. Backwards. Like the Bible. It was too much of coincidence not to be relevant, but I didn't understand how. The way the discovery made me feel was clear enough though. I was happy to be vindicated but increasingly uneasy at what the connection could mean.

'It's an acrostic,' the archivist said.

I looked back at him, blank.

'A word square,' he said, outlining the shape with his pen. 'And a palindrome. It reads the same up and down and left and right. See?'

My eyes descrambled, finally deciphering the words.

'Only you had it as Rotas,' he said, 'when it's usually Sator.'

'Usually?' Howard said. 'You've seen it before?'

'Oh yes,' the archivist said. 'There's another one not very far from here. Inside a house on a site of a Roman villa in Cirencester. And there are others, some of them abroad.'

I felt so deflated. I'd been certain it was unique to Stagcote, somehow linked to the manor and the book. But I was wrong. It was just my imagination after all. My isolation at Stagcote had got to me, made me receptive to nonsense and wild stories.

'So, what does it mean?' Howard said.

The archivist pointed to the caption beneath the photo in the book.

'"Translated it means 'the sower Arepo holds the wheel carefully'."'

'Who's Arepo?' I said. 'What's he sowing? I don't get it.'

The man laughed. 'No surprise, really,' he said. 'As a direct translation it's nonsense. But . . .' He took a piece from the pile of scrap paper on the desk and wrote out the letters once more. 'See what happens if you rearrange the letters?'

```
A               P               O
                A
                T
                E
                R
    P A T E R N O S T E R
                O
                S
                T
                E
A               R               O
```

'It's a giant anagram,' he said. 'Paternoster, Latin for Our Father. Twice. In the shape of a cross,' he said, 'with Alpha and Omega at the start and the end. Some academics say it's a symbol used by early Christians to let other Christians know they're around. A sort of code, or calling card, that sort of thing. Some say it's the Lord's Prayer in précis . . . Our Father and the alpha and omega indicating enduring faith.' He grinned at me. 'Clever, isn't it?'

No, I wanted to scream. It's infuriating. Unfair. Wrong. And that made no sense as what I should have been thinking was hooray, everything's fine. We're safe.

'Yes,' Howard said, tracing the letters with his finger. 'Fascinating.'

'Would it make any difference if the letters were the other way round?' I said, trying to hide the hope in my voice and not understanding why it was there at all.

'Transposed, you mean?' he said writing out a reverse 'P' and 'R'.

'No, if the *words* were backwards.'

'They're the same letters so they'd still make up Paternoster. Like I said, it's not unheard of having a Ratos square instead of a Sator square.'

'But devil worshippers recite the Lord's Prayer backwards!' I said. 'I've seen it in films.'

'Devil worshippers?' The archivist's smirk grated on me.

'My friend thought that this inscription might be magical,' Howard said. There was an edge of condescension in his voice too and I couldn't help cringing inside.

'Ah, well it has been used in that way,' the archivist said.

'See!' I said, leaning forward. 'I knew it.'

The archivist smiled. 'I wouldn't get too excited, I'm afraid. Where it has been thought to have been used in a "magical way",' he said, making speech marks in the air with his finger, 'it's in the context of protecting livestock from witchcraft.' He took a shallow breath. 'The fact that it's a word puzzle has some precedents in magic though.'

'How do you mean?' I said.

'People put beads or threads in large glass globes to entice the spirits into a game that would keep them occupied and stop them making mischief. So again,' he said with an apologetic shrug, 'it's more about deflecting bad things than inciting them.'

'Right,' I said. I felt as if I was deflating right in front of him. 'Thank you.'

He put the book back on the shelf and walked back to the enquiries desk.

'I think I'll take a look at that coded book whilst we're here,' Howard said.

'What for?' I said, defeated.

'It's still interesting, even if it doesn't tie up with the inscription.'

'If you say so. You can see it at home if you must,' I whispered, checking over my shoulder just in case. 'I copied it. Let's get out of here.'

'Well, that's that then,' Howard said when we were back in the car. 'Bang goes your theory.'

I pushed my head into the headrest, puffed out my cheeks.

'I can't believe it!' I said. 'I was convinced it would back my story up. I tell you, Mum's going to love this.'

'You *both* should,' he said. 'It's good news, isn't it?' He laughed. 'Crikey, it's almost as if you'd rather there *was* a curse just so you could prove a point to your mother!'

There may have been some truth in that but I wasn't going to admit it.

'The stone must be linked to the book, surely?' I said. 'They're *both* backwards. *Both* Latin.'

'Most things were in those days,' he said, flicking the indicator and pulling out to overtake a cyclist.

'What about the code though? That word square was a sort of code too. The archivist said so.'

'A code for Christians, yes. And even once it was deciphered its meaning was hardly diabolical. I mean, the Lord's Prayer? You don't get any less demonic than that.' He accelerated and the wind rushed in through the window. 'Sorry, Izzy, but I think you've had it.'

I should have been glad. Instead, I felt duped. The nonsense of that was confusing. Maddening.

There was no sign of anyone when we got back to the manor, which was a relief as it postponed my apology to the Fletchers and my admittance of defeat to Mum. It also gave me the chance to print off the photos of the coded book and give them to Howard.

I enjoyed the mix of surprise and curiosity in his face as he pored over them. And I recognised the frustration and impatience at not understanding what it said or meant.

'Well?' I said.

He rubbed his eyes and leant back, arms folded.

'It could be anything. A diary, maybe. Or notes on the Bible text. Sixteenth-century doodles. Even recipes.'

'No way.'

'It's interesting though. I can see why you might jump to conclusions about it. And why you'd link it to the stone.' He picked up a few pages and leafed through them again. 'I'm sure it's all quite innocent but . . . it's fascinating. I'd . . . I'd love the chance to go through it properly, though . . . you know . . . see if I can work it out.'

'You?'

'Why not? I've got as much chance as you have. More

chance than Olga had, probably. At least I'm a native English speaker.'

'It might not be English.'

'No, but . . .' He looked up at me. 'It's got to be worth a try. I did a smidgeon of Latin at school. And those screens on the bank's trading floor have given me an eye for trends and patterns, decoding information that looks like gobbledegook. A mix of logic, guesswork and leaps of faith. It might work.'

'Yeah, but why? What do you want to do it for?'

'I thought you'd want me to!'

'You don't have to humour me.'

'I'm not! I just need a bit of a challenge. Been a while since I've had a proper mental workout. What do you say? Can I keep this set of printouts?'

'Fine,' I said.

Despite my disappointment over the connection between the stone and the book, I was still interested in what the book said. When I suggested that Howard and I worked on it together, he pulled a face.

'I'm not sure *you* should be looking at it all,' he said. 'And anyway, you promised you were going to give it all up. Your mother will be watching you like a hawk from now on. She'll go mad if she finds out.'

'I'm used to that.'

Only I wasn't. Not any longer. Things had been better between us and I liked it that way. The row we'd had over Sasha and the Fletchers was a throwback to how it had been before and I didn't want to repeat it. But I didn't want to give up my search either, despite my promise to Mum.

'I work better on my own,' Howard said. 'I get distracted. If we worked together then we might influence one another and go down the wrong route.'

'Yeah, but we could bounce ideas off one another too.'

'You're missing the point, Izzy. *I* don't want to encourage you to do it, as there could be ructions with your mother. For both of us. Please. Leave it to me for a bit. Let me see how I get on and we'll take it from there. If I draw a blank, then we can look at it together. By that time, your mum might have taken her beady eye off you.'

'OK,' I said.

My agreement didn't mean I wasn't going to ignore the code completely – just that I wouldn't work with him. I still had the photos on the laptop and could print them off again when no one was looking. Maybe Howard didn't understand my agreement that way. I didn't put him right.

He rolled the pages up and put them in his back pocket.

'Let me know if you get anywhere,' I said.

'Absolutely.'

We heard Mum and the others come back to the manor about half an hour later and went to meet them in the forecourt.

The Fletchers stopped when they saw us and looked down at their feet. They were agitated, anxious. Mum was too; her eyes were red and her face puffy.

'We've just finished burying Sasha,' Mum said.

'Oh, I thought you'd have done that a while back,' I said.

'The ground's hard, miss,' Cedric said. 'It's been so dry lately. And I had to go deep, see. Stop the foxes getting at him again.'

Olga crossed herself and shook her head.

Mum coughed.

'Well?' she said. 'What did the inscription say?'

She stood there impassively as I explained.

'So there's nothing demonic about it at all,' she said crisply. 'The complete opposite, in fact. Exactly as I thought.'

She glanced towards the Fletchers then looked back at

me. She was enjoying her victory and my humiliation. The Fletchers were too.

'Isabella? Haven't you something to say?'

'I'm . . . I'm sorry,' I said, my cheeks burning. 'I was out of order accusing you. I just . . . I just got a bit overexcited. Emotional, you know? He was our dog.'

'We understand,' Brenda said.

'No offence taken,' Glenda added. 'No offence at all.'

'That's very gracious of you,' Mum said to them. 'Rather more than my daughter deserves, I think but . . . anyway, this is done now, Isabella. Over. I will not tolerate any more of this crap, OK?'

'Yes.'

'You promise?'

'I'm not a little kid!'

'Then stop behaving like one. Now, do you promise?'

I let out a long, irritated sigh.

'I promise,' I said.

'Good, then we're done here.' She walked towards the front door. 'I need a drink. Howard, would you like one?'

'No thank you,' he said. 'I should be getting back.'

As he walked away, he tapped the pages in his back pocket, turned around and winked at me. I didn't wink back.

As expected, Mum kept a close watch over me for the next few days. She kept me busy too.

She asked me to go through the auction house catalogues with her to see what I thought of the things she wanted to buy. A drab desk with lots of drawers and brass handles, deep-napped rugs swirling with pastel florals, paintings of galleons on grey listless seas, a Lalique perfume spray with black tasselled pump, vintage wines, gold boxes, a necklace fizzing with diamonds and rubies. My opinion didn't matter as she would have bought it all anyway. It was just a game, a distraction.

So too were the rambles around the house. There were still so many rooms that were empty of furniture and devoid of purpose. Mum had ideas for some of them – a billiard room being the most ludicrous – but the Long Gallery defeated her.

'The length and light would suggest it would be ideal for paintings . . . even the name says it. *Gallery*.' She turned to the windows. 'But all that sunlight wouldn't do the canvases any good, would it? Or wood. Or fabric.' She sighed. 'I'd rather not go for curtains but it's such a waste of a lovely space . . . Never mind, we'll think of something.'

It was strange to hear her talk of the light in the Long Gallery because to me it was predominantly shades of darkness. As we walked down the length of the room, our footsteps echoed, the light faded and shadow flickered. Warm air came in pulses through the open windows. I had the feeling of people rushing by me, the rustle of leaves outside like whispered prayers. My head reeled with the scent of frankincense. The cloisters of

Stagcote Abbey had never felt closer. I shuddered and walked on quickly.

Mum had plans for outside too and she dragged me round the grounds as she explained her preferred locations for a wildflower meadow, pasture for sheep and pens for the pigs. The grass was so brown and the soil so hard-baked I couldn't imagine it would ever support anything, but I manufactured interest and enthusiasm to match hers.

She couldn't keep me under surveillance the whole time though. At night I scrolled through the photos on the laptop, the eerie white light casting a beacon for moths and mosquitoes. The bites and buzzing and the soft flutter of dark wings around my head were as real as the shadows inside my head as I battled with the code, anxiety, certainty and doubt.

Eventually the drone and the bites became so intolerable I had to shut the window, but within minutes it was too hot to concentrate and I opened the window again, letting in more mosquitoes following the scent of blood. Letting in the hoot of the owl. The erratic church bell.

Once in a while there was a scratch behind the wall too but I was so accustomed to that it barely registered. I had other things on my mind now, things that unnerved me more.

The code was as impenetrable as ever. I couldn't spot any patterns or sequences and when I thought my head would explode I closed the photos down, revealing my desktop with my email, the inbox still empty.

My subterfuge with the code brought back the same feelings of excited panic I had when I was sneaking out of the house for a date with Cosmo. It struck me that breaking the code was as random and unlikely as Cosmo ever getting in touch.

Hopelessness made me tired. Sleep tugged at my eyes as I worked, my fluttering eyelids making the symbols shift and pitch, like boats on a paper sea. In between the pitch and swell, I saw me waving, calling Cosmo. Drowning. Eventually I was taken under and crawled to my bed. Into oblivion.

No owls or itchy insect bites could wake me then, nor the heat that pressed heavily upon me. My sleep was deep and dreamless and when I woke, I was dozy and lethargic, my eyes bleary and blank.

I'd never slept so well yet felt so tired.

The whole time I kept wondering how Howard was getting on. In the end my patience ran out and I went up to the Gate House. I found him lying under an apple tree, eyes closed, hands folded over his chest, a contented smile on his face.

'Not exactly putting your back into it, are you?' I said.

His head turned slowly towards me and he sat up, propping himself on an elbow.

'I'm knackered,' he said. 'I need to give my eyes a break.'

'Only joking,' I said, sitting down next to him, although that was only partially true.

'But I'm not shirking completely. I'm hoping the bees might help me.' He jerked his head towards the hive. 'We tell them stuff, so I thought they might reciprocate.'

'I thought you were taking this seriously?'

'I am,' he said. 'I promise.' He sat up and wiped his forehead with the back of his hand. 'Not that they're in any fit state to tell us anything. Cedric showed me earlier. He's worried about them.'

The queen was still alive apparently, but the eggs in the nursery were still and the caps over the cells were brown instead of creamy. Alarm gripped me, like a tight and sudden cramp.

'What does Cedric reckon it means?' I said, glancing anxiously at the hives.

Howard frowned. 'Well, it's been on the news enough

times. You must have seen or read about it? You know, hives collapsing, the bee population taking a hit from modern farming techniques, fertiliser, parasites. Whatever. They're not really sure which. Probably a mixture of all three.'

'No,' I said, 'I've heard all that stuff, of course I have! I'm not a complete dum-dum. What I mean is, what does it *mean*? The swarm predicted a death so what does the *bees* dying mean? That they saw their *own* death?'

It didn't seem possible that I could be giving any significance to the state of the bees, let alone giving it any credence – but my consternation had a vicious pinch.

His eyes narrowed.

'No. Cedric said bee colonies are potentially immortal. Back in the dim and distant though, he said that in order to get the honey from the old type of hives . . . you know, the sort of basket things . . . you had to kill the bees. I thought that was pretty much what happened anyway. Or that all the bees died at the end of the summer and new ones hatched each spring.'

'Me too.'

'But that's not how it works, apparently. The queen and some of the others huddle together to survive the winter and start again the next year.'

'If that's the case then there must be some omen attached to the bees dying! Are you sure Cedric didn't say anything?'

Howard reached over to me. 'Don't start freaking out,' he said. 'I shouldn't have said anything. I'm sorry.'

'I'm glad I know,' I said, looking at the hives.

The grass underneath the entrances twitched with walking bees, their droning low and intermittent. 'It's all connected . . . the fish are dying . . . now the bees!'

'Stop working yourself up, Izzy. It's not unique to Stagcote. Hives are collapsing everywhere.'

Logically I knew it made sense but that didn't make it any easier to accept or quell the rising tide of anxiety.

Howard sat up. He looked tired. Concerned.

'Look,' he said, holding his hands out, 'if this stuff is getting to you so badly then . . . maybe it's better if I stop working on the code.'

'No!' I recoiled at the urgency in my voice. 'Please,' I said more quietly, 'keep going. Just for a bit longer.'

'But . . . your mum's right. It's not doing you any good.'

'God! Why do other people always think they know what's better for me?'

'Maybe they're just looking out for you.'

'Or trying to control me.'

'That's not what I'm doing, Izzy. I want to do what's best for you.'

'Then help me!'

'But I don't know if all this *is* helping you.' He shook his head. 'You're getting all wrung out over it.'

'No!' I said, flushed with anger. 'I'm not . . . I'm interested, yes. Tired, yes. But . . . do you really think I'm daft enough to actually *believe* all this stuff?'

'Well,' Howard said, shifting uncomfortably, 'you do—'

I held my hands up.

'All I want is to follow this through. Out of *interest*.'

'Nothing more?'

I looked away.

'I thought so,' Howard said.

'It's not . . . it's not what you think . . . I just want to be listened to . . . and . . . not have people make decisions about what's best for me all the time. Like Mum does. Like *you* are now.' It was true, of course it was. But anxiety was driving me as much as my bid for independence. 'Please. Once I know what the code says I'll be fine. In some ways, understanding what it says is less important than actually cracking it . . . it's the—'

'The principle?' Howard said.

'Yes.'

He nodded. 'Yeah. I get that.' He gave a rueful smile. 'I was a teenager too, you know.'

'So you'll keep going with the code?'

He puffed his cheeks out and nodded.

Midsummer Day. It had never meant anything to me before. I always assumed it was the same as the summer solstice, but it turned out it wasn't.

Last year, I spent the solstice with Cosmo at Stonehenge, surrounded by hundreds of people in jumpers and hats who cheered as the lightening sky pinked and a weak, hazy sun slid above the huge grey stones. Mum had gone mental when she found out.

She was more enthusiastic about Stagcote's plans for Midsummer.

'They don't do anything for solstice,' Mum told me, 'but Midsummer, it's quite a party apparently. The Fletchers said they have a big bonfire and the whole community comes together. It's a time for letting bygones be bygones. Burying the hatchet.' She put a hand on my shoulder. 'And that's exactly what you're going to do with the Fletchers.'

I'd apologised to the Fletchers but my attitude towards them ever since had been polite but distant.

'I'm quite sure your picking on the Fletchers has been the gossip of the village. These are our neighbours, Isabella. We have to make amends and this is the ideal opportunity.'

It was the chance she'd been waiting for to play the lady of the manor too. A proper event. Rosemary's funeral hadn't given her the opportunity to lead the village or dress up. She didn't even host the wake. But the Midsummer gathering sounded typically English, *typically Stagcote*, and was sure to have a role for her.

'Of course, we'll be glad to have the bonfire in the grounds of the manor,' Mum said.

Brenda and Glenda shot glances at one another.

'No, please,' Mum said, with a shake of her head. 'I absolutely insist.'

'It's not *that*, ma'am,' Brenda said.

'I know,' Mum said. 'You think it will be work for us all. And it will be. But only up to a point. I'll bring some caterers in from London.'

'But—'

'I know what you're going to say, Glenda,' Mum said, 'but I won't hear a word about the villagers not coming to the manor because of the curse. This is our chance to put it all behind us. For *us* to fit in.'

Brenda smiled weakly. 'We appreciate that, ma'am,' she said, 'but if you want to fit in, the best way to do it is follow the custom and have the bonfire where it's always been held.'

'Which is where?'

'At Maidens' Reel.'

Mum frowned.

'The stone circle,' Glenda said.

Mum looked at me, bemused.

'It's just across the river,' I said. 'A bit like Stonehenge.'

My gaze collided with Mum's. I saw the memory of my trip with Cosmo last year, her anguish in my deceit, the ferocity of our row.

'Oh,' Mum said. 'I see. I had no idea there was such a thing nearby.' She scraped a strand of hair behind her ear. 'It sounds very . . . appropriate.'

'It's been held there for centuries,' Brenda said. 'People

wouldn't go anywhere else, especially not . . .' Glenda nudged her and she swallowed her words.

Mum raised her eyebrows.

'Well, Maidens' Reel it is then,' she said. 'I wouldn't want to flout local customs, would I? Even if some of them are a little far-fetched and out of date.'

Having lost out on the chance to host, Mum was determined to get involved as much as she could – which meant I had to as well.

I resented being taken away from studying the code but I knew the party was important to Mum, and that I had to make more of an effort with the Fletchers – for everyone's sake.

It was embarrassing the way Mum tried to take over. There was talk of a marquee, a string quartet, invitations.

'It's not *your* party, Mum!' I said. 'How many more times?'

'I just want it to be lovely,' she said.

'Well, they've managed to make it lovely enough without your interference for hundreds of years. I'm sure they'll manage this time.'

'But—'

'Just leave them to it,' I said. 'All you have to do is join in. You don't have to lead it.'

The Fletchers smiled at me, grateful for my intervention.

'Seeing as you've got the hang of it, miss,' Glenda said, 'perhaps you'd care to join the rest of us in collecting the firewood and doing the decorations.'

'We all go out and gather wild flowers and other plants,' Brenda said. 'Green birch, fennel, St John's wort and orpine. White lilies too, if we're lucky.'

'For garlands?' Mum said. 'Like the ones the little girls were wearing that first day we came here?'

'Sort of, miss,' Glenda said. 'Only this time we arrange

them around the cottage doors. It's tradition that it's done by the women of the village, although we don't expect you to join in, of course.'

'Why ever not?' Mum said indignantly.

'Don't take offence, ma'am,' Glenda said. 'It's just that there's lots of bending and stretching involved and your neck and shoulder aren't quite right yet, are they, and we don't want you to aggravate it, do we?'

'I'm sure I could manage.'

'With the decorating, maybe. Not the collecting.'

'And anyway,' Brenda said. '*You're* the lady of the manor. Won't do much for your nails scrabbling around in the fields and woods.'

My nails didn't matter, obviously.

The other women welcomed me with shy looks and hesitant smiles, as if they didn't really want me sharing in the custom – or were scared a careless word would help me learn something they didn't want me to know. I was nervy and awkward, embarrassed that maybe I had more in common with them than I would admit to – a creeping belief. Fear.

I didn't know what any of the plants and flowers we needed looked like, so just followed the others and picked what they did; broad yellow star-like flowers, tendrils of leaves cut from slender-stemmed trees, bulbs pungent with aniseed.

When we moved on to picking a plant with reddish-purple clusters of flowers, I felt the women watching me and heard some of them laugh.

'You need your Midsummer Men,' Glenda said. There was an unexpected note in her voice; flighty and fun.

'Sorry?'

'The orpine.'

I looked down at the bunch in my hands.

'That'll tell you all about your love life, that will,' Brenda said. 'And Midsummer Day is the best day to do it.'

'Do what?' I said.

'Love divination,' Brenda said.

'Just put two sprigs of orpine up in the joists of the house. If they bend towards one another, you and your sweetheart will be together. But if they don't . . .'

I smiled weakly and looked away.

'You don't have a boyfriend do you, miss?' Glenda said.

'No,' I said quickly, busying myself with the flowers. 'Not any more.'

'There's a pity,' Brenda said. 'It's not like there's anyone in Stagcote who'd suit either. They're all too old. Or too young.'

Glenda clucked her tongue.

'Seems to me you wouldn't want one of ours even if there *was* one, would you?' she said.

I had to be careful as I didn't want to offend them any further.

'Why?' I said as gently as I could. 'I'm not a snob.'

Glenda stepped back from me.

'No, I'd say you weren't, miss,' she said. 'But you *are* in love.' She put a hand on my shoulder. 'You still love him, don't you? I can tell. You want him back.'

I dropped the bunch of orpine into the basket.

'Doesn't really matter what I want,' I said.

'Oh,' Brenda said. 'He broke it off, did he?'

I said nothing but there were sighs of sympathy all around me. One of the women nudged Glenda and Brenda.

'We know a way you can get him back,' Brenda said.

'Crikey,' I said. 'I can't even get him to reply to my emails.' I tried to hide the hurt with a feeble laugh.

'We can help,' Brenda said.

The women nodded as one.

I was outnumbered, tired, keen not to offend them. Above all I was desperate to hear from Cosmo again. I might be able to persuade him to come and get me.

'OK,' I said. 'What do I have to do?'

The Fletchers asked me to meet them in the kitchen. Brenda rummaged under the bundles of leaves and loose flowers in her basket, and took out a bone, tatty with bloody gristle and muscle. The sight of Sasha's body flashed in front of me and I pulled away.

'It's a sheep bone,' Brenda said.

My mouth was dry.

'A sheep. Not a ram?'

I thought I saw a flicker of amusement in her eyes but couldn't be sure.

'A sheep, miss. We got it from the farmer whose pig we'll all be tucking into at the feast.'

'But what do I—'

'Don't worry,' Glenda said, taking a large saucepan from the sideboard and filling it with cold water. 'We'll help you prepare it so it brings your boyfriend back.'

'But it's just a sheep bone.'

'No. It's a love charm.'

'You sit down,' Glenda said, 'and we'll take you through what you need to do.'

The first step was boiling the bone clean. The shreds of meat bubbled in greasy water and gave off a smell that made my stomach turn. Once it was done, the Fletchers dried it off and put it in my hand, followed by an envelope, a small knife and a length of white ribbon.

'You need to go up to your room, open the envelope and do what's written down on the note,' Glenda said.

'You must do it to the letter,' Brenda said, 'or it won't work.'

Up in my bedroom, I opened the envelope slowly. Took out the note.

It was folded like in a game of consequences, each instruction revealed in turn.

Make a hole in the bone.

The blade of the knife slid through the thick, misshapen triangle of bone easily. It made a rasping kind of pop that made me flinch.

Tie the white ribbon to the bone.

I threaded the ribbon through the hole, tied a series of knots and pulled them tight.

Tie the ribbon up the chimney as securely as you can. Leave it there until next week's full moon.

I remembered the last time I'd looked up a chimney, the scratching, the bones. The screams. I remembered who it was that had given me the love-charm instructions. The Fletchers were playing another awful trick. There was no way I should trust them and follow through.

But I also remembered how anxious and jumpy I'd become. How much I'd missed Cosmo. I was beginning to lose sight of who I was and what I believed in; Cosmo might bring me back. Then he could take me away. If there was something to the curse, then there could be something to the love charm. I was desperate enough to try it.

I closed my eyes, reached up the chimney and tied the ribbon tight around a nail I'd worked into a gap between two bricks.

Wiping my hands on my legs, I went over the checklist one more time, making sure I'd done everything necessary. There was one last instruction to follow.

Read this rhyme before you go to sleep every night until

the full moon. Your beloved will come to you needing help with a cut he sustained in the last seven days.

I coughed, clearing my throat. Took a breath.

"'Tis not this bone I means to stick
But my lover's heart I means to prick
Wishing him neither rest nor sleep
Till unto me he comes to speak.'

A shiver ran through me as I finished. I willed the words to fly up the chimney and out to Cosmo, like the children's wish list for the perfect nanny in *Mary Poppins*. Their wish came true. Mine might too.

It was ridiculous. It was laughable. But at least I'd shown willing.

Even if the spell didn't work, it was worth doing just for the tingle of expectation running through me. It made me feel alive. Part of something big, mysterious, ancient. Something simultaneously silly and futile.

Abandoning myself to it was liberating. It made the whole world and everything in it as malleable as molten plastic. As hot and sticky too. Easy to get into. Hard to shake off.

On Midsummer Eve, Mum and I cut through the churchyard to get to the village. We found Cedric hovering outside the church door.

'Bit late for church, isn't it?' Mum said.

He turned around slowly.

'I was just wondering if anyone would be here come midnight, ma'am.' He licked his lips. 'If *I* would.'

Mum looked surprised.

'Oh, why? Do they do a special service for Midsummer

then?' She turned to me. 'Like Midnight Mass on Christmas Eve?'

Cedric laughed, a dry, humourless laugh.

'It's no service. Oh no. Nothing godly about it.' He shook his head. 'I won't come. I don't need to. I know something's coming. That's all I need to know.'

'What?' I said.

The certainty was bright in his eyes as he pointed into the porch. A dried-out husk of a spider hung limply from a web above the church door. I could smell the rust on the hinges.

'Porch watching,' Cedric said. 'If you sit here at midnight, you'll see the wraiths of all the people in Stagcote come up the path in a procession and file into the church.'

Mum flinched.

'I might have known we wouldn't get through the evening without some of this nonsense,' she said, as she started to walk on. 'Come on, we'll miss the party. And if there's any more of this hocus-pocus lark, we're going straight home.'

'Mum. We need to listen. You're the one who said we had to make an effort to fit in. *This* is part of our home. Our community. You can't pick and choose what you want to play along with.'

If I'd told her that I wanted to know too, that there could be something in it and we could be vulnerable if we ignored it, she'd have turned around and gone home without a moment's thought. As it was, she shrugged and kept walking.

Cedric put a hand on my arm and walked alongside me.

'Wraiths aren't ghosts of the dead as such,' he said, 'more like . . . apparitions of the living. They'll go *in* the church. And some will come out just as they went in. But others, well . . .'

'What?'

'Them that goes in on their own and comes out with some-body else, will be courting – maybe even married – before the year is out. But, them who don't come out at all will be dead within the year.'

Mum looked over her shoulder and laughed.

'Honestly, where does all this stuff come from? I mean, it's very interesting in a way – or would be if it didn't have the potential to hurt people and cause trouble, but . . . ghosts popping in and out of church? *Really?*'

'Oh, yes, ma'am. It's real.'

'You've seen it then? You've actually seen this happen?'

Cedric mumbled into his beard.

'No, ma'am. Not me. I'd rather not know, see. The bees tell me as much as I'm happy with. And anyway . . . there's risks to watching.'

'Like people doubting your sanity?' Mum said, laughing.

'Mum, please! Have some respect.'

'Once you've watched once, you've got to do it every year,' Cedric said. 'There ain't no going back, see. Plus,' he added, taking his hand from my arm and raising his forefinger, 'you mustn't fall asleep when you're watching. If you do, you'll be dead within the year.'

'It's all nonsense!' Mum said. 'Far too gloomy for such a glorious evening. And on our way to a party too.'

Cedric tilted his head.

'As you wish, ma'am,' he said. 'But Old Bess won't be at the feast tonight on account of being on her deathbed.' He looked around him. 'She fell asleep whilst watching last Halloween.'

Mum shook her head. 'I don't know this poor woman, of course,' she said, 'but given that she's called *Old* Bess it's not unlikely that she might pass away sometime soon, is it?'

'Ah,' Cedric said, rubbing his chin. 'Well, that's the thing, ma'am. Old Bess ain't so old, you see. Just fifty-two. But you'd never guess it if you saw her. Hair's all white and wispy. Skin wrinkled like dried out apples.'

'Clearly she's got some medical problem,' Mum said. 'It stands to reason. People don't just age like that overnight.'

Cedric raised his eyebrows. 'If you say so, ma'am.'

We walked on in silence. I wanted to turn around and look back at the porch but didn't dare. I thought of the charm in my room and shivered. *Wondered.*

'I didn't know Midsummer had such dark connotations,' I said. 'Halloween, yes. Everyone knows that.'

'There's good and bad days for all sorts of things all year round,' Cedric said. 'Midsummer's especially good for matters of the heart.'

I didn't feel reassured. Doubts dogged me.

The village was quiet as we walked through it, aggravating my sense of unease. The High Street had never been lively but now there was a sullen broodiness to its silence. The air felt heavy and thick despite the breeze that made the hanging baskets sway like pendulums and drip dust, the flowers inside them brittle and withered, crackling in the wind. The ram's horn looked down on us from the creaking pub sign like a twisted eye. Crisp leaves hissed and scratched along the ground; scabs of bark rattled as they dropped from drought-stressed trees.

Crossing the bridge, Cedric stopped and pointed at the river. In the half-light, the surface looked muted and glossy, but there were occasional flashes of silver that I took to be moonlight but then realised they were the bellies of upturned fish.

'Everything's dying,' I said. 'What's wrong, Cedric? The bees, the fish.'

'I can't say about the fish,' he said. 'But the bees . . . they can die if they're not told the local news. And I make sure I tell them everything. Everything I know, anyway. So maybe there are secrets in the village.'

I looked away.

'The bees are dying everywhere,' Mum said quickly. 'Nothing unusual in that, unfortunately. And as for the fish' – she peered into the water – 'lack of oxygen maybe? The water looks quite low and they said on the news that levels have dropped significantly. We really could do with some rain. Let's hope we don't get a hosepipe ban or we'll never get the garden going.'

Cedric sucked his teeth.

'This river's prone to drought. Used to serve the well up at the manor at one point – back in the day that is. Now it's dry. Only good for dust.'

'And ghosts.' Mum joked with a sly grin.

The bonfire glowed in the distance, the flames like orange fingers ripping at the sky. Beneath the rolling, boiling smoke, shadows crept and jumped. A string of lanterns stretched between each of the stones in the circle to the elder tree in the centre, forming a delicate wheel of fire.

Beneath it was a long line of tables and chairs. Chatter and the clatter of cutlery mingled with the crackle of the fire and the spit and sizzle of the hog roast. The smell of smoke and hot fat hung in the air.

Mum's face lit up brighter than the fire when she was ushered to the head of the table. Olga sat further down the line. She raised her glass to me in invitation to join her but the seats beside her were taken. The Fletchers waved me to the empty seat between them halfway down the table.

'How did you get on?' Glenda said. 'With the love charm?'

'I did it exactly as you told me,' I said. A full jug of cloudy yellow liquid was pushed along the table; thick white suds slopped over the side. Brenda poured me and Glenda a glass then filled her own.

'Then within the next seven days,' Brenda said, 'your beau will be in touch.'

She and Glenda raised their glasses and waited for me to join the toast. Their eyes danced with reflected shadows and flames. Greasy lips split into smiles.

'Cheers,' I said and chinked my glass, hesitantly.

The cider was potent and the slabs of succulent, apple-glazed pork were tender, moist and plentiful. There were bushels of lush, plump salads and wedges of thick crusty bread. Foil-wrapped jacket potatoes were retrieved on a shovel from the embers at the foot of the bonfire, like eggs from a dragon's lair.

It looked festive. But it didn't feel like fun.

Beneath all the merriment I detected an echo of my own anxiety. There was an ambivalence to the gathering; the laughter seemed a little too loud and hearty to be real, and the buzz of conversation frequently became muted, as if secrets were being swapped. The fiddler's tunes had a sharp, grating edge and the penny whistle's notes were so shrill they made me wince. At least there were no trumpets.

In the end, I had to get away from the noise, the relentless press of the hot, flame-lit sky, the skulking sense of threat amidst the pleasure. I took out my pouch of tobacco, rolled a cigarette and stood up from the table.

'I need to stretch my legs,' I said.

I edged away from the gathering, from underneath the circle of lanterns, and leant against the dark side of one of the stones. My lighter fired a thin, yellow flame. The smoke from my mouth was a thin ghost.

A hand on my shoulder made me jump. I wheeled around, fist clenched.

Howard pulled back.

'Jesus! Don't do that!' I said, slowly relaxing.

'How are you enjoying Midsummer?' Slurred words rode on meat and cider breath. 'I think it's been great. Better than last year.'

'Where were you?'

He pointed over his shoulder and nearly lost his balance.

'Next to Evelyn Cooper, God help me. That's what you get for being late. But even she was interesting after a few glasses of that cider.'

He gave me a silly kind of smile. Flames reflected in his red-rimmed, glassy eyes.

'What? I said.

He wobbled again.

'It's the code, isn't it?' I whispered, trying to steady him.

'What else?' He shook his head slowly. 'It's totally consumed me. Bizarre . . . almost like it hypnotised me . . . or possessed me. Once I started I just had to keep going.' He rubbed his eyes. 'I've barely slept since you gave it to me. Or eaten!' His hands slipped down and patted his belly. 'No wonder that hog roast hit the mark.'

'And? Did you make any sense of it?' I said. My words were rushed, my eyes wide.

He pulled me deeper into the darkness, the pair of us almost toppling over.

'I think I might have, yes,' he said, quietly. 'I could be wrong, I mean, I've never done anything like this before . . . who has? But it sort of adds up. To me anyway.'

'What does?'

He yawned. The veins in his eyes were red and raw. He leant against the stone and rested his head.

'Don't you dare go to sleep on me!' I hissed. 'Tell me.'

'Are you sure you want to know?'

'Of course I do. What are you talking about?'

'There's a warning right at the start. Revelations . . . book

. . . oh, I don't know . . . somewhere in there anyway . . .' He wiped his mouth. '"And if anyone will have taken away from the words of the book of this prophecy, God will take away his portion from the Book of Life."'

His head lolled. His grin slackened.

'You still want to know?' he said.

'Yes.'

'It is done now,' he said.

'I know! You told me! But what does it say?'

He groaned and slid down the stone. I shook him hard by the shoulders.

'Howard? Come on. Tell me.'

I gave him a few taps on the cheek. His eyes fluttered open.

'I *am* telling you,' he said. 'That's how it starts.'

'It is done now?'

He nodded, his neck loose, his head heavy.

'It is done now,' he mumbled. 'It cannot be stopped. It is God's will.'

His eyes closed again and he fell into a sleep so deep I couldn't wake him.

'Help!' I cried. 'Help!'

Ed and Nathan came running over. They squinted as their eyes adjusted to the dark.

'Hello?' Ed said. 'Who's there?'

'It's me,' I said. I ran my thumb down the wheel of my cigarette lighter. The flint rasped, igniting the flame. I held it up, close to my face. 'Isabella.'

They moved closer.

'You all right, miss?' Nathan said.

The men stopped as Howard groaned. I pointed to the ground.

'Can you help me get him up, please? He's pissed out of his head.'

They hesitated then heaved him to his feet, hooking their shoulders into his armpits and linking their arms across Howard's back.

'This way!' I said, pointing back towards the Gate House.

'Too far,' Ed said. 'He can sleep it off here.' His tone was grudging and they were less than gentle as they lowered him to the ground near the fire, close enough to benefit from its warmth, but not so close that he might roll into it.

I splashed some water on his face but he was out cold, his skin clammy.

'He'll be fine,' Nathan said.

The two of them walked off, back to the feast.

I shook Howard. He grunted and began to snore. I rolled him onto his side, tipped his head forward. It was a warm night, the heat boosted by the fire. With any luck he'd come round before the last of the revellers drifted home and he'd find his way back to the Gate House.

'Damn you!' I muttered.

It was ungrateful of me. Selfish. He'd helped me, not slept for days and forgotten to eat. No wonder the cider had hit him so hard. He was entitled to a break and it was wrong of me to begrudge him that. I'd waited so long, another few hours wouldn't make much difference.

I patted his shoulder.

'See you tomorrow.'

Back in my room, I stood by the window, staring at the sky. The moon glowed, a grubby opal snagged by skeins of wispy cloud. I thought of the bone in the chimney, how I could complete the love charm in a few days' time, when the moon was full.

I thought of Howard, sleeping it off by the fire, his head no longer full of dots and squiggles but words and sentences. Secrets.

I lifted my hand until it cradled the moon then let it go, prodding and pushing at it with my finger, willing it to shoot across the sky and for the sun to rise and shed some light.

My heart quickened at the prospect. The flush of excitement. The thump of fear.

I lay awake, looking for imperceptible shifts in the darkness, a thinner, subtle hue stirred up by a stretching sun. The scratching noise distracted my scrutiny of the sky. Although the noise was still faint, it was slightly faster than before. The tempo matched my heartbeat.

Shapes and shadows twisted in the night; dry leaves blew a sibilant hiss. And on the hour, the flat clang from the church bell, its random ring more regular now. When the reverberations faded, an owl screeched.

The dawn took forever to come.

I was up and out of the house before anyone else was awake. Given the state Howard had been in there was no way he was even going to be conscious, let alone coherent. But I couldn't contain my impatience. Not any longer.

I ran along the driveway towards the Gate House, startling the birds in the hedgerows. My breathing was quick and hard by the time I got to the end of the driveway. The beech hedge around the garden had thinned and withered, and through the crispy leaves I could see Cedric, hands on hips, staring despondently at the hives. He looked up as I opened the gate. Shook his head.

'Morning, miss,' he mumbled. 'Not a good one though.'

'Is Howard OK? He did make it back last night, didn't he?'

'As far as I knows,' Cedric said. 'I came by Maidens' Reel this morning and he wasn't there then, so . . . he must be home. Safe.' He sighed. 'Not like these poor buggers.'

'What?' I said, approaching cautiously. 'They're not all dead, are they?'

'No, but they're not right neither. Listen.'

The timbre of the drone was flimsy and hollow. The grass around the hives was flecked with bees; many of them were dead but lumbering among them were bees with crispy, curled up wings or lacking wings altogether.

I stepped back as he lifted off the roof of the hive and slid out a rectangular wooden frame meshed by honeycomb. I'd never seen inside a hive before but even I could tell the crusty brown caps over the cells of honeycomb didn't look right. The bees crawled over it lethargically, occasionally losing their grip and slipping, like slow drops of rusty rain.

'There's the queen,' Cedric said. He pointed to a bee, larger and more active than rest. The red spot on her back made her stand out. A splash of blood on the sickly symmetry of honeycomb.

'She's still alive. Looks healthy too. So there's hope.' He peered in closer, gazing at her fondly. 'She's been a good queen this one. Not as uppity as some. Still a killer though. Does for all her rivals before they're even born.' He looked at me. 'And she don't die when she stings you neither, not like the others. So *she* can sting again and again and again.'

I didn't like the gleam in his eye, the punch in his tone of voice. I wasn't sure if he was threatening me. Or warning me. Or just telling me facts about bees.

I turned away and walked towards the house. I didn't like what it all might mean. If anything. Fear crept through the gaps in my understanding and the cracks in what I thought I did and didn't believe. What was possible. What was real. What was actually happening and what was happening only inside my head.

There was no answer when I knocked on the door so I tried the handle. The door opened.

'Howard?'

I poked my head around the door and called again. The kitchen was warm, the air sour. There was a groan from the front room.

'Don't come in. I'm not decent. Give me a minute to get my head together. And my notes. Be out in a bit.'

'Right,' I said, stepping into the kitchen and closing the door behind me.

His head popped around from the front room door. He was dishevelled, bleary-eyed.

'Outside, eh, Izzy?' he said. 'I need the air.'

I went back outside and sat by the wooden table in the shade, my legs jiggling with impatience. Howard came out a few moments later wearing the same clothes and expression as the night before. He slipped on some sunglasses but not before I caught a glimpse of his eyes; they were glassier than last night, the veins thicker and redder.

He sank into the chair, placing a glass of water and a bundle of papers on the table. The printed pages were grubby and dog-eared, covered with scribbles and scrawls in different-coloured ink. Arrows pointed up and over the page, or swooped down to the bottom, linking passages or symbols.

The breeze teased the edge of the top sheet into a curl. Howard rested his hand on the pile to keep them from blowing away.

'What does it say?' I was so tense my voice came out in a husky whisper.

He took a greedy glug from the glass and licked his lips.

'Before I start, I've got to give you the disclaimer. I *could* be wrong about this . . . way off the mark, so you can take it or leave it, but . . . I think that archivist got it wrong about the inscription on the stone. And *you* were right. It's too much of a coincidence that both the Bible and the inscription were back to front.'

The pages fluttered beneath his hand. He spread his fingers wider.

'I think this is all about flipsides, Izzy. Opposites. The inscriptions the archivist mentioned may well have been some kind of "calling card" so Christians knew there were others around but . . . I think this is the reverse of that.'

He lifted his hand and slid the top sheets from the pile of paper across the table.

'Here. This is what I think the first page of the code says. Just my opinion of course . . .'

He sat back in the chair, took another sip of water. Despite the sunglasses I felt his strong, insistent gaze.

There was a tremor in my hand as it reached for the papers. They were as cluttered with marks and arrows and scratching-out as the original document but, in between, words began to appear, like a tree in a fog, the shapes vague at first, then darker, more definite, each one leading to the next.

There were words – recognisable words, *English* words. They flew out of the page at me, fast and dark, like bullets from a gun.

It is done now. It cannot be stopped for it is God's will. He has taught my hands to war. Even now they are sticky with blood and glisten in the moonlight that blazes bright as haloes.

My ministry is murder. My prayers are for despair, destruction and damnation. They will be heard by God. I know it. He has been at my shoulder these last fifteen days, judging my diligence as I set about my labours.

He watched as I whittled wood to fashion a plough small enough to sit in the upturned palms of my hands. He guided my fingers as I sculpted a ram's horn into tiny traces and weaved tough, flat, hairy stems of dog grass into long reins and close-fitting bridles.

I saw the Holy Spirit move between the clouds of steam and

smoke that have billowed from the concoctions in the pots upon my stove. My incense has been the noxious stench of tansy, chicory, red elder and vervain steeped in urine and then set upon the fire until they spat and bubbled. They have been skimmed and boiled again with lark's hearts and crooked pins, then cooled and decanted into jars as slowly and carefully as communion wine is poured into the mouths of the faithful.

And as one brew fermented, God goaded me to another and set me to farming adders, harvesting their slimy venom into cork-stoppered vessels. Then He delivered to me seven toads and guided me to christen them: Jehovah, Sephiroth, Netzach, Hod, Yesod, Malkuth and Arepo. I fortified them for duty with flies and spiders that were snatched from my fingertips by unerring tongues as eager for the sustenance as I was for the toads to grow.

When all was ready, He set the moon to swelling and summoned me to circle Stagcote Abbey like Joshua at Jericho.

For six days, Joshua marched around the city with his priests. On the seventh day they blew loud and hard on rams' horns and brought the city down.

For six nights, I harnessed a single toad to my plough and carved furrows in the grounds of Stagcote Abbey, sowing an unbroken line of scathing brew. For six nights, I matched the red of sunrise with the blood of a toad, my faithful servant skewered with a knife and left bleeding into the soil.

On the seventh night, I hitched Arepo, the strongest of my toads, to the plough, and followed him through the ruins of Stagcote Abbey, beneath the once mighty spires and arches, down deserted aisles and abandoned cloisters, the walls collapsed, the cold wind threading through them where once there had been prayers.

My prayers.

And as we neared completion of our circuit, of our duty to God, I fell to my knees at the battered altar stone and sang out from the Book of Psalms, like I had done many times before, with my sisters by my side – but never more fervently than now.

Let him be condemned: and let his prayer become sin.
Let his days be few.
Let his children be fatherless, and his wife a widow.
Let his children be continually vagabonds, and beg: let them seek their bread also out of their desolate places.
Let the extortioner catch all that he hath; and let the strangers spoil his labour.
Let there be none to extend mercy unto him: neither let there be any to favour his fatherless children.
Let his posterity be cut off; and let their name be blotted out.

For once I did not feel the force of prayer rushing up to couch in God's ear. I knew He needed more from me. I drew a long, deep breath to fill my lungs and blew my curse as long and hard as Joshua's priests had blown upon their trumpets.

'Make those who lay claim to this land, these bricks, or any part of Stagcote Abbey, who rob God and dispossess the faithful, suffer plague, misfortune, despair and death in all its guises.

'Let it rain poison. Let crops fail and livestock starve. Let any who dare to claim the title Lord to suffer disease, injury, poverty and dishonour. May their women be barren.

'Let bad fortune be all that prospers here, and graves the only flowers.

'Make this my Jericho!'

This time, as the last breath left me, I shuddered as the walls of that great city had, and took it for God's pleasure.

I unhitched Arepo from the plough then sliced him with a knife. His warm blood trickled through my fingers as I watched life slowly drip away. When he was still and the flow of blood abated, I took the knife and scratched upon the blunt nub of the Abbey's altar.

```
R    O    T    A    S
O    P    E    R    A
T    E    N    E    T
A    R    E    P    O
S    A    T    O    R
```

As the dawn robbed the full, fat moon of its glow, I rubbed Arepo's blood into the letters and bowed my head.

I turned for home. Psalms sang repeatedly and joyously in my ears.

'Come behold the works of the Lord, what desolations He hath made in the earth.'

It is done now. It cannot be stopped. It is God's will.

My heart was in my throat. Its detail was too convincing for Howard to have made it up or transcribed it incorrectly. Dread fought with disbelief, the turmoil making me blink at the pages, as if staring at them would help make things clearer. But it didn't. My head swam.

'It's . . . the curse!' I said, looking up at Howard, hoping for some certainty but fearing it too. 'I . . . can't believe it.'

'I could have got it wrong,' he said. 'But . . .' He held his hands out in surrender.

'No,' I said. 'The details . . . the seven rams' horns. The trumpets that brought the walls of Jericho down. The inscription on the stone.' My hand flew to my mouth. 'Oh God! The stone. Sasha *was* sacrificed. I knew it!' The din of thoughts clamouring in my mind was deafening.

Sasha. The Fletchers. Rotas. Sator. Satan. Paternoster. Monster. Death.

'I've got to tell Mum!' I said, pushing back my chair and jumping to my feet.

'Whoa,' Howard said, getting up and putting a hand on my shoulder. 'You can't go jumping to conclusions. Again.'

'But it's all there! In black and white!'

'It is in *your* eyes. Your mother might not see it that way.'

'Do you?'

The pause was interminable. I needed the reassurance that I wasn't going mad. That I wasn't on my own. But there was no reassurance. Not really. If he rejected my claims then I was back where I was started. If he accepted there was something to them, I was in danger. There was no comfort either way.

'Yes,' he said. 'I do. Although . . .'

'Although what?'

'I'd like to know more before we take this as gospel.'

I shrugged his hand from my shoulder and picked up the pages.

'But *this* is gospel. *This* is the truth.'

'If it *is*,' Howard said, 'then . . . whose truth is it? Your mother's going to need a bit more detail to convince her.'

'Doesn't the book say who wrote it?'

He snorted with laughter.

'I've only got as far as the first few pages. There are loads more to go. But,' he said, calmly, 'my guess is it was written by a nun. A former nun. Kicked out of Stagcote Abbey after Henry the Eighth dissolved the monasteries.'

My mind ran with snippets of history at school. The king. An heir. A divorce.

'Right. Which gives her a motive, *and* explains the religious stuff. The backwards Bible. Starting with Revelations, which *also* goes on about prophecies heralded by seven trumpets.' I nodded. 'It all adds up!'

Howard angled his head.

'I suppose it explains why the villagers don't tell us much either. Not because we're incomers, but because of the warning

244

at the start of the book. "And if anyone will have taken away from the words of the book of this prophecy, God will take away his portion from the Book of Life." They can't tell us because it affects them too.'

'I've got to tell Mum,' I said. 'Now.'

'I'll keep translating the rest of the book, shall I? There's got to be more in there.'

I ran to the gate. Stopped. Turned.

'Thank you.'

He cocked his head.

'Go.'

The hot, dense air pressed hard against my lungs as I ran back to the manor. My breaths were quick and deep. Branches of the trees along the driveway seemed to lunge after me or stand in my way; shrubs scratched at my face. Shadows shifted and darkened.

My tread echoed around the hall of the manor as I ran across it, shouting at the top of my voice.

'Mum! Quick!'

I threw open the door of the drawing room but she wasn't there. Nor in the dining room or the office. Olga appeared at the top of the stairs, wiping her hand on her apron.

'Miss Isabella,' she said. 'What is it?'

She hurried down the stairs without looking, her gaze focused on me.

'You cut your face,' she said as she reached the last step.

I put my hand to my cheek, saw a smudge of blood.

'Where's Mum?'

'She's out riding. First time since the accident.' Olga pressed her hand against my forehead. 'You're very hot, Miss Isabella. Upset. What is it?'

I thrust the baton of paper at her.

'The code!' I said. 'It's the curse!'

Olga recoiled from me, knocked my hand away.

'I don't want to see,' she said, hurrying along the corridor to the kitchen.

'But you must.' I ran after her, unfolding the paper. 'Look. It's really real. Howard worked it out.'

Olga shrieked. 'Stop it! I say I don't want to know. You're like a mad woman!'

'What on earth is going on here?'

I turned around. Mum stood in the hallway, a black riding hat and crop in her hand, her face glistening with sweat.

'She's . . . she's scaring me,' Olga wailed. 'Make her stop, Lady Lindy.'

The Fletchers appeared at the other end of the corridor, one with a duster and the other a broom.

'Isabella?' Mum said.

I ran towards her.

'We're in danger,' I said, waving the pages. 'The curse . . . it's real . . . right here . . .' Each word made the panic rise in me further.

The slap on my cheek brought me up short. I stopped and looked into Mum's face. It was creased with anger, tinged with pity.

'Stop this right now!' she said through clenched teeth.

'But—'

She yanked me by the arm towards the drawing room.

'Thank you, ladies,' she called over her shoulder. 'You can go back to your work now. Show's over.'

She slammed the drawing room door behind us, tossed her riding hat and crop on a chair and pointed to the sofa.

'Right, you're going to sit there and tell me what this is about.'

I was too wired to sit. When she put a hand out I flinched,

thinking she was going to hit me once more. But she simply pressed down on my shoulder until my legs gave.

'Now,' she said. 'Tell me.'

Her face grew more tense the more I told her. The colour drained away; by the time I'd finished she was like a stone at Maidens' Reel; grey, still, silent.

Finally she leant forward and took the translated pages from me. She gave them a cursory glance then tore them up.

'No!' I tried to snatch them from her but she moved her hand away, folded the pages in half and tore them again.

'There,' she said. 'Done.' She looked up at the ceiling then back at me, bemused. 'See. No lightning bolt. No fire and brimstone. No troop of flying monkeys. It's nothing.'

'I can get another copy,' I said. 'Howard's got it on his computer.'

'Then I shall ask him to delete it.'

'You can't just go round telling other people what they can and can't have on their computer. It's none of your bloody business!'

'Oh, but this *is* my business.'

'*Yes!*' I screamed. '*It is.* It affects all of us here.'

Mum sniffed impatiently.

'It doesn't affect any of us as there is nothing for us to be affected by.'

'But you've just read it!'

'Nothing more than a silly little ruse . . . an initiation . . . for the amusement of the villagers,' she said. 'One that I shall ask Howard to bring to an end. It's gone far enough.' She stood up. 'Really quite irresponsible for grown adults to play around with the head of an impressionable girl, *any girl*, let alone one with your history.'

'I haven't told him anything about my past.'

'Then maybe I should. He'll see the danger of it once I have.'

'If he does, he'll be quicker on the uptake about being in danger than you are.'

'There is nothing to be scared of. Other than you being so gullible and filling your head with nonsense. I can't wait for school to get under way. You've got far too much time on your hands and not enough to fill it with. I'll put that right for damn sure.'

'No! We need to get out of here.'

'Ah, and that's what all this boils down to, isn't it?'

'I'm scared!'

'No, you're bored. Frustrated at not getting your own way. Angry at being stuck in the countryside. Angry at me.'

'I'm scared for both of us. Olga too!'

'I tell you,' she said, opening the drawing room door, 'I don't know whether I should be pleased you've got the imagination to believe this crap, or upset that you're so gullible. You used to be as level-headed about all this as I was. What happened?'

'This place!' I yelled. 'It's . . . it's . . .'

'What?'

The scorn in her eyes was withering. I pulled into myself.

'Evil,' I said, looking around me.

There was a sneer in her laughter.

'Oh honey, really . . .' She jerked her head at me. 'Come on.'

'Where to?'

'Up to your bedroom. We're going to delete the photos from your computer. And from your phone.'

'Yeah, that's typical of you, isn't it?' I bawled. 'Anything inconvenient like, say, a baby? Just hit delete. Sorted.'

A muscle in her cheek twitched.

'Let's go.'

'No, I won't do it.'

'Fine,' she said, 'I'll go up there and do it myself.' She held her hand out. 'Phone please, Isabella.'

'No way!'

'Suit yourself. I'll just take it out of action.'

I was going to say she wouldn't dare but we both knew she would and I didn't want to give her the satisfaction. A couple of calls to some colleagues and competitors of my father's and I would be blacklisted by every mobile phone company. Beyond Cosmo. Beyond calling for help. Permanently.

I stood up and gave her the phone. She raced through the menus, found the photos and deleted them without a moment's hesitation. She did the same to the photos on the laptop once we'd gone upstairs.

'Right,' she said, 'let this be the end of it. No. Scratch that. This *is* the end of it. Period. OK?'

I threw myself onto the bed and glared at her.

'OK?' she said.

I turned over. She groaned and shut the door.

I curled up into a ball. Why couldn't she see the truth? Even if she didn't believe the curse existed, she should at least be able to see that *I* did, that I was scared. But she just saw my emotions as ploys to thwart and aggravate her plans. Comfort was beyond her. Compassion a weakness. Control everything.

But it was her pig-headedness that made us vulnerable now. I took out my phone and called Howard.

He didn't sound surprised at Mum's reaction and said he'd take me into town if I needed anything else from the archive.

'Our secret, of course.'

'Thanks,' I said. 'I don't think we need anything else. The rest of the book is what matters now.'

'I'm on it.'

I was reassured by his competence and companionship. Maybe he would help Mum see sense where I had failed. But perhaps I didn't have time enough to wait for that. She might never come round.

I could run away.

I'd done it before, after all, and I was underage then so the police had come looking for me. They found me at Cosmo's flat within a matter of hours. And they were waiting for me at that pub in High Wycombe, the third stop on Cosmo's tour. His bandmates were embarrassed by the fuss and attention and wondered at the sense of inviting an underaged girl on a tour whose dates were easy to find online. I'd had no choice but to return home.

This time it was different. I was over sixteen so the police wouldn't be compelled to interfere. Trouble was, I had nowhere to go. And even if I did, it would mean leaving Mum behind.

As angry as I was I couldn't just abandon her. She was still my mother and although I wouldn't rush to admit it, least of all to her, there was something in my heart for her that looked like love.

I kept wondering what Dad would do. Then wishing he was here. But if he had been, we probably would never have moved to the manor in the first place. My heart snagged with regret twice over.

At least I had Howard.

My gaze slid over to the fireplace. I couldn't see the sheep bone but I knew it was there. Just like I knew about the trumpets, Rosemary and the rest. Maybe it was the significance I attached to them that gave them the power. They could just be harmless. They could be potent and connected only because my imagination made them so. Or not.

The fact of them was enough to make me fear them. And

the fact of them meant they could not be forgotten.

I got off the bed and sat down by the fireplace, looked up the chimney. The sheep bone was pale against the brickwork, hovering, like a ghost. Or someone hanging. Or a white flower petal. A butterfly.

My skin was ice.

I reached up and yanked the bone down.

Retaining my phone and laptop was more likely to bring Cosmo to me than a love charm made from a sheep's bone. On the instruction of twins who'd killed our dog at the spot where a curse had been cast.

They'd not been helping us with their 'little ways'. They'd been spinning a web entangling us even further in the curse. I looked around my bedroom. The bed had been repositioned, supposedly in a luckier direction. My pillows were always arranged so that the open end of the pillowcases were pointed outwards, allowing the bad dreams to escape. But what if they trawled for them like a net instead?

We only had the Fletchers' word for it that knives should not be sharpened after sunset to spare us from thieves in the night. The plants that looked like rosettes with little pink flowers that grew on the roof and walls might not be protecting the manor from thunder but inviting it to strike.

And maybe doing everything clockwise – stirring the pans, passing food and drink, *the route of Rosemary's funeral* – was the wrong way and we were actually reversing good fortune. Going backwards. Like the Bible and the stone.

And if *they* were connected then there had to be links between the other strange or macabre things I'd encountered in Stagcote. Rosemary. The church window with the optical illusion. The hassocks. The stone circle. The bees.

The book and the altar stone made seven.

Seven.

One for every ram's horn in the pub. Each a herald of the curse. A fanfare of catastrophe.

This was madness. This was truth.

But it sounded so absurd. Mum would never believe it even if I *could* get her to listen to me long enough to explain. She wouldn't leave Stagcote before, on principle. She was even less likely to leave now; it would be like giving in to a spoilt toddler, stamping their foot because they hadn't got their own way.

I got off the floor and pushed the bed to the other side of the room, rucking the carpet as I did so. The lamp on the bedside table wobbled as I moved that too. The pillowcases were rearranged on the bed, the open ends facing inwards.

From then on, I would do the exact opposite of everything the Fletchers had told me to do or done on my behalf.

If I dropped my comb I wouldn't step on it before I picked it up again. I'd make sure all the clocks in the rooms faced the fireplace and would put white flowers in the same vase as red ones. Catching my skirt on the doorframe was snagging good luck, not bad. And I wouldn't wait at the top of the stairs if someone were coming up. One by one, anything embroidered by the Fletchers would be surreptitiously removed.

I turned over the love charm with my toe several times, then stamped on the bone. There was a sickening crack. I scooped up the shards and splinters, shunning memories of Rosemary's bones, and wrapped them up in a towel, securing it with a couple of knots.

It might not have been much, but it was liberating. Empowering.

It did not last for long.

Despite myself, when I sneezed a few days later, I couldn't help but remember the rhyme I'd heard the Fletchers chanting to Olga.

If you sneeze on a Monday you sneeze for danger,
Sneeze on a Tuesday, kiss a stranger,
Sneeze on a Wednesday, sneeze for a letter,
Sneeze on a Thursday, something better,
Sneeze on a Friday, sneeze for sorrow,
Sneeze on a Saturday, see your sweetheart tomorrow,
Sneeze on a Sunday and the devil will have dominion
   over you all the week.

I sneezed on a Wednesday.

At first I thought I was imagining it. As with everything else I couldn't distinguish between what was real and what I thought I saw. What I wanted to believe and what I feared to.

But it *was* there. I squinted at the screen. Focused. No mistake. No hallucination. In my inbox.

Cosmo Dyers.

The name alone was enough to make my heart flutter, but the title of his email made me tremble: *Cuts Me Up*.

Cuts You Up was one of Cosmo's favourite retro goth songs. I'd first heard it in bed at his squat in Finsbury Park, my head nestling on his chest, the skin smooth and firm, the heart beneath it percussive, beating in time with the pulse of the music.

Smoke wreathed around us as we smoked, exhaling in unison, blue-grey tendrils rolling and blending, folding in upon each other like interlocking fingers. Neither of us said it was our song – neither of us had to.

I'd played it a lot since Cosmo deserted me and I had to fight the temptation to do as the title said; scratching my arms and legs with pins or slicing them with scalpels wouldn't bring him back. I'd discovered *that* when we'd split up briefly once before, and I'd sat in my bathroom, watching the thin arcs on my skin flood with blood and wishing I could feel something other than just empty.

I stabbed a finger at the email, impaling it so it couldn't escape.

Iz

Are you there? Is this still your email?

You probably hate me. I don't blame you if you do. But you've got to know this – I miss you, Iz. Going crazy with it.

That song – OUR song. In my head. I haven't played it since we split up – I couldn't. Way too painful. Now, out of the blue, it's everywhere. On the radio. Clubs. Shops. IN MY HEAD. On repeat. Over and over and over again.

Cuts you up. Cuts you up. Cuts you up.

I'm bleeding, Izzy. Tell me you are too.

Cosmo

x

I thought my heart would burst. My head too. Cosmo! He was missing me. He wanted me. He could rescue me. Give me somewhere to run.

The promise of it knocked the breath from my lungs. And beneath the surging thrill of being with Cosmo once again, of being safe, there was the nip of fear.

Somehow the love charm had worked despite me abandoning it before the specified seven days. Perhaps my intent made up for the deficiency; being willing to give it a go, being receptive, had been enough. Maybe it was just a coincidence that he'd emailed me at that moment. But why do it then, after months of silence?

Not only had the charm made Cosmo come to me within the specified period of time, it had also driven him to respond as he was meant to: complaining about a wound he'd received during the time he was enchanted.

256

In our relationship, love and danger had always run hand in hand – Mum's disapproval and snooping had seen to that. But this was different. Now that Cosmo's love was spiked with magic it was an even darker, more dangerous potion, all the more intoxicating and utterly impossible to resist.

The rush of it made my head swim; I felt the blood race beneath my skin, the tickle as the hairs lifted from my arms.

And, mixed with the flood of love was an overpowering relief that I'd thwarted the booby traps the Fletchers had set in my room and my head. *If* they worked – and I was sure they did as the charm had – then they'd been disarmed. I was safe.

Safer – although still not safe. If the charm was real and effective, so was the curse. The only way to be truly safe was with Cosmo, away from the manor.

I checked outside my bedroom door, closed it, then hit reply.

Cuts me up too, Cos. Here's my new number. Call me. Now.

There was enough signal. Not a lot – there never was – but there was enough. If he wanted to call he could.

If.

I sank back down on the bed. Maybe the email was just a joke. I imagined Cosmo sitting in the squat with the others, or on the tour bus, applauding him for being so irresistible despite everything he'd done. I could hear them laughing at me for still being there, hanging on for him, like a silly, desperate little schoolgirl.

A few moments later, my phone rang. There was no name displayed on the screen; just a number.

'Hello?' My mouth was so dry I was surprised any words came out.

'Iz . . . Izzy? . . . Is that you? . . . It's—'

That throaty, mellow voice that made even mundane words sound new and poetic. The timbre of it had tickled my ear as I nestled my head on his shoulder. How many times had I heard it in my head, willed it to be true and not just wishful thinking? Now here it was, real and every bit as sweet as I remembered it.

'I *know* who it is!' I said. Tears scorched my cheeks. 'I've . . . missed you, Cosmo.'

'Me too, Iz. Me too. You'll never know how much.'

I swallowed a sob, waited, let the words run out in a rush.

'Then what took you so long, Cos? Why did you go? Where? I've been going mad. I still am . . . this place . . . it's driving me crazy . . . it scares me. It's going to kill me. Where are you? Come and get me? Please! If I stay here any longer—'

'Whoooah, calm down,' he said, his voice slow and soothing. 'Take it *izzy.*'

I heard him chuckle. Cosmo had introduced me to someone he'd got talking to at some club once, and the guy had misheard him. *I'm Cosmo. She's Easy.* It had become a running joke with us although I knew Mum wouldn't be too impressed. Which was exactly why I'd told her.

But the warmth of a shared joke fell short this time. Either my fear hadn't registered with him or he was ignoring it. Just like Mum. Maybe he didn't want me back as much as I wanted him. Maybe I was pushing things – too much, too fast.

I caught my breath, let the thumping in my ears recede.

'What's up, Iz?' he said.

What's up.

Our love, I wanted to say, our baby, has seen me banished to the countryside, locked up with my overbearing, interfering, obstinate mother and an array of country bumpkins who killed our dog on a sacrificial stone and believe that the bees have told them me and Mum won't be far behind. Even the bees and fish are dying.

But get this – the best of it is that I believe them – the locals *and* the bees. Laugh, laugh if you want. I did too at first. But now, *now*, I feel madness reaching out from every brick of this unhappy house, see my confusion in the twisted branches of the trees. I cannot tell if the shriek of a pheasant or a crow is alarm or laughter. I'm no longer certain if my mind is mine.

There are noises at my window that you might take for an owl, only I hear a trumpet, one of seven, blown by a vengeful nun. The cacophony is deafening to me but no one else can hear it, like the scratching noises just before a skeletal girl fell down the chimney, into the grate of a long-cold fire, which might as well have been my heart.

And I buried the baby in a darkened churchyard where shadows hang dark and chilly, as overwhelming as the sense of despair. Some of it mine.

No wonder I jump at the shadows and things that aren't really there. No wonder I've taken to reading a Bible, backwards, and was so desperate to hear from you that I put a sheep bone up the chimney. And I've been slashing embroidered cushions too but maybe that's better than slicing up my own legs with a scalpel – although I can't say that for sure as I'm not certain of anything any more.

But of course, I couldn't say any of that. Not yet. If I did he'd be gone once again. Once and for all. I couldn't let that happen.

'It's . . . just the bloody countryside,' I said as nonchalantly as I could.

'Countryside? Where are you?'

'Stagcote. It's in the middle of nowhere. In the Cotswolds. It's doing my head in.'

'What, all maypoles and scrumpy, is it?'

'You wouldn't believe me if I told you.' But I have to tell you at some point, I wanted to say. And you have to believe me. You have to.

'Where are you?' I said, hoping he'd say Birmingham or Bristol, somewhere nearby so he could get here soon.

'Berlin!'

'Berlin?'

'Yep. The band's gone all European! Some bloke heard us at a gig in Hull. Said if we could get ourselves over here, he'd get us some dates. We'd have been stuffed if we hadn't got the new van. Looks like it's gonna be Amsterdam next.' He sounded buzzy. 'You should come and see us. We've really kicked on this last few months.'

'Sure,' I said, swallowing my disappointment. 'Sounds great.'

'We've got some new stuff too,' he said, his voice quieter, more serious. 'What happened between you and me it . . . it really ripped me up. I've been bleeding songs. You wouldn't recognise our set any more – it's all new.'

'I'm glad I've been good for something,' I muttered. 'It's gutting to know that people in pubs up and down the country know all about your heartache, when I don't!'

'Iz, please—'

'Maybe you can send me the lyrics? You know, so I can understand what happened.'

There was a pause. A sigh. His and mine.

'You know what happened,' he said. 'Your bloody mother.'

'But we were used to that!' I said. 'She was always against us seeing one another. There must have been something else.'

'No, there wasn't. Honestly. I just couldn't take the stress of it any more. Sometimes I wondered if it was really me you wanted or if I was just a good excuse to row with your mum.'

Maybe it was no different from my feelings right then. Did

I love him or did I just want someone and somewhere to run to?

'No,' I said. 'You can't mean that!'

'I used to think . . . you know, we probably spent more time talking about how unfair and evil your mum was, how much we hated her, the ways we could outwit her . . . than we did about our feelings for each other.'

'No, I loved you, Cos!'

The pause killed me.

'I know,' he said eventually. 'And I loved you. Songs like these new ones don't come from nowhere.'

'Does that mean you still love me?'

'Not a day's gone by when I haven't thought about you. Not one. But the last few days? Shit. It's been mental. I thought I was going mad.'

'I felt the same when you ran off.'

'Yeah. I did too. But this time . . . I've been like . . . I dunno . . . like a zombie.'

My eyes flew to the fireplace. My thoughts flew to the charm. To Rosemary.

'There was a . . .' I swallowed and tried again. 'A baby, Cos . . .'

His breath caught.

'You had it?'

The tone in his voice was unmistakable. Not the excited anticipation of a new father, but the dread of a young man, trapped.

'No! I wanted to, believe me, but now . . . now I'm not so sure. You could at least try and sound upset. It was *our* baby! And she killed it. She made me kill it.'

Tears welled, large wet drops of anger and regret that burned like acid.

'Oh God . . . I'm so sorry, Izzy,' he said.

A surge of fury knocked me from my feet and onto the bed.

'Sorry! *Sorry!*' My laughter was loud and hollow. 'You left us, you bastard! You left us! We could have been a family.' I rolled on the bed, phone to my ear, hand pulling at my hair. 'I could have died, for all you know. Like your baby did. *Or . . . or* I could have had it and you'd be a dad . . . and not even know it! You didn't even bother to find out either way. You're as bad as my mother is!'

I drew my legs up, curling into a ball, squeezing out more tears. I was *so close* to hating him and hanging up. Not close enough for him to hold me and love the hurt away. To take me to safety.

'But I couldn't reach you,' he said.

'My number changed. Not my email. If you'd wanted to find me, you could.'

'You're in the middle of nowhere. You said so yourself. How could I find you?'

'The same way you just have. You could have tried before. But you didn't. Why?' I couldn't bring myself to look at the fireplace.

I sniffed back more tears.

'I was scared, Iz.'

'Of what? My mother?'

'No, of course not!'

'Scared of being a dad, then?'

He caught his breath.

'I suppose. Probably.'

'Probably?'

'OK, definitely. It would have been a big step for me, Iz, what with the band and everything.'

'Yeah, and believe it or not, it was a big step for me too! Oh and by the way, killing a baby wasn't exactly a breeze either.'

I liked his silence. I could picture him squirming like a worm on a pin.

'No,' he said eventually. 'Are you OK now though? No . . . no scars or anything.'

'No scars?' I whimpered. '*No scars?* Shows what you know about how abortions are done. How they affect you.'

'Tell me then.'

'I can't, Cos. You won't understand. I . . . I just want to get out of here. Soon.'

It's what I always said to him back in London. The last few months might just as well not have happened. He had moved on. I had only moved. I'd never felt so far away from him as I did right then.

'I'll come and get you once we're done over here,' he said. 'A couple of weeks or so. A month tops.'

'I could come over there.'

'I'd love it but we're cramped in the van as it is. I mean, it's great but it's not big enough for anybody else. And anyway, we made a rule. No girls. Not this time.'

I heard noises in the background; voices calling, an engine revving. Lairy laughter, the crunch of a can.

'I've got to go,' he said.

'No, wait! What about the others? Gretchen? Spud? Where are they? I went round to your squat but it was all boarded up. Maybe I can hook up with them at their new place.'

'I don't where they are now, or the rest of them. It all got a bit messy.' He sighed. 'Just hang on, Iz. It won't be long. I'll be back before you know it.'

It was the best I could hope for. Better than losing him altogether.

'You will call me, won't you?'

'Too right.'

I'd tell him about Stagcote and the curse then. I had to.

'When?'

'Tomorrow,' he said. 'Email your Skype account. I really want to see your face. And I can't afford another mobile call from here.'

We'd have more time to talk that way too.

The engine revved and the voices called out, louder, more urgent.

'Bye, Iz.' He paused. 'Love you.'

My heart caught in my throat.

'Love you too.'

But the line was dead. I was on my own once more.

The clock on the screen said our video call had lasted for nine minutes. I had only a vague recollection of what Cosmo had been talking about. The tour, how the gig had gone the night before. How sick he was of pizza, how fond of German beer.

Not how I was scared and needed to get away, or how I wished I could convince Mum we were in danger. Every time I went to tell him, the words disappeared completely. It was as if I'd forgotten how to speak. I sat watching Cosmo's lips, as a child would a magician, hoping to see how his trick was done.

I was mesmerised. He hovered in front of me; my fingers left smears on the screen as they traced his face. Lingered around his lips.

His hair was teased into stiff spikes like it always had been; his eyebrows glinted with the bolt and the star studs I'd given him on our two- and six-month anniversaries. He was still pale but looked a little older, the prow of his cheekbones less pronounced.

The brown eyes were brighter, more alert and alive than I remembered, which only made me think he must have been unhappy when we were together in London. But then, it might have been finding me again that had put the fire in his eyes. It would go out once I told him about being confused, scared. Mad.

He'd told me I looked great, but I knew that wasn't true.

I'd barely slept since I'd taken down the sheep's bone and moved the bed, its new location placing me in direct moonlight. Brenda had warned me off sleeping there which just made me all the more determined to stay where I was.

'You don't fool me,' I said to her. 'Not any more. My mother might not be wise to you, not yet, but she will be. You watch.'

She and Glenda both said they didn't know what I was talking about, assured me I'd got them all wrong.

'We're trying to help you, Miss Isabella,' Glenda said. 'I wish you could see that.'

I told them they were not to come into my room again.

'If that's what you want,' Brenda said as they walked towards the door. 'Just don't sleep in the moonlight. It'll give you bad dreams and drive you to madness.'

Was it already too late? Had she just put the idea in my head? By thinking of it – taking remedial action – was I just reinforcing the chance of madness?

Since then, I'd spent the nights wide awake, the strong blue-white light smothering the bed, a torch beam searching me out. Hunting me down.

I see the moon
The moon sees me
God bless the priest
That christened me

I tried to silence the rhyme the Fletchers claimed would keep the dreams and madness at bay. But it was an endless echo. Useless too. For when I did sleep, I was plagued by dreams of

Father Wright at Rosemary's tombstone, the soil on the grave disturbed by a ram's horn scratching at it from beneath. And when I woke, it was to the sound of scratching, the call of an owl, the occasional clang of the clock bell.

'Izzy? Hello?'

I squirmed in my seat.

'Izzy? You OK?' Cosmo said. 'You were miles away.'

He put his hand to his screen and our fingers touched; mine were trembling. If only he could reach through the screen and grab me.

I turned quickly as the door to my bedroom opened.

Mum stood there for a moment, her gaze sailing past my shoulder and landing on the laptop screen. The line of her jaw hardened. What colour she had in her face quickly drained away.

'I *thought* I heard voices,' she said.

'Iz!' Cosmo called.

I slammed the laptop lid closed and stood up.

'Mum! I—'

'Don't even think about lying,' she said, striding quickly across the room towards the desk. The effort made her breath-less.

I tried to stand in her way but she pushed me aside and flipped open the screen. Cosmo's face was so close it was pix-elating. He jumped back.

'Leave my daughter alone!' The hiss in her voice was hate trapped in struggling lungs.

His face vanished. The message on the screen said the video call had been terminated. Mum leant a hand on the desk and took a breath.

'What . . .' she gasped. 'What are you doing . . . with that creature?' Confusion raced around her face. 'How did he . . .'

Her voice trailed away. 'He said he . . . you changed your phone number . . . email . . . how . . .'

'How did he find me?'

Now I saw my chance. I could prove the Fletchers were guilty, working against us, brewing up trouble.

'A love charm,' I said. 'Given to me by the Fletchers to bring Cosmo back.'

Mum tried to laugh but couldn't spare the air.

'And guess what, Mum? It worked.'

She shook her head.

'Don't be ridiculous.'

'He's here, isn't he?'

'Coincidence. Somebody must have told him.'

'Nobody knew. I'm telling you, if the charm can work, so can the curse!'

'I am *not* going to talk about that crap now! That's not the issue. I don't really care how he found you, although I will be talking to the Fletchers about their silly little prank. What's important is *why* he found you. Why you're talking to him. After he left you. With a baby!'

'Because I'm scared! And you're not listening.'

She swept the laptop from the dressing table and onto the floor. It landed with a heavy clunk and a rattling. The screen shattered.

'Now look what you've done!' I screamed, bending down to pick over the pieces.

'What *I've done*?' Glass popped under her feet as she walked towards me. 'You stupid, stupid girl.'

I backed away.

'You've broken my heart, Isabella. Again. How could you do this? Not just to me but to yourself? He's using you. And you're letting him. How could you be so weak?'

Her face contorted as if she was shedding tears of broken

glass. She wiped them away, swept her hair back from her face. Gulped in air.

'Mum, please, take it easy. Sit down. Get your breath. You'll trigger your asthma again—'

'Don't even think of pretending you care about me. Not now! Not after this!'

'After what? We haven't even seen one another, let alone slept together.'

'Nor will you. Believe me. He's had his chance. He should have stayed away.'

'Only he couldn't, could he?' I said. 'Why? Because he loves me!'

Mum tossed her head back; an awful guttural sound caught in her throat. Part sob. Part laugh. Part gasp. Her lips sneered.

'He loves you, does he?' she said.

'Yes.'

'Well, if he loves you, answer me this. Why did he practically take my hand off when I offered him a nice fat pay-off to stay away from you and get out of London?'

I reeled away like I'd been punched. My eyes searched Mum's face and my lips quivered.

'Pa-pay off?' I whispered.

'That's right, honey. When it came to down to a choice between you and a lump of cash, he didn't think twice! Said something about a new van for a tour. How his bandmates would be made up. Yes, he chose them over you. Over your baby. He was off and gone and never mind you – the pair of you. *That's* how much he loves you.'

'No, no,' I said, clutching fistfuls of air. 'No! He wouldn't do that . . . you're making it all up!'

'Every word is bang on the money. Just like Cosmo.'

'No. He loves me! Why is it so hard for you to understand

that someone might actually love me? And *if* I am so unlovable, whose fault is that?'

'Unlovable?' she said quietly, her mouth trembling. 'Oh,
Isabella, it's *because* I love you . . .' She put her hands out,
let them drop, defeated. 'Everything we've been through. All
this. It's all out of loving you . . . but you . . . all you see is a
trap.'

'That's because your love feels like punishment,' I said
through clenched teeth.

Her legs gave slightly and she steadied herself with two
hands on the dressing table.

'That's an awful thing to say,' she said, tears streaming.

'Yeah? Well, so is using threats and cash to break my heart
. . . running the father of *your own grandchild* out of town
. . . and then . . . then making me abort it. And for what? Your
Barbie Princess dream! *Your dream.* You won't listen to me
ever. I'm scared, Mum! Scared! And you just sweep me aside.
How can you dare lecture me on love? You don't even know
the meaning of the word!'

'And how can you be so stupid? Goddammit, there's nothing to be scared of. How many more times? It's all in your
head. Just like the deep feelings Cosmo's supposed to have for
you. He's not back because he loves you. He's back because
gullible girls with plenty of cash don't come along very often
– they're just easy to get into bed when they do. *You're* the
one who told me his joke about Izzy and Easy. Well, the joke's
been on you for a long time now! And even though it hurts
so, so much, this time *I'm* laughing at you too.'

I flew at her. My fists and hands were a blur of amber rings
and black nail polish. Like angry bees.

Every blow was a sting for every hurtful word she'd ever
said, for every painful thing she'd done. For robbing me of
Cosmo, my baby, the life I wanted. For not hearing me and

ignoring my fear. For not being satisfied with who I was and trying to make me into a Disney princess. For not stopping Dad from working so hard, for letting him die. For money being easy to make. Easy to give. For love being so much harder.

Each blow had a shockingly satisfying resonance. The shock of it reverberated along my arms, triggering an electrifying surge deep within me. It was fused with fear and shame and guilt, charged with the relief of letting go.

I'd been so close to lashing out several times before but had never been able to do it. Instead I'd turned my fury on myself; the cuts on my legs alternated – one slice for me, one for her. The guilty thrill of it ran like blood.

Eventually the swarm of blows and slaps subsided. I could see as if for the first time. What I saw withered me.

She was on the floor, curled into a ball. Sobbing. Shaking. Fighting for breath.

'Mum?' My voice was barely there.

Slowly, she lifted her head. Her face was red and puffy; an imprint of my palm bloomed on her left cheek and the cut beneath her bottom lip glistened red. Through the effort of trying to breathe, there was a look that tore straight through me; dazed pain, distrust. Fear. In all the rows we'd had over the years, I'd never seen her look at me like that. She'd never seemed breakable.

Now I could see that she was. The realisation winded me, taking my legs from under me, until I too was on the floor, by her side.

She flinched and moved away, terrified I was going to hit her again.

'I'm sorry, Mum,' I said, wiping away snot and tears. 'I'm so sorry. I didn't . . . I don't know what . . .'

I could hear thunder. Not through the open window, but

270

from the hallway, the stairs, the corridor as Olga and the Fletchers raced to my bedroom. They stood at the door, mouths open.

'Lady Lindy!' Olga said, dashing into the room. She bent down and put her arms around Mum, her body absorbing Mum's shudders as she fought for oxygen, her mouth opening and shutting as if biting chunks of air.

Olga looked up.

'Get her inhaler!' she shouted. 'On the bedside table.'

Brenda ran out to get it. When she returned Olga snatched it from her and passed it to Mum. Her breathing slowed, settled.

She lowered the inhaler. Olga wiped away the drool dripping from Mum's chin, gasped at the blood on her lower lip. Her eyes scanned the room, faltered on the broken laptop and its shards of glass. Glenda went to get a dustpan and brush.

'This isn't just asthma,' Olga said. 'You fight?'

The accusation seared. I couldn't look at her.

'Miss Isabella!' Olga said. 'She's your mother.'

'I . . . we . . .' The words wouldn't come, as there were no words to justify what I'd done. 'I'm sorry.'

I brought my knees up and buried my head.

Olga asked Brenda to help her get Mum to her bedroom. The grunts of their efforts, the soft encouragements, faded along the hall. Then came the quick, dry rasp of a brush on the carpet, the tinkle of glass in a plastic pan.

'Get out!' I screamed, scrabbling to my feet and pushing Glenda towards the door. 'Get out!'

Glenda cringed and wrestled her arm free from my hand.

'You've got the devil in you!' she cried. 'You were cursed long before you ever came to Stagcote, from what I can see.'

I slammed the door behind her, fell onto the bed and wept into the pillow.

I wondered how Mum was and would have gone to her room if I'd thought it would do any good. But it wouldn't. The reverse, probably. She'd panic at seeing me. Get angry. Get breathless.

It was better to wait. Torment grew in me, like the bruises I imagined ripening on Mum's face. Maybe they wouldn't be too bad.

Bad?

What was I thinking? Of course they were bad. *I* put them there. Her own daughter.

Of all the things I'd put Mum through, this was by far the worst. The school exclusions. The self-harming. The overdose. Even Cosmo and the abortion. They distressed her, of course, but they were ultimately acts against myself and she was just caught in the line of fire. Had my overdose been successful she'd have been remorseful, devastated, angry. The pain would have been overwhelming but it would have diminished, bit by bit, over the years, although never fade entirely.

My assault would always be in the here and now, the threat of a repeat lurking behind every argument or potential flash-point. I would tell myself – tell her – that it was a one-off, unrepeatable. A singular mistake. But I couldn't *know* that – neither of us could. And that doubt would gnaw at us both, keep us at arm's length – just in case. She'd flinch when I reached out to hug her. She'd see a headbutt in my kiss. My love would be an assault.

I tried to shake the thoughts from my head. It would all be OK. *We'd* be OK. We would. Getting away from the manor would help. It was the curse that pushed me to hit her. It had to be.

If only she could see it.

*

272

At some point I must have fallen asleep. I saw my dreams through a veil of what looked at first like falling snow, only then I realised it was sheep bones. Then fluttering white butterflies. An open palm – pale and cupped, ready to receive. An open palm, twitching with a slap, curling into a fist.

I was woken by a knock on the door. I opened my eyes, squinted at the silvered glint of moonlight streaming through the window, bathing the bed in a ghostly glow.

The knock came again.

'Miss Isabella?'

It was Olga. I sat up and asked her to come in. She was silhouetted in a shaft of yellow light admitted from the hall outside. She looked smaller, tense. I pulled my knees up to my chest, wrapped my arms around them.

'Is . . . is Mum OK?' I said quietly.

Olga switched on the light, making us both blink. Her face was stern, the set of her jaw steady and unforgiving.

'She's sleeping,' she said. 'Breathing better now.'

'Shouldn't we call the doctor for her?'

Olga shook her head.

'She doesn't want the doctor. She's scared for you.'

'I'm scared for all of us.'

'No, not that . . . that stuff,' she said, rolling her shoulders. She sat on the bed. 'She's worried about what the doctor might think. Lady Lindy's got a cut here,' she said, pointing to her lip. 'And a bruise coming up on her eye. Doctor will know she's been in fight, so she . . . she embarrassed. And worried for you . . . worried he maybe call the police.' Her eyes flashed. 'Why did you do it, Miss Isabella? Why?'

I took her hand. Told her about the love charm. About Cosmo. About Mum offering him money. About him accepting it.

The grim fix on her face dissolved a little and she squeezed my hand.

'It's hard thing when the man you love is no good to you,' she said. 'My husband was also bad . . . but I . . . I didn't attack him! It's very bad of you. Your own mother! *Anybody*.'

'I know!'

'It's not like you. Not the Miss Isabella I know, anyway.'

'No, it isn't. I don't know what I'm doing. And that's because of the curse. Can't you see?'

'Stop,' she said, turning away from me and taking back her hand.

'You feel it too, don't you?' I said, my hand firm on her shoulder. 'You think I'm right. About the horns. The Fletchers. Everything.'

She shrugged my hand off.

'No need to worry about the Fletchers no more. They've gone.'

'Gone?'

She nodded.

'Lady Lindy told me to tell them to go. She's very angry about the . . .' She jabbed her finger towards the chimney. 'You must be careful, Miss Isabella. These things . . . they're not toys . . . dangerous.'

'So you *do* believe me!'

She folded her arms and shivered.

'All I know is this house makes you and Lady Lindy fight worse than in London. Maybe that's a curse. Maybe not. But it's bad.'

'She won't leave.'

'No. She likes it here . . . for you and for her.' She sighed. 'So if *you* stay, *I* stay. It's my job . . . a good job. And I like looking after you, even if you are very bad sometimes.'

'I don't mean to be. Glenda said I had the devil in me.'

Olga snorted.

'Well, no matter what she says no more. She's gone.' She walked to the door. Turned off the light. 'Goodnight, Miss Isabella.'

I rested my head on my knees. Screamed silently.

There was a noise behind me. A low, intermittent hum. Like a prayer. Or a bee. I froze. There it was again. I waited, hoping it might go away.

It didn't.

At least it wasn't coming from the fireplace. I turned around, slowly at first, trying to catch whatever it was in the corner of my eye. Scared of what I might see.

There was something under the bedside table. Glowing.

My phone. I'd muted it after I first spoke to Cosmo just in case Mum wondered who was calling or texting me. It must have fallen off the table during the tussle – the assault – with Mum.

Relief swept over me, warm and sweet. It wasn't bees or prayers I'd heard. I wasn't going mad. I picked up the phone. There were twelve messages from Cosmo, a couple of them alerting me to calls on voicemail. I refused to let my eyes read what he had to say but a couple of words filtered through.

Your mum. Well freaked out. Are you OK? Skype/call me.

There were emails too. I didn't read them either. There was nothing he could say to me that would make me want him back.

I hit reply.

You bastard. I know what you did. That van you're driving around in was paid for by mother. With the cash she gave you to abandon me. I don't know who's worse. Her for offering it or you for taking it. But at least I don't ever have to see you again.

I never thought I'd say this but I'm glad now that I got rid of our baby. It had a narrow escape. It deserved better than me and certainly better than you.

Don't think I'm crying over you. You can't hurt me any more. But you will always disgust me.

Stay away.

Don't even think of calling me or sending emails or messages. Don't try and find me. If I see or hear anything from you again, I will tell the police about your habit and the dealing you do. And that you knew I was underage when we first slept together.

I never thought it possible to hate someone so quickly, so completely. The way I hate you now – and always will.

I sent it without a second thought and deleted all the emails.

There was a voicemail message from Howard too. I was about to listen to it, when the phone rang.

Cosmo.

Fury gripped me in a tight, quick fist. I threw the phone into the fireplace. The glass broke, the light went out. The grate was silent.

Then there was a tapping noise. Quick but quiet. Different from the scratching noise I'd become used to. I peered into the fireplace. Jumped as the bedroom door opened.

'I forgot to tell you something,' Olga said, abruptly. 'Howard called in earlier . . . on his way back from the church. Said he wanted to see you. But you were asleep and I didn't think it good to have anyone else around after . . . after, well . . . you know.' She rummaged in her dressing gown pocket. 'So he wrote this out downstairs and asked me to pass it on.'

I took the envelope from her. She lingered, as if hoping I

might share the contents of the envelope with her. I yawned and put the envelope on the bedside table.

'Thank you,' I said and yawned again. Olga took the hint. As soon as she'd closed the door I ripped the envelope open.

Need to see you. Tomorrow. At the church. Ten o'clock. Not before. I still need to check a few things and I'm knackered – I need a clear head to explain properly.

I've managed to work my way through a fair bit of the book but not all. I can't vouch for the accuracy of everything that I have to tell you – I've had to skim over some parts as the code was beyond me. But I was able to establish patterns and sequences.

What I've ended up with is not exactly guesswork – it's much more informed than that. A mix of fact and hunches. But mostly facts. There's one thing I'm certain of though:

I KNOW WHO ROSEMARY WAS.

I was desperate to get to the church to hear what Howard had to tell me, but my conscience wouldn't let me leave the house the next morning without checking on Mum.

I knocked on her bedroom door sheepishly, half hoping she was still asleep or would tell me to go away. I wanted to see her, to apologise. But I was also wary of the slap of shame I would feel at the sight of her bruises and cuts.

I was perturbed and relieved that there was no answer. Her bed was empty, the pillows flattened, the duvet twisted – just like mine were after my agitated, anxious sleep. Used tissues were piled on her bedside table, full of tears that I'd caused. Dotted with dabs of blood too.

I closed the door quickly.

She wasn't downstairs either. Olga sat at the kitchen table with a pencil between her lips, poring over a crossword puzzle, an eraser and a mug of steaming coffee in front of her. She glanced up quickly; her eyes were red and narrow.

'Where's Mum?' I said.

She slipped the pencil from her mouth.

'She was up early.'

'To the doctor?'

She shook her head and filled in an answer on the crossword grid.

'Could be the police,' she said. 'You think of that?'

I swallowed hard.

'The police? But I thought . . .'

Olga waved me away.

'She's not at the police. But she *could be*. That's the important thing. You remember that.'

I relaxed.

'So where is she then?'

'Riding.'

'Riding?'

'I know,' Olga said, with a sigh. 'I told her stay in bed. Take things easy. But no. I made sure she took the inhaler though.'

'How is she?'

'How you think? Her own daughter attacked her.'

'Don't,' I said, and looked at the floor.

Olga glared at me. 'Lady Lindy is breathing better now. But she has black bruise here,' she said, tapping her left eye. 'Doesn't look good. The horse won't mind, I suppose.' She put the pencil down. 'You want to eat now?'

'No, thanks,' I said. 'I'm not hungry.'

'Good. I don't feel like making it this morning.'

She picked up her mug and sipped from it studiously, eyes fixed ahead.

Her rejection unnerved me. She had always been so constant, no matter what. Even when I was in the wrong, or the few occasions she was angry with me, she still let me know I had a way back and would always find her there. I wasn't so sure any more. The uncertainty rocked me; the world beneath my feet could not be guaranteed and the thoughts in my head were just as mutable and erratic.

I hurried to the back door.

'Where you going?' she said. 'Lady Lindy will want to know when she gets home, or she'll worry.'

'Maybe she won't,' I said. 'She'd probably prefer it if I ran off and never came back.' I grimaced. 'She'd probably feel safer if I did that too.'

'She loves you, Miss Isabella.'

'Even now?'

'Even now. Just like you love her.'

I opened the back door.

'You didn't say where you're going,' Olga called out.

'Church,' I said.

'Good. Go ask God to forgive you. He may answer your prayers.'

'I doubt it. He hasn't done so far.'

I went to pull the door closed but Olga asked me to leave it open.

'Let some air in,' she said. '*Very* hot today.'

I left the door open and ran through the garden to the gate. I was sweating before I even got halfway. The weather felt different. Before, it had been broad sweeps of deep blue sky, odd puffs of cloud dawdling on a cooling breeze.

Now, the sky was lower, paler. Heavier. The sun was washed-out too, as if it had burned off its orange shell and exposed a mildewed core. The air was hot and stale, dense with humidity. I had to breathe in harder and quicker and wondered how Mum was coping. Thank God Olga had made her take the inhaler.

Howard was walking among the graves in the shade of the northern churchyard, stopping at each one then flicking through the pages in the A4 file in his hands. He'd give a little nod, make a note and move on, like a surveyor inspecting a site.

He looked up at the sound of my footsteps. His brow buckled with a frown.

'Izzy,' he said, 'you look awful.'

I wanted him to hug me and say everything was all right. That I was safe. And good.

'I know . . . last night . . . I . . .' Words became whimpers.

He pulled me to him. His shirt was damp, the flesh beneath

it warm and soft. I breathed in the zing of citrus, beneath it, a trace of sweat.

'I heard,' he said.

I looked up, ashamed.

'Oh God.'

'You know how quickly news travels in Stagcote,' he said. 'Sometimes, anyway. The Fletchers set the whole pub gossiping last night.'

I pulled away from him.

'I didn't mean to hit Mum. You must believe me! I'm not evil. Violent. Not got the devil in me like Glenda says. I don't know what got into me.' I buried my head in my hands. 'No, that's not true . . . It's . . . it's the curse! It has to be.'

The arm around my shoulder was back. It felt good.

'I think you're right,' he said, tapping the cover of the file. 'This makes sense of it all. Your fight. Sasha.' He pointed along the line of graves. 'Rosemary.'

I looked up. The marble of her gravestone shone in the sunlight. It looked wet, as if it was sweating with fever. The butterfly looked like a burst blister.

'You said you know who she was?'

He nodded. 'I do. And you're not going to believe me when I tell you that Rosemary actually *was* her real name.'

My skin was suddenly cold; the sweat on my brow not from the fierce heat of the sun, but from fear.

Howard's eyes widened. 'How did you know?' he said.

My lips moved but no words came out. I remembered the moment I'd chosen her name. The scent of the crisp, white roses outside the drawing room window. Their tap upon the glass.

'I don't really know . . . she . . . it was as if . . . the house told me.'

I screwed my eyes up, trying to dredge up any more details.

'At the funeral,' I said, 'the people behind us . . . the villagers . . . they murmured when Father Wright first said her name. Like they recognised it. And . . . and you . . .' In the shadows in my mind, I saw Howard with his thumb up in approval. 'You said it was a good name.'

'And it was. *Is*. Rosemary would have been a popular name of the time.' His face clouded. 'But there was another reason she was given that name.'

He stopped in front of her grave.

'Rosemary used to be planted on graves to bring immortality to the dead.' He tapped the file again. 'It's all in here. Rosemary's influence was meant to last forever, only in this case, it wasn't a positive thing. The reverse, in fact. No surprise there, I suppose . . . Like I said before, this is all about flipsides.'

I looked at the file then at the grave. Then back again. The red of the file and the white butterfly ricocheted in my mind, backwards and forwards, bouncing, blurring. Red. White. Blood. Purity. Life. Death.

He leant in close.

'She *is* part of the curse, Izzy. Just as you always suspected. It's as real as you and I are.'

I felt the earth tilt beneath my feet as if it had slipped into a dubious equilibrium, where gravity wavered, like sanity.

'Who was she?' I said quickly. 'Who put her there? Why did they dig her up? Tell me!'

'Let's go inside the church. I'll be able to explain it better there.'

I stayed close to him as we walked around the graveyard. The tombstones seemed to shift and wobble. Above us, rooks circled, their raucous calls a rolling echo of alarm.

I glanced up at the window with the optical illusion as we went past. Judas stared back at me, the pile of coins in his palm glittering. His eyes were defiant. Disdainful. Like Cosmo's probably. I could practically hear the chink of the money as he counted it and slipped it into his pocket. I could hear his snorts of laughter too. Anger and resentment boiled.

Howard lifted the latch on the church door. The cool of the church was welcome but there was a sense of uneasy expectancy, something brooding. A trap.

The feeling intensified once Howard shut the door and silence settled. I could tell from the way that he cocked his head that he felt it too. We were not alone. There was a presence. Lingering. Out of sight.

'Hello?' Howard said hesitantly.

There was a rustling noise. A clunk of something against wood. The echo hung in the air. A head popped up from behind one of the pews up by the altar.

'Mum!'

She recoiled from the word. From me.

'Olga said you were out riding.'

'I meant to go riding,' she said, her voice breathy and distant. 'But . . . well, I just wanted somewhere to think.'

'I'm . . . I'm so sorry,' I said, walking quickly up the aisle.

She sat up in the pew, reached to her side and stood up. She had her riding helmet in her hand and was dressed in jodhpurs; the black singlet intensified the translucency of her skin. Her face, though, was darker, shinier.

As I drew closer I could see the faint line on her neck where her natural skin colour met the foundation on her face. Tears were traced in black smudges beneath her eyes. Bruises too. Blue-black. A pinched-out yellow. None of them quite masked by the make-up. The cut above her mouth matched the glossy red of her lipstick.

'Oh God,' I said. 'I'm sorry. I feel so ashamed.'

'So you should be. If it's any consolation, I'm ashamed of you too.'

Tears welled in my eyes.

'Please,' I said, 'tell me . . . you can forgive me.'

Her lips twitched.

'That's what I came here to find out,' she said. She coughed a wheezy cough. 'And to pray.'

'For me?'

Her laugh was thin and joyless.

'For both of us, Isabella.' She sounded so hollow, so defeated. 'Somebody has to. After all, I don't suppose you came here to pray, did you?' She tilted her head at Howard.

'No,' he said. 'Although, all things considered, it might not be a bad thing to do.'

Mum waved him away. 'I don't need any more gloom and misfortune, thanks very much,' she said, edging out of the pew. 'I've had enough – *more than enough* – already.'

Her riding boots sounded gritty against the stone floor as she walked towards us.

A bolt of hope shot through me.

'So we're leaving the manor?' I said.

She stopped. Her shoulders dropped. Once again I saw the fragility that had shocked me the night before.

'God,' she said. 'How is it . . . how is it that after everything we've been through, you still don't understand me? Any more than I understand you?' She shook her head. 'We don't really know one another, do we, Isabella? If your father . . . He wouldn't know who we are.' She smiled sadly. 'Or maybe he would. This might look very familiar to him. Perhaps . . . perhaps that's even sadder.'

My cheeks burned.

'I said I'm sorry.'

'And that's meant to make it all right, is it?'

I looked at the floor.

'No.'

'No,' she said firmly, as she drew alongside me. 'Sorry won't make it all right. How could it? Any more than leaving the manor would. All I'd be doing would be rewarding your . . . your *assault*.' She closed her eyes as if that word was dancing in the air before her. 'Setting a precedent. Isabella doesn't like something, mother gets thumped until Isabella gets her own way.'

'No! It won't be like that. I promise. I never meant to . . . I won't do it again . . .'

'But you can't guarantee that.' She clenched her jaw. 'You know, there's part of me that thinks it might be for the best if I reported you to the police. Maybe they – or the threat of a stint in a young offenders' institution – could do what my love and concern have clearly failed to do: get you on the path to a happy and fulfilling life.'

I hadn't even thought of being liable to prosecution.

'No, please!'

'I probably should do it. For your own good. But,' she said, tipping her head and looking at the ceiling, 'that story would get out eventually . . . into the gossip columns . . . broadcast by you, probably.' She looked into me. 'We'd be no further on than we are now. Just a little bit older. But no wiser. Stalemate. And if that's the case, then we might just as well try to work our way through this once and for all, away from prying eyes. Here. At the manor.'

'But can't you see? The manor's part of the problem!'

'We had our problems before we came here. Let's not air-brush the truth.'

'But this place is making it worse! Because—'

'Because of this curse nonsense? Please. It's just the gullible girl crying wolf. Yet. A. Gain. And guess what? There's nothing there!'

Howard held the file up.

'But there is!' he said loudly.

The words echoed around the church. *There is. There is.*

'He knows who Rosemary was,' I said. 'And that Rosemary *was* her real name.'

There was a flicker of interest in Mum's eyes. I stepped towards her. She leaned away, subtly, the move barely perceptible – but it was there. I brushed past her, ran to the church door and pushed my back against it.

She stopped about an arm's length away but wouldn't come any closer. Her gaze dropped to my hands. I flexed my fingers, more out of nerves than as a threat. Her body stiffened.

'Hear what he's got to say. Then see what you think. If it's all crap—'

'*If!*'

'If you think there's nothing to it then . . . I'll drop it. Totally. Once and for all.'

She arched an eyebrow, shifted her weight.

'You've said that before, and yet here we are.'

'I mean it this time. Really. I promise this will be the end of it. You said we've got to work our way through this. Well, we can't! Not if you won't listen . . . It's not going to go away. Please.'

She held my gaze. I was trying not to look at her bruises and cuts, and she knew it. She hesitated to let the guilt grip.

'No more bleating about moving away from the manor and finding any old excuse to make it happen?' she said.

'Yes. I promise.'

'You'll knuckle down at school? Maybe get some anger-management counselling?'

'I told you, I won't . . . *that* won't happen again!'

'Yes or no, Isabella?'

'Yes! All right!' I pressed my head against the door. 'Now, can we get on with it?'

Mum looked at her watch. 'Let's get it over with.'

Howard coughed and held the file up.

'I don't have the time or patience for you to read all of that,' Mum said. 'Just give us the gist of it.'

'You already know that,' he said. 'But I'll need to put some flesh on the bones for you to consider it properly and see it for the very real threat it is. The devil's in the detail, as they say, only in this case, it's a nun.' He extended his hands towards the pews in invitation. 'Let me explain.'

I took a seat in the pew across the aisle from Mum so I could block her path should she dip out of her side of the bargain and try to leave before she'd heard the whole story. At least that was part of the reason. I wanted to be closer to the door too, even though I knew there was no escaping the doubts and demons running loose inside my head.

Howard put his file on top of the Bible in the lectern at the front of the church, flicked over a couple of pages, flicked them back again, coughed.

'It's hard to know where to start really,' he said. 'But maybe I should kick off by reiterating that I had my reservations about this curse business too. But, going through this lot,' he said, tapping the file, 'I had to cut some slack. Subdue my twenty-first-century sensibilities. My judgements and preconceptions.' He looked straight at Mum. 'I ask you to do the same.' He paused. 'For your sake.'

My mouth was dry, my skin like ice. Mum crossed her arms.

'The code I've been working on is the work of Agnes Tump . . . At least, she started the book. It seems it's been passed down through the generations, a sort of family history, diary, almanac and prophecy all rolled into one . . . Now, Agnes wasn't from Stagcote originally; she was born in Ashtonbirt. The date isn't mentioned – but the time of her birth is. Three o'clock in the morning.'

'So what?' Mum said.

'It's a time, apparently, every bit as auspicious as midnight. The chime hour. When bells would ring in monastic orders, summoning the faithful to prayer.'

Three o'clock. The time the scratching in my bedroom always started.

'Sounds like a good thing to me,' Mum said.

'You'd think so, wouldn't you? But that isn't the case, it seems.' He turned a page of the book and read aloud.

'"For chime hour children like me are plagued by visions more customary to the darkest dark of night than abroad upon the daytime. Spectres, ghosts, goblins, imps and demons haunt our wakeful eyes.

'"And in our blood, the prick of stars, the churn of planets, the spiteful twist of Fate that levers open unknown futures like a knife upon an oyster, inside of which are pearls – but not the white shiny kind favoured by fine ladies, but hard black nuggets of the occult."'

Howard looked up.

'But that's not all,' he said. 'Agnes was the seventh child of a seventh child, a fact which gave her another unfortunate birthright. A natural talent for magic.'

'I thought you said she was a nun?' Mum said.

Howard nodded and held his hand up, asking her to be patient.

'It was an auspicious – ominous – double whammy. The circumstances of Agnes's birth determined a life to be spent hovering in the twilight between good and evil.

'Agnes knew it too. She prayed for so long from such an early age that people joked her kneecaps would be dented and her neck permanently cricked. And they were right . . . Agnes grew up hunched and hobbled . . . bent by both her devotion to God and the burden of the devil.

'As soon as she was old enough, she sought refuge in the vows, piety and sisterhood of an order of Cistercian nuns at Stagcote Abbey. She quickly fell in with the regime of fasting and prayer, and worked long and hard in the abbey's fields . . . rearing crops and cattle and horses which they sold along with their cheese and bread . . . and the honey Agnes harvested from the abbey's hives.

'Agnes took the bees' chastity and industriousness as her example. There'd be no time for idleness, no room for sin or the supernatural and she'd always be part of a community working for the common good.

'But . . . she felt the devil on her shoulder and around every cloistered corner. Even the clothing favoured by the Cistercians was testament to the battle Agnes fought with herself; a white habit with a black scapular pulled over the top. Good and evil on her skin, good and evil within.

'Then came the Reformation . . . The Abbey had lots of land, a source of clean running water, and stone . . . tons and tons of good sturdy bricks, perfect for building a manor house befitting royal favourite Thomas Drysden, newly created First Earl of Windrush.'

Howard turned over a couple of pages in his file and began to read.

'"How it pulls my heart asunder to see that happy haven, God's own house, stripped then dismembered brick by brick, only to see those selfsame bricks rise again, reordered into the revolting pomp and vanities of Stagcote Manor.

'"Corridors that once ached with heartfelt prayers and

meaningful devotions now ring with vile obscenities. My sisters have been replaced by jewel-encrusted whores and greedy, bloody villains. The wine that flows there may be red but is indisputably not the blood of Christ, and anyone who claims it so will roast upon the hottest fire in the deepest pit of Hell."'

Howard looked up.

'Agnes didn't just lose her home,' he said, 'she lost her purpose, her friends . . . the comfort of rituals, relics and icons . . . the balm of regular, organised, communal prayer. Everything that had kept her on the right side of God had been swept away in a cataclysmic rush. The devil rushed into the void.'

My hand ached and when I looked down I saw the skin, white and knuckled as I gripped the edge of the pew. This was right. This was real. This was madness.

'So she cast a spell!' I said, turning to Mum. 'For revenge. Just like we thought.'

Howard nodded. 'On what had been the Abbey's altar stone,' he said.

'A black mass,' I said quietly. 'A sacrifice.'

Mum drummed her fingernails on the wooden pew.

'All very imaginative, I'm sure,' she said, 'but the archive confirmed there was nothing demonic about the inscription on that stone.'

'They were wrong,' I said, throwing my hands up in frustration.

'Why? Because you say so?' Mum said. 'I'd take their word over yours anytime.'

'Both the archives and Isabella are correct,' Howard said. 'The archivist told us the inscription was the letters of Paternoster scrambled up. A sort of shorthand for the Lord's Prayer, yes?'

I nodded.

'And that's what Agnes intended people to think, should they discover it. But, in this instance, what matters is the literal translation of the *words* rather than playing around with the letters. "The sower Arepo holds the wheel carefully." And the book tells us Agnes sowed the spell with a plough pulled by toads, the last of them, the seventh, named Arepo.'

He looked down at his file and read from the pages.

'"I unhitched Arepo from the plough then sliced him with a knife. His warm blood trickled through my fingers as I watched life slowly drip away. When he was still and the flow of blood abated, I took the knife and scratched upon the blunt nub of the Abbey's altar. As the dawn robbed the full, fat moon of its glow, I rubbed Arepo's blood into the letters and bowed my head."'

'Come on, Isabella!' Mum said. 'You can't possibly believe this.'

'Why not?'

'Because this sort of thing doesn't really happen. Not in real life! The silly sort of films you watch maybe, but—'

'As I said at the start,' Howard said, 'we need to put our modern-day logic behind us. We assume – hope and pray to God – that this sort of thing doesn't happen nowadays, but, back then, when things were less certain, life was lived on the brink . . . people had to take chances . . . precautions . . .'

'By killing toads *maybe*,' Mum said. 'But kids? *Infants?* Come on! Not in England. Not even back then.'

Howard's expression darkened.

'Rosemary's death wasn't ritualistic. No blood and knives and so on. And it didn't take place at the altar stone.'

'Right,' Mum said smugly. 'So it's not a sacrifice at a black mass, after all, is it?'

'She was still murdered.'

'Where?' I said, half hoping he didn't know or wouldn't tell me if he did.

'Agnes's house.'

'She killed her own child?' The words ripped me apart.

'Not her child, no. But it was still her flesh and blood. The child was her sister's, you see . . . Ursula. *She* had been sent by her father to bring Agnes back to the family home in Ashtonbirt after the abbey was destroyed. But Ursula stayed in Stagcote . . . not with Agnes, mind . . . she was too alarmed at the change in her sister, appalled at her taste for magic and revenge.

'She could've decried Agnes as a witch but Ursula couldn't betray her; it was just a . . . temporary aberration. The sister she knew and loved would soon be returned to her. Until then, she would make sure the targets of the curse were kept safe. So she . . . found work at the manor. In ensuring nothing happened to Lord and Lady Dryden, Ursula could keep Agnes safe too.'

I was struck by the similarities with the Fletchers. Maybe they had been motivated for good, like Ursula, just like they always claimed. And there were echoes of my inability to abandon Mum in Ursula's loyalty to her sister. The past was repeating, stamped into the bricks, the air of Stagcote Manor.

'But,' Howard said, 'in looking out for Agnes, Ursula failed to take care of herself.'

He read once more.

'"Not satisfied with throwing off the one true God for the promise of a bauble from the King, of bringing down the walls of Stagcote Abbey and banishing its harmless sisterhood into untold torment and danger, Lord Dryden's vile passions have found another target in my sister. And, as in the other matters, where consent was not forthcoming, force would do."'

Howard cleared his throat.

'Agnes was mortified . . . racked with guilt that the first manifestation of her curse should be the rape of her sister. But it brought them closer together, uniting them in hatred for the Lord of Stagcote Manor. Ursula asked for instruction in witchcraft from her sister and made a curse of her own at the abbey's altar stone, sealing it with the sacrifice of a stoat. Then Agnes set to work on inducing a miscarriage with compresses of white hellebore and dilutions of rue and juniper, aided with fervent incantations and charms of wood, stone and bone.'

I lowered my gaze. Mum shifted, the clunk of her foot against the pew echoing around the church.

'None of their methods worked, so the two sisters concluded that for *some* reason God wanted the child to be born . . . that it was somehow part of their curse. They could not understand why God would ask them to raise Dryden's bastard child, but obeyed his will as always.

'The child was born with supernatural powers by virtue of the time of its birth – three in the morning. A chime-hour baby, just as Agnes had been. Now the sisters understood why God wanted the baby to survive and found confirmation of his will in the book of Psalms.'

He looked down at the book, turned a few pages, and read.

'"He shall cut off the spirit of princes: he is terrible to the kings of the earth."'

'Ursula and Agnes took it as an instruction to use the baby's powers against the lord. The child, a girl, was smothered a day after her birth. Infant mortality being as high as it was in those days, the baby's death wasn't questioned by anyone. But Ursula had to follow Christian practice and allow the corpse to be buried, which it was, in an unmarked grave in the northern churchyard. Although not baptised, Ursula had given her a name.'

'Rosemary,' I whispered through the scald of tears.

'Named after the rose of Mary,' Howard said. 'Ursula hoped it would invite the Virgin Mary to watch over her daughter. But . . . there was another reason for the choice of name too . . . the herb rosemary is believed to repel evil. They exhumed the girl's body and Ursula, now returned to work at the manor, hid her daughter's remains in the chimney, where it would work from within to drive out Lord Dryden.'

Howard picked up the file from the lectern and walked along the aisle, stopping near the door to point at the church window.

'This is the work of one of Ursula's descendants who, in the sixteen hundreds, convinced the then lord of the manor that the new window's optical illusion would be a marvel for the church. It does, in fact, depict the sisters' deception. The Virgin Mary on one side, Judas on the other. Ursula and Rosemary were like the Trojan Horse, attacking the manor and the lord from the inside.'

'Right,' Mum said, 'so now, after killing her own child, Ursula gets to work bumping off the lord and lady with poison and axes, yes?' Her tone was slow and sarcastic and she tilted her head at him defiantly.

'Yes,' Howard said, 'only not with poison or axes. The sisters were too careful for that . . . they *had* to be. Anything too obvious would arouse suspicion. So too would any blatant witchcraft which could see them hanged or burned at the stake. That's why they wrote the book in code and used the word square for the inscription on the altar stone.'

'So just how did our diabolical duo set about it, then?' Mum said.

Howard smiled weakly.

'Agnes used her spells. Ursula . . . she used—'

'Embroidery!' I said. 'Yes, of course.'

295

Mum blinked and turned to me, dumbstruck.

'Excuse me? *Embroidery?*'

Howard pointed at the kneelers hanging on the panel at the front of every pew.

'Ursula was expert with a needle and not just for darning holes and making neat, quick repairs. Lady Dryden noticed her maid had a flair for needlework and encouraged her to embroider samplers.'

He read from the file.

'"She took domestic items for her subjects; a pan boiling above a fire, a gleaming sickle, a hunter's knife. These were her spells, made right under the nose of their intended target. She turned her samplers into covers for cushions and insisted My Lord and Lady made use of them at church, where the reeds upon the floor offered scant support or warmth to the knees of the faithful.

'"They were glad of her thoughtfulness and mindful of her skill but blind to the import of the images on the cushions, ignorant of the Psalms and sprigs of witchbane, hellebore and elder sewn within. So, the intensity of prayers for the salvation of their souls gave wing to the spells for their damnation beneath their knees."'

'Like the Fletchers,' I said.

Mum's laugh was wheezy, short-lived.

'God, it's just as well you weren't around back then, Isabella. You'd have been the one leading the witch-hunt. I thought you'd be the last one to start accusing other people of being different. The Fletchers have done nothing *wrong* . . . they've got a great knack for needlework and you . . . you go and turn it into something nasty. No, not nasty . . . stupid.' She laughed again. Through gritted teeth. 'You know, I feel kind of cheated. We don't get witches with magic wands.

Ours have magic needles. Still, at least it's original. You've been using your imagination. The pair of you have.'

She pointed at the hassocks. 'I mean look at these things,' she said. 'Do they look like they've been knocking around for the last couple of hundred years? No. And no matter how brilliant this Ursula was meant to be at sewing, even she couldn't have cracked all these out.'

'You're right, of course,' Howard said. 'I doubt if any of them are originals. They'd have fallen to bits by now. And as for the quantity, *these* were done by the villagers, past and present. Spilling blood ends the curse on the latest residents of the manor – but it also renews the curse, replenishes it, so that it's potent and ready for the next lord and lady.'

'Oh right,' Mum said sarcastically. 'So now *everyone* in the village is a witch too!' She shook her head. 'Why in God's name would they be involved in this nonsense?'

'Because,' Howard said quietly, 'they want the manor to be empty as the curse affects them too. Agnes sewed her curse on the abbey's estate and the bricks that had once made up the abbey itself. *They* were used to build the manor – *and* the houses in the village.'

'Yours included,' Mum said, standing up and walking towards me. 'And you seem to be doing OK, although I'm beginning to doubt your sanity.'

He nodded. 'I've been thinking about this myself,' he said. 'I mean, obviously I'm still alive, but my marriage fell apart in Stagcote. And at times there are things that have been . . . odd. *And*, I realise now, *those* times coincided with the manor being occupied.' He counted on his fingers. 'There was that near miss with the lorry on the A40. *Very* near miss.' His eyes screwed up as he relived the moment. 'Then I lost loads of important stuff – personal and business stuff – when my computer wiped itself clean . . . the chickens I had when I first moved here all died within a month . . . as did most of the plants in the garden.'

'And we had the crash swerving to miss the dog,' I said. 'Then there's Sasha—'

'An accident. All of this stuff is . . . it's just life!' Mum said. 'The sort of thing that happens every day.'

'Absolutely. But here's the interesting thing. Nothing like it has happened until recently – when the manor was occupied once again.' He counted out on his fingers again. 'The bees are dying. The plants and fish too. Then there's the stuff in the village. The river drying up. Old Bess taking a turn for the worse. Again. Suddenly. Just as suddenly as she rallied after the Gilbeys had gone.'

'If they didn't want us in the manor,' Mum said, 'then why go to all this trouble with the kneelers? Why not just tell us right at the start?'

'Like you'd have listened!' I said. 'You're not even listening now!'

'And of course,' Howard said, 'as it says in the preamble in the book, they *can't* tell anyone the details. If they do, they die.'

Mum looked exasperated, bored. Baffled.

'I'm done with this,' she said, reaching for the latch on the door. 'Isabella? You're not staying to listen to any more of this garbage.'\

It wasn't a question.

'Yes,' I said firmly. 'Yes, I am.'

Our eyes clashed. She blinked.

The door slammed behind her. The rattle of the latch echoed.

I looked down at the kneelers hanging in front of me, in the next pew and the next, at the altar rail. Everywhere.

'They're all spells?' I said.

'Or stories of spells that worked. Celebrations. Like the Bayeux Tapestry, I suppose.'

'Tell me.'

'I'll start with the first one to work,' Howard said, walking along the aisle scanning the hassocks. He stopped two rows from the front.

'Ah, here,' he said. 'A sickle.' He went to unhook the kneeler. Panic rushed me.

'No!' I said. 'Don't touch it.'

My insistence startled him. My fear made him wary. It made me feel ridiculous. How could I be afraid of a cushion?

Even so, I crept along the aisle and peered over the back of the seat to look at the kneeler. An arc of gleaming silver on a bed of red.

'It'll be a copy, of course, not the original,' Howard said.

'I don't think that matters. Just don't touch it.' I leaned closer. 'What happened?'

He found the right page in the file, then read out the tale of Thomas Dryden's first harvest from the manor's estate. It had not grown well, the seemingly fertile soil coughing up tufts of thin, pale corn. Despite the meagre yield, he joined the estate labourers in the fields to mark the end of the harvest with the customary game, where a few stalks of the last of the standing corn were tied together and the men, blindfolded, took turns to throw their sickles at it.

Arcs of sharp steel flew. Lethal half halos. Thomas Dryden was fatally wounded, his blood drenching the stubs of blighted corn.

I pulled away, half expecting the sickle to fly at me. It must have been the light that made it look as though it were spinning.

'What about this one?' I said, sliding and ducking along the pew to an image of a sheep. 'It couldn't be the lamb of God, could it?' I knew it was unlikely but I needed reassurance, however vague that might be.

'No,' Howard said, flicking through the pages. 'I can't find the right bit here but I seem to remember it was to do with the plague . . . A merchant from Gloucester brought plague to the manor . . . in a . . . in a bundle of infected cloth.'

So much for God. I pursed my lips and moved along the line.

A black spade. Not used for digging graves, Howard explained, but taking Arthur Simpson to it. He was found at the foot of Stagcote Hill, the spade sprouting from his shattered skull, the work of Elizabeth Monkton, lady of the manor in the 1700s who, mad with jealousy, despatched her wayward lover and was executed herself soon afterwards.

I stood up and leant over the pew in front of mine. My fingers clenched.

'A white rose,' I said in a whisper. 'Rosemary.'

'Ah, no,' Howard said. 'I thought the same when I first saw it but it's nothing to do with Rosemary.' He scrambled through the pages. 'It's not a rose, you see. It's white hellebore.'

A plant, he explained, that both irritates the nasal passages, making you sneeze over and over again – *and* slows down the heartbeat to the brink of coma. A lethal combination for Arnold Baines, ten-month-old son of the lord, who, in 1793, crawled through a patch of white hellebore, and whose repeated sneezes drained him of air, his slumbering heart too slow to fill his struggling lungs.

Another dead child. I lived among bones. Restless bones. Their clatter filled my ears.

'What . . . what about the Gilbey's son? Is there one for his leukaemia?' I asked.

Howard frowned.

'I'd not thought of that. But you're right, I suppose there should be one.'

It was at the back. A microscope, alongside it a circle of red cells overwhelmed by a rash of blue dots. The yarn was still bright and thick and taut. *New.* The other kneelers told stories that were centuries old. This one happened only recently. The curse was as much about the present as it was about the past.

'Oh God.'

I didn't want to look any further but felt my eyes drawn to a kneeler in the next row.

A grey-white ring on a green background.

Not a ring, as it turned out, but a stone. A hag stone, placed in stables to prevent witches riding the horses at night and leaving them too tired to work in the morning. An object the lad put in the stable of the lord's favourite horse before every big race, and helped it win by a country mile.

The lord, a highly successful gambler, was so encouraged by his horse's easy victories, he bet his entire estate on a repeat performance in the Derby. Only the lad neglected to put the hag stone in the stable and the horse finished last. The lord lost everything, including his wife, who committed suicide.

The chill of recognition made me sit upright.

'I . . . found that story in the archive. The lord . . . he was the one who had the coded book . . . Crichton-Stuart. His wife's grave's outside.' I stood up. 'This . . . this is what I needed! It's proof. The archive and the gravestone corroborate what's in the book! Mum won't be able to argue with it.'

Howard looked doubtful.

'The facts might be consistent but I doubt that will be enough for your mother. People have been blind to the warning all along. Even though the bees were seen swarming before each tragedy.' He held up the file. 'It says so in here.'

He led me along the aisle and stopped at a kneeler on the very front pew. A single bee on a beige and orange honeycomb.

'No one's going to notice a single bee, are they?' I said.

'Subtlety is not what you want in a warning, I agree. Which is why they spell it out en masse.'

He beckoned me towards an alcove to the right of the lectern and opened a wooden door. The walls of the room behind it were a head-high mosaic of kneelers – all with the same image of the single bee on the honeycomb. There were so many of them the stripes of amber, beige and orange all merged together and the black antennae seemed to tremble. The buzz in my ears was only the rush of blood. *Wasn't it?*

He grabbed the door handle and closed it gently, as if wary of disturbing the bees. His caution heightened my anxiety.

'There's something else,' he said. 'Outside.'

I cowered under the heat as we stepped out of the shade of the porch. The sky was a light grubby grey, the air heavy and still. Howard led me to the usually chilly northern churchyard but that was just as stifling, its shade darker and denser.

He stood by the line of graves, wiped his head with the back of his palm, then fanned his face.

'It's the dog days, according to Cedric.' he said. 'When the Dog Star rises with the sun . . . it makes the earth a furnace. He says it drives dogs mad and sets evil walking. He's not wrong.' He wiped his brow again. 'The dog days are mentioned in the book too.'

Howard pointed to the graves.

'Look at the inscriptions, Izzy,' he said. 'You can't see some of them for moss and wear, but look at the dates on those that *are* legible. What do you see?'

I looked at the first grave, then another. My head was fried. I was dripping with sweat. A cold sweat. I couldn't see what I was supposed to be seeing and wasn't sure if what I *was* seeing was actually there or in my mind – or halfway between the two.

'I don't need any more fucking codes and riddles!' I yelled. 'Just tell me.'

Howard coughed.

'Of the former lords and ladies of the manor buried here, *all* of them died during the dog days. In the month of July. The *seventh* month. Now.'

Terror was an icy fist, holding me still. I couldn't take my eyes from his face, hoping for a smile to precede the punch-line. Ta-da! Fooled you. Just joshing. But he was serious, unblinking.

'We've got to get out!' I said, turning away from him, beginning to walk quickly to the manor. 'I'm going to give it one last shot with Mum. I have to! If she doesn't listen this time, then she's on her own.'

'OK,' Howard called after me. 'If she insists on staying, I'll wait for you at the Gate House.'

'You?'

'*I've* got the car. And believe me, I want to get out of here even if your mother doesn't. This affects me too.'

I ran back to the manor in a haze of panic. My feet flew across the ground, the dull thud of each step juddering within me. Shaking me up. I'd never felt so heavy and so light. So certain. So confused. The mix was maddening; the buzzing in my head grew deeper and louder, like disturbed bees.

I crashed through the gate into the garden.

'Mum!' I yelled.

It was worth one more try to get her to leave. There was

only so much I could do. Only so long I could wait for her to see the truth and change her mind. If she couldn't – if her stubbornness wouldn't let her – then I had no choice but to let her take her chances. Just like I had to take mine.

The figure ahead brought me up dead. Cedric. With his arms out. Holding a length of rope. His face was red and sweaty and he had the look of a hunter in his eyes.

'Get away from me, you bastard!' I said, circling around him. I was younger. More agile. Alert to any lunge.

'Miss?' he said.

I ran in a wide arc around him and through the back door, locking it behind me.

'Mum! Olga!' I bawled, tearing through the kitchen and along the corridor. 'We've got to go. Now!'

The house was quiet. Empty. Waves of panic overwhelmed me.

'Mum!' My voice echoed in the hallway.

There were footsteps. I whirled around quickly. No one was there. *My* footsteps.

I locked the front door but as soon as I'd done it, I freaked out; there could be someone in the house. And I'd just locked myself in. My hand dithered with the lock.

Upstairs, the squeak of an opening door. Olga's voice. Gently cooing.

'Olga!'

She appeared on the landing and peered over the balcony.

'Where's Mum?' I shouted. 'We've got to get to the Gate House. Howard's waiting.'

'Miss Isabella,' she said, waving wildly with her hand. 'Come. Come quick . . . Lady Lindy.'

It was like treading water as I climbed the stairs, each step slow and tentative and seemingly getting me nowhere. When

I finally reached the top, Olga took my hand and dragged me to Mum's bedroom.

The curtains were closed, filling the room with a diffuse, gloomy light. I heard a groan. The rustle of bedclothes.

'Mum?'

I ran to the bedside. She was too pale, too still, her breathing shallow. Her hand was cool and clammy, too weak to squeeze mine back.

'She's sleepy. Doctor gave her a painkiller.'

'Doctor? Why . . . why did she need the doctor? What's wrong with her?'

'She fell off the horse. Cedric was holding it as she got on and . . . whoosh! It run off. Very fast. Lady Lindy wasn't ready. And . . .' She smacked a fist into her palm. 'Lucky she had her hat on but that couldn't stop the rest of her getting hurt. Cedric's out now, looking for her horse.'

Cedric. Whispering in the horse's ear, telling it to bolt. I remembered there was a horse embroidered on one of the samplers Brenda had made.

'How bad is she hurt?'

Olga whirled a finger at her temple.

'She got a little bit of con . . . concussion, doctor said. Be worse without the hat. A broken rib also . . . that makes breathing hard. And . . . and she fell at a funny angle. Twisted the ankle under her.' Olga lifted the sheet, revealing a heavily bandaged foot and a glistening ice pack, supported by a couple of pillows.

Mum gave several feeble coughs; her breath was hot and sour.

'Why didn't he send her to hospital?'

'No need, he said. Painkillers can take care of it. And plenty of rest.'

Dread chilled me.

'Where did this doctor come from?'

'He's in the village. Cedric went and got him.'

'Shit! Why did you let him in?'

'Why?' Olga cried. 'Because . . . Lady Lindy's hurt, of course!' She threw her hands up. 'What's wrong, Miss Isabella? You're scaring me . . . you—'

There was a blue glass bottle with a cork stopper on the bedside table. I grabbed it up and popped out the cork. It smelt sharp and floral.

'What's this?'

'Oil. To help the bruises go down.'

'Where did it come from?'

'The doctor, of course!' She looked bewildered. Scared.

'Have you put any on yet?'

Olga just stared at me, as if she hadn't understood.

'Olga! Answer me. Have you put any of it on her?'

She shook her head and went to take the bottle.

'I'm sorry, Miss Isabella. I'll put it on right now.'

I snatched the bottle away from her.

'No!'

'But it will help her,' Olga whined.

'No it won't.'

Her face hardened.

'You're just trying to stop her get better!' she said. 'Why? She's your mother. Why do you want to hurt her – *again*? You said you were sorry!'

'I *am* sorry. And I'm trying to help Mum now. *Really*.' I held up the bottle. 'This might not be good . . . if it's from the village it almost certainly isn't . . . it's part of the plan . . . the villagers' plan . . . the curse!'

Olga rolled her eyes. 'Stop!' she cried. 'Stop it.'

I put the bottle in my pocket.

'You've got to listen to me, Olga. Now, did the doctor give Mum anything else?'

'Only painkillers,' she said, pointing to the box on the table.

I opened the box and slipped out the silver strip of foil. The pills behind the blisters of plastic were whole and uniformly round, their colour a consistent white. In the middle, a hoop of letters: Codeine.

'How many did he give her?'

'Two.'

I checked on the box. Adults: two pills a day, up to six times a day. May cause drowsiness.

Mum's eyes fluttered open.

'Mum?' I said, leaning closer.

She coughed, grimaced and closed her eyes.

'She'll be like that for a while,' Olga said. 'I had those pills before.'

'You're *sure* it was only two? He couldn't have slipped her any more when you weren't looking?'

'I was here the whole time.'

Perhaps it was better that Mum was completely out of it. At least she wouldn't be able to argue or resist. I whipped the duvet from the bed.

'What you doing?' Olga shrieked.

'We're leaving. Right now.'

'What? No! The doctor said she can't be moved. Needs rest.'

'I bet he did,' I said.

I swept away a strand of hair from Mum's face, let my hand slide around the curve of her cheek and jaw. I tried not to think how she would flinch if she woke up and saw my hands so close to her face. I tried not to notice the bruises under her eye. I tried not to remember that I'd been on the point of abandoning her at the manor.

I knew then that I couldn't. We would all have to leave together. But there was no way I could get Mum to the Gate House, even with Olga's help. Force of habit made me dig into my pockets, looking for my phone. Then I remembered the pieces in the fireplace where I'd hurled it to avoid Cosmo's call.

'Damn!' I said. My eyes flew around the room. 'Where's Mum's mobile?'

'Downstairs,' Olga said. 'On the hall table, I think.'

I stood up.

'Stay with her. I'll ring Howard. Get him to come and pick us up here.'

'But why, Miss Isabella? What's wrong?'

'The curse! How many more times?' I yelled as I ran down the stairs. 'It's real and it's happening now. Cedric. The Fletchers. The doctor. They're all part of this.'

The phone was on the table just as Olga said. My fingers shook as I tapped through the menus and the contact list. He wasn't under 'H' so I tried T for Thompson. He wasn't there either. I ran through the full contact list, just in case she'd put the name in wrong or given him some nickname. She hadn't.

'Fuck!' I put the phone down and ran to the bottom of the stairs. 'Olga! I can't call Howard. I'm going to the Gate House to get him, OK? Just stay where you are.'

'Yes, Miss Isabella,' she called back, her voice distant, strangled. 'Don't be long. You've frightened me now.'

I unlocked the door and leapt down the steps, throwing up a spray of gravel as I ran across the forecourt and up the driveway.

'Howard!' I bellowed as I got closer to the Gate House. My heart was thumping, my chest heaving. I flung back the garden gate and ran to the back door. It was locked firm so I pounded at it with my fists. Thunder rolled. I stopped. Waited. The thunder came again. Not from my fists, I realised, but from the glowering sky.

I dashed round to the front of the house and was relieved to see Howard's car was in the driveway. He was still here. But the front door to the house was locked.

'Howard!' I yelled, hammering at the door.

Nothing. There was no sign of any life through the windows either. My fear now had another nuance, a harder, tighter grip. Something must have happened to Howard.

Another roll of thunder. Then, above it, the dull, tuneless clang of the bell at Stagcote church, only this time it wasn't erratic but consistent, fast and unrelenting. Like someone raising an alarm.

Howard.

I had to get to the church. Fast.

A flash of lightning ripped through the darkened sky, the vein of brilliant light stretching for the earth. Great gusts of wind came out of nowhere, sweeping me up and pushing me along. Leaves were ripped away from the trees and branches clacked and rattled, the erratic rhythm enhanced by the splat of fat drops of rain. The booming bass of thunder. Then the deafening applause of torrential rain. I was drenched in moments, my clothes tight and clingy.

I slowed as I approached the churchyard. My lungs were screaming for air, the need for stealth making my breath even shorter. There was no one around but I ducked behind a gravestone just in case. Rosemary's gravestone, I realised. The stone glistened and the rain bounced back from the soil as if the earth was spitting. Or something beneath it was boiling.

I ran on, to the other side of the cemetery. The church door strained and trembled against the rusty hook that held it open. A cascade of drops draped the porch in a veil of silvery rain.

And still the bell rang out. Loud and insistent.

I crept towards the door. Peered in. Heard the hum of mumbled prayer. The pews were full of people, all of them with their backs to me, all of them still, staring at the altar, where a white-robed Father Wright stood, arms outstretched – in front of a coffin.

On top of it, all around it, smothering the altar, the chancel and the aisle – a carpet of kneelers. A swarm of orange and black bees. A perfect mosaic; all of the bees facing towards the manor, primed.

My gasp was lost in thunder and the clang of the bell.

'Offer the sacrifices of righteousness and put your trust in the Lord,' Father Wright said, crossing himself.

The congregation's 'Amen' echoed around the church. Their hands moved in perfect, robotic unison as they repeated the sign of the cross.

The thrum of rain on the roof intensified, the low buzz of bass growing stronger, louder, the pitch growing higher. Angrier. A flash of lightning made the light in the church jump; the Virgin Mary – *Ursula* – looked down on me disdainfully, her eyes a cold, clear white. The bees' antennae twitched. The stings quivered.

They'd got Howard. All because he was helping me. One outsider to another. It was my fault. First my baby, now Howard. If it hadn't been for me they'd still be alive.

Guilt dragged at my heels, slowing me down as I ran back to the manor. Fierce, cold rain slapped and stung my face but didn't wash away the heat of tears or quench my panic.

They'd be coming for me and Mum next.

I charged through the manor's door and slammed it behind me. The bolts and locks had a reassuring timbre.

'Olga! Quick!' I called as I ran up the stairs. 'They got Howard. They're all under the spell. They killed him, oh God, they killed him.' I sniffed back snotty tears. 'We've got to go. Hurry.'

Mum's room was silent save for the rain dripping from the curtain billowing in front of the open window.

'Olga?' I said, stepping further into the room.

Mum was still sleeping; she looked peaceful, comfortable. Panic ripped through me and I leant in to touch her, my hand shaking. The skin was warm; the hand I put in front of her nose was stroked with breath. I patted her gently around the face. She moaned and turned her head away from me. I shook her harder.

'Mum! Please. Wake up. We have to get out of here.'

She groaned and twisted in the bed.

'Mum. They're coming for us. Where's Olga?'

Her eyelids flickered open, then closed once more.

I walked around the bed and grabbed the telephone on the bedside table, my mind racing with the story I was going to tell the police. A curse cast by a belligerent nun six hundred years ago. Its calamities foretold by a swarm of bees and recorded on a set of church kneelers embroidered by deranged villagers.

Was I mad? It sounded ludicrous – even to me. The police were bound to be sceptical. But they'd understand murder. That's all I needed to say.

The phone line was dead.

I hung up and tried again. Nothing but the faint crack of static. I followed the wire back to the socket, pulled it out, put it back in and jiggled it. Tried the phone again. Still nothing. So I ran downstairs to use the one in the hall, only there wasn't even any static on that one. Just a long and empty silence.

I threw back my head and wailed. Sank to my knees. As I straightened up, I opened my eyes and glimpsed a creamy white sheet of paper, folded in half, on the floor. The wind must have blown it off the table when I opened the front door. The paper felt thick and heavy. It had my name on one half of it, the handwriting rushed.

Dear Miss Isabella
I'm sorry. I can't wait any more. You scared me then left me, all on my own. With sick woman. I waited but you'd been gone so long I think you not coming back. Or maybe something bad had happened. I hope you're safe.

This is a bad house. You always say it and I believe it. But I couldn't say anything or Lady Lindy would get angry and laugh at me. Or I lose my job like the Fletchers.

I hate leaving Lady Lindy when she's ill. But I can't stay. So sorry. Please tell her. Please pay what you owe into my account. I'll go back home to Riga. Maybe forever. I miss there. It won't frighten me like here.
Olga

I couldn't believe she was really gone. Only a few days ago she'd said she would stay. That she'd never leave.

'Olga!' I called and ran back up the stairs to her bedroom. Arms and legs dangled from the chests of drawers, socks left an erratic trail across the floor. The wardrobe doors were wide open, the hangers gone.

'Damn you!' I sobbed. 'How could you leave us?'

It wasn't just that she'd gone. She'd taken *her* car with her. Mum's was still in the garage but as it hadn't been repaired since the accident, what use was that? And even if it had been roadworthy, I didn't know how to drive it and Mum wasn't able to. We were stranded. Caught in a trap. Alone.

The bell chimed on and on.

I stood in the room, frozen. Light dwindled as the storm hurried in an early dusk. Everything around me began to lose shape and become indistinct, consumed by deepening darkness.

There was no reprieve when I flicked the light switch. The light in the corridor wasn't working either. Or in Mum's room. Her electric clock was blank, the red eye of the television stand-by button extinguished.

Darkness came in a rush. I felt in my pocket and pulled out my lighter. Sparks jumped as I flicked the wheel, the rasp it made an echo of Mum's breathing. The flame sputtered. Chairs, paintings, curtains mutated in the shadows. Was that a twitch of the curtain or a trick of the light? The walls closed in.

Clang. Clang. Clang.

I remembered that Olga kept a torch in a kitchen drawer, and used my lighter's hazy, yellow glow to get me to the top of the stairs. The handrail guided me down, my feet tentative, searching for each step. Panic made me want to hurry; caution wouldn't let me. I put my hand out and followed the line of the wall, around the hall, down the corridor to the kitchen, along the dresser to the Aga.

I found the rubber-handled torch. It was heavy with batteries. I fumbled for the switch and pressed. A bright cone of light burrowed into the darkness, chased by my sigh of relief. There were some matches and a box of long, slim candles in the drawer too.

I turned and followed the beam of the torch back along the corridor. The torchlight strafed the hall. The locks on the front door. The closed windows. The useless phone.

As I swung the light towards the stairs, it grazed the fireplace. I stopped dead.

In the black maw of the hall fireplace were the yellowed

bones of an infant's skeleton, among them a ram's horn and a silver rattle topped by a jester's hat.

Rosemary.

It couldn't be. It was just the shadows. The lightning. My mind getting the best of me.

I stepped closer, the light of the torch trembling, a miniature strobe. The rattle glittered.

It *was* her.

A scream caught from my throat, then came again. Louder. A hybrid of horror, confusion, madness, the impossibility of it all. The screams rang out through the house, hung in the air with the din of the bell and the booming thunder.

Rosemary had escaped from her grave. *Again.* She hadn't been exhumed last time or this time – she'd been pushed up by the hand of the devil and carried back to the manor on the wings of demons.

If I was to stand any chance of getting away, I had to get rid of her, once and for all. She was a magnet, a talisman. Deadly.

I put the candles and matches on the hall table and crept towards the fireplace, eyes wide open, half expecting the tiny, bony hand to reach out and grab me. I tipped out the tongs and poker from the basket next to the fireplace and tossed in Rosemary's brittle bones. Then I raced to the door, unlocked it and ran through the garden to the well.

Rain pelted into my face. The wind howled in the trees, a long, loud note of tuneless air. A rousing blow of a trumpet, that came again and again. A chorus. Calling for catastrophe. Like Joshua at Jericho.

I flashed the torch across the top of the well. Rain-slicked lichen shimmered. I caught my breath and sagged against the wall, the top stones shifted and swayed. I pulled away then tipped the skeleton into the void, the tumble of bones clattering, echoing. Gone.

I shone the torch down into the well. In the circle of light at the bottom, a spray of tiny bones.

Amongst them a hand. Large. Fleshy.

I jumped, moving the torch beam to the right.

A twisted leg. A buckled torso. Olga's eyes, pale and wide. Unblinking.

I fell to the ground, scrabbling away from the well on my hands and knees. I opened my mouth to scream but terror wouldn't let me.

Olga. Oh God, Olga. First Howard. Now her. We were next. I had to get back to Mum. Protect us. Somehow.

It flashed into my head from nowhere. The gun! The rifle Cedric had got for shooting foxes. He hadn't wanted it – said he didn't need it, he could just ask the foxes to go – but Mum had insisted.

I scrabbled to my feet and ran towards the outbuildings, past the stables to the shed. It was dank and smelt of rusty metal, damp bricks, soil and creosote. Cobwebs grazed my face and hands as I felt around for the gun.

I found it in a cupboard, the smooth wood giving way to a long, thin barrel of metal. Next to it, the rattle and heft of a box of bullets. I'd never held a gun and the thrill of it shocked the breath from me. I felt powerful – but only momentarily.

I'd never used a gun before. And if it wasn't the villagers who were coming for me but spells and demons, what use would a gun be then? But I took the rifle and the bullets anyway.

I locked the manor's door behind me, stood with my back against it, panting. Having got rid of one part of the spell, I had to get rid of another and raced around the house collecting the Fletchers' embroidery, ripping off seat covers, cushions, snatching place mats from tables and dressers, breaking up screens and bundling up counterpanes. I tried to read them for clues, as if they made an embroidered zodiac or fabric runes. A horse. A well. Bees.

They looked so innocent before. Why wouldn't a house in the Cotswolds be embellished with symbols of rural life? But now every single one was threaded with threat and danger. The reds ran like blood. The blacks were pitch. The whites ghostly.

I tossed every image into the hall fireplace. A fiery shower of lit matches fell onto the pile; the samplers blazed in a roar of orange flame. The heat pulled me forwards; I was freezing, shivering wet. Trembling with fear.

I picked up the candles from the hallway table. The bullets rattled as I climbed the stairs, the rifle under my arm, its half-cocked shadow like a broken finger. Wet clothes leeched at my skin, left trails of water on the stairs and corridors. I went into my bedroom, shucked off the clothes as quickly as I could and pulled on some jeans and a jumper.

As I was about to leave the room, frantic scratching broke out – behind one wall, then stopping before beginning behind another. Then two walls simultaneously. Three. Above my head.

I peered out of the door. I didn't dare go up to the room where I'd first found Rosemary. I didn't dare cross the Long Gallery. I just stood there, my nostrils filled with the scent of frankincense, my eyes blinking into the expanse of nothingness. Lightning flickered. White against black. The flash of Agnes's habit and scapula as she rushed by, her prayers, her curses, hissing in the rain.

I fled along the corridor, into Mum's bedroom and locked the door. By the time I'd placed lit candles around the room it looked almost cosy, the yellow glow of serenity belied by the drama of the gun propped against the wall beneath the window. And by the wheezy breathing from the bed.

In the light, I spotted Mum's laptop tucked on the bottom shelf of the bedside table. I switched it on; the icon for internet connection was a faint grey but the battery symbol was solid and black.

I went to the window, picked up the rifle. My fingers shook as I slid the shiny, copper-coloured bullets home. I was ready. For whatever it was that would come.

All I could do was wait.

Howard turned over the page then looked up quickly at Detective Sergeant Barr sitting on the other side of his kitchen table. Sleepy brown eyes held Howard's gaze.

'Extraordinary,' Howard said. 'Where did you find this?'

'The silver vault.'

Howard's eyebrows arched with curiosity.

'In the basement,' Barr explained.

The fluttering lines of yellow hazard tape around the manor had stopped the villagers getting too close, but it was clear to see that the blaze had destroyed a lot of the house. Shards of blackened wall jutted from the ground like rotten teeth. Blistered timber and twisted iron made grotesque shapes through skeins of milky smoke. Fire officers picked through rubble and damped down mounds of smouldering debris. Broken glass crunched underfoot and the sharp, acrid air gripped lungs.

But the back of the building had escaped the worst of the blaze. It was still streaked and singed but the walls were intact. A fireman, down in the basement, had seen the open vault door.

The laptop had been found on a large tray directly opposite the door, ensuring it couldn't be missed. So too did the red and shiny writing on the lid of the laptop.

This was not an accident.

'I thought it was blood at first,' Barr said. 'But it wasn't. Lipstick.'

He'd had the laptop photographed in situ then taken it back to his car and booted it up.

Right in the centre of the desktop was a single Word document.

READ THE TRUTH

'Like Aladdin's cave in that vault,' Barr said, with a touch of envy. 'Blinded me for a minute, the torch beams . . . bouncing back from all that silver. Candelabras and goblets, cutlery, ornaments and salvers.' He pointed at the pages on the table. 'Whatever happened at the manor, it certainly wasn't theft.'

Howard's eyes narrowed.

'*Whatever happened?*' he said. 'You mean . . . there's some doubt about it?'

Barr flicked up an eyebrow and folded his arms.

'A lot of what Isabella says in there doesn't add up at all.'

'No, of course not,' Howard said. 'How could it? Crikey! A curse! Come on. But, from what you said . . . you might be taking that seriously.' He cocked his head at Barr. 'You really don't think it was just an accident?'

'That's what we'd like to clear up. Like I said, there are some discrepancies in Isabella's story and we need to sort those out.'

'Right.' Howard coughed and leant towards Barr. 'So, how can I help?' He gave a quick smile and pointed at himself. 'I know I'm probably past my best but I can assure you that I am very much alive.'

Barr's thin slipped smile was fleeting.

'So I see, sir,' he said. The smile faded. 'Unfortunately the same can't be said of Isabella and Lady Griffin-Clark.'

'No,' Howard said. 'It's dreadful.'

He'd stood behind the hazard tape with the other villagers, their murmurs of conjecture silenced by the sight of two body bags being carried out of the manor. The fire crew had recovered Her Ladyship's charred body from her bed, Barr told him. Isabella was found crumpled at the bottom of the stairs with a broken neck, the charred stub of the rifle nearby.

'Oh Jesus!' Howard said, clamping his hand to his forehead. 'That poor girl! And her mother! I hope they didn't suffer.'

'The initial report from the police surgeon would indicate that they didn't. It appears Lady Griffin-Clark never regained consciousness and Isabella died instantly.'

'Thank God for those small mercies at least.' Howard shifted in his seat and frowned. 'What about Olga?'

'Ah,' Barr said, tapping his fingers on the table. 'That's where we hoped you might be able to help.'

'Me? How?'

'When did you last see her?'

Howard puffed out his cheeks and looked at the ceiling.

'Well, I wasn't a frequent visitor to the manor . . . and Olga certainly never came here but, let's think . . . erm . . .'

'The day of the fire?'

Howard shook his head.

'No, I was in the garden for most of the day.'

'Right, so you would have seen her if she'd driven by?'

'Of course.'

'What about when you weren't in the garden? Did you see or hear any car then?'

'No. And I wouldn't have missed it if one had gone past. I was in the conservatory or the kitchen the whole time and can see the drive.'

Barr nodded.

'So, how well did you know Olga?' he said.

Howard looked startled.

'How well? Crikey! Not at all really. I only met her a few times.'

323

'I see. And what was your impression of her?'

'Impression?' Howard wrinkled his nose. 'Like I said, I barely knew her . . . but she seemed a nice woman. Friendly. Smiley. I know Her Ladyship thought very highly of her.'

'So you'd say she was loyal then? Reliable?'

Howard shrugged.

'Yes, I suppose so. As far as I know anyway. Why?'

Barr glanced up at Howard and held his gaze.

'Curious thing,' he said. 'She's not been seen since the fire . . . since *before* the fire. And there's no sign of her car.' He coughed. '*Or* her body. And yes, we have checked the well. Nothing down there but twigs, damp soil and pebbles. No slabs or bricks from an unwanted house-warming present. And *definitely* no bodies. Not the housekeeper's. Or the little girl's skeleton.'

Howard stared back at Barr. Blinked.

'You're not telling me you thought there would be?' Howard said.

'However ludicrous this curse business might sound, we had to check it out,' Barr said firmly. 'And there *was* a little girl's skeleton found at the manor. PCs Simpson and Craven vouched for that . . . *and* for there being a funeral for the girl at Stagcote church.' He held his arms out. 'I've even seen the grave.'

It had been easy to spot it, he said, as the stone was dazzling and pristine, the butterfly unmistakable. But the soil on the surface was intact, unbroken by a spade, fork or scrabbling hands.

'Whoever Rosemary was,' he said, 'she *was* real – and she's still resting in peace.'

Howard drifted towards the Aga, waggled the kettle at Barr.

'Tea?' he said.

'Thank you,' Barr said. 'Milk. No sugar.'

The splash of the water from the tap into the kettle broke the silence in the room. There was a hiss as Howard placed the kettle on the hot plate.

'Of course,' Barr said, 'the skeleton isn't the only real thing to crop up in Isabella's story. Other bits are true too . . . like Maidens' Reel and the Seven Trumpets.'

'Yes, well, it's not easy to hide something like Maidens' Reel or an altar stone, is it, although . . . seven trumpets . . . not a phrase I've ever heard before . . . I'm sure I don't need to tell you that the altar stone wasn't a sacrificial site.'

'No?'

'It couldn't have been. There was no sacrifice as there was no dog!'

Barr's eyebrows shot up in surprise.

'Oh? That's very interesting,' he said.

'At least,' Howard continued, 'I never saw one, although, like I said, I didn't go to the manor often.'

'I see.' He took a deep breath and exhaled slowly. 'The horns in the ceiling of the pub are real enough too,' Barr said.

'Ed – the landlord – he reckons they're just decorations,' Howard said, taking two mugs from the drainer and dropping in a couple of teabags. He stepped back to avoid the steam that billowed as he poured water into the mugs. 'The wool industry was a big thing in this area, after all. Just a way of reflecting that, I suppose. And like you say, they're hardly secret, are they?'

'Couldn't be more public,' Barr said.

Howard fished out the tea bags and stirred in the milk.

'My hives and the kneelers are too,' Howard said. 'Although there aren't as many kneelers as Isabella's story would have you believe. And then there's the church window.' He put the mugs down the on the table. 'Easy to miss that one, I suppose. Quite subtle. Like the book in the archive.'

'You've seen that then?'

Howard blew across the top of his mug.

'Not the real thing. Only the pictures Isabella took of it.'

'And you didn't try and help her break the code?'

Howard snorted.

'I'm no code breaker, believe me! I haven't the patience for that. Even a crossword puzzle is pushing it for me. I get bored too quickly. There's no way I could sit down for days trying to suss a code out, even if I did believe in the curse.'

'Which you don't?'

Howard laughed again.

'Come on!'

'You are on the archive's register,' Barr said, sipping his tea, eyes hazed by steam.

'I don't deny I was there,' Howard said. 'I wanted to help Isabella. Show her the book with the acrostic, put her mind at rest. She was . . .' He scrunched his face up at the memory. 'She was wound up . . . jumpy. Needed a lift. I was happy to help only . . . seeing what she did with all this stuff . . . maybe . . . maybe I shouldn't have.' He rested the rim of the mug against his lip and stared into the distance.

'You think it's all nonsense?'

'Of course! How could it not be?' Howard said. 'Poor kid. I had no idea she was so disturbed by the manor.' He stopped, lifted a finger. 'No wait, that's not true. I knew she didn't like being here, *and* that she was freaked out by the whole thing with the skeleton. That's why I wanted to help. But . . . what she says happened . . . it's just a lot of fantasy sprinkled with bits of the truth. I had no idea she had such an imagination.'

Barr took another sip and placed his mug on the table.

'So you wouldn't say you knew her well then?'

'Clearly not. I didn't know anything about an abortion, school expulsions, self-harming or the overdose. Why would

I? I was only a neighbour and they'd not been here long enough for us to get to that level of intimacy.' He stopped and let his eyes focus. 'That stuff *did* all happen, did it? Or was that made up too?'

'No,' Barr said. 'Isabella did have her problems. And some counselling to deal with them.'

'Right, well . . .' Howard said. 'I'd no idea. She never mentioned anything of the sort.'

'Did you spend time together?'

'Some, yes,' Howard said. 'Not as much as she says in that document, mind. Makes us sound as though we were bosom buddies. What would a teenage girl see in me? A middle-aged ex-banker who keeps bees and potters around in the garden? Who sups a couple of pints at the local pub once in a while? It's not exactly going to do much for a teenager, is it? Especially one as . . . *individual* as Isabella.'

'What did you make of *her* though?'

'She was . . . a teenager! What more can I say? You know . . . a bit sullen and moody . . . then next time she'd be quite sparky but . . . overall, I'd say she wasn't very communicative. Bit vague when she *did* talk. Who knows what goes on in their heads?'

'Indeed. Especially one with Isabella's history.'

'*And* with her interests . . . you know she dressed to make herself look like the living dead?'

Barr nodded.

'Something of a goth, I understand,' he said. 'Vampires and zombies . . . all that. I suppose witchcraft and curses isn't too much of a leap.'

'Especially not for a bright girl like Isabella.'

'How did she get on with her mother?'

Howard glanced at the floor.

'There *was* tension there, no doubt about that. They rowed

a couple of times when I was around – about Isabella believing in the curse. That's why I offered to take her to the archive. I hoped it would settle the argument once and for all and they could get on with their lives.' He laughed cynically. 'Look how well that turned out.'

'You can't blame yourself.'

'No, I know,' Howard said quietly. 'But . . .' He shrugged away the rest of his sentence.

Barr leant forward.

'You say they rowed,' Barr said. 'Was it ever . . . physical?'

Howard looked up quickly.

'Did Isabella actually assault her mother that time, you mean?'

Barr nodded.

'That bit of the story was true too,' Howard said. 'The Fletchers told me about it. *And* I saw the bruises.'

There was a grunt of understanding from Barr.

'What?' Howard said.

'I was just thinking about the films Isabella would have seen,' Barr said. 'The books she read. Horror stuff . . . can have an effect on you, that sort of thing.'

He let his words hang in the air then continued.

'Isabella was very angry with her mother. The move. The abortion. The pay-off to the boyfriend. Her refusal to listen . . . interfering. She was mad enough to assault Lady Griffin-Clark, so . . .'

'So . . . so what?' Realisation drained through his face. 'Are you? You're not suggesting Isabella killed her mother?'

'Or Olga. Maybe the pair of them together. They were very pally, it would seem.'

'Yes, from what I saw I'd say they were but . . . but to do that? Jesus!'

'It's a line of inquiry,' Barr said. 'Isabella was unhappy

about the move. Very angry. Stood to cop for a mega inherit-
ance with her mother out of the way. She and Olga could have
weaved together the true, *real* elements of the story – the
trumpets and whatever – to cover their tracks. Only one of
them – Olga most likely, seeing as there's no trace of her –
double-crossed the other. There was a fight, Isabella fell down
the stairs and broke her neck. Olga took the laptop with the
decoy story down to the silver vault, as per the plan, helped
herself to some of the goodies seeing as there'd be no pay day
from her heiress accomplice, then vanishes into the mist.'

'But Izzy was mortified about the assault!' Howard said.
'*And* she bangs on about not being able to leave her mother
. . . that she loved her . . .'

'Protesting too much, possibly,' Barr said.

Howard stared at him, eyes wide.

'Are you really saying you think Olga . . . that she started
the fire?'

'Fire*s*,' Barr said, his lips curling back to emphasise the 's'.
'One in the bedroom – caused by candles – the other downstairs, caused by burning material falling from the fireplace,
catching a rug, onto the staircase . . . lots of wood in the manor.
Upholstery, silks, paintings . . . plenty to feed the fire.'

'Arson?'

'It's one line of thought,' Barr said. 'Do you think it's
something she – *they* – were capable of?'

Howard stood up, walked the length of the kitchen, a palm
clamped to his forehead.

'No!' he said. He spun on his heel. Confusion raced across
his face. 'But then . . . how well did I know her? *Any of them*
come to that. It's just . . .' He shook his head again. 'I can't
believe this . . . No, no, you've got it wrong! All we've got
here is a tragic accident. An imaginative but jumpy girl on her
own in a big house full of lit candles. End of.'

Barr didn't look convinced. He stood up, walked to the kitchen door.

'Thank you for your time and cooperation, Mr Thompson,' he said. 'You've been most helpful. I'll be in touch. Let you know what the guvnor makes of it.'

The wood creaked as Howard eased himself into the garden chair. He placed the bottle of whisky on the table and sipped from the glass in his hand, the glow in the pit of his belly matched by the warmth of the late afternoon sun on his skin.

The weather had been fresher since the storm. The air was light, the baby-blue sky cloudless, the sun full but forgiving. The scent of jasmine and roses rode the soft puffs of breeze and full-leafed trees threw dense shadows across sweet lush grass. He should have pointed that out to Barr too.

'Not a curse. Just drought. See how it's all green again now that we've had some rain?'

He took another sip of whisky, let it linger in his mouth. The flower beds hummed with the intermittent buzz of bees.

The plants in the garden had been chosen to provide good foraging for his bees for as much of the year as was possible; apple trees, grape hyacinths and gooseberry bushes for early sustenance, the white clover and dandelions left to thrive in the lawn instead of being blasted with chemical killer. In the summer, the intoxicating scent and subtle hues of sweet peas and honeysuckle were infused with base notes of marjoram and mint and purple fronds of lavender. And as the days grew shorter, the bees gorged on garish sunflowers, blue and white campanulas, dahlias, ivy and clusters of phlox. There was usually little need to support them over the winter with strong, sugary syrups.

He couldn't accept the credit for the choice of plants. The range had always been the same. The design may have altered once or twice and there'd been experiments with different locations for some of the plants and the introduction of new varieties but, fundamentally, nothing had changed.

Even the bees were the same. The direct descendants of those from the hives at Stagcote Abbey. He was proud – relieved – that he'd managed to keep them alive this time. It had been close. Closer than ever before, in fact. Which was why he'd had to help things along. And in doing so he'd also come close to making a mistake.

The look on Olga's face when she answered the front door at the manor had almost broken his heart. It wasn't that she looked so scared, although her terror was clear enough – wide staring eyes and cringing posture. What had struck him was her sense of relief that he was there at all. Like a lost child catching sight of a familiar face in a crowd.

'Thank God!' she cried. 'Come quick. Lady Lindy's hurt.' She looked over his shoulder. 'Where is Miss Isabella?'

'She's not going,' Howard said, his voice light but firm.

'What do you mean, not going? She's not staying here! She's too scared.' She pushed past him, out onto the step. 'Where's the car?'

'I'm not leaving either, Olga,' Howard said.

She grabbed handfuls of his shirt and shook him.

'But you must! The people here are crazy people. Because of the curse!' She pushed him away from her. 'Go and get the car and Miss Isabella. I wait with Lady Lindy.'

He gripped her wrist. Tight.

'You don't understand,' he said, pushing his face close to hers. 'Nobody's going anywhere. It's just not possible, you see. History says so.'

That's when he saw the understanding in her eyes. The bright light of hope dimming to a glow and finally flickering out.

She was feisty, her feet lashing at his ankles, trying to raise her knee to his groin. He jumped back then lunged for her, clamping a hand over her mouth and dragging her through the garden, each step accompanied by the jangle of keys from the pocket of her apron. He snatched the keys then lifted her clear of the wall well. Her hands scrabbled at his shoulders, caught on the straps of his backpack. He prised her fingers away, tipped her up and let her fall, head first.

The power was out when he got back to the manor so he had to use his phone to light the way, the eerie glow ushering him into the drawing room where he dashed out Olga's resignation letter. With the lack of light and Isabella's state of mind, she wouldn't notice the difference in handwriting, he was sure of that. And, it turned out, he was right.

With the letter propped on the hallway table, he went upstairs. The Fletchers had already told him who slept where, so he found Lindy Griffin-Clark's room without any problem. It would have been so easy to place a pillow over her face and hold it there. She was already so weak there'd be little struggle. Or he could have sat her up, made sympathetic noises and slipped her a few more painkillers.

Instead he did neither – not out of squeamishness or lack of aptitude, more a reluctance to take any more unnecessary risks, actions that might be detected. Agnes and Ursula would understand that. Removing Olga had been unavoidable but her death was easily hidden too.

Nothing was stealthier or more discreet than a spell. He would leave it to Agnes and Ursula to take care of Her Ladyship and Isabella. He closed the bedroom door and moved on to Olga's room, hastily pulling out the contents of the wardrobe and drawers, scattering them across the floor.

Satisfied that it was a convincing scene of a hurried

departure, he closed the door and dashed downstairs again, ready for the next part of the plan.

Only there were footsteps on the gravel in the courtyard. Someone running. Sobbing.

Howard darted into the drawing room and slipped behind a curtain just as the front door was thrown open. Slammed. Locked.

'Olga! Quick!' Isabella called as she ran up the stairs. 'They got Howard. They're all under the spell. They killed him, oh God, they killed him. We've got to go. Hurry.'

It was all he could to stop himself from laughing. Just like he had when they'd discovered Sasha's body. Or when he'd let her find it rather. Cedric had skewered the dog with a garden fork and they'd both knelt on the altar, glad of the chance to anoint it with blood once again and so replenish the spell.

Izzy had been overwhelmed back then. As distraught as she was as he listened to her panic, screaming to Olga that they had to get out of the manor. It wouldn't take much to push her over the edge. And he knew just the thing.

When she ran up the stairs, he came out from behind the curtain and crept to the drawing room door. He heard her begging her mother to wake up, asking where Olga was.

Just as he was about to leave the drawing room, her footsteps thundered along the corridor. The landing. The stairs. Howard jumped back behind the door, watched through the gap in the door frame as she read Olga's letter, ran upstairs again, turned at the top of the landing towards Olga's room.

'Damn you!' she cried. 'How could you leave us?'

Again he was about to step out into the hallway. Again he heard her footsteps on the stairs. He ducked back behind the door. Watched her go towards the kitchen. It was his best chance. Possibly the only one he'd get.

He crept into the hall, to the fireplace, opened his backpack and took out the bundle inside it. Unwrapped it. Placed a tiny skeleton in the grate. He felt the kick of history as he followed in Ursula's footsteps. In his ancestor's footsteps. The bones in his hands were his kin too.

Thomas. Rosemary's twin. Named after his father, the First Lord of Windrush and smothered along with his sister soon after they were born – at three in the morning. The chime hour. Just as Agnes had been. And as the hour approached each morning, it would set the twins scratching in their hiding places.

She was placed in the chimney. He was laid to rest beneath the floorboards in the same room, doubling the potency of the spell – a power that had been diminished by Rosemary's discovery and burial.

Howard had to get her back into the manor and Thomas could help him do it. The wraiths had shown Howard the way when he watched the church porch on Midsummer's Eve, the laughter from the village feast echoing across the village, the rich scent of roasting pig dripping from the air.

It was something he'd done every year since the age of three, when his mother had taken him along with her and told him to sit quietly and wait and watch. Just like she'd been taught to do by *her* mother. The gift – the magic – was stitched into them by history and practice, linking them to generations of Tumps, a name which, over time, had morphed into Thompson.

Isabella had never made the connection with his family graves in Stagcote churchyard. He distracted her whenever they passed even though he'd been unable to stop the automatic dip of his head as he went by. And she'd totally bought his lie about his job in banking, the move to Frankfurt, his German wife and their retreat to a simpler life in Stagcote.

If only she'd been better at checking facts. Even though it

had caused him some anxious moments, her curiosity was commendable. But she wasn't rigorous enough in its application. An easy mistake at first, he conceded, but once she'd established that not everything at Stagcote was as it first appeared, she really should have looked deeper.

As deep as he had looked into the pitch on Midsummer Eve.

At midnight the darkness in the churchyard shifted shape until it was no longer just a flat bank of black but a sculpted space with depth and perspective. A landscape. With movement. A series of ovals and lines moving in sequence. Heads, bodies, limbs. *People.* Only not. Their features were twisted, like smoke from a candle in a draught, and they trooped into the church treading on nothing but air.

Ed, Nathan, Cedric. The Fletchers. Howard himself. The wraiths of all of those who would live for the following year came out again; Old Bess, Olga, Her Ladyship and Isabella did not reappear.

As the procession snaked into the darkness, the shapes dissolving into nothing, Howard was drawn to the church window. Judas stared down at him. Only it wasn't really Judas, of course, any more than the image on the other side was the Virgin Mary. It was a family portrait of the twins, Thomas and Rosemary, each of them working against the lord from inside the manor.

Howard had been reluctant to remove Thomas from the manor but he knew it would be for the best in the end and, as the dog days were drawing closer, he knew it wouldn't be for too long either. Under the pretence of checking for wasps' nests Cedric had been allowed upstairs, unsupervised, lifted the floorboards and brought Thomas to the Gate House.

There was no way Isabella would notice that the child was male. She'd only see the bones, the ram's horn and the jester rattle Glenda had removed from the coffin on the day of the funeral. Isabella's mind would do the rest.

The torch beam strafing the corridor had sent him diving back into the drawing room.

He expected Isabella to scream and she did; long and guttural. He knew she'd need to look at it and would step closer to the fireplace, nervous and hesitant. But he panicked when he saw her remove the tongs and poker from the basket by the fireplace, toss in the bones and run from the manor.

He slipped out of the door and squinted into the darkness, tracking the torch beam. Towards the well.

He let her go. She couldn't escape anyway. He'd already seen to that. He ran back home to the Gate House, into the front room. An embroidered map of the manor lay on the floor, at its centre two hessian figures, stuffed with pungent rosemary, and speared with needles. Pinning them to the spot. They could get no further than the village boundaries.

Howard checked his watch. It would be another hour before the stars and planets slid into the right position to give the curse maximum potency. Another hour before the church bells would stop ringing and signal the end of the villagers' vigil.

He bent down and lifted the lid of a wooden chest by the fire, took out two ovals of creamy-coloured wax, each roughly sculpted with eyes, a nose and mouth. One sprouted a clump of auburn hair, the other black, all the strands harvested from hairbrushes by the Fletchers. He lifted the heads out and placed them on the pile of elder wood in the fireplace.

It had been no surprise to see that Isabella was a natural redhead just like her mother. Redheads were unlucky. Cain, Shylock, Mary Magdelene, Judas Iscariot – all of them redheads.

He placed the effigies into the fireplace, fumbled around at the bottom of the wooden chest, and pulled out a photograph. Isabella and her mother. In their car, pausing to chat with him before they drove off to town, apologising for disturbing the woodpecker Howard had claimed he was trying to photograph.

The picture was put among the sticks of wood and kindling. Other personal items followed; opaque crescents of finger- and toenails, lipstick-smudged dog ends, balls of hair, mismatched earrings.

He watched in silence as the effigies blistered in the heat of the flames, sticky pus bubbling and dripping, the sharp stench of burnt hair filling the room.

At the moment the last of the feeble orange embers dwindled into fine, grey ash, the church bell stopped ringing. Howard stood up and stared out of the window towards the manor. Watching. Waiting.

His heartbeat was steady and true, confident of success. And in his blood he felt the hot rush of history, of ancestry, the breath of Agnes and Ursula, the hectic swirl of stars and hexes, the scratch of claws, darkness, destiny, death.

A coppery glow singed the sky above the manor.

The rest was simple.

Before Howard called the fire service, he stood and watched a couple of the men from the village lower Nathan down the well. He collected Thomas's bones, the ram's horn and the silver rattle and brought them up for Howard. Then he went down again and brought up the stones left in the fireplace. Not a house-warming present, but a spell to make the hearth – the home – barren, unlucky and cold, the eggshell on the top of the pile not a wish for the occupants never to go hungry, but for them to be easily broken.

Olga's battered, bloody body was carried to the village, where she was lowered into Old Bess's coffin, her broken limbs easily twisted into shape to make room for Old Bess's body, which was laid on top of hers, and the lid of the coffin sealed. Everyone agreed that Old Bess would be glad of the company and they were buried a few days later.

As the coffin was lowered into the ground, Howard looked over at the charred ruins of the manor. Men were sifting through the ashes, poking at debris, taking samples. Spells left no fingerprints or DNA. They'd find no trace of anything suspicious.

Or so he'd thought.

Isabella's account of events had been a shock but he'd hidden it well from Barr. Thank God people didn't believe in witches and curses any more.

Howard smiled. Poured another whisky. He had to imagine what had happened after Isabella had written the last word of her account of events, as she would have had no time to write it down. It was a report, not a commentary. She'd taken the laptop down to the silver vault, the safest part of the house, and then gone back up to be with her mother and keep watch from an upstairs window.

Something must have made her grab the gun and run downstairs. A noise. Terror. The urge to flee. Ghosts and spells. A glimpse of Agnes in the Long Gallery. In the panic of it all, in the stuttering, shifting light on the stairs, she'd lost her footing. Fallen. Snapped her neck.

It was all possible – likely, even. But no one would ever know for sure. No one. Barr included.

But Barr's theory left the door open to further investigation. The case should have been straightforward. Closed within days of the fire. But now it seemed that Barr's imagination was just as agile as Howard claimed Isabella's had been.

Howard would go down to the pub to alert the villagers to be on their guard. But first he had something to do. Spells didn't leave any traces, but he had. He could feel the shame of his ancestors. If he'd been as careless in their day he would have hanged or been tossed on a fire.

Howard got up from the chair, gulped the last of the whisky in his glass and went into the front room. He opened the lid on the wooden chest by the fireplace and took out the bundle of Thomas's bones, the ram's horn and the silver rattle. Then he reached to the bottom of the chest and removed a tray of embroidery threads, a black cloth stiff with long silver needles and a length of blank canvas.

He carried it all to the end of the garden and set it down on the ground by the hives. The hum of bees filled the air. He picked up the smoker on the ground close to the hives, dropped in some grass cuttings and a lit match, and gave a few quick blasts on the trigger. The hives' population was recovering now and he could hear their contentment, feel it in the honey-heavy weight of the hive as he moved it aside.

He lifted the paving slab underneath, revealing a hole a few metres deep. It wasn't as elaborate as a silver vault but it had proved just as effective at protecting valuables for hundreds of years. Watched over by thousands of guards, armed with wings and stings.

He knelt down and placed the threads, needles and canvas at the bottom, then gently lowered in Thomas's skeleton. He would lie there until Rosemary could be safely exhumed and the pair of them returned to the manor. The site was sure to be developed. A new Manor house. With an old story. The same Heartbreak Hall.

Howard slid the paving stone over the hole and replaced the hive. He tapped the roof gently.

'It is done now,' he said. 'It is God's will. It cannot be stopped.'

The buzz within reverberated, a deep, long blast of bass. The hive walls shook.

Acknowledgements

A huge thank you to my editor, Jemima Forrester, and my agent, Oli Munson at A M Heath, for pushing me and believing in the book. Thanks too to everyone at Orion, especially Juliet Ewers, Sophie Painter, Marissa Hussey, Gaby Young, Ruth Sharvell, Julia Silk and Abi Hartshorne.

Mum, Sue and Ellie who put up with my absence, distraction and impatience.

The villagers of Lower Slaughter for their interest in my book, particularly Tony and Anne Keats, Rachel, Ken and Janet Barber, Stuart and James Mace, Robin and Jane Cochlan and, for interesting chats over tea and biscuits, Nadine Taylor. And lots of wags to Max the Labrador, for the company and fun on walks in the Gloucestershire countryside.

Bee Urban for giving me an insight into the lives of bees and Roots & Shoots for letting their bees star in the book's video. Chloe Thomas and Richard Gillespie, without whom the video would never have been made.

For too much to go into, thanks: Lynne Barnes, Polly Beale, Candy Bowman, Judith Buck, Claire Collison, Marietta Crichton Stuart, Len Dickter, Jean Dobson, Sarah Evans, Kerrie Finch, Rick Gem, Jo Hadfield, Suzanne and Betty Jansen, Gordon and Jill Johnston, Paul Kitcatt, Jadzia Kopiel, Maureen

Landahl, Diane, Graham and Aiden May, Lorna, Patrick, Oscar and Maddie Mills, Jane, Laura and Elen Morgan, Ant Parker, Consalvo Pellecchia, Kathryn Penn-Simkins, Mark Rogers, Mark Russell, Linda Tibbetts & Luca, Marnie Searchwell, Dave Sellers, Claire Dissington and Albert, Carolyn Solomon, Andy Tough and Cathy Brear, Ginny Tym, Richard Vessey and Judith Weir.

Thanks to my Twitter pals for keeping me entertained and to book bloggers everywhere for your passion, commitment and support.

And, Boosie – ta always.